OF WITHERING DREAMS

FATE OF THE EMBERED
BOOK ONE

ROWYN ADELAIDE

Copyright © 2025 by Rowyn Adelaide

All rights reserved.

No part of this book may be reproduced in any form or by any electronic or mechanical means, including information storage and retrieval systems, without written permission from the author, except for the use of brief quotations in a book review.

This is a work of fiction. Names, places, characters, and incidents are the product of the author's imagination and are fictitious. Any resemblance to actual persons, living or dead, events or establishments is solely coincidental.

Without limiting the author's and publisher's exclusive rights, any unauthorized use of this publication to train generative artificial intelligence (AI) is expressly prohibited.

Cover Design: Rowyn Adelaide

Edited by: Katie Awdas, Spice Me Up Editing

Ebook exclusive epilogue edited by: Ashley Bartlett, Ash Tree Editing

Map Art: Melissa Nash

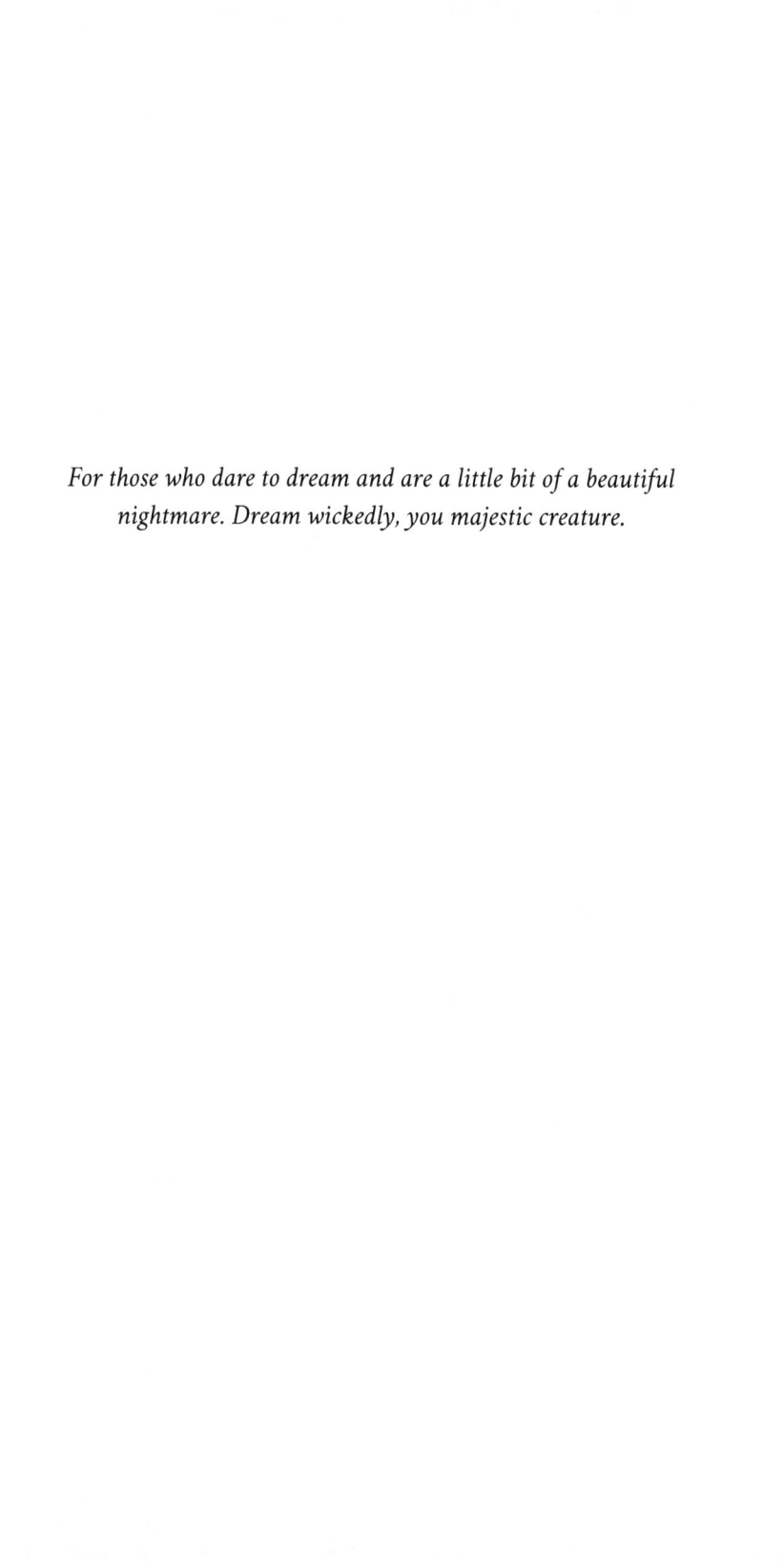

For those who dare to dream and are a little bit of a beautiful nightmare. Dream wickedly, you majestic creature.

Here you'll find me,
    In the withering mist between trees.
    There, I'll find you,
    In the blooming embers of your dreams.

— ROWYN ADELAIDE

CONTENTS

Of Withering Dreams	x
Playlist	xii
Author's Note	xv
Content Warning	xvi
Prologue	1
1 *The Withering*	5
2 *Thirteen Frogs*	12
3 *Crumpled Petals*	18
4 *A Ravenous Spider*	24
5 *Hazy Dreams*	28
6 *Stygian Murk*	35
7 *Fireflies in a Jar*	42
8 *Embedded Stones*	53
9 *Harrowing*	65
10 *Pinch Me*	73
11 *Ancient History*	84
12 *The Heart: A Fickle Creature*	92
13 *Sleepless in Surrelia*	106
14 *Sparring with Blades and Words*	121
15 *Buckle Up*	130

16 *Like a Cat Lapping Up Milk*	141
17 *A Sense of Control*	149
18 *Fated Khorda*	157
19 *Blood Oaths*	163
20 *Meadows and Mirages*	175
21 *Beyond the Veil*	185
22 *The Dawn Does Not Fear the Night*	197
23 *Blood and Rebellion*	209
24 *Toxin and Tonic*	218
25 *Pruned*	229
26 *Fated Promises*	234
27 *Shattering*	243
28 *Golden Bridles*	254
29 *Entombed in Amber*	263
30 *Bits of Ash*	275
31 *Unbidden Memories*	284
32 *Frayed*	291
33 *Winnowing*	303
34 *Midst Falling*	316
35 *Shedding Skin*	325
36 *Astra Poppy*	333

Glossary/Pronunciation Guide	339
Acknowledgments	347
Want more?	349
About the Author	351

OF WITHERING DREAMS

WHERE DREAMS COME TRUE ... AND NIGHTMARES, TOO.

Enchanting, atmospheric, and addictive—Of Withering Dreams is a steamy dark fantasy romance set in a dying world where dreams, magic, and corruption intertwine.

DREAMS DECAY.

The Dormancy was meant to be the mortal realm's salvation. From autumn to spring, citizens must enter a magically induced slumber to conserve dwindling resources. The divine Ancients, who gifted mortals magic, disappeared long ago, leaving humanity at the mercy of the Elders. These powerful and elusive oligarchs have one motto: "Through Dormancy, we blossom!" Yet, this seems more like a cruel jest than a promise.

For Seryn, this Dormancy will change everything. Except for the little details... you know, like her realm progressively decaying and people vanishing. As the threads of reality unravel, she soon discovers her hidden identity as a Druik, one who wields magic. But her abilities are... unusual. Unpredictable.

DESIRES BLOOM.

While her inherited powers bloom, so do her desires for her charming best friend, Kaden. She wouldn't dream of risking their friendship, but the Fates can't be bothered with mortal dreams.

DESTINY UNRAVELS.

Navigating a treacherous path where dreams and nightmares blur, Seryn must confront haunting truths. Her newfound courage and magic might be the key to saving her realm, but will they be enough when even dreams can wither into oblivion?

Don't miss this captivating debut in the Fate of the Embered series—a spellbinding tale of passion, peril, and profound sacrifice—where every twist and turn challenges the heart and the soul.

PLAYLIST

Books are life. But so is music—at least to me! In no particular order, the following songs inspired me while I wrote this story. Below, come find me and my book playlists on Spotify!

- "Mad World (cover)" - Andie Case
- "Dreams" - Fleetwood Mac
- "Supermassive Black Hole" - Muse
- "... Ready For It?" - Taylor Swift
- "Sweet Dreams (cover)" - HANZO
- "Fade Into You" - Mazzy Star
- "Broken Man" - St. Vincent
- "Nothing Matters" - The Last Dinner Party
- "Supersad" - Suki Waterhouse
- "The Man Who Sold the World" - David Bowie
- "I Put a Spell on You (cover)" - Annie Lennox
- "Glory Box" - Portishead
- "You're Standing on my Neck" - Splendora
- "A Thousand Years" - Christina Perri
- "The Most Beautiful Thing" - Bruno Mars
- "Boombastic" - Shaggy

- "Can't Help Falling In Love (cover)" - Kina Grannis
- "Ocean Eyes" - Billie Eilish
- "Wildest Dreams" - Taylor Swift
- "Wicked Game (cover)" - Trevor Something
- "Bring Me to Life" - Evanescence
- "War of Hearts" - Ruelle
- "Unrequited Love" - Lykke Li
- "Mad World" - Gary Jules
- "Linger" - The Cranberries
- "Unintended" - Muse
- "Mother Mother" - Tracy Bonham
- "Wicked Game (cover)" - Jessie Villa
- "No Rain" - Blind Melon
- "You Think I Ain't Worth a Dollar, But I Feel Like a Millionaire" - Queens of the Stone Age
- "Sweet Dreams (cover)" - Mecdoux
- "Happy Together (cover)" - FLOOR CRY

Of Withering Dreams Spotify Playlist

AUTHOR'S NOTE

This debut *Of Withering Dreams* is the first book in the *Fate of the Embered* series. I am thrilled to finally get this story out into the world. I've always loved romance novels, especially ones with atmospheric world-building, magic, action, quests, and mystical beings. While there are elements and names that may be similar or very loosely related to Greek mythology, this is not a retelling or close representation of those tales or culture. This is a dark fantasy romance that was inspired by nature, magic systems, the world of dreams and imagination, Fates and Oneiroi (Dream Gods), etc.

At the back (*because spoilers*) of the book, there is a **glossary** and **pronunciation guide**. If you utilize the glossary and pronunciation guide, **PLEASE** be mindful that they are together and may contain **spoilers** if you look them up before reading.

Please enjoy my debut dark romantasy, and keep an eye out for the rest of the series. Read on for an important **content warning**.

CONTENT WARNING

Of Withering Dreams is a dark fantasy romance (a.k.a. dark romantasy) with morally-gray characters, explicit content, themes or hints of trauma and abuse, scenes with blood and gore, violence, characters struggling with mental health and/or well-being, anxiety, and other complex emotions. There are open-door sex scenes, parental deaths, loss and grieving, cussing, characters with dark pasts and dark deeds, and supernatural elements.

Dark fantasy is a subgenre of fantasy that explores darker themes and worlds that may be considered disturbing, unsettling, traumatic, or frightening to some. However, it is not considered the same as dark romance, which often explores the darker side of love and relationships, power/control dynamics, fear, obsession, violence, abuse, etc.

I want to be clear that *Of Withering Dreams* is NOT considered a dark romance.

I think the difference is important to note for those who enjoy dark romance specifically. I don't want to lead you astray if you were expecting certain tropes and themes that are often included in dark romances and the relationships therein.

Your mental well-being is important, so please review any trigger warnings before reading. If you are sensitive to scenes with the noted content, then this isn't the book for you. I want you to stay safe and love what you read. If you decide to read this story, then buckle up and enjoy this enchantingly wild ride!

N
W E
S

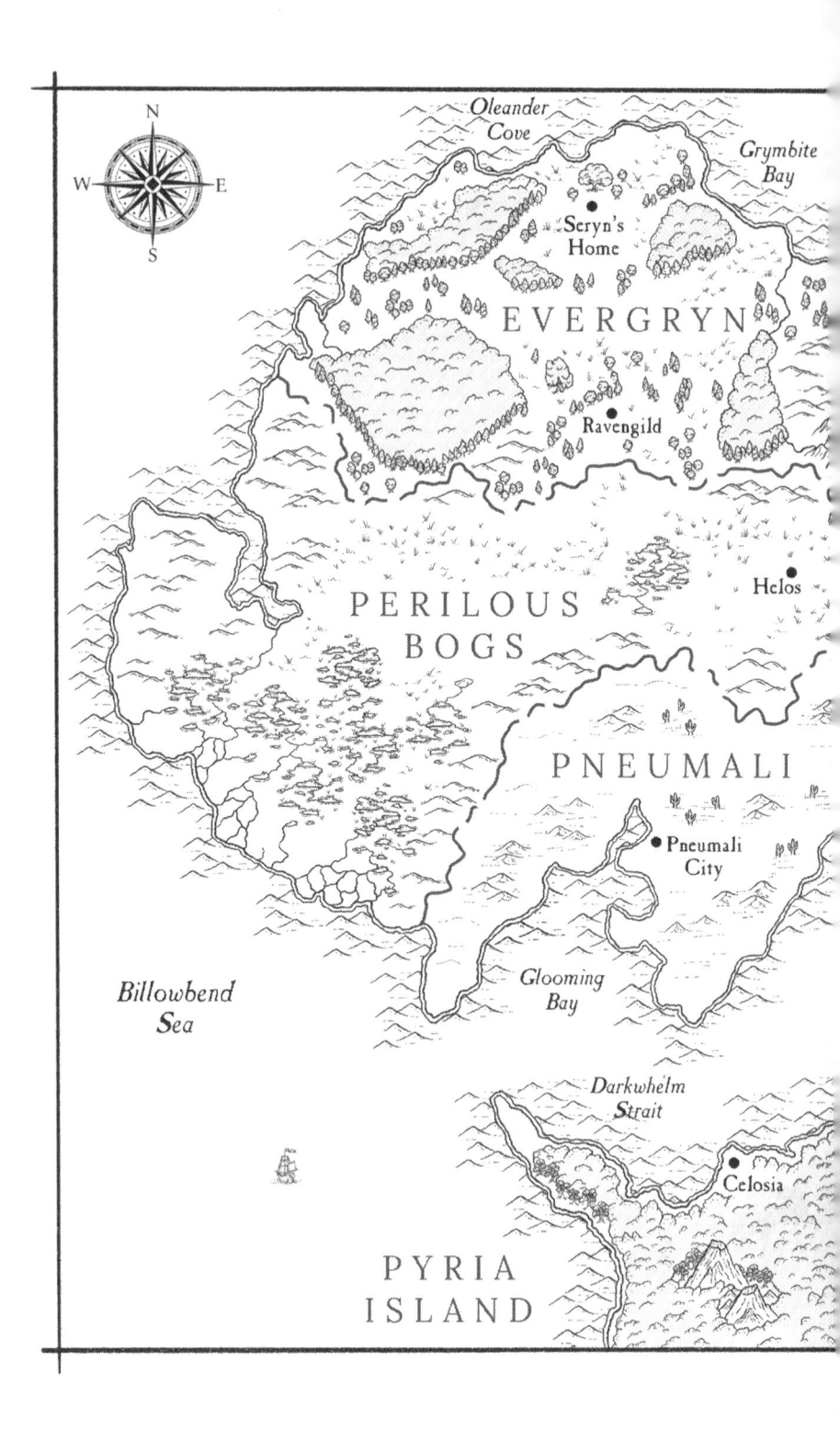

Oleander Cove

Grymbite Bay

Seryn's Home

EVERGRYN

Ravengild

Helos

PERILOUS BOGS

PNEUMALI

Pneumali City

Billowbend Sea

Glooming Bay

Darkwhelm Strait

Celosia

PYRIA ISLAND

MIDST FALL

Ourea Peaks

Lotus Loch

Oneiroi Abyss

Inksalt Loch

• Ceto

HAADRA

Aerides Loch

Gulf of Eidolon

PROLOGUE

BACK THEN

"But, Mama, why? Why do we gotta go in the pods again? I don't want to go to sleep for a hundred months *every* turn!" I flung my seven-turn-old body on the rickety wooden chair in our kitchen for dramatic effect, in case Mama didn't understand just how serious I was.

The storm outside sounded furious, rain thrashing against our cottage's tiny round windows. I must have upset the Ancients because the rain was thumping against the glass as if they were trying to break through it with stones.

I squirmed in my seat, waiting for Mama to finish braiding my little sister's flaxen hair, curls fleeing from her fingers with every crossover. My chair creaked impatiently with each second that passed without a satisfactory response.

Mama sighed when sections of hair escaped her hold as Alette squirmed to look back. Alette promptly shouted in the way only a four-turn-old can, "A hundid months every turn, Mama!"

"Maya, why are the girls causing such a racket? Hush now, girls. I'm trying to concentrate on fixing this leak," my father Gideon called from my parents' bedroom.

Our cottage wasn't large. Sound carried through the open-plan kitchen and sitting area to the two bedrooms and washroom in the back. Father was always fixing something. He also didn't appreciate it when I was being too loud. In solidarity, the wooden walls groaned with exertion; grumpy storm winds relentlessly shoving against them.

"Sorry, Father!" I replied and then turned to look back at Mama with eagerness in my gaze.

Earlier this week, my best friend Kaden said our teacher, Magister Barden, told him what snow was. About how slippery it was and that you could slide down the big hill in the woods if it was covered in the cold, white stuff.

We never got to see snow because we always went to sleep in the pods every turn. Honestly, it was the most unfair thing I had ever heard in my entire life.

My ice-blue eyes glared toward the back of the cottage, imagining them burning through the walls to the backyard's overwintering shed—a detached conservatory made of glass and shiny metal—where the closest Dormancy pods were sheltered. That glass shed never needed repairs for Father to fix.

I grumbled, "Mama, I just don't understand why we gotta go to sleep for so long. I'd rather be playing with Letti and Kaden in the snow. Kaden said we could slide down the big hill if bunches of snow were on it. You know, the one by the meadow with all those froggies and butterflies in the summer."

Mama let the rest of Alette's golden curls slip from her fingers as she looked at me with a soft smile. "That does sound lovely, Seryn. Remember when we talked about the Elder Laws?" Mama sat between Alette and me; her eyes softened as she looked at each of us. She wrapped her arms around our shoulders, cradling us. "For the last century, the mortal realm has followed them. When it's Autumn Equinox, everyone goes into Dormancy pods and rests inside until the Spring Equinox."

"I knoooow, Mama. But why do we gotta? I'd be really good and not do anything to upset the Elders if I could stay awake." My cheeks flushed with determination.

"I know you would, my little star, but it isn't a choice. If a person doesn't go into a pod, it's reported to the Elders, and they're put to sleep forever," Mama said while smoothing her palm down my deep-auburn curls. She continued when I opened my mouth to ask another question, "And, yes, the Elders know all, even though they live far away from Evergryn on Pyria Island. They have a whole lot of"—Mama looked up and scrunched her forehead—"helpers who ensure the Dormancy is done correctly ... so no one is hurt."

Mama's hand paused on the back of my neck under the thick curtain of my hair, then traced along the small scar beneath my hairline. She stared straight ahead at the front door, her hazel eyes glassy and reflecting the lightning flashing through the windows.

I jolted when Father appeared behind us, my chair croaking in surprise. He placed a hand on Mama's shoulder and leaned forward to kiss the top of her head. Her scarlet-colored hair gleamed in the cottage's candlelight as if it drew power from the flames. Mama leaned into him for a moment, and then Father put away his tools in the nearest kitchen cupboard.

Without moving, Father added, "Besides, girls, you wouldn't want everyone in Midst Fall to starve because you wanted to play in the snow. Would you?" He turned around and arched one eyebrow, looking at me. My eyes shifted to focus on my toes curling in my worn stockings. My shoulders hunched inward as if a heavy pile of wet blankets were plopped onto my back.

Mama made a clicking noise and swatted her arm in the air toward Father. "Don't be so harsh, Gideon. You don't need to scare them." Father's mouth tipped up on one side as if he was trying to smile but was also sucking on a bitter lemon. He often looked like that, but more so when looking in my direction.

"I don't want everyone to starve!" Alette shouted as her eyes glistened with upset. Her hazel eyes, so much like Mama's, appeared more golden when she was distraught. I leaned over and grabbed Letti's little hand, squeezing gently.

Mama kissed the top of my sister's now frizzy curls and tightened her arms around us. "What your father meant was that we need to participate in the Dormancy every turn because it's everyone's duty. We must ensure everyone has the resources to survive when we're not in the pods. It's just the way it is, my loves."

I thought about this for a moment, concluding I wouldn't get anywhere else by asking more questions tonight. I let go of my sister's hand and blew out a soft breath. "All right, Mama."

Like a cat stretching after a nap, my shoulders uncurled. I leaned against the back of my chair as straight and tall as I could, taking care not to tip it over. I wanted everyone to be safe. Mama said it was what we needed to do and had always been done, so I'd do it. Still, I wouldn't stop wondering how it would feel to live without being forced to sleep half of my life away.

The thunder cracked through the silence in our home, lightning flashing through the windows for one brief moment. One day, I hoped we'd all dream when we wanted to. I didn't realize then that nightmares could be mistaken for dreams. And by the time you realized what was happening, it was already too late.

1

THE WITHERING

NOWADAYS

*A*ncient grymwood trees towered above me like primordial sentinels of the forest. They made a meal of the sunlight breaching their bristly crowns, devouring the dappled rays before they reached the ground below. Their massive, ashen trunks consumed any shadows cast close to the earth. A murky film of fog, which often lingered in the woods, reverently caressed their tangled roots.

A drop of perspiration slipped between my shoulder blades. Damp, moss-scented air swirled into my lungs as my neck craned upward, my gaze searching the underside of the thick tree canopy. I squinted, trying to find any light at all. The packed treetops were so dense, it was like glimpsing glimmering stars poking through the night sky.

Though most trees clutched dying, cord-like branches and bundles of parched, awl-shaped needles, there were still several clinging to life. Various shades of green painted the wiry, pointed leaves closest to the canopy, even though their brethren below were pallid shades of beige and yellow. There was resilience in sporadic patches of healthy bark, ripe with an auburn shade as deep as the color of my windswept curls.

When the trees looked healthier, I knew we were closer to home, their graying trunks not yet defeated. My little sister Alette used to say our entire cottage could fit inside the base of a grymwood tree trunk. Our upstairs neighbors would be the critters surviving in the branches grasping at the sky.

A small smile threatened to overtake the straight line of my lips, pressed together in determination. I peeked at the back of Letti's golden hair, sweeping her shoulders with every step. Her back straight as a grymwood, she walked well ahead. Our father Gideon was beside her on the northern path toward home, toward Evergryn. Even without the rays of light, her messy curls still shimmered like a sunset's reflection bouncing atop ocean currents.

She wasn't so little anymore, going on eighteen. Tomorrow, I was turning twenty-one, and I longed for those times when her big hazel eyes shone brightly. When we both were full of mystical notions and endless hope.

I sighed and looked toward the obscured dirt path we traversed, adjusting the bulky bag on my shoulder. We had been hiking home for the last couple of days without enough rest, food, or water. The Larkins, our closest neighbors, journeyed with us.

My body was so fatigued that if I stopped walking, I thought I might sink into the desiccated dirt and never move again. I'd be buried under dead grym needles. Held down by the colossal roots, draining me of my body's moisture.

Just as my macabre musings spiraled further, something tiny but solid bounced off my cheek. I jumped in surprise, causing my bag to fall off my shoulder and onto the dirt. "By the Ancients, what was *that?*"

"Ah, there you are, Seryn. I was wondering if you were still with us." Kaden, my soon-to-be ex-best friend, chuckled, dropping the rest of the small pebbles he had ready in his palm. His words always sounded like they were hanging on the tail end of a grin.

His older brother Gavrel was a few steps ahead of us but glanced back at me, my hand still touching my cheek where the pebble had struck. Assessing there wasn't any real danger or damage, he glowered at Kaden and then turned back, marching forward while muttering something like, "You know the Ancients aren't listening anymore."

I lifted my bag with a wry grin pasted on my face. Brushing off the dead needles and dirt, I flicked the remnants at Kaden. "You could have hit me in the eye, you brute. I have a mind to stab you with grym needles right in your tender bits, Kade Larkin!"

He pivoted to the side of the path, avoiding the small spray of earth. My scolding didn't hold any weight, and he knew it. His smirk made that clear. I could never stay upset with him for long.

Kaden came to walk next to me again, adjusting his own bag and helping me pull mine atop my shoulder. I plucked a random bit of dry moss from the end of his dark, shaggy hair, the color of rich soot left after a burned log.

"I would never dream of poking you in the eye! How dare you. You wound me," he declared, clutching his chest.

I scoffed and thumped him on the arm, mirroring his bright smile. We trudged on wordlessly, the crunches of pebbles and brittle twigs breaking beneath our feet audible. A few solemn ravens scrutinized our progress, perching on petrified grymwood branches. Kaden scratched the back of his neck and broke the quiet. "What were you daydreaming about, Ser? It looked pretty dire."

"Just thinking about when we were little and thought we

could live in the grymwood trunks. So many more of them were alive back then." I shrugged my shoulder free from the weight of my bag. "Remember all the birds and animals we used to see? Especially in our meadow with the big hill? Everything is disintegrating around us nowadays," I huffed, swatting at an errant curl tickling my forehead. "The journey back from this Rationing has been ..."

"Absolute shit?" Kaden scoffed.

I snickered, nodding in agreement. "Not to mention the food rations aren't as helpful as they used to be. It doesn't even matter we don't have a horse and wagon anymore—everything we're provided fits on our backs." My eyes stung thinking of our old, chestnut-colored stallion, Alweo. He passed on several turns ago.

Kaden's brows furrowed, and his ever-present grin faded. "It's absolute rubbish that the Elders and their followers live comfortably while the rest of us scrounge together for food and water."

"Keep your voices down, you two," Gavrel hissed, spinning around. His scowl etched deeper into his lips. "Are you trying to get yourselves culled?"

"Take it easy, Gav." Kaden slapped a big hand on his brother's tense shoulder. "Who is going to report us? Ah, watch your back. That little gnat by your ear looks damn suspicious." Kaden wiggled his fingers near his brother's ear.

"Be serious." Gavrel brushed Kaden's hand away. "We know the Elders have ears everywhere. Not to mention the reach their embers have." His visage fell and softened for a fleeting moment. I blinked, wondering if I had imagined it.

"We all miss her, Gav. We miss ... all of them. We'll be more cautious," I murmured, gently squeezing his hand. Gavrel's emerald eyes flashed, and his gaze diverted to our embracing hands. Blinking once, he dipped his head and turned, walking faster ahead.

Kaden and I continued onwards. "He's right, you know. You need to be careful with how you speak of the Elders," I muttered.

"I think you should be less careful." I bumped my shoulder into his arm, squinting my eyes at him. He sighed, dipping his head. "Fine. I'll try, but I won't like it." After a moment, he murmured, "He's never been the same since Ma was culled."

"I know." My arm slipped around his waist. Their mother, Hestia Larkin, had been accused of using ember, or mystical powers, to help her family avoid the Dormancy. This was back when Gavrel was eighteen turns, and Kaden and I were thirteen.

No one knew who had made the accusation—most likely one of the Somneia, the Elders' covert network of spies. It's not like it mattered when the consequence had been so swift and without inquiry. Their father had unexpectedly died the following turn. A heart condition was the suspected culprit.

"I know you do, Ser, and I'm sorry for that, too." Kaden took my bag from my shoulder and carried it in one hand, relieving me of the burden. Around my shoulders, he draped his other arm, solid as the thick trunks surveying us. His warmth soaked into my side, easing the dull ache burrowing inside my chest.

The fog was thinning a bit. I noticed the faint, sweet floral scent mingling with moss in the air. We were almost to the meadow we played in as children, and home was less than an hour's walk beyond that. The meadow wasn't bursting with life as it was then, but it was clinging to life all the same. Like most of the people in our realm—Midst Fall.

As we approached the field, I paused and breathed deeply in awe. A small red astra poppy emerged from a patch of tall, dried grass. I caressed one fanned petal, the vermilion hue melting into its midnight-colored center. A vibrating energy hummed along my fingertips, and I longed to absorb some of the bloom's courage.

"These always were your favorite," Letti whispered,

crouching to smell another cerise flower. "Isn't it incredible that something so vulnerable can survive—can find the strength to grow—even when the world is crumbling around it?"

"It is." The corners of my mouth curled, my head tilting as I considered my sister. She wiggled her fingers at me, smiling, and I pulled her up, leaving the tiny flower to bask in the sun.

We were all together, walking as a unit now. The meadow had mesmerized us, convincing everyone to slow their pace and remain cognizant of its tranquil beauty.

From the side of my vision, a hovering, soft greenish glow startled me. My hand flew up to touch my bottom lip as if to hold in a gasp. I swung my gaze toward it but only saw Kaden keeping in step with me. I shook my head, my soft curls dancing around my ears. My hand dropped to my side, and a small giggle slipped past my lips. I must have been more exhausted than I thought.

As another raven flew across our path, I concluded if ember existed anywhere, this meadow would nurture it. But it was a rarity in our realm, at least over the last century—unless you were an Elder or one of their Druik enforcers, the Akridais. According to the law, if someone developed powers once they reached twenty-one turns, they were required to register as a Druik without delay.

Sometimes, I wondered what it was like to be a Druik. Having powers would be unnerving. If the Ancients had gifted me with ember abilities, I wasn't sure I would have taken the path Hestia was accused of. Yet, I couldn't condemn anyone for protecting their family. My eyes glanced at Gavrel, his steps never faltering, never relenting.

As we came to the opposite edge of the meadow, I stole one last look at the small clusters of astra poppies peppering it. A sea of toast-colored grasses and moss covered the big hill, sloping into the meadow like the crest of a wave frozen in time.

It was a matter of time before this place fell, conquered by the Withering—the progressive death of our lands and everything within them.

2

THIRTEEN FROGS

BACK THEN

*K*aden, Letti, and I had spent nearly all day in the meadow. It was the perfect way to celebrate my thirteenth birthday. I lay in a patch of tall, fresh grass, feeling blissfully content. A spotted moth fluttered above me.

I was grateful Father had gone without me, taking our wagon and horse, Alweo, to the Rationing. It was rare that I indulged on my birthday. It always coincided with the Autumn Equinox—when the Dormancy pods awakened. Since Mama wasn't around anymore, I usually went to the Rationings. However, Father had gotten a late start and didn't want me to slow down the journey. This wasn't the first time he had made it clear that my presence was unwelcome.

My eyelids scrunched shut for a moment, squeezing out memories of my mother and the effortless dismissal of my father. Over the last six turns, I'd gotten adept at pushing those feelings away, deep down into a hidden place within my chest. *Not today, Seryn*, I ordered myself. Today was a good day. A day to enjoy the vivid blue sky and the butterflies dancing among the flowers.

I sat up, watching Kaden help Letti catch frogs. Earlier, Letti had presented me with a handmade box, declaring it was for my birthday. It was crafted of grizzled grymwood bark, held together with tall blades of grass and bendy catbane reeds. I stroked the side of it. A cozy warmth spread through my chest at the memory of her excited smile. My second gift was the team of frogs they were catching—thirteen frogs, one for each turn of my birthday.

"Thirteen, Ser!" Letti bounced toward me with her hands cupped in front of her. Placing the frog in the box, she shouted, "Happy birthday! Wait … where are the other ones?" She sounded dismayed as Kaden walked up beside her, a goofy grin on his face. His light-green eyes sparkled with mischief. He had the most striking eyes. They reminded me of soft fern leaves stretching up to the sun.

I smiled at my sister. "I think they wanted to leap around in the little pond over yonder, but I chatted with each one before they went. Thank you so much, you two."

Letti plopped beside me as the last frog leaped out of the box. A giggle drifted along her exhaled breath.

"We should probably head back home," Kaden said with an exaggerated pout. "Your father should get home before dark, and I have to help Pa get things ready before the Dormancy tomorrow."

"I suppose you're right, Kade. Let's head home," I sighed, agreeing.

Kaden snapped his fingers and stepped backward, strands of dark hair falling over his forehead. "Hold on a moment while I grab some flowers for Ma. I think that'll cheer her up a bit." I grinned at him and reclined, resting my forearms on the soft grass.

Kaden's mother had been feeling ill lately and often needed

to rest. Kaden was helping a lot more around their home and never once complained about it. I knew he lost sleep worrying about his mother and brother. The youthful, usually fawn-colored skin under his eyes looked smudged with dark exhaustion.

Gavrel had been away for a few months after joining the Elders' warrior legion, the Order of Draumr. He'd already be training to be a warrior ... if he had survived the journey to Pneumali City. I often pondered how Gavrel was doing. He must have been experiencing so many wonders in the southern desert-like metropolis.

I squeezed my eyes closed for a moment, squashing any doubts about his survival. If he had perished in the Perilous Bogs, he would be another bloated body floating in a peaty swamp. I grimaced, praying to the Ancients for his safety.

The Perilous Bogs coated the center of the realm, spilling into the western lowlands. Most of what we knew of the area was passed down in whispered warnings. Few people from the northern or eastern regions chanced traversing the bogs—unless they had no other way to reach the south.

Before he left, there were missives, delivered by harbinger starlings, that Haadra, the eastern region, was flooded, its rivers engulfing much of the land in brackish water and sludge. To ensure they made it to training on time, Gavrel and a few other young men from our village agreed that passing through the Perilous Bogs was their only practical option.

"Ready, miladies?" Kaden bowed theatrically before us using a haughty Eastern Pneumalian accent our teacher once demonstrated.

Magister Barden tried to keep us interested in his lessons, enthusiastically teaching us what he could of the different regions, the Ancients, and the history behind ember. Of course, that was all layered with reminders of the Elder Laws and why

OF WITHERING DREAMS

the Dormancy was so vital. I rolled my eyes to the sky and then over to Letti.

Laughter burst out of us simultaneously as we made eye contact before looking at Kaden. He was brandishing his bundle of flowers and doing some little dance, feet moving back and forth swiftly.

I didn't want the beauty of this day to end, but alas, time marched on. I sat up and brushed off my plain, mud-colored kirtle. My linen chemise dipped down over my shoulder.

Kaden handed the flowers to Letti and then gave me his hand to pull me up. His other hand swept along my shoulder, righting my chemise. My breath hitched, and a wave of prickly heat washed over my face as I stood.

"Uh, sorry," Kaden mumbled and dropped his hands. He nodded in the direction of our homes. I could have sworn his cheeks were flushed a deep shade of crimson as he turned to walk ahead. Shaking out my hands, I reached out and pulled Letti up.

As we made the trek back home, my thoughts drifted like a leaf losing its battle atop a river current. My musings often circled one main focal point ... the Dormancy. How could they not when Midst Fall's survival depended on it? At least, that's what the Elder Laws decreed.

Every turn, seven days before the Autumn Equinox, we knew the Dormancy would begin when a pulsing amber glow spilled through the conservatory's glass walls. The light was so bright, it was difficult to sleep if your home was near one.

During this window of time, everyone had the opportunity to attend the last Rationing of the turn. Most made the journey if they could guarantee to return home in time.

Growing up, there were tales of those who didn't make it back. These were shared around spooky campfires in the dead of night. Parents would tell their children the stories as cautionary tales meant to instill a healthy, respectful fear of the

Dormancy. It was common knowledge that failure to enter a pod in time would result in culling. I wasn't sure what that entailed, but I didn't want the experience firsthand, regardless.

Kaden kicked several stones into a grymwood ahead of us, distracting me from my thoughts. "I wonder how much your father was able to get this time. I know Ma and Pa appreciate him helping us this Rationing."

"He doesn't mind. I just hope it's enough," I murmured, looking down at my hands fiddling with the fabric of my dress. During the Rationing, each family was allotted a small amount of grain and pickled vegetables to supplement their provisions for a few months. When feasible, it was also prudent to barter food and other resources with the others who made the journey.

Our small village only had forty-eight inhabitants. Each family tried to contribute food and supplies for trade at the biannual Rationings. Unfortunately, the last few months had been taxing, and our village hadn't had many viable crops. Nevertheless, I was grateful to live where everyone tried to help each other when they could—even when we were all struggling.

Father said we were lucky to live in Evergryn because it wasn't overcrowded—unlike Pneumali City, where people were supposedly starving in the streets. My fingernails clenched into the fleshy parts of my palms through the scratchy linen I was clasping. People were going hungry, and it wasn't right. Children were languishing with nowhere safe and warm to go at night.

I peeked at Letti and gave her a quick side hug as we strolled along the wooded path. She leaned into me a bit, her warmth a salve on my burgeoning ire. If I were a Draumr warrior, I would make it my mission to protect and help those who couldn't. Gavrel and I had that in common.

Members of the Order of Draumr directed and managed the Rationings. Many young people joined the Order with starry-eyed visions of heroism, hoping to become warriors. I'm sure some were not ecstatic to be assigned to such mundane tasks. Evidently, not every role within the Order could be an exciting adventure. I smiled, imagining Gavrel handing out jarred pickles all day, an insolent glower plastered across his face.

I often teased him that his face would stay that way, and then his emerald eyes would flash with mirth while the line of his mouth buttoned firmly together. He probably didn't want anyone to know he could express joy. *Ancients forbid he release a chuckle out into the realm*, I mused.

I snickered on his behalf as we neared my family's grymwood cottage. It almost reminded me of the box Letti and Kaden had made me for my birthday. All weathered and patched up, but still cherished.

My breath caught inside my throat as we all paused and stared. The pulsing, honey-colored light from the conservatory throbbed behind the cottage. Gleaming radiance repeatedly caressed its worn edges, winking at the sun overhead on its way to the west.

Even after all these turns, the sight of the awakened pods still stole my breath away. My limbs twitched with the urge to leap away—back into the safety of the meadow with my birthday frogs.

3

CRUMPLED PETALS

STILL BACK THEN

*K*aden grabbed my hand and pulled us toward the conservatory. Letti skipped after us. Her bouncing golden curls seemed to meld into the pulsating glow.

Absently, I reached back and rubbed the flat, star-shaped scar on my nape like Mama used to. It often beat in time with my heart... and the illuminated Dormancy pods.

The conservatory was hauntingly beautiful, despite housing such ominous items. Ten thick, adjacent glass panels formed a perfect decagon, and the shiniest metal I'd ever seen crept along each connecting point. From the outside, the glass walls curved slightly inwards, giving the impression it was imploding. Its silver base was just large enough to house the starburst of pods within. The glass roof was rounded, like a soap bubble caught on a spoon.

When the pods were inactive, there wasn't any way to enter the conservatory. Kaden and I had spent countless hours trying over the turns, but the aqueous metal seams fused with the glass, making it impossible to find a crevice offering a way in.

I had often watched the sleeping vessels with my face pressed against the concave glass. Their glossy obsidian shapes reminded me of human-sized dewdrops gently stretched out. To Kaden's dismay, I sometimes joked that the Dormancy pods were staring back at me, like the giant eyes of a lurking spider. Kaden loathed spiders.

Finding an available vessel in a village our size was easy. There were five of them within an hour's walk. We were lucky we had the one in our backyard. The Larkins always used this one, too, as it was the closest for them. It was incomprehensible how they were built. They'd been scattered across our world for as long as anyone could remember. At least, that's what Mama had always said.

I squeezed Kaden's fingers, his hand still wrapped around mine. He looked into my eyes with an unreadable expression, which I found unnerving. His irises looked varnished in shades of umber with the bright light coating them. I turned back to the conservatory; its surreal energy coaxing my focus.

Tomorrow was the seventh day. It was when the dazzling beams would be suctioned into the pods. The dark, solid forms would transform into swirls of smoky mist confined within amber-colored glass. Within a few thumps of a heart, the golden glass would rotate on its axis and evaporate from view, fading into the void without a sound. The inky, twirling mist would slither and hover in the pod's shape as if still encased.

That's when you knew your time was up. There was nothing else you could do but plant your whole being within the dark unknown—cradled inside one of the suspended caskets made of churning nightmares. My head felt stretched and fuzzy thinking about it. I was sure Kaden could feel the moisture slick on my palm.

I was about to grab Letti's hand when a sobbing shriek sliced through our numb fixation on the conservatory. The three of us whipped our heads toward the disturbance. Letti gasped, and my hands flew up to cover the startled cry clawing its way out of my throat.

"What's the meaning of this? Stop this madness!" Kaden's father, Emmet Larkin, bellowed as he struggled against two armored Draumr guards. They were holding him back by the shoulders.

A sobbing Hestia was floating parallel to the earth, her paralyzed body in a stiff line as if made of ice. Hazy ropes of milky light wrapped around her figure.

On her left was a stern-looking woman and, on her right, a grim-faced man. They shared matching tattoos that covered the front of their necks in black ink. Each looked like a mishmash of geometric shapes and lines, the pattern vaguely creating a hieroglyph of a locust.

They were Akridais. I was certain of it. It was my first time seeing the Elders' elite Druik enforcers. They wielded their gifts at the discretion of and on behalf of the Elders and their laws. The strength of an Akridai's ember was immense though still significantly weaker than an Elder's.

My heart tried to crack through my ribs as logic overtook my initial confusion. There was only one outcome when you were in their custody. Kaden must have realized this as he lurched toward the path they were on. I tried grabbing the back of his tunic, but he jerked out of my grip.

The Akridais' thick pewter-colored robes and capes whipped behind them as they marched the group to the conservatory. A menacing fluorescent-yellow aura clung to each of their bodies. Ebony shades slithered within the glowing air around each like grymseed oil creeping atop a puddle. The epicenters of their powers were pulsing orbs of light suspended between their open palms. The slippery, twisting auras breathed, siphoning in and out of the orb.

"Halt, dirtling!" the female Akridai commanded, neither breaking her stride nor dissipating the energy between her hands. Kaden did not stop his trajectory. "Halt, or they will perish this instant!"

Kaden stilled, his body tense. His parents, the guards, and Akridais reached us and the conservatory. I tugged Letti behind me. She still clutched the sweet bouquet Kaden had picked, cradling the petals against her chest.

"Pa, what is happening?!" Kaden's voice was frantic. Mr. Larkin swung his head from left to right, desperation blanketing his eyes. He had stopped struggling when Kaden ran toward them.

Upon reaching the sealed conservatory, the male Akridai lifted one hand away from the energized globe in his other palm and touched the center of the concave glass wall. His ember crept over the panel in oily tendrils. The glass devoured the writhing energy and then dissolved into nothingness from the center outwards.

The male turned around and waved his hand toward Hestia, who was whimpering now. Her body glided through the created doorway and paused next to the closest Dormancy pod. The glow from her bindings was consumed by the pod's pitch-black shell, no reflection in its glistening form.

"Listen well, dirtlings, for I will only say this once. Hestia Larkin is accused of using unregistered ember. Furthermore, she is accused of wielding said ember to tamper with the Dormancy pods." The male Akridai looked bored with the entire ordeal. Everyone was holding their breath as he went on. "The punishment is culling, which we will proceed with immediately."

Letti started crying and dropped the astra poppies to the earth. The ground felt like it was tilting, but my legs locked, keeping me upright. My breathing was labored. "Go, now, Letti! Get inside the cottage!" I cried, pushing her toward it. To my relief, she listened and ran. Out of the corner of my eye, Father arrived and caught Letti in his arms. His head moved subtly from side to side in disappointment as he glimpsed the scene. He brushed the back of her hair and carried her back home without a second glance.

Kaden was shouting, his expression burning with anguish. He was now being held back by his father. Solemn tears were streaming down Mr. Larkin's cheeks, pooling in his beard. I couldn't feel my legs as they carried me over to Kaden. We all understood there was nothing we could do to stop this.

With the wet taste of salt lining my lips, I took Kaden's hand. "Kade, let's be here for her," I implored. He looked at me, his eyes like a wild animal caught in a snare. Then he stopped struggling, defeated.

The Draumrs flanked the doorway as we approached the entrance. The Akridais stood at either end of the pod, feeding it their ember as the male did with the glass panel earlier. As the pod drank in their energy, the amber glass appeared, the murky mist within alive.

Simultaneously, they brushed their fingertips in a circular motion over the ends of the now amber surface. A burst of neon-yellow zipped from their dimming auras down through their arms and hands. The glass spun and vanished.

Together, the Akridais guided Hestia's incapacitated form into the pod, glowing power streaming from their hands and creating the path. Kaden cried, "We are here, Ma!"

Hestia strained her eyes toward us as far as she could, her head immobile. Her eyes were shiny. She blinked once. One solitary tear crept down her cheek. "I'll save a spot in Surrelia for each of you. I love y—"

As the pod's encasement reappeared and twirled into place, her last word was cut short, wrapping her in a morbidly beautiful cocoon. Placing their outstretched hands on the vessel once more, the Akridais closed their eyes in concentration.

Behind their hieroglyphic tattoos, their skin burned bright before fading. The last of their waning, oily auras absorbed into their arms and surged through their hands into the glass. The Akridais each slumped, looking drained. Without another word, they left the conservatory and walked away into the dusk, the Draumrs obediently following.

Before we could step inside, the glass wall reappeared, entombing Hestia. Kaden, Mr. Larkin, and I pressed our bodies into the glass as close as possible, not breaking eye contact with her. I didn't want her to be alone. This couldn't be real. She was a second mother to me.

Within a few breaths, the pod emanated a twitching, golden light. Hestia was screaming in what looked like pure agony, but only deafening silence met us. The inky mist slithered into her ears, her mouth—any pore that could be found. Then, without warning, her body turned to ash and burst into stardust. The pod turned solid and dark. The curtain had been drawn.

Mr. Larkin sagged to his knees, weeping onto the glass. A scream tore out of Kaden as he charged into the woods. I was a grymwood, silent and planted into the earth. My feet tingled, ready for movement. They carried me back to my cottage, crushing the rest of the flowers Letti had dropped. In my stupor, I didn't notice Gavrel approaching.

As he took in the scene before him, his eyes blazed, making them appear as if they would combust anything in their path. His fists clenched so tightly at his sides that I thought they might implode. He wore the standard, soot-colored Draumr uniform, a sword strapped across his back. He looked older somehow. More rugged. More broad. His shoulder and chest muscles were straining against the fabric of his structured overcoat with every ragged breath he took.

I murmured breathlessly, "Gavrel, I don't..."

And I passed out, Gavrel catching me before I hit the petal-strewn ground.

4

A RAVENOUS SPIDER

NOWADAYS

*D*arkness scratched my insides, clawing its way out of my skin. I heard my mother's voice as if she were shouting my name underwater. I couldn't see her. I couldn't reach her. The stifling atmosphere around me was directionless and suffocating. I was going to drown in this black hole with her.

Out of the corner of my eye, a shimmer flickered, a beacon in the void. I jolted in my bed, gasping for air. Wild wisps of damp hair clung to my neck. My starburst scar pounding in time with my heart.

"What's happening?" Letti's sleepy whisper anchored me firmly in my body. I brushed my fingers over my hair and wiped the sleep from my eyes. A slice of dawn slipped through the top of the curtains in our room. There was no pulsing glow, only the steady rays of the morning sun. It was time for the Dormancy.

"Just a nightmare. Sorry I woke you," I sighed and stretched my arms, shifting out of bed to plant my feet on the ground.

"It's all right, Ser. I wasn't sleeping well anyway. I'll check if Father needs anything before we head to the conservatory." Letti gave me a quick hug and left, leaving me in silence.

Enforcing my resolve, I pushed to my feet. My deep inhalation propelled me upward as my feet pressed into the wood floorboards. I began preparing myself for our long, relentless slumber.

"Hurry up, girls. Let's get this over with," Father chided as if we were taking a quick trip into the village.

"We're ready, Father." Letti's melodic voice floated down the hall. I left the washroom and followed her to the kitchen.

Father placed a kiss on Letti's head and nodded once toward me. For someone with such rich brown eyes, the color of warm catbane reeds, his gaze left a chill in its wake. He rarely looked my way, as if I was an apparition just out of his peripheral. His eyes softened when he looked back at Letti.

It was always a pleasant surprise to see any show of warmth from him, even if it wasn't directed at me. I didn't recall a time when he was especially affectionate toward me. No one could accuse Gideon Vawn of being a tender man. When Mama had disappeared all those turns ago, it was like he hid himself away—deep beneath layers of ice—rather than breaking into tiny fragments.

I would never scrub the memory of him frantic and searching the conservatory so long ago when I was a girl of seven turns. My thoughts had been muddled as I awoke from our six-month coma. I recalled him clawing his fingers within Mama's pod, the cloying mist sticking to his hands as he pulled them out. We had all gone into the Dormancy pods as usual that autumn but had awoken with one less body in the spring. Mama had disappeared from our lives that day as if she had never been—an illusion called back to the murky abyss.

"All right, onwards." Father straightened his already rigid spine, turning and ushering us into the damp, cool morning.

We made our way to the conservatory. The Larkin brothers were already waiting near the now-open entrance. Kaden put his arm around my shoulders and ruffled Letti's hair. She let out a quiet laugh and swatted his hand. Gavrel greeted us with a solemn nod, not a wrinkle apparent in his dark Draumr uniform. He always tried to be home for the Dormancy instead of stationed elsewhere.

Letti brushed the back of her hand along the back of mine. "I wish we remembered … well, anything when we're in there." Her small, pert nose crinkled. "It's like waking from a fuzzy dream that slips from you the moment your eyes wake."

"You can almost grasp the memory, but it floats away just as you almost catch it," I murmured in agreement.

"Enough, girls," Father snapped. "Let's move on. Why discuss things we will never understand and have no control over? The Elders know what's best, and we'll continue to follow their laws without useless whims." He waved his hand toward the pods, his direction final.

Cheeks burning, I sealed my lips into a tight line. Even though I wasn't a child any longer, he still had a way of making me feel small. I lifted my chin and followed Letti into our glass tomb. Perhaps this was the turn I would vanish like Mama. Maybe I was made of mist as well. Or a fragile seedling caught in a dark gale, never given the chance to bloom.

I was floating in a murky, gelatinous stew. My limp body was suspended in the languidly coiling matter. *Might as well be a turnip ready to be devoured.* I clenched my eyes shut.

The dusky haze wasn't particularly damp, but if I attempted to move, tendrils licked against my skin, clinging to it. The sensation reminded me vaguely of walking into a spiderweb sprinkled with dew. I forced myself to breathe in deeply and exhale slowly. It took a few moments for the glass to rematerialize.

On my fifth exhale, the vessel's encasement locked into place with a soft swish of air. I was a fly entangled in spider silk. I bit my bottom lip hard, trying to distract myself from the mounting panic bubbling in my gut.

We were taught not to fight this process. Just breathe. Let the ember envelop your body. Let it soak into your mind. I was convinced whoever drafted those instructions had *never* been through the Dormancy. *They could go straight to the fiery pits of the Nether Void,* I thought bitterly.

Shadowy tendrils surrounded me, now frantically whirling. Clinging mist slithered under my clothes as if trying to melt into my skin. The feeling was oppressive, like being too sticky with sweat on a sweltering summer day.

The amber glass was cast in its glow again, the back of my eyelids flashing in shades of apricot. I forced myself to open my eyes. To face the churning terror sinking into my rigid muscles.

All at once, the mist burrowed within, deep into the marrow of my bones. I tried to scream but couldn't as scorching pain ripped through every tendon, every joint. I was a paralyzed fly being consumed alive by a ravenous spider. Then everything went black.

5

HAZY DREAMS

A bright burst of light snapped me into awareness. I could move my arms. My fingers were tingling and stiff, but I still wiggled them. My eyelids felt pasted to my pupils and were reluctant to open. A crisp breeze wafted over my face; the scent acrid with decay.

Scrunching my cheeks toward my forehead, I opened my eyes, squinting and adjusting my sight to the gloom around me. Pushing myself into a sitting position was a burden—my muscles were achy and my bones creaky. A cough scratched my throat, and I unglued my tongue from the roof of my mouth. *Had I drunk a gallon of honey wine?* I wondered.

With effort, I stood. I hugged my arms protectively around my curves as I absorbed my surroundings. Between patches of dense haze, stony islet landforms appeared suspended and rocking in the sky. They weren't supported or tethered to anything—simply hovering high above in the churning, stormy firmament. Below my feet, cracked clay plains stretched far beyond the horizon. The land was pocked with massive shadows cast from the swaying islets. Every so often, a massive stone would plummet from a jagged base, cracking the ground on which it landed. Deeper fractures around the fallen rock splintered out from the impacts.

What the Ancients am I looking at? Am I dreaming? Panic bit into my spine, the chilly air slicing its way into my veins.

I took a few deep breaths, flexing my chilled fingers in time with each exhalation and extending with each inhalation. I rubbed my eyes, thinking I could no longer see in color. Everything was smoggy and bleak. Watching my hands as they skimmed down my kirtle, I realized nothing was wrong with my vision. My skin, hair, and clothing were muted shades of gray. *Did this place bleed the pigments out of all that it touched?*

A whimper escaped my lips. I was wide awake but had lost my mind. I couldn't grasp any other explanation.

"Seryn!" I jumped as Letti erupted from a cloud of mist and tackled me.

"Letti, thank the Ancients. Do you know where we are? Is the Dormancy over?"

"I'm not sure what's going on. I saw a sparkling light and ran toward it." Her shoulders slumped as she stepped away from me.

"Ah, well, let's pick a direction and look for others." I turned, looking behind me. Far into the distance, a mass of jagged mountains bracketed the entrance of a valley. A furious, storming squall heaved over the vale, casting it in sinister shadows. The floating islets closest to its entrance juddered violently but also progressively decreased in size until they disappeared.

Acid frothed in my belly, my nose crinkling. I faced Letti and nodded stiffly to the pallid plains behind her, heeding the urge to evade the ominous valley entirely.

We drifted through the lifeless terrain, chalky dust clinging to our tattered leather slippers. Storm clouds rolled above as we avoided walking under the islets. Being crushed or impaled by crashing cobbles wasn't high on our list of things to do.

"My legs feel too heavy. I'm so tired, even though we haven't been walking long," Letti grumbled, her last word caught in a yawn.

"I think it's this place. Maybe it's made of nether ember or cursed," I offered with a shrug, the gesture taking more effort than it should have. I wondered where everyone else was and if they were safe. *How long had we been here?* My sense of time had ceased to exist. There was no sign of the sun to guide me. *Was it day or night?* Perhaps something had gone amiss with the pods' ember. *Was this the Nether Void?*

A vibrant glimmer ahead of us startled me from my spiraling theories. "Did you see that?" I asked, swatting Letti's shoulder.

She yawned again, her eyelids drooping over her faded eyes. She rubbed her shoulder, glowering. "Huh? No, what're you talking about?"

"Up ahead. There's a bright-green light!" I exclaimed, pushing my legs to move faster.

"Are you all right, Ser? I don't see anything." Her mouth curved slightly downward in confusion.

Maybe I was hallucinating, but I didn't care at this point. My breath quickened at witnessing such a vibrant hue mar the monochrome gloom. As we approached the glow, it shrank inward. In the mist, a person-shaped outline formed. I slowed and called out, "Hello?"

"Hello? Seryn, is that you?" a gruff voice responded.

"Kade!" I shouted and ran to the opaque form in the haze. Our bodies collided, and his sturdy arms scooped me up, twirling me through the fog. I moved to kiss his cheek, but he turned his face toward mine at the same moment. My lips brushed his, and heat raced through me, making me forget how cool the air was. His hands tightened on my waist before he set me down, his ears turning a darker shade. I glanced away and went to Letti's side, a smirk drawn on her pale face.

"Uh, I can't believe we found you," I said, shifting my feet. "Do you know where we are or what's going on?"

"Sadly, no. I've been walking around for who knows how long. A while ago, I thought someone was following me. It's all shadows here ... maybe I was seeing things." He scraped his hand down the dark stubble covering his strong jawline. He usually was clean-shaven. *Why am I so distracted by his facial hair?* I shook my head, my own hair falling over my shoulders. A sleepy smile carved through his stubble, his mouth full and wide. "Let's keep moving that way. There wasn't anything from where I came, and I'm guessing there wasn't anything in the direction you left. I'm hopeful we can find your father and Gavrel since we've found each other."

"Agreed. I don't think we should return to where I woke up." I shivered. "There was a creepy valley that way. It felt ... off."

Letti snorted. "Like everything else here."

I smiled, nudging her shoulder. "Obviously, but it was ... I don't know. More threatening somehow."

"Well, let's skip that part of the adventure then. Come on," Kaden laughed and moved perpendicular to the path we had been on.

WE WALKED FOR HOURS, or was it minutes? Days? I wasn't hungry or thirsty. I counted this as a blessing since there was no food or water to sustain us. The desire to lie down on the splintered ground, a sleeping corpse, was overwhelming. My thoughts were bobbing in a sea of dreary murkiness. *What was the point of going on?* I stretched my neck from side to side, trying to dislodge such notions. I glanced at Kaden and Letti beside me, forcing my shoulders back and marching on.

My eyes were playing tricks on me. I didn't bother mentioning the occasional glimpses of shadowy specters lingering in the margins of my vision. We didn't converse with each other. We were all depleted, weighed down with the unending mystery of our situation.

At last, we approached a craggy landscape speckled with imposing boulders. The haze dispersed. Closer to the horizon, the grounded boulders grew. This correlated with the gradually shrinking, suspended islets.

The sky was now mottled with black, agitated clouds, occasional streaks of lightning slicing through them. Odd, considering this region didn't appear to have seen water in centuries. Intermittently, a furious clap of thunder would explode in a mighty tantrum.

"Look over there!" Letti exclaimed.

I squinted in the direction she was pointing. A sturdy-looking woman slouched against a huge, wedge-shaped boulder. We walked to her, leaden legs hindering our pace. I couldn't tell if she was breathing. Her eyes were closed, and her head slumped against her shoulder.

Kaden leaned forward with his pointer finger leading the way. I rolled my eyes and smacked his finger away, snickering. "You goon, don't poke her." A sheepish smile pulled across his teeth as his hand swung back to his side.

The tips of my fingers touched her shoulder, covered in a tattered, dusty tunic. Around her waist, a leather belt cinched baggy trousers to her slim form. She looked to be in her late twenties, but it was hard to tell with everything so layered in shadows. Her straight, chin-length hair was a mess. Most of its dark strands were resting against her rounded cheeks.

"Hello, miss. Are you all right?" I jiggled her shoulder. Her head bobbed, her chin bouncing off her chest, and she yelped, rolling away in an unsteady crouch. Her hands reached toward her belt, grabbing air. Not finding what she wanted, she growled. My mouth fell open in surprise as a faint cherry-colored aura shimmered around her body. I glanced at Letti and

Kaden. Their gaze appeared wary; however, they did not seem startled. *Can't they see her lit up like a damned candle?*

"Come near me, and I'll claw your faces off!" she threatened, calling my attention back to her. The glow brightened with her exclamation.

I believed her.

"We mean you no harm. We were checking if you were still alive," I said gently, backing away. My hands opened in front of me, palms facing her. One of her eyebrows arched, and she rose, eyes still tracking us. The red shimmer around her dwindled.

"All right then. You seem fairly harmless, and that one is easy on the eyes." She nodded at Kaden with a smirk. Her accent was reminiscent of Magister Barden's Pneumalian impression but cheekier. *She must be from near the city in Southern Pneumali,* I thought, tilting my head.

"I'll put my claws away for now, but no funny business. I'm Breena Cadell; you can call me Breena. Unless you think of a marvelous nickname that I approve of." She snapped her fingers for emphasis and put the other hand on her cocked hip.

"Uh, nice to meet you, Breena," I replied, still bewildered, pushing one hand toward her. "I'm Seryn Vawn, and this is my sister Alette. My best friend, Kaden Larkin."

At once, Breena shook my hand in a powerful grip. She grabbed Kaden's hand but lingered, a sassy smile stretching her mouth wide. Kaden let loose an awkward chuckle, gulping. Somehow, he freed his hand from her grip, stepping closer to me as if for protection.

"Oh no, Kade. You aren't using me as your shield," I laughed, and so did Breena. Her grin brightened her pretty, heart-shaped face.

Kaden rolled his eyes to the skies, a lightning flash reflecting in them. "Anyway, shall we get moving again?"

"Yes, let's," Breena purred, clapping her hands together.

"How do you have so much energy? You were just passed

out, and I feel like I'm made of cement," Letti muttered, one side of her mouth tipping up.

"Must be the battle fever you all inspired within me ... or my sparkling personality." She smirked as a clap of thunder boomed. I chuckled, blowing out a small breath through my nose. Letti and Kaden smiled politely. *Sparkling, indeed.*

6

STYGIAN MURK

For what felt like days, we meandered through the landscape. It didn't trouble us that we neither ate nor drank. We succumbed to the weighty, dismal burden of this place. Even Breena's *sparkling personality* was fizzling. At times, we rested on the barren ground, chilled and numb. When it was time to move again, we dragged each other back from the depths of overwhelming despondency.

Along the way, we stumbled upon a few people in varying stages of defeat. Bodies were strewn across the broken earth, melding into the landscape. At best, they were incoherent; at worst, catatonic. We tried to help them, but they would not be moved. Eventually, we stopped trying. Or maybe we stopped seeing them, everything a shadow, an illusion. Our minds and bodies were drained of hope—of our will to go on.

We passed a man on our left, his form bent and unmoving. His body was a husk, desiccated skin stretching across a bony frame. Breena paused for a moment, staring at the withered body. "That's how my grandmother looked ..." Her bottom lip trembled, but she bit down on it.

"I'm not sure how long I was lying there before you found

me or how much time passed after I left 'er. Yesterday? Maybe days ago, I saw a light. Ran to it." She wiped her nose with the back of her hand. "But she was gone. It was too late."

I took her hand in mine, squeezing. "I'm so sorry, Breena."

She squeezed back, releasing her hold. She waved her hand in the air. "Thank you. When it's yer time, it's yer time. I'll see 'er again one day."

"Do you have anyone else you're looking for?" I murmured.

"No. It was just me 'n Gran." She pinched her lips inward between her teeth and wandered a short distance ahead of us. I left her to her grief.

If she wanted to talk, it seemed like she was the type of person who would seek me out. Something about fear and sorrow had a way of binding people together like water droplets in a storm cloud.

Images of shadowy phantoms loomed in our peripherals, lurking behind every rocky mass. Each lightning strike erased the shadows around their forms. "What are those?" Letti's voice was raspy, her raised hand limp.

"You can see those?" My eyebrows shot up, but my eyelids were still heavy with fatigue.

"Yeah, they've been following us for a long time," she replied, her voice drifting away. Kaden and Breena's heads bobbed in agreement.

"Ah, I thought I was hallucinating. I, um, think we need to move faster."

Now that we knew we were all seeing these creatures, our situation was more alarming. Kaden winced, his eyes clearing while he looked deeper into the hidden spots surrounding us. "I think you're right, Ser. They seem to be getting closer."

Without further discussion, we all pushed forward. One specter was getting fairly bold, stalking closer than the others. It wasn't bothering to hide within shadows any longer.

It was twice the size of an adult human. Glowing yellow eyes were the only things stable within its form. Undulating above the parched terrain, the creature's figure was a dense mass of twisting, black smog. The very shadows around us had come alive, agitated and hungry for any light they could touch.

My scar stamped a tattoo on my nape, urging me forward. The thunder punctuated my growing fear. Far off on my right, one of the shadow creatures engulfed a person who lay motionless on the ground. The person was flickering with a gloomy shade of blue, but their aura was dimming. The creature was slurping the person's radiance, its core shimmering the same blue before being devoured by the churning shadows of its silhouette. Its yellow eyes beamed brighter momentarily before it left the human husk, heading in our direction.

A green flash snapped my attention back. "Watch out!" Kaden yelled, pushing Breena and me to the left. The creature stalking us swooped past my right, missing me. It paused and turned toward Kaden, its smoke darkening.

Letti was to my left, running as fast as she could, screaming. Breena grabbed my hand, pulling me in that direction. Her body was burning red again—a look of determination set on her grim face. I glanced back at Kaden, his body now shimmering in the color of spring clovers.

"Run, Kaden! Don't let it touch you!" I cried out.

With his lips set in a steely line, he feinted to the left and then pivoted to the right, catching the specter off guard. Kaden ran toward us, a flicker of his aura sticking to the shadow creature as he flew past it. The being's eyes blinked brighter momentarily, its shadows imploding wildly. It pursued us without haste.

Fear was fueling us, propelling our bodies forward. Up ahead, there was a gigantic, grounded islet. Its jagged mass arched before the stormy horizon. A flare of light illuminated the skyline behind it, unveiling a passageway carved through its center.

We all rushed toward it, hoping it might offer us safety. As we got closer, a blinding light erupted from the arched opening, and a man came bursting forth, charging in our direction. This didn't deter us as we ran. Whoever it was would be much easier to handle than the terrifying creature behind us.

As we neared the stony arch, a stunned gasp tore from me as the man's determined features became recognizable.

Kaden bellowed, "Gavrel, get back!"

At full speed, Gavrel raced toward us, a sword in his clutches. A bright white glow emanated from his right hand, skittering along his weapon. Any living shadows in his path slinked away from the blade's radiance. His brow furrowed, and his arms pumped in determination.

In my momentary surprise, my feet faltered, giving the shadow creature a chance to wrap its smoky tentacles around my slender waist. I lurched forward and fell. Landing on my knees, my scream carved the air as sharp pain bit into my skin. Kaden, Breena, and Letti spun toward my sound of distress but were well out of reach of me and my captor.

I tried to dislodge its suffocating grasp, my nails clawing and tearing through its form. It was of no use. My fingers slipped through the seething smog. It was cold and gummy. A buzzing sound rattled through my ears as if a swarm of bees surrounded me. The creature wrapped around me, muffling my cries and obscuring my vision with turbid fog. It probed my starburst scar with a clammy caress.

Spinning shadows zipped across my vision, but for moments at a time, there were choppy glimpses of the others. Gavrel reached us, his blazing sword keeping the other monsters at bay. There was muddled yelling, incomplete shouts, and enraged orders. The chaos of sounds and images disconcerted my senses.

"If you miss, you'll stab—"

Kaden held his brother back, their faces crunched inward in frantic worry.

"Get out of the—"

Darkness cloaked my eyes.

"It's kill—"

Tears streamed down Letti's face, Breena holding her sobbing form.

Sticky mist slapped me in the face, stinging my eyes shut again. I clung to my waning energy, but it still bled from me into the phantom. My very soul was being peeled from my body. Suddenly, the shadow beast clamped razor-sharp teeth into my nape, and my nerves burned as the flesh severed. I howled, thrashing around, but to no avail.

As the shadow creature consumed my essence, my body crumpled to the ground. *This is it,* I thought. *This is how I die.* Slinking blackness was creeping over my mind. My eyes sealed, recalling my nightmare about Mama just days ago. *Was this what happened to her?*

"Seryn!" Letti's terror broke through the darkness. Gavrel ripped away from Kaden, his glowing sword swinging forward as he ran to me.

A blaze of flaming heat erupted through my muscles, from the crown of my head to the tips of my toes. From the dusty clay, my body arched like a scorching lightning bolt ripped from the stormy sky above. Energy zipped through me, my limbs tingling with its charge.

The being froze, its jaws releasing my neck, its smoke motionless. Then, all at once, a blast of iridescent, blinding beams burst from my body, disintegrating the shadow monster. The force of it hurled Gavrel backward, his sword flying out of his hand. I slumped back to the earth, my body exhausted once more.

"Seryn!" Lettie cried at the same time Breena shouted, "Fecking void! Are you alive?!"

Everything was a scrambled blur as Gavrel scooped me up and propped me against the nearest cobble. When my vision cleared, everyone stared at me, concern etched on their faces. Gavrel's scowl was ever-present. His voice sounded defeated. "I'm very sorry, Seryn. I couldn't get to you in time." He looked into the distance, his eyes glassy.

My voice was gravelly, scraping up my throat. "It's okay, Gav. There wasn't anything anyone could do. I'm all right." Letti was clinging to my side, rubbing my shoulder. Kaden leaned down to kiss the top of my head, then stood next to Gavrel. He put a hand on his brother's tense shoulder, handing him his unlit sword. Gavrel took it, and I glimpsed a mark on top of his hand, in the curve between his thumb and forefinger. It was glowing under his skin.

"You gave us quite the scare," Kaden said, blowing out a shaky gust of air.

Breena was crouching beside me and slapped her hands on the tops of her thighs, then rose. "Well, my little firefly friend. You definitely know how to put on a show!" She chortled. Letti glared at her, continuing to rub my shoulder.

Breena's aura wasn't shimmering any longer, nor was Kaden's. I peered at my trembling hands, turning them palms up—no signs of glowing skimmed my grayish skin. Closing my fingers, I looked up in confusion. "What in the Nether Void is going on? Why are we all lighting up like bloody lanterns?!"

Kaden shifted awkwardly on his feet, and Breena pursed her lips, not meeting my gaze. When they remained silent, my narrowed eyes shifted to my sister as she shrugged, her nose scrunching.

Gavrel coughed as if his words were sticking to his windpipe. "The shadow creature that attacked you is a shade," he informed us, sliding his sword into the scabbard on his back. "We're in the Stygian Murk, a kind of limbo or portal realm.

And whoever is ... lighting up like a bloody lantern is a Druik." His eyes surveyed our surroundings, chiseled jaw clenching.

A sharp squeak left me, my mouth gaping and eyes wide. Kaden's eyes found something particularly interesting on the clay earth beneath his boots.

Breena started, "How do you—"

Gavrel interrupted, his voice firm, "I'd love to delve further into all that, but it looks like there are more shades interested in us. We have to move. Follow me, everyone." He turned without further delay, expecting us to follow him despite the astonished looks washing over our faces.

Kaden reached out his large, steady hands and pulled Letti and me to our feet. I rubbed my forehead, trying to rid myself of the lingering fog clouding my mind.

Kaden shifted my hair to one side. With concern, he whispered, "You're bleeding, Ser."

I gingerly touched my nape and let out a hiss. My fingers came away coated in congealed blood and clay dust. "It's all right. I'll take care of it when we get ... wherever we're going."

My forced smile was not convincing as I had hoped it would be, and Kaden moved his head from side to side in reproach. But he moved on regardless, dropping my hair to my shoulder. A few tangled curls cascaded down my back when I wiped my hand on the stone beside me.

I packed my lingering questions and panic deep into the base of my spine, enforcing its bones and forbidding it to bow—refusing to allow it to break.

A putrid breeze caressed my face as another crack of thunder roared, reverberating through the soles of my feet. My weary legs carried me after Gavrel and the others, advancing to the looming arch ahead.

7

FIREFLIES IN A JAR

The stony archway towered before us, commanding attention. Several creeping shades loitered at our backs but did not press forward.

"Are we safe from them?" Letti's voice trembled, and she leaned her shoulder into mine.

"They won't come near the passageway. They'll disintegrate if they come too close to its ember," Gavrel replied. He positioned himself near me, his broad shoulders and chest blocking the Stygian Murk from my peripheral. "Let's go, everyone. Walk through, and you'll be free of this place."

"What's on the other side, Gav?" Kaden tipped his head toward his brother, rubbing a palm over his flat belly, one eyebrow arched.

"It's Surrelia." Gavrel squared his feet.

An audible chorus of gasps flew through the air. My stomach lurched as I gawked at the rocky egress, shoulders frozen in place. I held my breath, hearing only the whooshing of the wind through the arch. He didn't continue.

Breena broke the silence, her sarcasm dripping through a

toothy grin. "So ... you mean we're all dead? Meeting the Ancients, as they say."

"No, we're not dead ... at least, not yet. Let's go," he insisted as he placed a hand on the small of my back, urging me forward.

"Are you bloody serious?" I demanded, digging my heels into the dusty ground. "We're going to need more than that, Gavrel Larkin."

He'd known me long enough to know how stubborn I could be. I wasn't budging. He stepped in front of me, making eye contact with each of us. "I promise many of your questions will be answered in the next few weeks."

He turned to the side, holding his arm toward the entrance in an invitation. "Please, let's head through. We'll talk more there. We're running out of time." His mouth went soft, his dark eyes pleading. Gavrel didn't plead. I didn't recall his mouth ever looking so full, considering it was usually trapped in a scowl.

"Fine. But I won't forget your promise." I stomped around him to the entrance. When the others followed, Letti grasped my hand in hers as we moved.

"I would certainly hope not," he muttered, herding us into the portal that led to where the Ancients once presided.

Many people believed the Ancients had deserted us long ago after cursing Midst Fall with the Withering. Several people still followed their old ways, praying harder and performing rituals in desperate repentance—trusting that the Ancients would never set such a scourge upon our lands. They believed the Ancients were, in fact, protecting us through the Dormancy. Some naysayers doubted the Ancients ever existed. I didn't know what to think. Most of my time was consumed by thoughts of surviving the days ahead.

Upon reaching the center of the narrow passage, I looked through the arch to the dusty horizon beyond. In the next moment, a snap of glaring light enveloped us like a tidal wave crashing over everything in its path. I found the sensation strangely soothing, similar to sinking your body into a warm pond.

When we stepped out of the arch, my hand shot up to cover my eyes. Brilliant azure hues painted the sky; not a cloud was in sight. I sucked in a deep breath, my stomach and chest expanding with the fresh air.

I spun around, my tangled auburn curls twirling around me before settling on my back and shoulders again. The Stygian Murk had vanished. We had exited a tall, vaulted archway. Dense amber glass—like that of an active Dormancy pod—formed its outer frame. Its edges were glazed in silver, liquid-like metal. Spinning mist and twinkling luminescence filled its interior, resembling hundreds of dancing fireflies trapped in a hazy jar.

My feet stood firmly on a pristine platform made of sparkling white marble, curving ahead of us. Stepping down a few bow-shaped steps, a path created from copper-colored glass continued from the platform, forming a narrow lane through the center of a semi-circular grove of lush trees. The leaves were rich shades of orange and red, creating massive domes that sheltered the mossy ground below.

The glass pathway was big enough for four people to walk shoulder to shoulder. Lining either side of the trail were deep, glimmering aqua pools that ended before the grove. I'd never seen such an electric color before.

Sparkling sand covered the bottom. Movement caught my eye as a fish with iridescent white scales swam beside us and under the glass walkway, one violet eye curiously assessing us. It was the size of a chubby cat that had roamed freely in our village for turns.

I didn't realize my mouth was hanging open until Kaden's fingers nudged it back into place. He walked toward the grove, following Breena and Letti, his shoulders shaking with laughter.

My eyes found Gavrel's fixed on me. They were deep green

again, stark against his tanned skin. It was startling seeing the world in color once more. A quick puff of air left me. "This ... this is beautiful."

"It is. You're safe now." His gaze was warm and reassuring, reminding me of home.

"How long were we there? It felt like days, but I'm not entirely sure."

"Time moves differently there. While it's been only a day in the mortal plane and Surrelia; it was roughly three days in the Stygian Murk," he explained.

I hugged one arm across my chest, holding on to the other. I nodded in understanding, even though I didn't understand anything at all.

"It'll take some time. The ember in that place is malignant. It drains you of your will to hope—to *live*. Don't let it win." He brushed his hand over my shoulder, a warm path lingering under my skin in its wake.

"I have so many questions, but they all feel too overwhelming." The weight of bewilderment pressed down on me. My eyes closed for a moment.

"I know. I'll do my best to answer them when you've rested. I'm here if you need me."

My gaze fell on my dress, covered in crusted blood and grime. "Thank you, Gav. I do need something ..." An embarrassed smile lifted the corners of my mouth. "For the love of Ancients, lead the way to a bath."

His full lips smirked, his cheeks pushing the skin around his eyes into crinkles. My face flushed, and I stammered, "I mean ... for me. Alone. I, uh ... You can take a bath. By yourself ..." I trailed off, flustered and looking at everything but him.

"Thank you for allowing me a bath." He chuckled.

"I meant—"

"Take a breath, Seryn. I knew what you meant. Shall we?" he asked, holding out his arm. I placed mine in the crook of his elbow, pressing my front teeth into my lower lip. The heat in my cheeks abated.

We strolled through the grove, everything around us bursting with life. The curious fish from earlier followed us under the transparent trail, swimming in lazy circles under the glass.

If pigments were drained from the Stygian Murk, I wondered if Surrelia was where they culminated. The vibrancy of the flora, sky, and water brimmed over as if the hues would spill into you if touched. I dipped my head. Perhaps I was used to Evergryn, which was pallid and depleted.

I glanced at his right hand, curious if the mark was still visible. It was, but it was no longer glowing. I unthreaded my arm from his elbow, pausing a moment under the orange shade of the grove. He shifted slightly toward me with one eyebrow raised.

"What is this on your hand?" I took his thick wrist in one hand and the toughened tips of his fingers in the other, flattening his palm to get a better look. His skin was warm as he allowed me to inspect it.

It was an intricate, geometric tattoo drawn in silver metallic ink—a ten-point star with delicate lines crisscrossing between the vertices. In the center was a perfect decagon—the sacred figure of the Ancients. An image of our ten-sided conservatory flitted through my mind like a distant memory.

My thoughts were distracting me as I brushed my thumb over the tattoo. A soft light underneath the mark illuminated it for a moment. Gavrel pulled his hand from mine, covering it with his other.

He cleared his throat. "It does that sometimes." He faced forward, and we continued on the path. "I'm part of a specialized Order of Draumr unit granted augmented abilities through tattooed runes. It's useful in battle—it enhances our strength and agility. Connects with our weapons, enabling them to deflect or destroy lesser ember forms." He hesitated, a heavy exhale falling from his lips. "The mark is only visible outside Midst Fall."

"Oh. Well, that's amazing, Gav. I'm so proud of you. I didn't realize that was even possible. The runes, I mean." My eyebrows lifted in interest.

A small smile crept across his lips, the slightest color blushing his ears. I noticed he kept his wavy ebony hair trimmed neatly. It was long enough for the top to be swept back casually, loose waves from the sides teasing his nape and ears.

"Thank you," he said after a moment. His smile faltered and fell into a flat line once again. "The Elders and their ember can do many unimaginable things."

I looked at him. "Well, I'm grateful for it. Yours kept the shades from attacking us further." One corner of my mouth ticked upward. "Thank you for finding us, by the way."

"The Nether Void couldn't keep me from finding you, Little Star." His eyes swept over my face. Under his piercing stare, heat flared across my rounded cheeks. He was the only one who still used my nickname. For a moment, I wondered what he saw.

Mama gave me the moniker as a child. She used to say my scar was a star-shaped kiss from the Ancients, then would smack a smooch on my cheek and tickle me into fits of laughter. A smile spread across my face at the memory.

As we exited the trees, my hands came together to make a steeple in front of my lips. I wasn't sure if I was praying or holding in another breath. The aqua-colored water appeared again, hugging the mossy land of the grove. However, this water was flowing, a broad river moving steadily. More of the enchanting, iridescent fish glided through the depths.

In the distance, our glassy footpath met three others, rooting into the edge of an overhang. They reminded me of dribbled lines of honey floating upon the water, the currents licking at their borders. The river vanished over the precipice, rushing around the edges of the burnished glass. At the brink, the four glass walkways melded together to form an enormous bridge, sinuous silver creating delicate guardrails on either side.

My examination followed the trails, curious about where they led. A wide field of grass met my perusal. A dense forest bordered the sprawling field, packed with domed, sunset-colored trees and splashes of vibrant but unfamiliar flora. Several long buildings stretched along the edge of the field, adjacent to the wooded expanse.

"That's the mainland, with the barracks and training field. Beyond that is an expansive stretch of woodlands—the Reverie Weald," Gavrel mentioned, noting where my line of sight had strayed.

Several people were milling about, working in a large garden, and sparring with weapons. Among them, a few auras sporadically flickered into view one moment and then disappeared the next like flames in the wind.

"Can you see their auras?" I asked.

"Not unless someone is using ember."

"I keep seeing them, even when they aren't. It started a while ago, back home. I'd see flashes of Kaden's aura but didn't realize it then. I ... I think something is wrong with me."

His lips pressed together as he shook his head, eyes softening. "On the contrary, it seems like a very useful ability. The Druiks I've met can't do that. Perhaps it has something to do with your gift. Only time will tell."

I nodded once, my attention drawn to a young woman throwing a ball back and forth with some children. A small child with unruly hair bent to catch the rolling ball, but it escaped through his fingers, bowling toward the edge of the field. The child wobbled after the tricky ball. His little feet were surprisingly swift but not quick enough as the plaything zipped under the wooden post-and-rail fence that skirted the edge of a sweeping bluff. The woman scooped up the toddler as he reached his arms out toward the steep precipice, crying for his lost toy.

My brows scrunched downward. "Gav, what happens to children in the Stygian Murk?" I asked him, my voice thick with unease.

He rested a warm palm on my shoulder, turning to me. "Fortunately, the younger you are, the closer you materialize near the portal. Those under twenty-one do not stay in limbo long. Very young children are maybe inside for a moment; older children usually no longer than fifteen minutes. The shades aren't drawn to those without ember." I bobbed my head in understanding, the pressure in my chest subsiding as we approached the bridge.

I gulped, my stomach clenching as I watched the aqua water rushing over the overhang in a curtained cascade. Through the translucent base, plummeting water smashed into a furious river far below. Its currents meandered around another imposing cliff, isolated from the mainland entirely. The sun reflected off the islet's glassy black stone, dancing along the conchoidal fractures scattered over its surface.

My knees wobbled, and tingles raced from my belly to my toes. I pressed my heels and the balls of my feet more firmly into the glass with every step, ensuring I wouldn't topple over the tenuous handrail.

We met the others waiting in the center of the bridge, their necks craning to take in the mesmerizing scene before us. Once more, I peeked at the faraway river below as it spilled into a churning turquoise sea. "Is … is that the Insomnis Sea?" I murmured, unsure if Gavrel heard me.

"It is—the one and only," he said, a gentle smile tipping his lips.

I exhaled, my trembling breath floating toward the fabled waves.

Beyond the other end of the bridge, a palace made from moonstone towered above, its bottom half directly embedded within the cliff face. Various turrets pierced the sky, free from the obsidian crag. The luminescent walls of the fortress were captivating—splashed with shiny flecks and shimmering iridescent patches. Depending on the angle, the colorful spots looked lit internally, blue and gold shifting in the sunbeams.

My gaze dragged further upward, squinting against the sun. A copious number of spires lined the top of the palace and its turrets. They were narrow, made of brilliant crystals of varying heights. When the light hit the quartz just right, the prisms split the rays and cast a spray of rainbow-colored tessellations.

"Can we live here now? Forever?" Breena laughed; her quiet words somewhat drowned under the rumbling waterfall.

Gavrel made a dismissive sound in his throat and led us to the massive gatehouse entrance, which was flanked by two Draumr warriors. He nodded to them, and they moved to open the metal gate made of silvery posts fused in an elegant, arched grid.

"High ranking, eh?" Kaden smiled as he bumped his shoulder against his brother's. The motion didn't budge Gavrel one bit.

"Something like that," he grumbled.

As we approached the palace's vaulted entrance, Gavrel said, "I'll show you to your rooms, where you can get washed up and rest for a bit."

He looked at a Draumr standing near the doorway and waved her over. Then he looked at Letti, his lips scrunching and releasing a quick puff of air. "Letti, you'll have to go with this guard. She's one of my best."

"Xeni Reed." The guard dipped her head in a slight bow toward Letti.

Gavrel went on. "Those who aren't Druiks are required to stay in the mainland barracks. I'm sorry. I wish you could stay in the palace."

"Absolutely not," my voice bounced off the moonstone walls.

He grimaced. "I don't control this, Seryn. The Elders' procedures are stringent. Almost everyone stays in the barracks, besides the Elders, my unit, and Druiks." The sound of his boots shifting sifted through the air. "She'll be well taken care of, I assure you. You'll see each other daily."

"What do you mean? The Elders are here in Surrelia? I thought they didn't have to endure the Dormancy," Kaden blurted, one brow arching. Of course, he fixated on that part. I crossed my arms across my chest, glaring at both men.

Gavrel's jaw set in a stony square. "It means, brother, we have to follow procedure. More will be revealed in due time."

"This is ridic—" My retort was cut short by Letti's soft but firm voice.

"It's all right. I'll go. Please, lead the way," she said to the guard before wrapping her arms around me in a steady hug and then standing straight, aligning her back. Ever the peacemaker. "I'll find you later, Ser. I'll see if Father is there."

"Thank you, Letti. Xeni will watch out for you, won't you?" Gavrel glowered at the young guard. It wasn't a question. "At sunset, everyone must meet in the Great Hall," he added. Standing tall next to Letti, the young warrior nodded firmly, her chin-length, wavy black hair and tawny brown skin gleaming in the sunlight.

I hugged Letti again before she turned and walked over the bridge. A stray rainbow-colored beam weaved within her golden hair. My worried gaze lingered on it until I could no longer see them.

I had to trust Gavrel. He was the only one who seemed to know what was going on. I wondered how often he had done this for us during the Dormancy.

Had he helped us escape from the Stygian Murk every time?

I didn't want to imagine being trapped in that nightmarish

landscape endlessly. My insides squeezed into knots, forcing acid up my throat.

Inhaling through my nose, I let the pure air soothe me and slow my thoughts. I knew deep within my bones he would never put any of us in harm's way. He'd always watched out for Letti and me. He took care of Kaden after their parents had died.

I'd pick a different battle later if I had to. This wasn't it. I set my shoulders back and put one foot in front of the other. We passed through the beckoning entryway—unwitting flies settling in the gaping maw of a beautiful snapwyvern plant.

8

EMBEDDED STONES

A grand set of obsidian staircases hugging the center of the foyer greeted us. They curved along the moonstone walls on either side. A landing connected them at the top, an undulating balcony overlooking the vestibule below.

On either side of me, a long hallway stretched, its black stone floors leaking into the shadows. All of the shiny doors were adorned with intricate etchings like someone had dragged the tip of their finger through a still silver pond, the ripples freezing in place.

Movement caught my eye, swinging my attention toward the landing above. I could have sworn wispy smoke slithered away from view. I blinked twice. Perhaps I was still seeing things.

I shook out my hands, releasing a shaky breath. Kaden stepped closer to me, putting his arm around my back and rubbing a soothing pattern along my shoulder. I rested my head against his warm, solid chest.

A breathtaking chandelier made of hundreds of pristine, star-shaped crystals dangled over the foyer, sprinkling sweeps of refracted rainbows over every stony surface they could reach. The vaulted quartz ceiling hovered above us, giving us views of the roof's gemmy spires.

"Ahead is the Great Hall, where we'll meet later." Gavrel turned to the left. "Follow me, please. Your rooms are this way."

"Have Seryn and I stayed here before, Gav?" Kaden asked.

"You've always stayed in the barracks." Gavrel dipped his head, pushing forward.

"So, you remember everything when the Dormancy is over?" Breena questioned, her voice an octave higher and her eyebrows flying to the ceiling.

Upon reaching the end of the long hallway, Gavrel stopped, opening the door to a sprawling bedroom. "This is you, Ms. Caddell."

"Why, thank you, handsome. You can call me Breena," she purred, giving him a jaunty wink. "But you didn't answer my question."

"Yes, I remember everything," he admitted hesitantly, his voice low.

"Very interesting." She twirled around, sauntering into her room. "Catch you later." She closed the door with a sharp click. Kaden and I stood side by side, gawking at Gavrel.

He shrugged one shoulder and pushed a hand through his thick hair. "Everyone has three days, in Stygian Murk time, to find the arch. Once they get close enough, guards on-duty from my unit help them through. If a person doesn't make it, they're trapped in limbo. Whether they successfully return to the mortal plane after the Dormancy is another issue." His brow furrowed as his teeth clenched together.

Was that what happened to Mama? I thought, my insides churning.

"That's ... amazing, brother. You being some elite Order leader, I mean. Being trapped in the nightmare place, not so much." Kaden wrapped Gavrel in a hug, thumping him on the back a few times. Gavrel's eyebrows shot up in surprise, but then his body seemed to melt, and he embraced his brother. They stepped apart, Kaden's hands on his brother's shoulders. "So, I'm guessing a benefit of you being the big boss of your fancy unit is …"

Gavrel nodded once. "Remembering everything. Yes. To be honest, I think it's so the Elders don't have to reeducate us every turn."

"Wow. Just wow, Gav," I murmured. That responsibility seemed overwhelming. Deep within the shadowy pockets of my mind, I buried the image of my mother shriveling in the Murk, my molars gnawing the inside of my cheek. "How long have you been doing this?"

"Five turns now. Luckily, you've all been in Surrelia for the last five cycles, except for your father." He grimaced, anticipating my dismay.

My heart crawled into my throat. "I understand." I rubbed his arm briefly. "If he's been trapped in limbo, at least he wouldn't remember his time there, and he has found his way home every turn."

"Indeed." His brows knitted together.

I blew out a puff of air. "Maybe I can find more answers while I'm here. Not that I'll recall them when we're home." A halfhearted chuckle fell to the stones as I shrugged.

Kaden gave me a side hug, then asked, "Are we in any of these rooms, Gav?"

"No, let's head upstairs."

Kaden let out a whistle and smirked. "The mysteries never end in this place. Here's one more: Where do the Elders stay?"

Gavrel's eyes look upward, probably asking the Ancients for patience. "Their quarters are in the opposite wing near the Great Hall."

Kaden nodded, his shoulders slumping a little. Gavrel rolled his shoulders back, adjusted his scabbard, and then strode to the wall, marking the end of the wing. I thought he would barge right through it until a metallic door rippled into view, his tattoo glowing faintly in response. That section of the wall had been a mirage. As he approached, the embedded door slid into the wall. When we entered, it slipped back into place behind us soundlessly.

We climbed a winding silver staircase. We reached the landing for the second floor, and another door appeared and slid open, shutting as we exited. Gavrel led us to each of our rooms. Kaden's was a few doors down from mine, and my room was close to the foyer balcony.

"If you need me, my room is next door. My team also has rooms throughout the palace; they'll have runes like mine." Gavrel lifted his hand. "Someone will bring you fresh clothing soon." He hesitated, lips parting as he sucked in a breath and sealed any further words behind the firm line of his mouth. Tipping his head once, Gavrel turned toward his room.

"Thank you," I called after him, entering my room when he didn't turn around.

My eyes widened at the sight of my quarters. My whole cottage at home would have fit inside it. Light trickled in through the vaulted quartz ceiling. Sparkling rainbows bounced off decorative metal beams that arched delicately below the gems. I ambled over to three large, circular windows, which lined the wall.

The Insomnis Sea stretched into the horizon, its watery crests rolling and sparkling. Looking down, cerulean waves pounded into the side of the craggy precipice. Glossy black shards crept up the moonstone under my window. The back of the palace burrowed higher into the cliff than the front.

Glancing to my left, an enormous plush bed beckoned me. A sweeping canopy sloped over it. The sheer silvery material caressed the corner posts as it flowed to the floor beneath. A sigh escaped my lips, and I brushed my hand over the pewter bedding, its velvet caressing my fingertips.

I needed a bath before I could snuggle into the bed. A pout pulled down the corners of my mouth. Turning reluctantly, I noticed a semi-circular glass tub built into the opposite wall. Sunbeams melted into its golden glass.

A quick knock startled me, making my shoulders jump and the crunchy fabric of my kirtle rustle. I moved to the door, opening it to a petite, older woman. Her bluish-gray strands swept into a neat braid down her back. Her mouth tipped into a bright smile, crinkling the lines around her eyes and forehead.

"Hello, Miss. I have some clean clothes for you. I'm sure you'll be wanting a bath right quick!" Her voice was lyrical, words swift. She swooped past me and placed the fresh clothes on the bed.

She rushed to the tub and turned the faucets on with a flick of her hand, a soft teal aura simmering around her. Steamy, bubbly water poured into the transparent basin, and the scent of lavender floated through the room. She spun toward me, her blue dress twirling around her legs.

"Thank you, Miss …" I paused, slightly dazed from her quick movements and casual display of ember. She was a busy little bluebird flitting about.

"Oh, call me Derya. Derya Atwater. And you are Seryn Vawn, you are," she chirped without allowing breaths to interrupt her. "Isn't the bath just lovely? I thought of the scented bubbles myself! I do love making concoctions. I can manipulate water … well, small bits of it. Things in it, around it … if you couldn't tell," she tittered as she swept toward the door.

"That's fantastic. Are you from Haadra?" I asked, recalling Magister Barden's lessons once again. If I wasn't mistaken, water-based powers originated there.

"Why, yes, I am! I miss my homeland, as I'm sure you do, but you'll be back in no time." She clapped her hands twice in front of her. "If you'll be needing anything, touch that sapphire by the door and I'll be right up."

There was indeed a sparkling blue gem embedded in the wall. My head bobbed in understanding as she swished her hand above her head. The water stopped flowing from the faucet as the metal door clicked behind her.

In disbelief, a brief laugh escaped me as I undressed and immersed my aching body in the basin. The heat soaked into my tired muscles, the steam drifting around me in a dreamy mist. A faint giggle dove from my lips as I skimmed my fingers over lavender-scented bubbles.

I couldn't believe I was here. That I was a Druik. I'd always wondered what it would be like to have ember. What would happen once the Dormancy was over? Would my gift resurface … or stay hidden until the next cycle?

Breathing in, my unrequited thoughts tucked into the recesses of my mind. I dunked my head under the water and scrubbed the grime and dried blood from my curls and face.

As my head broke the water, another knock sounded on my door. "Come in!" I shouted, swiping some errant bubbles from my brow.

The door swung open and closed. *Those don't look like Derya's slippers,* I mused before my eyes jolted up to see Kaden's smirking face. A loud squeak escaped me as I wrapped one arm around my breasts and used the other to hug more bubbles around me. "Kaden, what the void?! Can't you see I'm bathing?!"

"Absolutely … but need I remind you, you bade me come in?" He chuckled and walked over to the basin.

"I thought you were Derya!" My cheeks blazed, matching the temperature of the water.

"Ah, don't fret, Ser. I can't see anything interesting through the bubbles and steam." He pouted as I glowered at him. "Besides, I wanted to check on your neck wound."

I huffed, relenting. "All right. Thank you." I flicked my soapy hand at him, splashing droplets onto his white tunic. "Don't make me regret this."

"I would never." He grinned; one dimple visible on his now clean-shaven face. I wanted to poke him right in it. He swiped his wet, shaggy hair from his forehead as he squatted beside the tub.

I pulled my knees to my chest, wrapping my arms around my shins. The frothy bubbles covered my skin as my eyelids closed.

My initial embarrassment washed away as Kaden massaged my head with gentle fingers, untangling the auburn knots. A soft purr vibrated through my throat.

I wondered if it was peculiar that I wasn't more concerned about etiquette ... but this was Kaden. We'd grown up together, seen each other at our best, and held each other in our lowest moments. The last several days had been terrifying, but in this moment, I felt safe and cared for.

He carefully scooped water over my hair, brushing his hand down my curls and back. Goosebumps rippled over my skin, chasing his touch. A warmth spread from my chest and rippled through my limbs. My purr morphed into a soft groan.

Kaden's hand stilled under my shoulder blades. "Your hair, it's untangled. Let me, uh ..." He paused and cleared his throat, shifting on his knees.

I opened my eyes, gazing at him with a dreamy smile. "Huh?"

His eyes looked darker, as if they were glazed in steam. His thumb drew tiny circles on my back, sending a shiver down my spine into the water below. He licked his bottom lip and continued, "Your neck ... lean forward so I can take a look."

I did as he asked. Slowly, his warm palm slid up my slick skin, pushing wet strands of hair over my shoulder. I trembled despite the warm steam still draped around my skin.

He cleansed my neck with the soapy water. I could tell he was being as gentle as he could be, his fingers feathering over my skin. Still, a sharp sting of pain ran across the bite wound as he worked.

I whimpered as he touched a particularly sore area. He let out a hiss of air and growled, "Damn the shades to the void!"

He took a deep, deliberate breath and asked, "Are you all right? I can patch this wound up, but something is embedded in your scar."

"What?!" I yelped and reached along my nape. My finger slid along something razor-thin protruding from the scarred tissue. "What the Ancients is it? Get it out!"

"I'm not sure, hold still," he commanded, nudging my hand away. His face moved closer, his warm breath gliding over my skin, leaving goosebumps behind.

Locking my muscles in place, I held my breath, attempting to ignore the discomfort as he worked. My breath whooshed from me as my scar released its grasp on the object—a sharp burn burrowed in its place. Kaden's eyebrows scrunched as he handed it to me. "It looks like a pebble."

I took the tiny object from him and cleaned it in the water, running my thumb over its flat surface. "It looks like the pods when they're inactive. Look, there are markings etched into it."

His eyebrows flew up toward his hairline. "Uh, looks like an ember talisman. I saw something similar once."

"What are you talking about, Kaden? You seem to know much more about ember than you've let on. Not to mention why you looked so guilty in the Stygian Murk."

"What are *you* talking about?"

"When I asked about us all glowing. Don't play the dunce with me. Start talking."

He sighed, "All right, but let me heal your wound first."

Kaden closed his eyes, concentration coating his features. A green light encircled his hand, his skin glowing like smoldering pieces of coal. He moved my hair from my nape again and covered it with his palm. A tingling warmth skittered over my skin, knitting the edges of my wound together.

After he finished, I touched my neck, gliding over it. My now sealed starburst scar remained, the dense skin pressing into my fingertip.

"What the bloody void!?" I cried.

"Ah, come on. Get dressed, and we'll chat. Unless you want me to get in there with you?" He laughed as I thrust my finger toward the door. He turned with that annoying grin still pasted on his face, swaggering out of my room.

My body lurched out of the tub, water and bubbles splashing to the floor, too distracted to care about the mess I made. I clutched the obsidian stone in my hand as I threw on the soft undergarments and dress Derya had left for me. My palm slid over the clean white fabric. It was the softest material I'd ever felt.

Closing my eyes, I took a deep, calming breath. There was too much information tumbling around my skull. The Stygian Murk. Surrelia. My best friend keeping secrets. *This damned talisman.*

I studied the delicate sliver in my palm, prodding the engraved rune. The pebble was no bigger than my pointer finger's nail bed. The etching was a simple eye shape with a slanted *X*-mark through it.

I set it on the small table beside the bed and went to the door. "Come back in and spill all of your lies," I ordered, sweeping my arm out. Kaden blushed and lowered his chin, sighing. He walked to the side of my bed and sat on the edge, the velvet crushing under his solid weight.

"I never lied to you, Seryn."

"Help me understand then."

Kaden fidgeted on the bed a bit as I sat next to him. "In the months before the culling, I caught Ma in the woods one night. I couldn't sleep and went for a walk. There was this light shining in the trees ... It was her. Her body sparkled all over as she focused on a dying grymwood. The colors were amazing. Like honey-colored stars and caramel swirling together." He rubbed his hand across his forehead, then rested it on his muscular thigh. The fabric of his tunic and breeches rustled against his movements.

"She wasn't even ashamed or frightened, Ser. She told me right away she was a Druik. I was only thirteen, so she wasn't sure if I'd inherit any abilities, but I think she suspected I would. I've always felt connected to the woods, and I've always healed quickly." He shrugged, shifting to face me.

"In those months, she tried to prepare me the best she could in case any ember manifested when I turned twenty-one. She was proud of hers and said it was nothing to be ashamed of, but I needed to be safe. She wanted to teach me more ... but she didn't get the chance." He looked down, his mouth dipping.

"She made me promise not to tell anyone, not Gavrel nor Pa. Not even you." He grabbed my hand, his eyes pleading. "Please understand. I wanted to tell you, but then she was ... gone. I didn't want to break my promise to her. I didn't want to put you, or anyone else, in danger."

"Thank you for being honest with me. I ..." I paused, squeezing his hand. "I understand. It'll take a moment for me to work through all of this. It's all happening so quickly. I'll always be here for you, Kade. Even if you are trying to protect me, you should know by now I can handle whatever you share with me."

"I see that now. Forgive me?"

"All right, I'll forgive you ... for now." I smirked. We both shifted on the bed and laid back on the pillows facing each other. "So, what else is there to tell? Why didn't she register?"

"Well, she made it sound like registered Druiks were in more danger than those in hiding. She said if the Elders knew you had powerful ember abilities, which I think she did, you'd be given an ultimatum. Join their Akridai force or—I don't know—disappear or be culled. Maybe they leave Druiks who aren't formidable alone." One shoulder shrugged. He twirled his hand in the air. "I can heal small wounds. Before your wound, I tried it on myself earlier this turn, but I couldn't get it right. Maybe you were the motivation I needed. I'd call that a success." A grin split his face.

"Happy to be your test subject."

He chuckled, then went on, his eyes alight. "I also can sometimes help plants grow, but only small ones. As in, I once grew a leaf back on a clover. Not enough to help Evergryn or be a threat to the Elders, I'd say." His smile wilted.

"Well, I blew up a shade. I'm not sure that's very useful in Midst Fall either." He snorted at my comment. A small smile flitted across my face before settling in a line. "After hearing about Hestia ... let's keep our abilities to ourselves as much as possible. Just to be safe." He nodded in agreement. I reached for the stone sliver on the side table. "So, tell me about talismans."

"Ah, yes. Ma showed me some runes she had etched into rocks once. Said they were talismans for protection. Don't know what happened to them, but this reminds me of Ma's. Different symbol, though." He plucked the pebble from my fingers, studying it. His other hand itched the side of his jaw. "If I had to guess, this has been in there the whole time."

"I think you're right," I agreed, taking the stone from him and putting it in my pocket. "Someone put it there on purpose. It must have been when I was too young to remember. From what Mama told me, I've had that scar since I was a baby. The shade's bite forced it out." I sighed heavily, sinking further into the plush comforter.

Kaden picked up my hand, enveloping it in his larger one, wrapping my ragged spirit in unspoken comfort. We lay like that for a while, processing what we had been through in the past several days, listing all the questions we needed answers for.

I wasn't sure what I would do without Kaden. He was a solid rock beneath my feet, keeping me stable on unsteady ground. We grew weary as the moments ticked on, and soon, our energy ran dry—finally depleted from days of panic and confusion. We drifted asleep, our hands still embracing one another. The clouded bath water remained forgotten on the floor, mingling with our spilled secrets.

9

HARROWING

"Welcome, citizens of the mortal realm!" The woman's voice echoed through the Great Hall, bouncing off the metallic arches weaving intricately throughout the crystallized cathedral ceiling. Instantly, the whispers buzzing through the crowd were silenced. Impressive, considering there were hundreds of us clustered in the massive space. Luckily, Kaden, Letti, Breena, and I had found each other, a unit once more. Everyone's faces were rapt with interest, our collective breaths held.

Most of us wore outfits made of the same white fabric. There were those scattered throughout the masses dressed in similar clothing but in shades of red, blue, green, or yellow. Breena wore a tunic and loose breeches in a ruby shade, the color of astra poppies. I glimpsed a faint cherry glow dancing around her. I surveyed the room, spotting several other auras, their colors corresponding with each Druik's attire.

Draumrs lined the walls, encircling the crowd. Their spines were stacked in sturdy lines as if made of immovable stone. Gavrel stood at the front of the crowd, guarding the stairs leading up to a substantial platform.

Akridais lurked in every corner, their pewter robes shimmering. Each of their necks was branded with a matching geometric tattoo that extended from the line of their jaw to their collarbone. The intricate runes—for that is what I now realized they were—sank into the shifting shadows cast upon them. A few of the enforcers' symbols were glowing, an eerie yellow smoldering behind the black ink.

Acid boiled within my belly at the sight of them. I breathed through my nose and exhaled from pursed lips, willing my body to calm, trying not to recall Hestia's culling.

My attention diverted to the polished stage. It had been carved directly from the cliff rock the palace melded with. The obsidian of the platform crept into the shadows, then surged diagonally up the back wall. The blackened stone was cut jaggedly, fusing with the moonstone of the palace.

Down the center of the two-toned surface were seven windows aligned vertically, their shapes depicting phases of the moon—a waning crescent at the top to a waxing crescent at the base. Beams of orange and pink filtered through the moon-shaped windows, the full moon at the center filled with a glowing, neon blush.

I looked back at Gavrel. His face was so impassive that it made me want to touch him to see if he was still in his body. I clutched my fingers into the fabric of my skirt instead, feeling the stone talisman resting in my pocket. I pulled my shoulder blades together and regarded the five figures atop the gleaming dais.

The woman who had called out the greeting was perched on a grand, black throne. It was also carved directly from obsidian, its base a part of the stage. Intricate swirls and etched adornments embraced her lithe figure, the room waiting with bated breath for her to speak again. The four other people on the platform also sat, two flanking each side of her. Their Gothic wooden chairs looked out of place, less spectacular than the throne.

Shining orbs floated along the walls with the help of an enchantment. Amber fire licked over them from their bases, providing gentle illumination throughout the hall. The flames flickered over the woman's face, making her gray eyes flash.

She was the most beautiful creature I'd ever seen. Her nose was straight and regal, her red lips supple. Not a strand of her platinum hair was out of place as it cascaded in sleek lines down her back. The sunset's rays draped over her, making her pearly hair glow.

She wore a gorgeous raven-colored gown. The glossy bodice clung to her breasts and thin waist. Sheer pewter-colored fabric draped from her bare shoulders, flowing past her wrists to the ground. Her skirt was made of layers of wispy fabric, melting away from her hips and flowing to the stone below her feet. A wide, shiny black ring circled her thumb, almost touching the joints it sat between.

When the shuffling of fabric and feet crescendoed throughout the hall, she finally broke the suspense. "Congratulations on surviving the Stygian Murk and finding your way to Surrelia. That alone is a feat worthy of your presence here for the next six months." She clasped her delicate hands in front of her. "I'm sure each of you has questions, and I'm here to give you a brief introduction to the expectations of your stay."

She stood from the intricately carved throne, moving as if she were made of honey wine being poured slowly into a delicate goblet. Opening her arms wide, the fabric around her wrists dripped to the platform. Her smile was broad and taut, incisors glinting in the radiance from the hovering firelight. "We are your Elders."

The sounds of choked breaths and gulps fluttered throughout the room as everyone bowed or crumbled to their knees. Our small group followed everyone's example, lowering our upper bodies respectfully. The majority had never had the chance to see the Elders despite them being in power for almost two centuries. The elusive oligarchs were rumored to rarely leave Pyria Island—an untamed, volcanic landmass sitting in the southern sea, far from Pneumali City.

Kaden scoffed under his breath, his whispered words skimming my shoulder. "I know Druiks age way more slowly, but this is ridiculous."

"You may rise," the woman instructed after a moment.

He was right. Druiks aged significantly slower than mortals. Our ember burrowed deep within us, fusing with our breath, blood, and bone—delaying death's march. The oldest Druik ever recorded was a shocking three hundred turns.

Each of our Elders didn't look a day older than fifty. It was … odd. The woman in black didn't look as if she had yet crossed thirty; her unlined skin was milky and lustrous.

"To my left is Elder Ryboas Ash, representing Pyria Island." She flicked her fingers toward the man wearing thick crimson robes. Breena stiffened, her hands fisting at her sides. As the male elder stood, his look of disdain was palpable, pale lips twisting within a neatly trimmed red beard. His short, swept-back hair had probably been the same reddish shade at one point but was now ashen with flecks of orange, as if all the color had seeped into his beard.

She waved toward the man next to him in a robe of lemon yellow. "And Elder Endurst Guust of Pneumali." He rose from his seat but with more effort, his dark, wavy hair swaying just below his clenched jaw. He nodded once, his dark eyes distant and uninterested.

"On my right is Haadra Elder, Marah Strom." She wiggled her fingers toward a fidgeting woman in royal-blue robes next. Her limp and disheveled light-brown hair gave me the impression of a nervous mouse. The woman's mouth twitched as she pulled her body up jerkily. I wasn't sure if her lips were attempting to smile or escape from her face.

"And Elder Lucan Craven of Evergryn." She clasped her hands in front of her again as the man in dark-green robes dug his ornate wooden cane into the platform, his eyes boring into the crowd while rising. Lucan's gaze landed on Kaden, a flash of jade flickering in his pupils. Kaden coughed as his soft clover aura shimmered over him briefly, and he shifted his eyes to the ground.

"I am Elder Melina Harrow of the Perilous Bogs." She seemed to glide to the edge of the stage, her movements as fluid as the fabric of her dress. She dropped the volume of her voice, everyone going still so as not to miss a word. "Let me be clear. There are rules. Follow them. Otherwise, the Stygian Murk will claim you once more." Her lips stretched again, hanging off her perfect teeth.

A dark, smoky aura languidly drifted around her body before dissipating into the air. Her pewter eyes flashed once before her mellifluous voice rang above us. "This is for your safety. The survival of Midst Fall depends entirely on your complete adherence to Elder Laws."

Breena crossed her arms across her chest, exhaling her breath in a slow, controlled stream. Kaden's shoulders became frigid boulders under his tunic. Letti glanced at me; her eyes wide. I tilted my head, pressing my lips together in a firm line. She blinked a few times, and we both paid attention to the Elders.

"Over a century ago, the Elders knew our lands were dying, the Withering sinking in. We tried everything but learned we needed more than our combined embers ... no matter how mighty they might be." Her delicate hands hung in the air. She curled her nails into her palms and remained standing. The other Elders returned to their armchairs, the wood groaning as they settled.

"We appealed to the Ancients for a miracle. Morpheus, Ancient of Dreams, agreed to an arrangement offering our domain relief from the burden—the strain we put on its resources by simply living. He granted us access to the limbo realm and Surrelia. To his palace. He guided us through how the Dormancy would operate," she went on.

This wasn't new information, at least not to those who went through primary education. *Thank you, Magister Barden.* Scanning the crowd, though, there were enough expressions of confused wonder to conclude not everyone had the opportunity or access to such teachings. Regardless, it probably wasn't surprising to anyone that Morpheus would agree to help our realm. He was said to be a benevolent Ancient with a fondness for humans, unlike his brother Phobetor, Ancient of Nightmares.

"In return, Morpheus was offered unlimited access to our collective, extended dreams. For this is what the Dormancy essentially is ... a living dream fueled by celestial power. Our astral bodies are but guests roaming this dreamland. The Ancients call this "soul-wandering". Your physical flesh, muscle, and bone rest safely in your pod." She paused, scanning the crowd as a thick wave of gasps permeated the air. "Thrilling, isn't it?"

My eyes caught Gavrel's for a moment, his face unreadable. If I didn't know him so well, I would've missed his head shift subtly from side to side, a pulsing vein ticking on his temple. I relaxed my scrunched forehead, mirroring his expression.

"To honor the sanctity of this divine gift, you won't recollect anything upon waking from the Dormancy with two exceptions: Druiks will retain the knowledge of their abilities and must register if not already."

She pressed her red lips together. Her pink tongue darted between the seams, making them look glossy with claret. "Second, few have been granted the privilege of keeping their memories throughout the turns."

Her eyes narrowed. "Continue to follow the Elder Laws, and you never know if you'll be granted such a boon." She paused, her voice lifting and her arms sweeping in front of her in a fanlike arch. "Through Dormancy, we blossom!"

A few people began chanting, "Dormancy! Dormancy!"

One woman near the front clutched her hair, shouting frantically, "Bless the Elders!"

Kaden choked on his next intake of breath. I patted him on the back, glaring daggers at him so he'd shut up and not do anything obnoxious.

Melina held up one finger, dipping her head a fraction and closing her eyes. The chanting ceased. "If you've displayed recent signs of ember and are wearing white, never fear." I was startled when she made direct eye contact with me, her metallic gaze boring into my icy blues. "You'll be provided with identifying attire once we learn more about you and your gifts." Her eyes released mine as she scanned the hall again.

"Last, you will each be assigned daily chores while residing in Surrelia. Think of it as your privilege—a way to earn room and board in such an enchanting plane of existence. In your free time, you can do as you please. If you attempt to leave the grounds ... it'll be clear if you've gone too far." A giggle slipped from her lips.

"Dinner will be served in this hall in a couple of hours. Although your astral forms don't require it, you may eat and drink if you so wish. If you have questions, please direct them to the Draumrs. Dismissed!" Melina clapped her hands together once and spun, her gown twirling around her legs. The other Elders departed abruptly behind her, disappearing through a door at the back of the platform.

The crowd stood together in a stupor before a wave of bewildered murmurs spilled across the hall.

"Fecking raven shite on a twig," Breena rasped.

"So many words. So little information," Kaden groused.

"What? Are your ears stuffed with wool? She just told us we're spirits stumbling around willy-nilly." My voice squeaked as I poked him in the arm, his biceps a stone wall.

"This doesn't make any sense. I don't feel any different," Letti grumbled, running her hands over her arms, her eyes dazed.

"I mean, ember and Elders ... We're not meant to understand how it all works. Keep the masses ignorant. Wiggle your fingers over here. Shoot off some ember over there—we'll stay in line. Am I right?" Kaden's wry chuckle slipped off his last word.

Gavrel made his way through the dispersing crowd, ushering us out. His harsh whisper was low. "Not here. Be careful what you say and who you say it around."

Kaden rolled his eyes and breathed in. He swallowed his retort, noticing the interested glare of a male Akridai shuffling closer to us, pewter cape slithering along the dark floor behind him, his neck glowing. The Akridai toyed with a long strand of his dark hair, licking his lips as he slunk closer. Kaden snapped his mouth shut, retreating down the hall with the rest of us.

10

PINCH ME

That night, we shared a meal and honey wine with anyone who braved returning. Wooden tables and benches stretched across the Great Hall. Lively stories were shared, both strangers and acquaintances conversing about their lives. It was odd to think we didn't need to eat or drink. Still, my stomach was grumbling angrily by the time we dove into massive piles of savory meats and colorful vegetables scattered across the tables.

"Is that you growling … *and* humming?" Breena smiled, looking at my belly and stuffing a piece of flaky bread between her teeth.

I laughed. "Yes, my astral body didn't get the notice. I'm starving." I savored a tender bite of meat, the flavors bursting on my tongue. This was the most delicious food I'd ever tasted. The overabundance of it all weighed on me, a heavy guilt bending my shoulders inward.

"She always hums when she eats." Kaden's lopsided smile found mine.

"That's what they tell me." I chewed happily, my shoulders

bouncing. "I rarely notice I'm doing it. What can I say? I love eating."

Breena said, "I can't fault you for that. I don't mind a 'lil entertainment when I'm stuffing my face. That tune, it's a bit gloomy, innit?"

I shrugged, swallowing a lump of bread. "It's a song Mama sang to us as children."

"Huh," Letti uttered distractedly, shrugging her shoulders and nibbling a carrot. "I don't feel hungry or thirsty, but I guess it's something to do."

An amused smile spread across my mouth. Letti was not usually inattentive, but she wasn't currently engaged in the group's conversation. Her focus drifted off as the vegetable between her teeth snapped. She peeked at the guards eating at the end of our table. Xeni was among them, her golden-brown eyes finding Letti occasionally, one side of her mouth tipping up.

"It is peculiar, isn't it?" a brawny man sitting next to Breena added. A thoughtful expression lined his bold, rectangular face; his skin was a rich umber. His hand boasted a silver rune tattoo like Gavrel's—in the shape of several decagons layered within each other, shrinking smaller and smaller until there was a single dot in the center. Each one was rotated a bit, so the points did not align. This gave the illusion they were spinning on his skin, leading into a craggy tunnel.

His Draumr uniform hugged his burly chest, which shook slightly when he chuckled. Breena had introduced him earlier as Rhaegar Hale, a friend of hers from home. Coincidentally, he was also Gavrel's second-in-command. He tipped his head in humble confirmation when she boasted this. And then promptly rolled his eyes when she imitated his formal, Eastern Pneumalian way of speaking.

He was friendly enough—quick to smile, with a playful glint in his eyes. His accent melodically stretched his vowels, at odds with the gravelly baritone of his voice. "I, for one, find it entirely vulgar. One of the greatest pleasures in this life is sharing a meal with kin." He raised his cup, acknowledged everyone at the table, and took a sip.

"Agreed. I'm not hungry either, but I won't pass up food and libations. Let's not forget the libations!" Kaden exclaimed as he set his empty goblet on the table.

Chatter and boisterous laughter filled the hall, which felt out of place somehow. Had everyone forgotten we were wandering around our scripture's most sacred realm ... in ethereal forms?

We were feasting on food we didn't need, laughing in what had once been the dwelling of an Ancient—Morpheus' home. He was one of the most celebrated and feared Ancients. Any divine being who could infiltrate the strange and clandestine corners of one's mind was to be revered.

My mouth twisted in curiosity. "Where do you think Morpheus went?"

"Who knows? Wherever the other Ancients ran off to," Kaden mumbled, slurping from his replenished goblet.

I rolled my eyes.

I planned on exploring the palace in the coming months. Perhaps there was a written archive that could shed light on our history or that of the Ancients.

Gavrel materialized behind us, wedging his bulky form between Kaden and me on the bench. He nodded at Rhaegar, the warrior tipping his head in acknowledgment. Kaden scowled at his brother as a bit of glittering, golden liquid escaped over his cup's rim. Gavrel picked up a pitcher of the Surrelian mead, filling Kaden's goblet with the sparkling spirits. Another lopsided smirk stretched across Kaden's face as he took a hearty swig, his irritation wiped clean.

"No one truly knows where any of them went." Rhaegar's voice was low. "Rumors have circulated, especially in Pneumali. Many people believe Morpheus is to blame for the Withering.

Whether he has a soft spot for mortals or not—maybe he and his siblings were bored and conspired to shake things up. They are celestial, after all. Existing forever would be daunting." He shrugged, his boulder-like shoulders pulling his overcoat taut. "Maybe they simply didn't care about their playthings anymore and buggered off to another dimension."

"Watch the little bugs squirm." Breena snorted. Kaden's head bobbed clumsily in agreement.

"Dreams and nightmares galore. Huzzah!" Kaden raised his glass. When no one responded, he picked up Breena's cup and clinked it with his own.

A scoff of amusement left me. "Looks like we can still get sloshed. I'm going to call it a night. Nice to meet you, Rhaegar." His lips curved into a smile, one big hand waving from his brow in a quick salute. I stood and helped Kaden up. "Let's go, you drunken gillytoad."

"Ribbit." Kaden bopped me on the nose with one finger, his tongue held in between his teeth. I shook my head with a chuckle, not bothering to correct him on the sound a gillytoad makes.

Gavrel stood and took Kaden from me, wrapping his arm around his brother's waist. "I've got him, Seryn. Let's head up."

We bid everyone good night and made our way to Kaden's room. We maneuvered his hefty body onto his bed. I tucked him in, kissing him on his forehead. As I moved away, Kaden seized my wrist, his fingers gentle yet firm. He tugged me toward him, causing my chest to topple across his.

"Kaden, knock it off," I giggled, wriggling away from him.

"Ah, Seryn. If you keep wiggling like that, I'll never let you go," he crooned, his gravelly voice laced with mirth and promise. A tingling blush crept over my cheeks.

Gavrel coughed. "Goodnight, brother."

Kaden pouted and mumbled, "Always ruining my fun, Gavie Gav. Very spoilsporting of you." He chuckled at his own words.

Then his body went lax. I slipped off him, righting myself. We left the room, Kaden softly snoring.

We reached my room, and I turned to Gavrel. His steady gaze studied my face intently. Had he always looked at me in this way? As if he was quietly cracking me open. Scooping out my secrets. This place was getting to me.

I let out a puff of air, glancing down. A vivid beam of moonlight split through the ceiling's prisms, casting delicate hues upon my dress. I smoothed one hand down the skirt and looked at him. "Thanks again, Gav. I'm grateful for everything you've done for us."

Although his smile was humble, it was enough to kindle the light within his eyes. He nodded and turned toward his room. "Sleep well, Asteria."

The Ancient of Stars.

I smiled at the new nickname, moving through my moonlit room. A fresh, pale nightgown waited upon my bed. I slipped into it and nestled into the silken sheets. I tumbled into a deep sleep, dreaming of shattering supernovas and spiteful deities.

THE NEXT MORNING, Gavrel accompanied Kaden, Breena, and me to the mainland, giving us a tour. The open land of the training field and barracks stretched well into the distance. It was comforting to see all the people bustling about, but a little voice kept prodding me in the back of my mind, reminding me so many more were missing.

We had not found our father yet. I suspected he did not make it out of the Stygian Murk. I rubbed my lips together, a crease forming between my eyes. *What can I do besides get through the Dormancy?* I prayed to the Ancients he was safe and found his way home.

As we made our way to the barracks, Letti waved us over. We met her outside her room, near the middle of an extensive stone building. She briefly showed me her space, expressing contentment with her accommodation. Her cozy, narrow bed sat against one white stone wall, her roommate's bed along the other. The room was clean and comfortably temperate. This put my mind at ease a bit.

"Thanks for the tour, brother." Kaden set his hand on Gavrel's shoulder, his voice hoarse. I imagined he was unwell after drowning in mead last night. "Now, tell us more about us wandering around as astra poppies."

Breena snorted as Gavrel lifted Kaden's hand from his shoulder. He didn't look amused.

"There isn't much to add." He kept count on his fingers as he spoke, starting with his thumb. "We're here in our astral bodies. Ember works because it originates from this plane. If you're injured while soul-wandering, your physical body won't be affected … but I don't recommend it. Injuries to your ethereal form still hurt like the void."

"Just rattling them off, all direct, eh? No warming us up with this one," Breena snickered, waving her hand toward Gavrel.

"Apologies. After answering the same questions for the last several turns, I find it more efficient to get the easy answers out of the way." He shrugged.

"I haven't noticed the Akridais or Elders lurking around since the gathering in the Great Hall. Where do they spend their time?" I asked.

"The Elders make themselves scarce. Akridais are usually sent on various missions." Gavrel frowned at the mention of the Druik enforcers. Hestia Larkin's terrified face flashed through my mind. "You won't see them until near the end of the Dormancy, during the Winnowing festivities."

"Winnowing festivities?" Letti wondered, her eyes swinging behind Gavrel.

"There are various ceremonies and events to mark the end of the Dormancy. A ball. Competitions. The Elders will round everyone up to provide more information in the future," he explained, turning at the sound of advancing footsteps.

Xeni approached Gavrel, a small smile lifting the corners of her mouth when her bronze-like eyes found Letti. Color rose in the apples of my sister's cheeks. Her gaze flicked to everything around us but the comely, young guard.

"Commander Larkin, here are the chore assignments," Xeni announced, handing over a crisp scroll.

Gavrel studied it for a moment and then pinned it to a tall stone pillar, marking the barracks entrance. "Thank you, Xeni. Please let the other guards know to spread the word. Make sure everyone identifies their roles within the hour."

He turned to our group, letting us know where we were each assigned. Letti was tasked with being a palace chambermaid. She shrugged, never one to complain or shy away from hard work. Breena and Kaden would be squires to separate warrior units, their matching smirks showing their delight. My heart thumped in gleeful anticipation when I was allocated to the palace library—precisely where I wanted to be.

Kaden and Breena went with Xeni toward a group of Draumrs assembled at the far edge of the training field. Various warriors were sparring or practicing their swordsmanship, those around them cheering and catcalling.

Gavrel led Letti and me to the palace. In the foyer, he beckoned a chambermaid with dark, wispy hair. He nodded a greeting when the sweet-looking young woman approached us, her big eyes rapt on his face. "Miss Linlee, would you please show Alette around and walk her through a chambermaid's duties?"

"Of course, Commander Larkin." Her head bobbed energetically as she curtsied, a glow brightening her round cheeks. Letti and I said our goodbyes, and she walked off with the besotted woman.

He walked on, his mouth cutting a stoic line across his face. Apparently, he was oblivious to the chambermaid's reaction to him.

As we strolled, I studied him from the corner of my eye. I had to admit, he was very handsome. Growing up with him over the turns, I suppose I hadn't always recognized this. It was too easy to take familiar things—and people—for granted, to cast them to the side to be obscured within the shadows.

His nose was straight and well-defined, perfectly in proportion. It was centered between high, regal cheekbones. The muscle and skin above his jawline dipped inwards slightly, sloping toward his solid jaw.

I didn't realize Gavrel had caught my curious examination until his dimple peeked from the side of his smirk. Kaden had the same dimple. An amused puff of air blew out of my nose as I looked forward, rubbing my lips together.

He led us through a labyrinth of winding halls on the ground floor. Numerous works of art lined the moonstone walls—a gilded assortment of otherworldly dreamscapes and Ancients in various stages of scheming. The hues were so bold that I thought the images might leap off the canvas. I did a double-take a few times, imagining the creatures in them were dancing among the paint strokes.

"Here we are," he announced, pushing open a set of massive, curved doors.

"Pinch me. I must be dreaming."

"Well, I suppose we all are ... technically."

I rolled my eyes, cuffing him on the arm as an excited grin swept across my face.

The elliptical library was vast. Countless columns and stacks of books covered the floor-to-ceiling walls, and rows of book-lined aisles stretched ahead of us. Two pairs of curling staircases, like contorted parentheses, stood at the entrance and back of the room, granting access to the second and third-floor balconies running along the walls. Every inch of the space was formed of glossy black stone and fluid pewter, arching protectively over stacked sections of tomes. Obsidian ladders scattered throughout the room, stretching toward the vaulted ceiling.

The bowed walls on the third level rose high into the ceiling, their arched peaks creating a diamond pattern along the center. Nestled between the pointed cutouts, a sea of crystal prisms coruscated defiantly, refracted sunlight bouncing over the room's glossy surfaces.

I breathed in the comforting musk of the leather-bound treasures, their yellowed pages and well-loved backbones beckoning me.

An older man tottered over, interrupting my daydreams. His puffy white mustache hid his upper lip. His bottom lip was tipped downward in a displeased scowl as he grumbled with every step.

"Commander, *what* have you brought me?" His words were like dry gravel scraping under a boot. His back bowed with age, and the dark green of his tunic rustled as he shifted uncomfortably. *He must have ember*, I mused, taking in his attire.

Before Gavrel could speak, I interjected, ensuring my voice was polite and unaffected. "My name is Seryn Vawn. I'm from a village in northern Evergryn. Pleased to meet you." I paused, holding out my hand.

He raised one bushy eyebrow, a faint brownish aura fizzling around his bent form for a moment. *Well, that settles that.* A gentle smile curved my mouth. He studied me, holding me hostage in an amusing staring contest. I tipped my chin up, not breaking eye contact.

He huffed and lifted a bony, arthritic hand, his grip surprisingly firm when he shook mine. "Iben Burlam. Evergryn. Eastern—bordering Haadra."

"Seryn is to help you in the library, Mr. Burlam."

"Fine, fine. Come this way, girl," he demanded, shuffling toward the long tables lining the center of the aisles.

Gavrel whispered, "He's not so bad once you wear him down, which I've no doubt you will excel in." He smiled, his viridescent eyes glinting.

"Absolutely. He's nothing but a grumpy little lamb." I winked and followed the prickly librarian, leaving the commander chuckling as he left the library.

"Pick up the pace, girl," the librarian chided. I smirked, considering I was already beside him. He moved slower than sap seeping down a tree.

"We get a lot of traffic in here. There isn't much else to do. Unless you want to take your chances in the Reverie Weald or swing a sword like an imbecile."

I bit my lip to hold in my smile. "Good to know, Mr. Burlam. How can I help?"

He regarded me as if *I* was an imbecile swinging a sword. "Help find books. Put away books. Organize books." He threw up his hands. "By the Ancients, girl! It's a library. What do you think you would do?"

"Ah, yes, of course. Well, I'll be off to do all the book things. Let me know if you need anything." He scrunched his face, his mouth disappearing entirely under his mustache. As I walked toward the back of the library, he muttered under his breath.

"And sweep the floors!" he called after me.

"Of course, Mr. Burlam!" I responded in a singsong. He hobbled over to a desk in the corner, a trail of grumbles drifting behind him.

Under his watchful glower, I worked for several hours— reshelving books, sweeping, dusting, and yet more reshelving.

When he seemed satisfied with my efforts, his lips buttoned together, a disgruntled huff whooshing from his nose. He nodded and then paid me no further attention. I took that as my cue to take a break.

I claimed a seat in the back of the library, far from the few people scattered throughout the space. My fingers trailed along spines as I meandered through the aisles, plucking out any title calling to me. Soon, I had collected a small stack of timeworn books, hugging them within the safety of my arms.

As I left the aisle, a faint rustle sounded behind me. I turned toward it but saw no one. Without warning, a book from an upper shelf tumbled to the ground, landing with a thud at my feet. Startled, I jumped back. A nervous laugh left me as I reached for the tome, curious how it had fallen. There didn't appear to be anyone on the other side of this aisle. I shrugged, placing it atop my pile.

When I deposited them on the table, a stale puff of air curled around me as I settled on my seat. Choosing the book that had tried to clobber my brains out, I smirked at the name, my tongue pressing into the wall of my cheek. My fingertips traced over the gilded letters etched into bumpy leather—*Ancient History: An Unabridged Bridge into Divine Yesterdays*.

11

ANCIENT HISTORY

I skimmed the book's pages, flipping through them haphazardly until one handwritten word caught my attention. *Oneiroi*. It was scrawled in elegant gold lettering above a beautiful illustration of three Ancients. Delicate strokes of black brushed over the yellowed parchment, gold-foil accents illuminating the ink.

The Oneiroi were the Ancients of Dreams: three celestial siblings who penetrated and manipulated the minds of every living being. They could influence a person's psyche while conscious; however, their divine ember was most potent when their target was sleeping—whether naturally or in an induced trance. *Thank you, Dormancy.* I sighed as my focus lingered on the image.

The male in the center was breathtaking, all chiseled muscles and robust angles. His frosty gaze was direct, staring down his aquiline nose at whoever viewed the drawing. His flaxen hair floated in a halo around a golden diadem atop his head. One powerful arm lifted above him; a shining globe in gold leaf floated above his hand. Stars burst from the glowing orb, levitating above and around the three figures. *Morpheus:*

Supreme Ancient of Dreams was written in crisp script under the male.

On his left was an equally attractive male, his form powerfully trim and lean. While Morpheus was golden light and stars, this male was made of shadows and the promise of misery. A slinking swirl of smog spilled from one palm, devouring the edges of the drawing under their feet and shrouding half of his face. A desiccated skull rested in his other hand. One dark eye was visible, piercing and narrowed as a smug look stretched across his gaunt countenance. *Phobetor: Ancient of Nightmares.*

The stunning woman on Morpheus' right was his sister. *Phantasos: The Ancient of Illusions.* Her face was obscured—a soft blur of gold and mist creating a subtle veil over her. Nevertheless, her lips smirked, her eyes twinkling with mirth as if she were withholding a secret. She wore a flowing gown, sparkling gold sprinkled over it, melding with the stars that Morpheus' orb released. A plump raven sat in her cradled palms, staring adoringly at her.

I eagerly moved on to the text, soaking in whatever information I could gather.

It is understood that the immortal Oneiroi maintain the balance between realms and minds. For what is the mind if not the inner world of all living creatures? Their divine embers are esteemed, even among other Ancients. Over time, there have been a few attempts to usurp the triplets; all have failed.

Morpheus reigns over Surrelia, welcoming the departed souls of mortals and immortals alike. Once the physical body perishes, a mortal's astral form may take refuge in Surrelia for all time unless banished to the Nether Void.

Furthermore, Morpheus drifts through dreams, shaping them to his whims and providing support, comfort, or pleasure when he feels charitable.

> *Phobetor presides over the aforementioned Nether Void. A dark and dismal fate it is for those who reside in his domain. He conjures up the darkest of visions within one's mind, tormenting the soul and punishing who he pleases.*
>
> *Phantasos is thought to wander through various planes, a trail of either bewilderment or surreal clarity in her wake. It is believed she prefers to dwell deep within wild landscapes, letting nature's ember permeate her essence. Her guidance, although peculiarly sage, is cloaked in cryptic riddles.*

I studied well into the afternoon, my eyes tired from the strain of reading the worn ink in the dimming light. It was clear Magister Barden had taught us the basics, but there was so much more to know.

"Seryn, there you are." Kaden's voice barged into my awareness, his call echoing down the length of the library. He plopped down next to me, bumping the table and making my tower of books lurch precariously. I steadied them with my hand, an embarrassed heat blushing my cheeks.

"Hush, this is a library, for Surrelia's sake!" Mr. Burlam shouted from the other end of the room. Kaden held up his hands in surrender, and Mr. Burlam scowled, turning his attention back to his desk.

"How was your day? Feeling any better, you little honey wine bandit?" I giggled.

"Feeling just fine, Ser. Just fine," he purred, rubbing his belly. "An average day in the life of a mighty squire."

"Ah, what a delight you are, Kade." My eyes rolled so far back that he probably could only see their whites.

"Honestly, though, I'm looking forward to it. I think we'll be training a lot with the guards. I wouldn't mind brushing up on my swordsmanship."

"It is fortunate Gavrel taught you early on."

"Perhaps you'll partake?" His voice was hopeful.

A small smile crept across my mouth. "Perhaps." I had never thought much of learning how to use a weapon. Over the turns, the Larkin brothers had taught me the basics of swordplay, but I didn't keep up with practicing.

I shifted, facing Kaden and pushing my book toward him. "Look at this. So much information about the Ancients and our realms."

"I bet Magister Barden would have wet himself with excitement." Glee shined in his eyes. I swallowed a laugh to avoid Mr. Burlam's attention again.

"All right, give it here," he ordered, pulling the book closer and flipping through the pages. A strand of black hair flopped over his brow. I longed to brush it back and run my fingers through his unruly strands. Instead, I watched him intently.

"Ah, here's a little history lesson. Listen to this then," he said, looking at me. He caught me staring, and a grin cut across his face. He read on, his voice imitating Magister Barden's. "When the Ancients first gifted ember to humans, the rise of untamed Druiks overwhelmed Midst Fall. There were no known orders to govern the use and misuse of such powerful, wild energies. The emperor was ineffective in controlling the scourge, and consequently, the empire crumbled."

I shifted closer to him, reading silently along.

"The Ancients were uninterested in managing the Druiks. However, they eventually agreed upon establishing a ruling body of Elders—supreme wielders, to prevent the extinction of the Ancients' acolytes. For without worshippers, the Ancients' immortality and power would dwindle. From each region of the mortal plane, the Ancients chose the most powerful Druik—selected for their extraordinary ability and capacity to endure ultimate levels of divine ember."

"All right, all right." I waved my hand at him dismissively, centering the book between us. He laughed at my impatience, nudging his shoulder against mine. I smiled as we read the rest of the passage to ourselves.

Henceforth, these original Elders possessed divine bloodlines, and future descendants, or Scions, hailed from their lineage. Only one Scion from each ancestral house will exist at a time.

The founding family names are:
OLEANDER OF EVERGRYN
LOTUS OF HAADRA
NIGHTSHADE OF PERILOUS BOGS
AERIDES OF PNEUMALI
CELOSIA OF PYRIA

To maintain balance, the Ancients decreed that each region must be represented consistently by an ascended Elder. When all five delegates are assembled, they take an oath sealed in blood. This bond grants them additional enhanced ember. If this celestial covenant is broken, their abilities diminish progressively until their gift is no more.

An Elder can often sense the new Scion's power. Once recognized, the Scion and Elder undergo Ascension—the ritual in which the Scion metamorphoses into the new Elder.

The retired Elder has two paths: either live out their days in Midst Fall, their ember weakened and ultimately fading, or join the Ancients in astral form immediately, their physical body rejoining the earth, their gift returned to the aether.

"Well, where do I sign up?" Kaden joked.

I blew out the breath I hadn't realized was stuck in my chest, staring at the yellowed paper.

"It's a heavy price. I suppose after leading for so long with enhanced powers, it would be hard to cope with such a loss.

Either way, they lose their ember." Pity moved my head from side to side.

"It is, but if it is a person's calling," he said, his tone sincere. "Then the choice to lead—for the good of the realm—outweighs the cost." He shrugged one shoulder, falling silent.

"Wow, Kaden. I don't think I've ever seen your philosophical side."

"One of my many hidden talents." He winked, rising from the table. "Want to head to dinner—sans the libations?"

I snickered, rising and gathering the books. "Sure. Help me put these away?"

He nodded, allowing me to fill his sturdy arms with the stack. We walked through the aisles, returning the tomes. Their leather-bound neighbors welcomed them with a rustling sigh. I took the final book, the one that had mysteriously fallen earlier, and stretched on my tiptoes to put it back in place.

I groaned in frustration, failing to reach the shelf.

"Let me help." Kaden stretched his muscled arm over my right shoulder. He gently took the leather volume from my fingers, lifting it and pushing it home.

The warmth of his chest seeped into my shoulders as he lingered behind me. His warm breath grazed over my temple, some loose strands of hair tickling my skin. He breathed in deeply, his exhale coming out with a sigh.

The library was tranquil. Kaden could doubtless hear the drum of my heart as it accelerated.

"Thank you," I whispered, still staring at the leather spines before me as if I had forgotten how to move my own.

From the side of my vision, Kaden's biceps contracted, and then his fingertips touched the back of my hand, which was frozen in mid-air. He gently skimmed them over my wrist. My arm. My shoulder. Goosebumps tracked his touch. My fingers gripped the edge of the shelf, steadying myself as my knees quivered.

His heart thumped against my spine, bringing it back to life. My arm fluttered back to my side as I tilted my head to the left. A faint, shaky chuckle escaped him.

"Anytime." He brushed his palm over my shoulder, gently gathering my hair and placing it over my left shoulder. His palm returned to the curve between my bared neck and shoulder. The wide expanse of his hand branded me motionless, as if he was memorizing the feel of our skin touching in the buzzing silence.

I turned into his touch, achingly slow. Our breaths mingled, hitching in time with each other in little gasps. His hand lingered, slipping along my skin as I faced him. His palm now rested on my collarbone, fingers cupping the other side of my neck under a curtain of dark-red curls. My back pressed into the shelved books, acting as my vertebrae and offering me stability in a tilted world. I closed my eyes as his thumb circled leisurely over the hollow of my throat.

My eyes fluttered open, dragging upward to meet Kaden's smoldering gaze. His clover-colored aura simmering around him, melding with his radiating heat. My chest was heaving, trying to break free from the bodice of my kirtle.

He stepped closer, placing his other hand on my waist, squeezing gently. As he leaned down, the air caught in my throat. My hands flew forward, gripping the front of his tunic. I wasn't sure if I was urging him toward me or holding him still. He paused, his full lips hovering a breath away from mine. If I licked my lips, my tongue would run over his, tasting him.

"It would seem ..." he murmured, his words flitting over my mouth, "all our stories are put away."

"I ... I hadn't noticed," I breathed.

"I notice *everything*, Seryn."

"Kaden," I whimpered.

All at once, both of his hands shifted, his fingers burrowing into the curtain of my hair and cupping the back of my neck and head. His lips crushed into mine, and he groaned. The taste of salt and mint danced in my mouth.

My hands clenched the fabric of his tunic, pulling his weight against me. The shelves dug into my back, but I barely felt their bite.

I lifted onto my toes, pushing our lips together more firmly. I was dazed. I was ravenous. I needed...

"Library's closed!" Mr. Burlam's voice boomed down the aisle, startling us as we jumped apart, our breathing erratic. Kaden's eyes bore into the side of my face, and my gaze whipped toward the cranky librarian. My face burned brighter than the sun.

"Uh, yes. Yes, of course, Mr. Burlam. We're leaving now. Thank you!" I stammered.

I rushed down the aisle, away from Kaden, as he called my name. I flew past Mr. Burlam, ducking my head and dashing past the endless rows of novels.

Hurrying through the doors, I sped through the winding halls, not looking behind me to see if anyone had followed. At the sight of my bedroom door, I moaned. My leather slippers slapped against the stones, echoing along the corridor.

I shoved my door open and tumbled into the safety of my room, slamming the door shut and smacking my palm against the blue gem in the wall. Derya wouldn't mind bringing me something to eat in my room tonight.

As I counted my breaths, calming the frenzied pace of my heart, the fog cleared from my thoughts.

Bollocks.

I had left my spine in the library among the others, after all.

12

THE HEART: A FICKLE CREATURE

"*A*ll right, so what if I kissed my best friend? It's no big deal."

I was talking to myself in bed the next morning. Out loud. The sun had risen, spraying fractured rainbows around the canopy, but I'd awoken hours before, restless and annoyed with myself. Accepting I needed to get on with my day, I shoved the quilt off me, huffing. After quickly bathing and dressing, I joined Letti for breakfast in the dining hall.

She was right; eating was something to do. It seemed like almost everyone ate at mealtimes. While trapped here, why not enjoy a little indulgence? It was a time to connect with others. Well, not the Elders, of course. I deduced they wouldn't join us for meals in the future since they hadn't done so yet. Why would they bother sharing a meal with us lowly minions?

I shifted on the bench, the wood grumbling under me. *Oh, shut up, bench,* I thought, gazing at the fresh muffin on my plate. We could all use these moments to distract us from the fact that we were not physically here in Surrelia. That our bodies were in ember-induced stupors—in terrifying black tombs, dreaming against our wills. All the while, our world continued its death march without us.

"Are you okay, Ser?" Letti stared at me wide-eyed. Her brows furrowed as she scooped a spoonful of oatmeal into her mouth. I glowered at her as she chewed in an aggravatingly slow manner.

I sighed and took a deep breath, calming my spiraling thoughts. *Get ahold of yourself, woman,* I scolded myself, sitting up straight and rolling my shoulders.

"Yes, I'm fine." I glued a smile on my face.

"I don't believe you."

I mumbled something unintelligible.

"What was that, sweet sister?" Letti asked.

I picked up the muffin and tossed it at her plate. "I'm fine, oh loving sister of mine. Eat your breakfast."

She laughed, picking up her muffin and taking a big bite. "Here if you need me. Besides, you're humming while you eat. So, it can't be that bad."

The corners of my lips curled as I nodded at her and continued eating. We left our table shortly after to start our chores for the day.

As we approached the exit, Kaden and Gavrel walked in. Kaden's eyes immediately found mine, imploring. My head swayed briefly as we greeted them. One of Gavrel's eyebrows raised at the formality of our conversation, but I was too worn out to mind. We each went our separate ways without further discussion. I'd process our little rendezvous later.

After I finished my work for the day, I longed to explore the grounds further. Throughout the day, Mr. Burlam hadn't sniped at me much, despite being as cantankerous as ever. Maybe he felt a speck of sympathy after seeing me scurry out of the library last night. Scoffing, I dismissed the silly notion.

The afternoon sunlight soaked into me as I wandered to the mainland. I went to the fence along the cliff, staring into the deep ravine below. The river crashed relentlessly into the jagged cliff. Leaning my forearms on the wooden barrier, I closed my eyes and lost myself to the whooshing of the waterfalls to my left, allowing the sound to wrap me in a buzzing haze of solace.

"Seryn," Kaden murmured, resting on the fence beside me. I hadn't noticed him approach. His hair was damp with sweat, making him look rugged. Strong. Stupidly handsome. *Damn him.*

"I'm all right. I needed to get my thoughts together."

"I'm sorry if I scared you last night."

"You didn't scare me. I … I enjoyed what happened." I looked over at him, a smile creeping along his lips. The very lips I had kissed last night. "But we're best friends, Kade. I don't want to ruin that."

"But—"

"Listen, can we just forget about it? Go back to normal for now?"

His lips pressed together, a glower etching into his face as he watched the violent currents below. "For now."

I'd known him long enough to appreciate the restraint he was showing. He wanted to say more but was giving me what I wanted. *For now.*

"Walk with me?" I bumped his shoulder with mine, and a cheerless smile lifted the corners of his mouth. We strolled silently for a while, observing others in the training field and taking in the vibrant landscape around us. My thoughts wandered as we moved, drifting in and out of various memories and musings.

I peeked at Kaden and then forward again, releasing a puff of air. Over the turns, I'd had dalliances with a couple of young men at home. Though it never went beyond kissing and touching. I still possessed my maidenhead, but it wasn't something I was concerned about one way or the other.

The heat—the burning desire—to go further with them had

eluded me. If I had wanted to, I would have. At the time, I had more pressing concerns; ensuring my family had enough to eat every day being the main one. However, it frustrated me that I had wanted—no, *needed*—to go further last night.

With my best friend.

Kaden certainly had broken some hearts over the turns, even if unintentionally. He'd bedded at least two women in our village that I knew of. One a few turns older than us and one our age. Both were left mourning the loss of a relationship that had never begun. I peeked at him from the corner of my eye, my gaze drawn to his plump lips.

Stop.

I looked ahead, concentrating on the colorful hues of the Reverie Weald.

One of Kaden's most admirable traits was his absolute candor—even when you didn't want it. I grinned. We shared almost everything, maybe to a fault. I wasn't sure anymore.

At the time, Kaden had told me he'd been honest with each woman, informing them he wasn't interested in a serious relationship. But alas, the heart was a fickle creature, digging its way through any sane person's sensibilities. I should know. If I was honest with myself, the random thought of Kaden and me being together had sporadically slipped into my notice over the turns.

But it was foolish. If our friendship had been left in shambles
...

It.

Would.

Destroy.

Me.

My chin lifted. It was better to be friends. And that was that.

When we reached the edge of the woods, Kaden and I paused, peering at each other.

"Shall we?" we both asked in unison. We laughed and strode into the trees, Kaden's hand on my back.

We explored the area for hours, wandering deep into the endless forest. I basked in the mellow beams of light bursting through the succulent leaves overhead. Sunshine bathed the canopy, the breeze making it look like flames swaying above us. Healthy moss and clusters of multicolored flowers covered the forest floor. This place—I sighed, leaning against a tree—took my breath away.

"Dreamy, isn't it?" Kaden chuckled.

"I miss home so much, but this is spectacular." I paused, watching a furry, hand-sized critter scurry past us and into a nearby flower patch. It studied us with six curious brown eyes, blinking in time with the frenzied swish of a long, fluffy tail. Its perky, triangular ears swiveled this way and that. Finding us harmless, it sat on its haunches, grooming its spotted, apricot-colored fur with tiny paws. "Doesn't it make you want to figure out what we can do for Midst Fall?"

Kaden's eyebrows rose. "Yes, it does. What do you think I've been complaining about all these turns? Contrary to popular belief, I don't like the sound of my own voice."

"I know, I know. But it seems impossible. Like we're just puppets dancing to the Elders' tune."

"Never a better time to cut the strings, I suppose." He bent over and picked up a bundle of broken flowers, its smashed petals the color of blueberries.

He cradled it in his cupped palm, closing his eyes. His aura gathered in a compressed, pulsing orb, radiating from his chest as if his heart were the source of his ember. His eyes opened, focusing on the flowers. Simmering from the orb, his power flickered over his arms and hands, and then the rest of his body. The green hue around him was so vibrant that it looked like he came from the moss beneath him.

He poured his energy into the bouquet, the petals and stems twisting and knitting back together. A grin spread across his face, and his brilliant aura faded. Handing the posy to me, his eyes glinted for a moment. "For you, milady."

My smile pushed wider, my eyes scrunching in awe and delight. "Have you been practicing?"

"I have—in between squire duties and sparring. Gavrel and some other Druiks have been sharing tips with me. You can learn a lot in a short time ... when you aren't hiding." He shrugged. "You should join us. Dig into what your ember is."

"I'd like that." A twinkle caught my attention, and I turned my head.

Not far ahead, a barrier of some sort fluttered over the path, stretching across the entire forest; a glittering, translucent veil draping from the treetops and through anything it touched.

"What is that?" Kaden asked, squinting. Our tiny, furry friend flicked its six rounded eyes in that direction, squeaked, and scampered off in the opposite direction.

We moved toward it, drawn by its mystic beauty. I grabbed Kaden as his outstretched hand reached for the luminous shroud.

"Careful—we don't know what this will do."

Upon closer inspection, it was a thin film of glimmering iridescent hues and sparkles. The delicate colors swirled and shifted in the light, sometimes disappearing from view as if made of vapor. The mesmerizing boundary was neither liquid nor gas, but it wasn't solid, either. I couldn't exactly grasp what I was looking at, my eyes playing tricks on me. It quivered in the breeze like a piece of wispy material drying on a clothesline.

"This must be what Melina was talking about when she said

we'd know when we'd gone too far." Kaden studied the veil, one hand cupping his chin.

"Well then, I'm not sure I want to test that theory." I laughed nervously.

"Come on, Ser. What if the answers to our questions are on the other side of these sparkle drapes? I think our astral bodies will be just fine."

I rolled my eyes. "Damn you, you hobgoblin."

A sound of nervous determination vibrated in my throat as I thrust my fingers into the twinkling vapor to show my annoyance with his logic. A rush of heat zapped from below my star-shaped scar, pulsing along my spine. It wasn't unpleasant, but it vaguely reminded me of the feeling in the Stygian Murk before I blew up the shade. I pulled my hand back, holding it against my chest with the other.

"Holy shit on a biscuit! Your eyes are glowing!" Kaden yelped and then proceeded to shove his hand through the veil. He yelped again and pulled it out.

"Yours, too," I responded wryly.

We shrugged, wearing matching, mischievous grins. Kaden winked as my eyes widened, and without further ado, we flung our bodies through the mist.

As we tumbled into the other side, I had the fleeting thought that we were being too reckless, but here we were.

I looked at Kaden and then down at my dress. Tiny beads of twirling light stuck to our figures like soap bubbles on wet glass. The hazy outlines of our shapes remained in the veil behind us, opaque silhouettes devoid of the veil's colorful, swirling sparkles.

The mystical glow within our eyes faded. Soon after, the dazzling orbs leaped from our bodies, fusing with the mystic mesh once more.

Kaden shook out his arms, clenching his hands. "It feels like my skin is vibrating."

"Same," I murmured, my vision wandering over the lustrous forest surrounding us. The trees, moss, flowers ... every living thing was bursting with illuminated, coruscating auras as if they could no longer bury their ember within them. I exhaled, creating a soft, glittering swirl of air in front of me. "Is this what the world truly looks like?"

Kaden shrugged and moved forward, smirking. Specks of twinkling light floated around him and his path, caressing but not making contact with him. I shook my head, brushing some errant curls from my cheek, and followed him. The neon motes frolicked around me in the same way.

As we walked, I wiggled my fingers through the air, mesmerized by its shimmering dance. With every step, a rippling glow swept through the moss. I brushed my palm over the rich bark of a tree trunk, its smooth knots and ridges prominent. It felt alive. I grazed my fingertips over pearlescent flowers dancing beside the tree, the petals warm and velvety. Each time my skin connected with the flora, its aura brightened, swaying away from my touch and settling back into the living thing like a wave upon the shore.

I closed my eyes and inhaled deeply, the energies around me sifting through my lungs and tingling along my skin.

Little Staaaaar.

My eyes snapped open, a trickle of panic zipping up my neck at the rasping voice creeping through the air.

"Kaden, was that you?"

"Huh? Did you say something?" Kaden's eyes bore through me like I was made of the same material as the glimmering veil. I reached my hand toward him, but he wandered around and past me—searching for something, forgetting I was there.

"Kaden—"

My voice caught behind my teeth as a chilled breeze washed over me. Irradiant specks of ember churned in a frenzy, as if trying to escape, but they couldn't stray far from the confines of the orbiting breeze. The creaking voice tangled within the wind as it twirled around me. My nickname echoed, slicing through my thoughts until I was dizzy, my mind spinning.

Liiiiittle Staaaar.

My little star.

I whipped toward the voice, now immediately behind me—melodic and feminine. Familiar. Nearly forgotten. I swept my fingers over my lashes, clearing away tears exorcised by the frosty memories clawing within me.

"Mama?" I rasped, my voice scratching.

She was there, a milky form materializing. The ember caught within the spinning air slurped into her shape as if it drank in the energy, extinguishing its light.

"Yes, Little Star," she said, a simper splitting her ethereal features. She looked both solid and made of vapor. Her gauzy white dress drifted to the ground, fading into hazy billows around her. The only true color saturating her was that of her wild ruby-colored hair floating around her shoulders.

My mind was made of vapor as well. I clenched my fingers into my palm, the pain a reminder to steady myself. Pulsing frantically, my scar sent tremors quivering down my back and over my arms.

"Where have you been, Mama?" I asked, my words catching in my throat, breathless. She glided toward me, her arms outstretched.

"Here."

"In Surrelia? Why couldn't you come home? What happened?"

Her arms wrapped around me, her skin icy and clammy.

She didn't feel right.

"Mama?"

"Littlllllle Starrr." Her voice slithered around me.

She didn't sound right.

I tried to shift within her embrace but found myself

ensnared. A tear freed itself, rolling down my cheek and freezing against my skin as I looked at her. No longer beautiful, but eerie and ravenous. My breaths were shallow; each inhale felt like tiny icicle shards sliced down through my windpipe.

A deep, rumbling terror rushed through me as my legs and arms numbed, my fingers bending into rigid claws, unable to move or extend. My mind filled with fog as my breathing slowed.

Little liiiitle.

Starrrrr.

The creature's voice was in my mind, its terrifying grin stuck in place, lips unmoving over glinting teeth.

The creature was wearing my mother's skin and lurking behind her voice.

Staining the memory of her.

Unacceptable.

Burgeoning fury sweltered in my belly. My teeth ground together as I concentrated on that fire, willing it to spread, to thaw my iced limbs. I thought of my mother. Her unique views of the world that were also instilled in me. The love that radiated from her.

This monster could never understand that. Could never mimic who she was deep within her soul. The blaze ignited, scorching through my body. My hair flamed around me in whipping tendrils. My scar throbbed as iridescence sizzled over my skin.

The being's eyes—a poor imitation of Mama's—widened. It released me with a moist pop, its sticky skin releasing from mine. As it stumbled back, the cloudy haze shrouding it flickered, revealing its true form.

A gelatinous, wiggling blob stood before me, balancing on its squishy, corpulent tail. Its muck-colored body, as tall as me, resembled a giant leech with several segmented rings circling its turgid mass. Through a slimy, semi-translucent membrane, its innards were on display, pumping and writhing—gluttonous.

Desperate to latch onto me, a gaping, viscid cavity, filled with needle-like teeth, sucked at the air. A myriad of tiny worm-like arms wriggled from its upper body, grasping for me.

I swallowed a lump of disgust and let power pulsate over me. My aura grew bright and then condensed, rushing down my forearms and hands in splintering, branch-like patterns of luminescence.

My prismatic glow reflected on the slime of the monster's body. Two glacial-blue orbs reflected in the ooze—my eyes were glowing again, filling with magnificent energy. A sense of relief and tranquility settled into my mind as if my ember welcomed my surrender. One word ached longingly through my awareness: *destroy.*

Destroy.

A curdling, moist screech cleaved the air. The creature crumbled before me, the blade of a shining sword piercing its bulging belly.

Destroy.

"Seryn!" A commanding shout pried through my consciousness.

Destroy.

Someone was in front of me, shaking my shoulders. I squeezed my eyes shut tightly, willing my mind to own itself—scratching through the muddied recesses of my focus.

"That's it. Come back to me now," his voice rumbled along my skin.

Steady hands cradled the back of my head and neck, and a soothing warmth radiated from the male's skin, blanketing mine. My scar hummed with the comforting energy, my aura greedily absorbing it.

The murk cleared, and my aura seeped into my body. My eyes, no longer blazing, focused as I opened them.

"Gavrel?" I murmured in confusion. He nodded, a grim line cutting across his mouth.

"Where is Kaden?" he asked.

"I'm ... I'm not sure." My heart thumped wildly as I took a wobbly step away from him. He went to the slimy pile, and a wet, slurping sound followed as he wrenched his sword free from the beast's mass. His rune tattoo burned brightly, and the radiance of his sword intensified as he adjusted his grip on the hilt.

"Gavrel—"

A howl of sorrow cut off my words.

"Ma! Noooo!"

"Wait here," he commanded. He gave me a stern look, knowing I probably would do the opposite of what he instructed. He was right. Grunting, Gavrel ran toward the sound of Kaden's pleas. I ran behind him on unsteady legs.

Kaden was soon ahead of us, defenseless and unable to move. My hands flew to my mouth, holding back a scream and the sick rising. Another parasite latched onto his limp form, its worm-like arms embracing him tightly. His back bowed as the oozing being curved over him. Its barbed teeth latched onto his chest as it gulped in his ember.

"Ma, why?" Kaden's ragged whisper broke my heart in half. His lips were pale, the same color as his now pallid skin. His aura was diminishing fast, the green of it barely visible.

Gavrel reached them, his hand and sword blazing as he stabbed through the demon's side. The monster hissed, unlocking its grip on Kaden. It writhed and shrieked in agony as Gavrel pulled his sword away, stabbing it again through its gaping mouth. It sagged, flaccid and lifeless, onto the glowing moss.

Kaden crumpled to the ground, and I ran to him, holding him in my shaking arms. His body was freezing, his limbs limp.

His upper body lay across my lap as I cradled his head in the crook of my elbow. He whimpered.

"Well, this is disappointing."

The female's voice startled me, jerking my body, jostling Kaden. Elder Melina Harrow leaned against a tree. Her snug black dress wrapped around her curves, the color marring the neon hues surrounding us. A steel-colored mantle hung from her slender shoulders and swept down, petting the moss beneath her. She casually inspected her dark, pointed nails. A striking, glossy ring wrapped around her thumb. Its intricately carved design resembled delicate lace sculpted out of black tourmaline. The ring's interwoven contours and crevices glinted.

She caught my stare from under her lashes and let her arm fall as she pushed herself off the tree trunk with a dramatic moan.

"Why did you have to spoil the best part, Gavie?" she asked with an exaggerated pout and then laughed as her mouth settled into a simper.

"Forgive me, Mistress Harrow. I wasn't about to allow my brother to be harmed," he replied, his expression unreadable, aside from his ticking jaw. I followed his lead, grinding my molars together, wary of saying something any of us might regret.

She dismissed him with a wave of her delicate hand as she approached Kaden and me. She loomed over us, tilting her head to one side, studying me with one eyebrow raised. "You put on quite the show … Seryn Vawn, is it?" She didn't wait for a response. "I've no doubt it would have been more riveting if Gavie hadn't intervened."

"Indeed, Mistress," I murmured, keeping the acid in my gut at bay.

She clapped her hands together, glancing at Gavrel, who stood at my side. "Ah, the little puppet speaks."

Puppet.

Heat gathered in my cheeks. I opened my mouth to reply but then thought better of it, slowly releasing my breath and sealing my lips. Kaden stirred in my arms, groaning and lifting his hands to rub his eyes.

"Kaden, it's all right. I've got you." I helped him sit beside me.

"All is well in the enchanted forest," Melina quipped as she twirled and took a few steps away. She turned back to us, her mantle twisting around her curves, her platinum hair draping down her back meticulously. She grinned again as her hands stretched toward us.

A wisping dark smoke smoldered around her, licking over her arms and hands. Her uncanny silver eyes pierced into mine. A deep throbbing began in my scar and clawed over my head. My mind was breaking free of my skull, pushing against the thick bones. I pressed my palms to the sides of my head, scrunching my forehead—trying to rid myself of the intrusive ache. My aura flickered over my skin, and I welcomed its presence. All at once, the pressure dissipated. With a sigh of relief, I dropped my hands. My ember fizzled out, evaporating as swiftly as it had appeared.

Melina squinted, tilting her head. "I look forward to observing your ember develop, little Seryn. You are quite intriguing. It wouldn't do for you to be trapped in the Stygian Murk when I'm just getting to know you. Perhaps you'll heed my warnings and not stray so far again. Be a good pet, like your mother, and all will be well."

I began to rise, ire pushing my limbs forward. Gavrel's heavy hand bridled my shoulder, and Kaden grabbed my hand on the other side. Before I could tug my body away from them, Melina's aura enveloped her in a billowing haze as she clapped her hands together. She vanished like a nightmare does upon waking. Her smoky ember drifted away into the neon leaves, joining the flames above us.

13

SLEEPLESS IN SURRELIA

*M*are wyrms. That was what those soul-sucking demon leeches were. We were nearly back to the training field, Gavrel leading the way. I assumed he was particularly displeased with our lack of critical thinking skills—if his scowl was any indication.

"They hail from the Nether Void. Over the last century, Void creatures have been trespassing into Surrelia. The Order's efforts to resolve the situation have been futile." Gavrel swung his head from side to side before glaring at the ground momentarily. Then he adjusted his scabbard, his sword snuggly sheathed at his back as he strode into the open field ahead of us.

"Are you all right?" I asked Kaden.

"Yeah," he muttered.

"Kaden ..." I put my hand on his forearm, encouraging us to pause. His muscles tensed beneath my touch.

"I'll be fine. Was it a shit experience seeing my mother? Yep. Would I recommend having your soul or whatever sucked from you? Nope. Now we know." He shrugged, effectively nudging my hand from his arm.

"I understand. You know I do. Seeing my mother was devastating," I murmured.

His eyes softened. "I know. Sorry. I'm grateful you snapped out of it—unlike me. I'm a jackass," he groused, plunging his hands through his messy strands. Kaden's bronzed complexion had returned, chasing away the chalky paleness the mare wyrm's attack had triggered. I studied him from the corner of my vision, looking for any lingering signs of affliction.

His nose, once straight like his brother's, was crooked after it had been broken. A rueful smile tipped one corner of my mouth. When we were sixteen, he had gotten into a scrap with another boy from our village. The boy had cruelly mocked me for not having a mother. Kaden tackled him, delivering several blows before the boy landed one good punch to Kaden's nose and ran away. The boy never ridiculed me again.

"I'm fine, Ser." He huffed, his face pinching. He took my hand, squeezed it once, and then rushed ahead to speak with Gavrel.

While I didn't condone violence, I recognized its value at times. Over the turns, especially since Hestia's culling, Kaden had battled his persistent temper. It was rare for anyone to sense the inferno bubbling beneath his amiable disposition. Kaden was quick to laugh, his humor provoking amusement within others.

He wasn't a violent man by any means, but was he impulsive? Absolutely. After having some rocky adolescent turns, he honed his self-discipline, diverting his simmering fury into physical labor, swordplay, and now—I realized—embercraft.

I glanced at the enigmatic forest behind me and squared my shoulders. Catching up to them, I positioned myself next to Gavrel, giving Kaden space. "Gav, you said Morpheus' sister, Phantasos, created the veil centuries ago. Was it for defense or to keep us mortals from straying?"

The corner of his mouth quirked upward. "Both. The veil keeps Void creatures out. It's a boon it has held up."

"It doesn't restrict Phobetor, I would suspect," I added, my brow creasing.

"Correct, only his realm's beasts. As for keeping us in. Yes, its secondary aim is to deter vulnerable souls from leaving the grounds before they're ready." His smile dropped. "Which you've both learned the hard way today," he grumbled, glowering at us.

"Ah, Gavrel, don't be so surly. I have no doubt you can join us in the fun next time," Kaden chided, his shield of humor back in place. Gavrel squinted at Kaden, his tongue pushing at the inside of his lips.

"I'd suggest learning more about Surrelia and the Nether Void before wandering off like unsuspecting children. Of course, there is more to this world, but it would help to be armored with details to avoid getting yourselves killed." Gavrel's chest muscles were so tense I thought he might be carved out of stone.

My mouth dropped at the insulting rebuke, but I snapped it shut when Kaden snickered, "Killed? Our astral bodies can't be killed, Gavie. Was that what Melina called you back there? Little Gavie Gav?"

A flush of heat tinged Gavrel's bronzed cheeks, reminding me of a crimson sunset shining over toasted wheat. He stood taller, stacking his already straight spine into a rigid column. "There are worse things than death for both physical and astral bodies. But, by all means, continue using your poor decision-making skills to test that, brother."

Kaden stepped forward, his aura flaring around him, but then clenched his fists and paused. Cracking his neck, he glared at his brother and then stomped off toward a group practicing with weaponry.

Gavrel sighed, looking at the ground and shaking his head.

I turned to face him. "I'm not a child. You would do well to remember that. Were we rash? Yes." I shrugged, taking a breath. "You are right, though. I'll study more. But you should be more forthcoming with information as well."

He nodded once. "I appreciate that. I'll try. There are some things I ... I can't share with you—yet. Despite what you may think, I don't know everything," he admitted with a sheepish smile, his eyes shifting to the left.

I gasped teasingly, "Say it isn't so."

His smile lingered for a moment, then melted. "I know you aren't a child." His eyes swept over my body, his direct gaze landing on mine. "But I worry about you both. What if I hadn't made it to you in time?" Unease swam freely in the viridian pools of his eyes.

I stepped into him, gathering his solid body to mine and wrapping my arms tightly around his waist. "Thank you. I appreciate not being unalived." His back stooped as he wrapped his arms around me, a soft chuckle vibrating through him.

"How did you find us, by the way?" My question was muffled as I pressed my cheek into his stiff overcoat.

"I ..." He retreated slightly away from our embrace, rubbing a hand along his nape. "I'm not sure. I was with Melina, and my rune lit up. Beyond the veil, ember is untamed. Wild." He ran his hand over his stubbled jaw, his metallic ink reflecting in the setting sun. "My tattoo grew brighter—burned—the closer I got to you, so I went where it and my instincts led me." He gripped the strap of his leather baldric, his fingers tense.

"Huh, well, that's interesting."

"That was Melina's sentiment as well. She insisted on coming." He looked back toward the palace and then at me with urgency. "Be careful around her, Little Star."

"Already on it; you don't have to worry. I mean, anyone who

can go poof into thin air is terrifying," I joked, making an explosive motion with my fingers, air puffing out my cheeks.

Gavrel smirked as we turned to head to the palace. "As far as I know, she can only transport herself short distances. She likely sent herself to the other side of the veil. She loves all the theatrics of it."

I chuckled, "Could've fooled me."

Gavrel took a deep breath. "In all seriousness—"

"Ah yes, one of your best qualities," I interrupted him, smirking. Noticing the worry still lingering in his gaze, I put my arm through the crook of his elbow. "I'll be careful around the Elders, Gav. Unfortunately, I have Melina's attention now. I'll tread lightly. Promise."

"All right, thank you." He tucked my arm closer into his side.

I drew in a breath. "It would seem you have her attention as well."

A sound suspiciously like a growl shuddered through his chest. "I'd rather not, Seryn."

"I didn't mean to pry."

He exhaled for three heartbeats. "I don't mind you prying, but her attention is something I don't want …" he muttered, glaring at the palace. "And I can't seem to escape. Let's leave it at that."

I leaned into his side for a moment as we continued in silence.

"Oh, I've also been thinking …" I hesitated and looked at Kaden, who was sparring with a guard. His sword furiously slashed and parried against his opponent's, a clover-colored glow pulsing around him.

"Yes?"

"Would you spar with me?" I asked, a blush spreading over my cheeks. "I'd rather not take up your or Kaden's time during the day when everyone is milling about."

His eyes softened. "Of course. I think it's a brilliant idea. It never hurts to learn how to defend yourself." He crinkled his brow briefly. "Let's start later this week. I can meet you on the training field shortly after sunrise. Agreeable?"

"Absolutely."

DURING DINNER, I shared what had happened in the Reverie Weald with Letti, Breena, and Rhaegar. Kaden had eaten his meal in grim silence. Gavrel never came to dinner. I wondered if he had gone to see Melina.

Later, after hours of failing to sleep, I went to Kaden's room to check on him. I figured he'd had enough time to stew.

"Kaden, it's me," I said, knocking on his door.

The door creaked open as he stepped aside and let me enter. His room was decorated similarly to mine, but the bed was drenched in shades of emerald and bronze instead of pewter. His bare chest was on full display, his white breeches hanging low on his hips. I swallowed, dragging my gaze to his.

"I wanted to check your bite wound," I blurted when he didn't speak.

A tired smile spread across his face. "Thank you." He waved his hand, a current the color of soft grass shimmering toward his chest. Only a rosy patch of sealed skin rested. "Healing ember, remember?"

"Oh, of course. It looks like your skill is improving." Without thinking, I skimmed my fingers over the mended mark on his strong pectorals, and we both inhaled at the contact. I pulled my hand to my collarbone as if I'd been burned. I rambled, "I, um. Are you all right? I know today was unnerving."

He rubbed the spot my hand had been near his heart. "I'll get through it. I'm out of sorts." He paused, shrugging and dropping his hand to his side. "How are you holding up?"

"I can't stop thinking about my mother, but what's new?" A weary sigh fell from me. The air buzzed with the sound of our gentle breaths.

"Well, I'll let you get some rest." I turned to leave.

He gently grasped my wrist. "Sleep here tonight?"

My breath hitching, I studied him with an arched brow, biting my bottom lip.

"Just sleep ... I promise," he drawled.

I hesitated as warmth spread over my skin. "All right."

"But stop biting your lip, or you'll make me a liar." He smirked, wiggling his brows.

A breathy, high-pitched laugh left me as I followed him. We settled under the soft bedding. No further words were needed. His arm was a comforting weight around me, soothing my pounding heart. I let myself mold into the cradle of his body, his heat and solid mass blanketing me. I drifted to sleep in moments, all thoughts of the day whisked away into the haze of a dreamless sleep.

THE NEXT DAY was a tedious blur of shelving books in the library. When I finally made my way to my room that night, I had hoped to rest soundly, but my mind had other plans. My bed was a heap of crumpled blankets wrapping around me. Restless thoughts bounced around my skull, twisting and turning with the rest of my body. Mama. Kaden. Mare wyrms. Shades. Ember. Kaden.

Kaden's lips.

Eyes.

The hollow that dipped beneath his throat.

Sitting up, I huffed and pushed wild strands of hair from my cheeks. Soft rays from the harvest moon of the autumnal equinox scattered about the room, casting halos around the solid objects strewn about.

I slid off my bed, pushing my feet into the slippers next to it. A sardonic chuckle stuck in my throat. *Who needs a harvest moon when we're not harvesting anything?*

I sighed. It was time for a late-night stroll to calm—and hopefully tire—my mind.

I meandered the halls aimlessly, running my fingers over the moonstone walls, studying the artwork, sculptures, and potted plants lining them.

My legs carried me to the library. I'd never seen it so empty and quiet, as if it had been holding its breath. The stillness blanketed the book stacks in reverence.

I went to Mr. Burlam's desk to borrow the lantern orb he kept on it. As I reached for the hovering glass sphere, its enchanted flames swept over it from the bottom, ready to be of service.

I stuck a finger out, hesitant to touch the embered flames as I'd seen the grumpy librarian do. Sucking in a breath, I grimaced and pushed my finger into the blaze. Relieved, I gasped as a pleasant, liquid warmth licked at my skin. Its energy briefly zipped over the back of my hand before returning to the lantern with a fizzle. I stretched my fingers wide, admiring the tiny, shimmering mark left in the shape of a flame. As I stepped away from the desk, the orb floated above me, lighting my way.

I moved through the library, going up the curling staircase to the third-floor balcony. I gathered books hinting at information about Surrelia and the Nether Void. About its creatures and history. The landscapes and regions.

I read for what seemed like hours, and it very well might have been for all I knew. I was tucked into a corner of the second-story balcony beside the staircase, cocooned in flickering radiance, immersed in my studies. The night sky still painted the crystal ceiling in twinkling blackness, the harvest moon's glow spraying sparkles of soft amber throughout the space.

Seryn.

I jerked forward, startled by the raspy whisper slinking through the air. My heart galloped as I set aside the book in my lap. *Was I still sleeping?*

Find me, the voice demanded.

Not a dream. I sprang up on shaky limbs, the lantern orb bobbing excitedly with my quick movements. I rushed to the banister, my eyes adjusting to the dimness and scanning the room for intruders. My heart jumped into my throat as a loud thud directly below me reverberated through the room. Stumbling back, I pressed into the shelves as if the books would protect me. I covered my mouth, holding in the sob that yearned to flee from me.

The flicker from the lantern's stamp caught my eye, and I clamped my lips together, holding my marked hand in front of me. I brushed at the twinkling spot with my other thumb frantically, and the mark crumbled into ash, fluttering away from my skin. Immediately extinguishing, the orb gently descended. I caught the glass and hugged it to my chest, using one hand to guide me to the shadowed stairs.

Another thump. Clammy sweat broke out across my forehead and neck. Sucking my trembling lips inward, I crept down the stairs as fast as possible, my knees locking when my slippers settled on the ground floor.

Seryn.

A smallish novel from a lower shelf dropped at my feet. My ember tingled along my nape in response. Looking ahead, I noticed two large volumes resting on the ground.

Below.

The disembodied voice sounded more insistent but not

threatening. Another book tumbled to the floor as if the fallen chronicles were creating a path to follow. Waiting for any sign of movement, I scrutinized the surrounding space. I breathed in, calming my senses and also keeping my gift engaged, just in case.

I pushed my shoulders back, dipping my chin and squinting toward the book-lined trail. My palms stroked over the smooth sphere cradled between them, activating it and its stamp once more. It levitated above me; a witness to the decision I was about to make.

With tentative steps, I followed the grounded volumes. Every so often, another book would drop ahead of me, guiding the way. I paused as a final novel landed in front of a small, arched alcove.

These nooks were carved sporadically within the library's perimeter, each boasting an intricate engraving. I ran my fingertips over the elaborate depiction of Morpheus' palace etched into the obsidian.

My ember tingled from my nape to my tailbone, and I shifted so one knee rested on the tufted bench as I traced the smooth lines and valleys of the image. My aura sparked and rippled over my body. It glided through my arm and fingertips, flowing over the etching. As it began to melt into it, the engraving faded away, revealing a tunnel cut into the glossy stone.

My mouth dropped open, and my eyes widened. I swallowed, looking behind me into the library and then back to the exposed passageway. A sense of foreboding prickled me, the hairs on my arm standing on end.

I shrugged, my curiosity holding greater weight than my apprehension. I stepped over the bench and into the passage, the glowing orb trailing behind me. My aura faded as I righted myself, thanking the Ancients that the ceiling was a bit taller than me so I didn't have to crouch.

The air inside the passageway was cool and stagnant. A warm breeze from the library hissed by me as the dark stone knit itself back together, trapping me within the tunnel.

I gasped, panic clawing through me. My hand swiped along the wall. The stone pulsed and rippled in time with my energy, still prickling under my scar. The wall vanished, exposing the entryway again, and closed once more when I removed my palm. In relief, a whoosh of air left me as I realized I could open the hidden entrance.

Turning back to the tunnel, I pushed myself into the abyss. Every step brought me deeper into the stony islet, along a series of gradients and carved stairs. I pondered how far this system of corridors burrowed under the palace and where they led. The lantern illuminated around me, but the gleaming black rock gobbled it up a few feet ahead.

I came to a fork in the tunnel, one stairwell heading up and one moving deeper still. I paused for a moment, wrinkling my nose. A draft of crisp air brushed over my right side from the downward path. I recalled the ethereal plea that led me to my current position. *Below*, it had directed. I chose the corridor on my right, my ember tingling in agreement.

As I descended, the air grew dense, its chilled pressure pushing into my form, urging me to turn back. My steps slowed as if I moved through water.

It was eerie, the reality of being entirely alone. Thoughts of being buried alive prodded my concentration. My courage wavered, but I pressed forward, my power coursing through sinew, holding me together.

At last, the stairs ended, a sculpted arch marking the entrance to a cavernous clearing. As I tentatively stepped onto the narrow landing, my breath hitched and a numbing sensation ran through my legs. A bottomless well burrowed down the center of the cave. I braced my hands against the walls of the archway to avoid plunging into the gaping pit.

Heights were not something I enjoyed. I gulped, my breath sticking within my throat, an unpleasant flutter somersaulting in my gut. Closing my eyes, I inhaled deeply and then blew out slowly through pursed lips. I opened my eyes, taking in my surroundings. The soles of my feet planted firmly into the stone.

Embered sphere torches hovered along the spiral-like ramp, descending along the pit's walls. Conchoidal fractures glistened whenever the firelight met their gleaming surfaces. I swiped at the lantern mark on my hand and allowed the snuffed lamp to float to the ground.

As I moved down the spiral slope, I kept close to the wall. Every so often, another archway would present itself. Nestled within were stairwells, tunnels, or barred cells of various sizes. This seemed like a dungeon. I paused to examine an empty chamber, wondering if the voice that led me here was imprisoned. *What if it's a trap?* A line of determination settled across my lips. There was only one way to find out.

I tightened my fists, ready to march forward, when distant voices rang through the air. I sucked in a breath, peeking over the edge of the chasm. Three people were swiftly rising through the center of the shadowy cavity. *What the Ancients?* I thought as I rushed to the next archway, tucking myself into the shadows.

"He does not appear to know," a deep baritone rumbled up the carved walls.

"That means nothing, Lucan," a melodic but caustic voice responded.

Melina and Evergryn's Elder, Lucan Craven. My scar itched, my gift scratching at the surface. I grimaced. *Not now! Calm down!* I swiped my palm over the scar, willing it to settle.

"Certainly. I'll have to resolve the problem if the imbecile figures out how to use his gifts properly. We can't risk ascension after all our efforts," Lucan snarled. They were closer now. Pyrian Elder, Ryboas Ash, was with them, his pallid lips sealed tightly. The thick disk of amber glass on which they stood rose, its edges writhing with swirling inky power.

"There will be no ascension. I've seen to that, as you know," Melina purred.

Lucan dug his cane into the glass with a grumble. "The girl is notable as well, eh? Another new pet, Melina? How tedious." A scathing smirk pushed his cheeks wide, his wrinkles digging into his skin.

Melina tittered, "Now, now, Lucan. Just because you don't have anyone to play with, there's no need to be sour."

He sniffed, his mouth stiff as he mumbled, "At least I didn't slaughter my own fated."

Her eyes flashed, and she snarled, "That's because you've never had one. I believe I've been clear that the topic of my khorda is off limits." Both male Elders shifted, putting more space between them and Melina. She brushed her hands over her hips. "Anyway, back to my new pet. Her ember is wild, like her mother's. I can't deny it intrigues me, and the reaction she pulls from my darling commander … it's too much to disregard."

A small gasp escaped my lips, clamping my palm over my mouth. The Elders' attention snapped in my direction. I froze, my feet stuck in the shadows. I didn't think they had seen me, but my presence was no longer a secret.

"Ah, what have we here?" Melina's words slithered toward me as the translucent platform drifted near the ramp's edge.

RUN! The otherworldly voice tore through my mind, my aura bursting over me as I whimpered. It was enough to snap me into action. I turned into the tunnel, sprinting as fast as my legs would carry me, paying no attention to the directional choices I made … as long as I went up.

Up.

Turn right.

The pressure dissipated.

Up.
Corner left.
The air warmed.

My aura lit the way, vibrating through the murky shadows as I ran. I didn't sense anyone following me, but the notion that I'd never find my way out clawed at my chest, turning my breathing erratic. As soon as the thought passed, I took another right up a steep incline, and a hazy, oblong halo glimmered ahead of me. My sob of relief rent the air.

As I approached, my forehead scrunched in concentration. I coaxed my ember through my arms, placing my palms in the center of the glowing outline, my hand meeting cold rock. My energy seeped into the stone and a sparking fissure swept up the middle, creating a person-sized crevice. I bolted through as the opening sealed immediately upon my exit.

I bent forward, one hand propped on my upper thigh, the other on my chest, willing my breath and heart to stop galloping. Blooming pink incandescence danced over the stage, stretching for my toes. My eyes flew up, realizing I was in the Great Hall. The sun's rising hues lined its moon-phase windows. I had exited from the back of the obsidian throne, not an inch of intricate design out of place.

It was still early; breakfast was not yet being set up. Not wanting to loiter any longer, I hurried to my room, closing the door as Gavrel opened his. If he noticed, I didn't hear him call out to me.

I slumped against the door for several moments before a brisk rapping rattled the cool metal. *Gavrel?* My heart pumped briskly against my ribs as I opened the door.

Bleary emptiness met me, the hallway uncannily silent. I leaned out, checking both ways. Nothing. My face scrunched, air huffing from my nose as I clicked my door back in place.

I stared into my room, not truly seeing anything despite the soft morning light spilling in. Confusion and exhaustion cloaked me as my scar tapped at the skin of my nape incessantly. Massaging my pounding temples, I stumbled to the bed.

With a groan, I leaped onto my mattress and turned onto my side, curling my limbs inwards. I squeezed my eyes shut, thinking my twisted, crumpled bedsheets now seemed more in order than the chaos stalking my every waking moment.

14

SPARRING WITH BLADES AND WORDS

It had been a few days since the mare wyrm incident. I hadn't seen Gavrel in that time. I wondered what kept him busy as a high-ranking commander within the Order—besides training, giving commands, and walking his rounds.

He frequently attended private meetings with the Elders. With Melina. I doubted he wanted her attention, considering what little information he had shared with me. But the idea of them together lingered. *They were both full-blooded adults ... with needs.* I swallowed, a sour taste lining my tongue.

My hands stretched to the sky, and I yawned. The rising sun painted it in shades reminiscent of ripe peaches. My stomach grumbled as my arms dropped. I was seriously questioning my sanity. *Why had I agreed to meet him so early in the morning?*

My thoughts drifted as my fingers fiddled with the end of my messy braid, fiery curls struggling against their weaved confines.

The even pace of steady footfalls sounded behind me, bringing my awareness to the present. Gavrel's bright smile met me. Mocking me, his dimple flashed.

"How dare you be so chipper this early in the morning," I

muttered, tossing my braid over my shoulder so it trailed down my back.

He laughed heartily. "And what a fine morning it is. Have you stretched?"

"Can confirm."

"Wonderful. We'll use these to start." He pushed a wooden sword into my hand. "I trust you remember the basics."

"Yes, but why can't we use real swords?"

He looked at me, clearing his throat. "You haven't practiced in a long while. I'd prefer it if you didn't cut off your own foot."

"How dare you!"

"I do dare, only when it's true." His smile was good-natured, disarming.

"I yield then. I wouldn't want to stand in the way of truth." I chuckled.

"Much obliged, Asteria." I grinned at his use of my nickname. And then Gavrel promptly knocked my wooden sword to the grass with his own.

"What the—"

"First lesson. Always be ready," he advised, his mouth a grim line of composure. "Your enemies won't wait for you to form a thought."

He slashed his ligneous weapon toward my belly. I dove out of the way, grasping my sword's hilt, blocking his downward attack.

"Ah, excellent. I see you haven't forgotten everything." He grabbed my hand, pulling me up. I showed my gratitude with a swift stab toward his thigh, which he deflected easily.

I huffed, balancing on my feet and body as he had taught me. Slashing, stabbing, parrying—urging my muscles to recall his earlier teachings and work through the discomfort. We continued until the sky was its azure hue. People were making their way to the palace for breakfast. I swiped sweat from my brow, pushing a loose curl behind my ear.

"What have we here?" Letti asked, trotting up to us from the barracks.

"Just some light torture," Gavrel deadpanned.

I rolled my eyes. "Practicing my fighting skills."

"I think that's best. We wouldn't want you to get attacked by any more slugs," Letti stated, her expression solemn.

I cuffed her on the arm. She laughed, kissing my cheek and taking my practice sword from me. "I'll bring you some breakfast if you want to wash." She smiled sweetly, returning the sword to the rack.

"Are you saying I smell?" I asked in mock offense, putting a hand to my chest.

"Yes. Yes, exactly."

I scowled at her, and then we both burst out laughing when I could no longer keep a straight face.

Gavrel dipped his head, a small smile threatening to spread as he looked at me from under his thick lashes. "Uh, I have to wash as well. Shall we head up?"

"But, of course, Commander Larkin. We wouldn't want to offend anyone with our musk."

We left Letti at the dining hall and walked to our rooms. We weren't in a rush, so I took in the mesmerizing paintings lining the hallways as we walked. One of my favorites depicted Morpheus.

It was in the hallway near our rooms, and I often stopped to study it. His golden hair and robes whipped around him as a rainbow of colors spilled from his hands, dancing and twirling through the air. Everything beyond him was in shades of white and gray—until his ember touched and filled them with sparkling, vivid hues. It's exactly how I imagined Surrelia had been created in all its brilliance.

"Thank you for the lesson," I said, turning my attention to Gavrel.

"It's no trouble. With enough practice, you'll be a fair

swordswoman." A note of pride laced his words. "Would you be interested in working with some other weapon? You're swift on your feet, so you might enjoy trying a smaller blade."

"Oh, that sounds intriguing. Yes, I think I would." A wide grin spread across my face.

"Brilliant. I'll enlist Breena. I've observed her over the last few days. She has quite the talent with a dagger."

"Good morn, early risers," Kaden called from down the hall, shutting his door behind him. He wore green attire now. I still wore white. I didn't think the Elders knew what to make of my gifts. Ancients knew *I* still didn't have a clue.

"How did your swordplay go? I see you don't have any new wounds," he teased, walking up to us. He tickled my side, and I laughed, swatting his hand away.

"I'll have you know, I did just fine. Thank you very much."

"She'll do well with more practice," Gavrel added, his mouth tilting to one side, his lips politely suppressing a smile.

Kaden chuckled as I huffed, crossing my aching arms across my chest. "I'll find you later, Kade. I want to practice with my ember after work."

He nodded, and I switched my focus to Gavrel. "Thank you for your help. Same time tomorrow?"

He dipped his head, looking at me through his thick, dark lashes. "Of course, Little Star."

Kaden squinted at Gavrel, a line of displeasure etched between his brows. I tilted my head to the side, my eyebrows lifting, my lips pressing together. Spinning, I entered my sanctuary and shut the door on the brothers.

My hand rested on my chest as a strange uncertainty pumped through my musings. I wondered if this was how the sun experienced its existence—bound between rising and setting—its power and path influenced by the cosmos.

"Thrust with your whole body, woman!" Breena commanded, standing behind me. She pushed and pulled my limbs into position like a doll made of straw. "You aren't just stabbing with your arm. Step into it. The blade is an extension of you."

I did as she instructed, stepping into my thrust and aiming for the soft parts. The belly. Neck. Eyes. If you wanted the heart, you had to go from under the breastbone and stab up. One could stab directly into the chest, but there were ribs and a dense wall of muscle to contend with.

I wiped the sweat from my brow, thinking of the combat advice Breena had poured into our lessons over the last few weeks; the information branded my thoughts. She delighted in describing the gory details of how a blade could damage the body. *I did this to myself*, I thought, a wry laugh escaping me.

"Shift your grip on the hilt, Seryn. The goal is to stab your opponent, not yourself," Gavrel interjected. I paused, turning my head and blinking at him once. He was lucky my eyes were the only things throwing daggers his way. One corner of his lips quirked in amusement.

I pushed an errant curl behind my ear, sighing, and stabilized my stance, ready to spar with Breena once more. Her eyes were bright with glee. I gulped, tightening my grip on the wooden dagger.

She enjoyed attacking abruptly, not one to wait for action to commence. I preferred to study my opponent. A quiver of their hand. A tiny shift in their eyes.

Escaped tendrils from my braid drifted over my cheeks, carried by a cool breeze. The corners of Breena's eyes crinkled ever so slightly, and I tightened my grip on the dagger's hilt.

Her weapon jabbed toward my chest with stunning speed, like that of a threatened snake. I twisted my torso to my left, using my hand to push the trajectory of her blade away from my body. In a fluid motion, I slashed the dagger in my other hand horizontally under her arm and into her flank.

Breena grunted, her eyes bright as she stepped away from me. "Finally! Well played." She clapped excitedly.

I rolled my eyes but laughed. "I've gotten many strikes in over the last few weeks."

"You've come a long way," Gavrel agreed, squeezing my shoulder.

"Thank you both for all your help. It's been … quite the journey." I smiled, putting my hand on Breena's shoulder. She grinned, shrugging my hand from her shoulder and pulling me into a tight, damp hug.

"Anything for a friend." She held my shoulders at arm's length. "I think we can all agree I'm the most qualified to teach you the majestic ways of the dagger. Without my intervention, I can't fathom what would've happened. These men and their toys. Am I right?" She stepped from our embrace and squared up again, her blade ready.

Gavrel sighed in resignation. "I welcome your feedback, Breena. It looks like the dagger master is ready to go again, Seryn." One corner of his mouth tipped up briefly as he surveyed the training field and barracks. "I'll be back shortly. I need to discuss something with Hale." He stepped toward his second-in-command.

It seemed Rhaegar was finishing his morning rounds through the camp. The strapping warrior smiled brightly at his commander's approach, thumping a large hand on Gavrel's shoulder in welcome. Gavrel returned the greeting.

"Rhaegar has been through a lot. I suppose as much as any of us." Breena's subdued voice brought my focus back to her. She stood unmoving, staring at her leather boots. Her hesitation falling thickly at her feet.

With a deep breath, she continued, "I ran into him turns ago in Pneumali City while he was on duty. I mean, I literally ran into 'im. I was outfoxing some Order twats after, uh, borrowin' some bread from the market. Ran smack into the hulking mass of 'im." A faraway smile flitted across her profile, her already strong accent thickening with unsolicited emotions.

I listened intently in absolute stillness, not wanting to deter her. It wasn't often Breena shared glimpses of her life—in such a sincere tone, at that. One wrong move, and I thought she might scamper away into the woods.

She continued, "I'm not sure what he saw in me, but he didn't give me up. He gave the guards some coins and directed them to pay the shopkeeper. Then he walked me home to Gran. She adored 'im." Her lower eyelids glistened with unshed tears I doubted she'd allow to escape. She sniffed and continued, "Made the big lug stay for supper, which was the bread with leftover pickled vegetables. More than most people have in the city."

"That's lovely, Breena." I hugged her sturdy side to mine.

She put her arm around me, squeezing before facing me and standing tall. She pushed her shoulders back, puffing out her chest. "Yes, well. It's something. Worthy pals are hard to come by. Rhaegar has my seal of approval. As do you."

"Awwww," I crooned, touching one hand to my chest. "I adore you as well, Breena."

She waved her hand at me. "Did I ever tell you Gran and I were originally from Pyria Island?" I shook my head, my eyebrows rising. "After my parents died in a volcanic eruption when I was young, she brought me to Pneumali. I don't recall the island much, but she said it was too dangerous to stay there. 'The land is too treacherous, my girl. It'll eat us alive,' Gran would say to me." A wistful smile came over her.

"I've only heard tales. It sounds like a harsh wilderness to survive in. I'm sorry to hear about your parents."

"Thank you, but don't fuss. I don't remember them." She

lifted one hand loosely, palm up, and let it drop to her side. "It was always me and Gran. I want to go back someday. Learn more about my people; where I'm from. I think she would have liked that."

"I think it's a must," I agreed, smiling brightly.

She touched my shoulder, giving it a little squeeze. "Right, so. Let's go again." Her form settled into a fighting stance once more.

"Now, Breena, you can't have all the fun," Kaden interrupted, strolling over to us. His hair was tousled as if he'd just woken up, which was probable.

"By all means, I'd love to watch her stab you," Breena goaded, handing over her practice weapon. She rubbed her abdomen. "But I'm going to head for breakfast instead. Dagger master, out! Toodles!" I waved a hand, chuckling.

"I'll take it easy on you, Ser." Kaden smirked. I rolled my eyes in reply, taking position across from him.

"No need. She'll prevail either way," Gavrel countered as he returned, a confident smile unfurling. A warmth seeped through my chest at the compliment.

"Stop the chit-chat, and let's do this. Unless you're worried I'll actually stab you in your tender bits this time," I taunted.

"I wouldn't dream of—"

I thrust the dulled blade toward him, but he feinted to the side, barely dodging my attack. He stumbled a bit before righting himself, holding his dagger in front of him. "Ah, I see how it is." He chuckled.

"Lesson one. Always be ready." I smirked. Gavrel's shoulders shook, one hand cupping his jaw and mouth.

"I was born ready. Especially for the likes of you." Kaden flipped the dagger in his palm, holding it in a reverse grip. He sliced his hand diagonally upward. I blocked his blade with my own, slamming my shoulder into his arm to create space. He lost his footing, and I swiped my weapon into the side of his neck.

"Defeated again, you braggard. My advice is less talking and more action."

Kaden exhaled, puffing out his cheeks and tipping his head toward me. He leaned into the wooden blade, grinning. He reached his left hand across his chest, enveloping my hand in its warmth. My heart flipped, forgetting how to beat momentarily.

His eyes held mine with a burning intensity, his grin dissolving. "I see I've underestimated you."

"Per usual," I murmured.

"I have no objection to taking action with you, by the way." Kaden's hand squeezed mine gently before sliding his palm over the top of mine. He took my dagger as his other hand, now empty, met the curve of my waist.

A blush swept across my face and chest. For simply standing still, my breathing was far too hurried. He dropped my dagger on the grass next to his, his other hand rising toward my cheek.

"Perhaps you are the one who needs further lessons, Kaden." Gavrel's disgruntled tone broke through the fog.

I hastily backed away from Kaden, his arms slumping to his sides.

"Perhaps you should pay Melina a visit. You're her pet, are you not?" Kaden's words lacerated the air. My eyebrows rose.

Gavrel pushed his shoulders back, tipping his chin up. "That's enough."

"It never is. I'll see you later, Ser." He strode away without another glance.

15

BUCKLE UP

After dinner, Kaden and I headed to the mainland.

"What's going on with you and Gavrel?" I asked, one hand propped on my hip, the other clutching a borrowed library book. After sparring earlier—with both daggers and words—and the bustle of the library throughout the day, a wary heaviness pressed upon me.

Fortunately, Mr. Burlam had stopped complaining about his missing lantern orb after finally receiving a replacement. Thank the Ancients for small miracles.

"What? Nothing," Kaden groused, his eyes shifting toward the garden beside us. A couple of older women were puttering around in it, gathering vegetables in a woven basket.

"Sure." I stepped to his side, in line with his vision. "You know I can tell when you're lying?"

He rolled his eyes, turning to me and crossing his arms. "He's being Gavrel. I find it annoying sometimes."

My mouth went slack, and I snorted, squeezing the bridge of my nose with my free hand. "What does that even mean? He isn't behaving any differently than he usually does. You, on the other hand, are provoking him more than usual."

"He ... he needs to mind himself and not worry about what I'm doing."

The women gardening attempted to ignore us, but I caught some side glances and raised brows. I put my hand on his forearm, gently leading him away from prying ears.

"Well, he has always worried about you. So, that won't end. Maybe you should have a chat with him," I suggested, my eyes pleading.

"Sure," he muttered, letting his arms drop, his lips tucking in for a moment. "Don't you think you should talk with him?"

"What are you on about? Please, just say what you want to. I'm getting dizzy from talking in circles." I jammed one fist into my dress pocket, using the book in my other hand to make a circle in the air before hugging it to my chest.

My knuckle bumped into my talisman. I kept it in my pocket every day—a little reminder to be steady. I huffed in frustration. Kaden was usually my rock, but he was working through something, trying to find his footing in life. I'd need to find solid ground on my own.

"You haven't noticed how he's been looking at you the last several turns, *Little Star*?" he mocked, leaning into my space. His nostrils flared a bit, his breathing shallow. "He barely smiles unless you're around."

"Ancients forbid Gavrel actually smiles," I snapped, my tone dripping with sarcasm. My cheeks burned. I couldn't believe Kaden's behavior. Pressing my lips together, I breathed in and out through my nose.

After several moments, I added, "For now, I won't continue this conversation because it's absurd, and it sounds like a *you problem*."

His jaw ticked as he ran both hands through his dark hair. I spun around, heading for the forest to calm myself. Prickling heat was tapping under my scar in time with my pulse.

After what had happened with the mare wyrm a few weeks

ago, I wasn't sure how dangerous my uncontrolled ember could be. The nagging feeling of being a puppet on a string sat heavily on my chest. My memories of the event were spotty. I still needed to discover if it was because of the Nether creature's influence ... or my gifts.

As I strolled, I focused on the people I passed, grounding myself. They smiled and greeted me, and I returned the sentiments. I waved to the young woman and toddler I saw on the first day we arrived—the ones who had lost their toy ball. During our time here, I learned they were siblings. Sadly, their parents had not made it to Surrelia. The child was giggling and running around his sister, chasing a butterfly, as she chatted with other people.

A gentle sense of hope nudged at my frustration with Kaden. It always amazed me to think about how resilient people were, their hope and perseverance refusing to break during times of uncertainty and hardship. Kaden had lost his way, but I trusted he would find the right path. I would be there for him while he did.

A smile danced on my lips, thinking of all the incredible people I'd met so far in Surrelia, but then it dropped as I mourned the eventual loss of their memory. The Dormancy would claim such reminiscences upon waking. My heavy sigh plummeted to the ground.

Once in the woods, my feet carried me, as they often did, to a heartbreakingly beautiful tree with a massive, gnarled trunk—the Elysium Tree. It was said to be the most sacred tree in all existence. A source of life-giving ember. A place to pray or offer oaths to the Ancients. It was a primordial form towering above the others nearby, its long, thick branches twisting over them as if gathering the smaller trees like children into the safety of its embrace.

Groaning contentedly, I sat and leaned against the trunk. A flicker of its power shivered against my back in greeting. The tree's dense crown of roundish orange leaves draped above me, hiding me from the setting sun. Patches of dangling vines clung to the branches, creating a sparse curtain.

I reached up and touched the back of my neck, stretching to the side. My star-shaped mark was calm but tingling.

In the last few weeks, I was more aware of the energies around me. Every day, more auras revealed themselves, clinging to Druiks, flora, and fauna. They were brimming with ember, elemental creatures at their core.

Each aura was unique to the living being it resided in. Swirling, sparkling, pulsing, floating. The world was a gorgeous display of the Ancients' gifts to mortals, an exquisite canvas bursting with vibrancy and color. It often reminded me of the painting of Morpheus near my quarters.

The leaves and vines above seemed to rustle and shiver in understanding. The sinuous bark of the Elysium Tree warmed, soothing energy nuzzling against my back.

My hands rested on the spongy moss beneath me, and I closed my eyes for a moment, savoring the peace flowing through me. I breathed in and out.

In.

Out.

Willing my ember to synchronize with my heart, I repeated the cycle several times. I'd been practicing, learning how to regulate it. Such concentration helped channel and redirect my power when it had a mind of its own. I was tentatively enthusiastic about my progress in managing and learning my gifts, even if I still wasn't entirely sure what they were.

A warm bulk settled beside me, leaning against the tree, fabric brushing against the bark. Without opening my eyes, I knew it was Kaden. I could *always* tell. His woodsy scent laced with mint. The way he moved his body.

His hip and thigh were snug against mine as he took my hand. "I'm sorry, Ser," he murmured.

I opened my eyes and turned my head toward him, the back of it still touching the tree trunk. My book forgotten.

We sat in silence, looking at each other. His countenance was highlighted in pink and violet—the same shades as the sunset in Reverie Weald.

When I didn't speak, he continued, "I feel like there's too much within me. My thoughts … my feelings … are bashing into my skull with nowhere to go." He looked up to the canopy above us, fingering a drooping vine for a moment. "And I took it out on you. On Gavrel."

"All right," I sighed. "I think you still need to talk with your brother, though. You've been through a lot, and you need to find ways to deal with it." I squeezed his hand.

"I know. I …"

I waited, not wanting to discourage his processing.

"I suppose I'm a bit envious of Gavrel. He's accomplished so much. What have I done? Nothing." He let go of my hand, rubbing his palms over his thighs. "And when he looks at you the way he does … I want to punch something."

My belly fluttered. My pulse eagerly tapping against my neck. I dipped my head, swallowing, sifting the jumbled sensations within me.

Shifting to face him, I crossed my legs. I took his hand again, twining my fingers with his and resting them on my lap. "You are as worthy as Gavrel or anyone else. You're one of the best people I know. And you care." I put my other hand on his cheek, and he leaned into it. "You care so deeply, which is why you feel so much. All at once."

He enveloped my hand with his, turning his lips to my palm and kissing it gently. His fingers moved to my shoulder, settling against the slope of my neck. My hand fell, resting atop our joined fingers.

Staring intently into my eyes, he leaned toward me, drawing me closer. My breath quickened as he moved his mouth next to my ear. "Thank you for knowing me," he whispered, resting his forehead against my temple. His rapid breaths tickled the side of my cheek and chest. Goosebumps sped over my arms.

His body was still as if he were a petrified piece of grymwood. I angled my head so our brows touched, swallowing as heat spread from my belly to my chest. My dress slid down one shoulder, and I shivered as it whispered against my skin.

His eyes were closed. I squeezed mine shut, willing my heart, mind, and body to stop battling and reach a unified decision.

Don't do it, Seryn. The last bit of my resolve put up a fight, but I was tired of listening. Tired of thinking. Exhausted by my relentless daydreams about him.

If only the Fates knew our future, I might as well buckle up and enjoy the ride while it lasted.

I wanted *this*.

To give myself to Kaden, break into a million pieces, and put myself back together afterward—a new woman.

I drew in a sharp breath, my eyelids flying open. His green gaze burned into mine as he licked his lips, pressing his fingers into my shoulder, branding me.

He began to pull away, but my hands whipped out, fingers burrowing into his messy waves.

His knowing smirk undid me, his dimple taunting me.

"Bloody void," I muttered before crashing my lips against his.

He grunted at the impact, his other hand gripping my waist. His mouth moved with mine, his tongue prodding at the seam of my lips. I parted them, my tongue dancing with his as it slipped inside.

A tingling warmth rocketed down my spine. All at once, I couldn't get close enough to him. I moaned, shifting to my knees and straddling his thighs.

We tasted each other—our lips, teeth, and tongues melding and clashing. Shifting. Nipping. Pressing into one another.

As my heart slammed into my ribs, I pulled away, catching

my breath. We stared at each other, panting, our breaths merging between us. I rested my hands on his chest as it rose and fell.

His eyes were glazed, a look of awe and raw desire swimming in them. His aura was softly glowing around him now, mixing with the dusky shades of violet and indigo settling over the forest. Twinkling fireflies fluttered around us like sparks of ember.

His huge hands grasped my waist, embracing my curves. He slid his palms over my stomach, fanning his fingers over my ribcage, under my breasts, and then to my back.

My head lolled to one side, tangled curls falling over my shoulder. A slight smile tipped one corner of my lips as I ran my hands over his chest and taut biceps. I leaned forward, kissing his dimple before moving back again.

He skimmed one hand beneath my breast, his thumb drawing circles on the underside of it.

My hips had a mind of their own as they rocked back and forth against his thighs. If I didn't quell the pulsing throb between mine, I'd go mad.

I bit my bottom lip. "What did I tell you about biting your lip, Ms. Vawn?" Kaden moaned.

He gripped my thigh with one hand, stilling my hips. His other hand crept upward, cupping the underside of my breast, his thumb now sweeping precariously close to my nipple, teasing me.

I dragged my teeth over my lip before releasing it and leaning into him. "I guess I'm making you a liar, Mr. Larkin."

A low growl vibrated in his throat as his fingers sunk into my hips, pulling me toward him. My core was fully seated against his erection, the skirt of my dress pushed high up my thighs. His breeches were straining, and his desire was clear.

It made me feel powerful.

Craved.

He smirked before swiftly wrapping his plump lips around the straining bud he'd taunted, sucking and licking it through my dress. I moaned without thinking, the sensation overwhelming.

Scorching tingles zipped from my nape to my belly. Liquid heat pooled at my apex. I rocked against him, and our groans mingled, vibrating against my sensitive skin.

Frantically, I grabbed his tunic, shoving it off his body and throwing it to the side of the tree. His hands ran down my shoulders, pushing my dress down so it hung across the top of my breasts.

My hands glided over his chest, relishing the feel of heated skin over chiseled muscle. I bent forward, nipping and kissing the side of his neck. He tangled his fingers in my hair, gently pulling on the strands when my hand neared the tie of his trousers.

"Wait," he croaked, scrunching his forehead. "I need …" He paused and took a deep breath, sliding his hands to cradle my throat. "I can't believe I'm the voice of reason right now … but we won't remember this after the Dormancy. Are you sure you want this?" His brows furrowed, his lips pressing inward.

"I know," I whispered, hooking my hands on his wrists. "I want this. I don't want to waste any more time. I'll take whatever moments we can get."

Kaden let out a relieved breath, looking down. His eyes met mine once more, green flashing within them. "Lie back." He slid his thumb across my bottom lip.

I smiled, slipping from his lap and resting on the cushioned moss. He knelt in front of me, looking at me in reverence.

He placed his hands on my knees. "Open for me."

My legs obeyed, and he stroked his hands along my inner thighs until he reached my underwear. After hooking his hands under the soft fabric, he paused, looking at me for approval. I nodded, resting my hands on my chest.

Slowly, he pulled my undergarment down my legs, his calloused fingers grazing my skin. I shivered, the cool air and his intense gaze skimming my bare womanhood.

He crawled toward me like a prowling beast, settling his face right near the juncture of my thighs. My breathing sped up, my fingers toying with the fabric covering my chest, grazing over my tender nipples.

"You're magnificent," Kaden murmured, his eyes shining. "I've thought about you—like this—for a long time." He looked at me under heavy eyelids, his pupils dilating. His tongue swept over his bottom lip. Without breaking eye contact, he lowered his mouth to my sex.

"Already so wet. What have I done to deserve such a gift?"

"Kade—"

His warm breath blew over my core, swollen with need, and I gasped at the sensation. He grinned and then licked me, through my center to the pulsing nub at the apex of my thighs. A feverish current blazed up my spine.

My hips squirmed, chasing relief. He wrapped one hand around me, nestling his cheek against my inner thigh. His lips sucked on my aching bud, nipping and licking it in circles. Back and forth. Up and down.

A building frenzy was swirling within me. I needed release.

I needed.

Needed.

He replaced his tongue with his thumb, rubbing in circles, flicking. He brought his tongue to my center, lapping and thrusting in and out at the same pace as his thumb. His other fingertips squeezed the round curve of my hip and bottom.

A throaty moan rumbled through me, my eyes rolling back. Tingling heat exploded through my every limb, every joint, condensing into my core. I sucked in a deep breath as if I couldn't get enough air and cried, "Kade!"

His mouth sucked one last time, pulling firmly on the throbbing bundle, and I shattered. My climax washed over me, tremors rocking through my body.

As my mind fluttered into awareness, my legs splayed limply, lying on the dewy moss. Kaden rested his head on my inner thigh, one arm under it, wrapping around my hip. His hand spread across my ribs. His other tenderly stroking over my mound and belly.

We lay there in silence, my entire being sated. My fingers played with the ends of his dark strands as his aura evaporated into the night air.

The leaves and vines swayed and rustled above us, the fireflies languidly floating around. I sighed in contentment, a giggle surging from me.

"By the Ancients, I didn't realize you were so talented."

A rumbling laugh left him, vibrating through my thigh. "I would never dream of keeping such a skill from you." He sat up, unwinding himself from my legs before plucking up my underwear.

"Wait, what about you?" I propped myself on my elbows, a playful pout dropping my bottom lip.

"Tonight was for you," he murmured, his tone sincere as he helped slide my undergarment back in place.

I sat up, reaching for his breeches, still straining from his hard length. He brushed my hand aside and grasped my hands, pulling me upright.

"Now, now. We'll have plenty of time. Besides, I've waited this long. I can wait a little more." He adjusted his cock within his trousers. "I'll have plenty of dreams to keep me company tonight."

He wrapped his arms around me, pushing his lips firmly against mine once more. I blushed, tasting myself on him.

He righted my dress, kissing my collarbone, groaning as he lifted his head reluctantly.

His hand found mine, and we walked back to the palace, our

strides buoyant.

I was filled with buzzing energy as if I were made entirely of phosphorescence.

At my door, we kissed each other goodnight, our faces beaming when he finally released me.

I watched him from my doorframe as he went inside his, winking before closing his door.

A cough came from behind me, and I squeaked.

"Ah, I didn't mean to startle you," Gavrel grumbled deeply.

My cheeks flushed. I wondered how much he'd seen. Had Kaden known Gavrel was there? We hadn't done anything wrong, but a strange ache sat solidly in my gut, nonetheless.

He pushed open his door, his hand affixed to the rippling pewter. He turned his head to the side, not fully facing me. Staring blankly at my feet, his shoulders sagged as if he carried something heavier than the sword upon his back.

"Sleep well, Asteria," he murmured. Then he moved into his room, closing the door with a firm click.

16

LIKE A CAT LAPPING UP MILK

A month passed by, slipping through my senses like sand through my fingers. I rubbed my thumb over the stone shard, staring at the edge of the forest from the training field.

In a way, it was comforting—to keep it with me as a reminder of who I was. The rune stone and I had been together for so long that I would feel odd without it.

It also reminded me of my mother and how she had often stroked my scar—whether in comfort or distraction, I'd never know.

My fingertips traveled over the etched symbol, a faint tingle of power kissing my skin with each pass. Mama had something to do with the talisman. I couldn't think of any other explanation. Sighing, I let the stone drop deeper into the pocket of my white dress.

"Mortal realm to Ryn-Ryn. Anyone there?" Breena asked, waving her hand in front of my face.

"Sorry. Bit distracted."

"Understandable. Kaden is *quite* the distraction." She tossed me a smirk, bumping my shoulder with hers.

Warmth spread over my cheeks as my gaze shot to my best friend a few steps away.

We had told no one about the developments in our relationship ... or whatever it was. We'd spent countless hours sneaking kisses, laughing, touching. I was blissfully content with my choices.

Kaden conversed with an older male Druik who was dressed in yellow. The man's aura glowed a soft golden hue. Kaden was attentive, observing the orb of ember spinning and palpitating in the man's palm. The Druik's other hand gestured animatedly in time with his words as he educated Kaden.

I shuffled my leather shoes on the grass. "I ... I wasn't—"

"No need to deny it. We all have eyes."

Letti snorted, hearing Breena's comment as she joined us. "She's right, Ser. Get on with it already. It's been a long time coming."

My blush spread over my neck. "I don't know what you're talking about. We're just friends. And that's what we'll continue to—"

"Hello, *friends*," Kaden interrupted, settling his arm around my shoulders. His fingers played with the end of a red curl.

"Why, hello, you delicious morsel. What have you been learning from that Pneumalian gentleman? Do enlighten us." Breena grinned, shifting her eyes between Kaden and me.

Breena was toying with him. She'd been working with her gift for turns and had been the one educating us for over a month.

Kaden went on without being phased, his lips tipping up. The heavy weight of his arm left me. He gestured toward the Druik in farewell as the male headed toward a group in the distance. "He was giving me some tips on harnessing ember. It's linked with your emotions, so you need to work on grounding yourself so it isn't as chaotic when you're wielding it."

"Makes sense," I said, nodding. "That's why my breathing

techniques help me. Also, I think that's what's going on when I see auras when people aren't using their abilities. They have strong, untethered emotions, and it triggers their power. I can see them simmering." I wiggled my fingers toward the group playfully.

Letti laughed. "At least that isn't a problem for me."

I shrugged, poking her biceps with my pointer finger. "I don't need ember to know when *you're* having a fit."

Letti rolled her eyes. "So hilarious, sis."

Someone passed our group, sneaking glances at us. It was Xeni, a shy smile tilting her mouth.

Letti noticed the young Draumr as well. "Ah, I'll see you later," she mumbled, stepping in the warrior's direction.

A knowing smile spread across my face.

"Oh, young love," Breena breathed. "What a wild and ridiculous ride."

A humming acknowledgment rumbled in my throat. I'd have to check in with Letti soon—be the nosy sister she knew and loved.

"All right, you two. Let's do this," I insisted, shifting my attention to the task at hand.

I focused on my gift's source within my body, which I had discovered was unique for each Druik. My nape tingled as I called upon it, my aura washing over and through me in iridescent ripples.

The constant drumming of my star-shaped mark against my spine worried me as if my power was a beast aching to be untethered.

I breathed through the distraction, binding my ember, only allowing it to simmer. I didn't want it to overpower me or cause irrevocable damage to others.

Breena focused, her body bursting in a bright poppy-red blaze. Kaden stepped away from her, his hands flying up to protect his face, his aura flaring.

Kaden was now able to heal minor wounds with little effort. His ability to influence plants and flowers was progressing steadily. Daily, he practiced in the forest, calling to and working with the vegetation around him.

His enthusiasm and pride for his evolving abilities were contagious. Hestia would have been proud. My lips tipped up, my eyes softening at the thought. My aura shimmered bright for a moment.

The other day, Kaden had summoned several twisting vines. They had crept toward him over the mossy ground, heeding his call. Groaning, the nearest trees had stretched their branches in his direction, wanting to join them.

We had screeched with excitement, dancing and hugging each other. That led to enthusiastic, frantic kissing. Hands scrambling all over each other.

Stop, I scolded, taking a deep breath and forcing myself to concentrate.

Breena grinned, cupping her hands as sparkling flames flickered over her, condensing into a sphere of swirling red sparks and hazy, heated waves within her palms.

I shuffled closer to her, mouth agape. "So, you're basically a giant fireball?"

Breena chuckled. "Sort of. I can control temperature. Make a shield around me and those close to me. I can pack my ember into this fun 'lil sparkle ball. If you find having an extra hole in your body fun, that is."

"Remember, I've been kind to you." Kaden winced, opening one eye and grinning. Breena chortled mischievously, one foot feinting toward him. Kaden ran behind me, gripping my waist.

I gasped at the contact, not only because his touch stirred something within me but because my power immediately tugged at his greedily.

Kaden released me as I spun to face him, a look of wonder flashing across his face. He had felt it, too.

I blinked a few times, gasping as a tumbling current of green streamed into my gleaming haze, my energy drinking in his like a cat lapping up milk.

He took a step back, holding up his hands. His awe vanished, an unfocused look slamming over his face.

"Something isn't right," he rasped, his voice shaky.

My aura gobbled up his energy, dazzling flashes and swirling rainbow-like flecks pulsing over me in time with the frantic beat of my scar. Glowing, branch-shaped patterns crept down my arms, my shaking hands illuminating.

"What the ever-loving feck?!" Breena squealed, her cherry glow extinguishing.

Kaden's eyes widened, his knees giving out. As he crumpled to the ground, my voice failed me, a silent scream ripping through me.

People from the training field ran toward us, my unchained abilities attracting attention.

My mind spun, my pulse erratic. I couldn't concentrate on breathing. On binding my power. Panic tore through me, my body trembling.

My body burned with the need to consume. *Mine.*

Mine!

"Seryn!" I vaguely heard my sister's voice, but I could not be bothered with the distraction.

Kaden was covered in sweat, his hand reaching out to me, his eyes pleading as I took and took and took.

His energy was potent, and I hungered for it.

He must be powerful if he isn't depleted yet.

Delicious.

"Breathe, Ser." His plea came out as a ragged whisper.

Yelling and gasping.

Frenzied movements.

They all whirled around my subconscious, my power swatting them away.

From the corner of my eye, Rhaegar's bulky form lurched away from me, his rune a shooting star through the air as my ember tossed him backward.

I blinked. Moments whizzed by me, then everything seemed to freeze in place.

Kaden was still, lying on his back, twitching. His hands clawed at his chest.

The pattern on my arms and hands burned brightly, dazzling sparks vaulting from my fingers as if they were kindling, ready to ignite.

Time sped up, a flurry of motion circling me.

Three of the Elders were at the front of the crowd now.

Lucan's glare burned with intensity, his eyes flicking between me and Kaden's incapacitated form. Ryboas stared impassively as if this was something he witnessed every day.

Melina's eyes shone wickedly as she sucked her bottom lip, her hands clasped gently in front of her. A wide grin sliced across her face, her teeth glinting.

A soothing voice cut through my awareness. "Little Star. It's all right. Let go of Kaden."

Mine!

More!

Kaden's eyes were fluttering, his skin pale, his aura diminishing.

I whimpered.

"That's it. Hear my voice. Pull your ember back." Gavrel approached, and another whimper escaped my lips. His tattoo was blazing as he reached for me.

"Don't!" I cried.

His eyebrows drew together, his hand pausing. Then he tilted his head, and the corners of his lips tipped up gently. His eyes softened as his fingers grazed my glowing arm.

My aura reared back from his touch but then curled into it.

His rune flared. My lungs inhaled deeply. I blew out a huff of air through pursed lips, willing my ember to release Kaden.

My aura shivered, flicking the green glow from its clutches. The light from my hands and arms seeped into my skin, and I panted, my power tucking within me, satiated.

Gavrel caught me as my knees gave way, my body wilting to the grass as if my muscles turned to jelly. I didn't have the strength to stand, but my attention flew to Kaden, my hands flying to my mouth.

His chest heaved fitfully from the exertion. He threw his arm over his face as he lay on the grass, catching his breath.

Filled with remorse, I took in the witnesses around me, my face and chest burning a deep shade of crimson. Hushed shock blanketed the crowd; feet shuffled, and heads dipped in dismay.

Xeni held Letti protectively, but my sister left her embrace to come to me, hugging me and smoothing my hair. A sob left me, and I gulped a second back. Breena approached, rubbing my shoulder for a moment.

Gavrel stood on my other side. His voice was clear as he directed the crowd to leave. "All right, enough. Please go about your day." He nodded at Rhaegar, Breena, and Xeni. They, along with other guards, immediately helped redirect everyone.

"Another good show, pet," Melina cooed. "Come to my chambers after the dinner hour tonight. Gavie knows the way." She spun, her hips swaying as she walked away.

A growl rumbled through Gavrel's chest, and I placed one hand on his calf.

Ryboas lifted a straight eyebrow; his mouth puckered as he studied me briefly. He departed, his red robes fluttering behind him like flames.

Lucan tossed a final sneer toward Kaden as he turned to leave, his twisted cane stabbing into the grass with every step.

I stood, Letti's supportive arms helping me to my feet. She

kissed my cheek and squeezed my shoulder. I offered her a small smile. "Go on. I'm all right."

One of her eyebrows rose, but she didn't say a word before walking toward Xeni, who was waiting at the edge of the barracks.

I looked at my feet, pushing them into the ground. My body felt unsteady, but my legs carried me to Kaden.

Kaden's arm slipped from his forehead as he looked at me.

"I'm so sorry," the tattered whisper fell from my throat. He sat up, wrapping his arms around my legs, burying his face in my thighs.

"It's okay," he uttered, his words muffled. "Looks like we need to practice more." He smiled, his green eyes finding my icy blues. I frowned, rubbing my hand over his thick mop of hair.

His arm fell heavily across my shoulders as he stood. My hand wrapped around his waist. I wasn't sure what else to say as we held each other, keeping one another steady.

Perhaps I was in shock; words and feelings ripped from my senses. Kaden was unusually reserved as we drifted to the palace, Gavrel trailing close behind. We were three restless shadows slinking away from the setting sun.

17

A SENSE OF CONTROL

An angry little creature was trapped inside my skull, careening into the sides, attempting to break free. I rubbed my temples, cringing at the relentless throbbing.

Soft multicolored splashes gleamed through the canopy, the morning light scattering around my room. I crushed my eyes closed, the brightness increasing the ache within my head. At least I had the day off from my chores.

A cheery rapping sounded on my door, and I winced. It burst open without my consent, and I squinted an eye toward it as a swirl of blue dashed into my sanctuary.

I flopped my arm over my eyes.

"Now, Miss. No use in lazing about. It's a lovely day, and it's running away from you," Derya chided, emphasizing the tsking she made as she flung my blankets off me.

"Let it run. I won't chase it," I grumbled.

"Up. Up!" She swatted my hip. A groan spilled from me as I rolled over and slumped into a sitting position. Derya wouldn't give up when she fixated on something—like a busy little bird nipping at a hidden worm.

I sighed, smoothing my hand over my untamed tresses and

closing my eyes. I'd be her worm if it made her happy. She deserved nothing less.

Derya's attention was rapt on me as her feet shuffled impatiently. I peeked at her, a wide grin spreading across her face as she swayed her hips, holding out a simple black dress toward me.

"What's this now?"

"Your new attire! Your gift is the talk of the palace. Quite exciting to be so mysterious," she giggled.

"Just what I wanted. More attention," I moaned, snatching my uniform from her.

I frowned at the garment in my hands. It was a symbol of failure—my utter inability to keep my ember in check.

"Embrace it, my dear. Never know when it might come in handy, yeah?" She wrapped me in a warm hug, squeezing before releasing me and cupping my cheek tenderly. "You've a long road ahead of you, my dear, but you'll manage it. I've no doubt."

My brows rose, a curious response on the tip of my lips when Kaden sauntered into the room.

"Good morning, beautiful," he drawled, oozing charm. Had he forgotten I'd almost killed him yesterday?

He tilted his head, looking at me. "Ah, Ser. Didn't see you there. Top of the morning to you as well." His grin was infectious, sullying my uneasiness.

"You cad." Derya swatted his arm, tittering and rolling her eyes. Then she gave him a stern look before shuffling to the door. "Take care of our girl."

"Always. I dream of nothing else," he crooned. He turned to me when the door clicked shut, wrapping his arms around me and pulling me close. I breathed in his woodsy scent, leaning into the warmth of his body.

"How did your mysterious meeting go with Elder Harrow?" he asked, kissing the top of my head.

I looked up at him, bringing my hands to rest on the wide

expanse of his chest. "Ah, she canceled. You know, important Elder stuff." I shrugged, wincing at the movement.

Kaden's warm hand gently kneaded my neck, and I moaned at the relief it brought. "That feels like a miracle. Don't stop."

"I aim to please." A laugh rumbled in his chest. He used his other hand to massage my scalp. Tingles raced over my crown, easing the ache in my temples. "Here, sit. I'll run you a bath."

He wouldn't hear any arguments from me. It sounded like a splendid idea. I laid on my side, watching him draw the bath, lavender-scented bubbles swirling out of the spout. I pushed myself off the bed, making my way to Kaden as he turned off the stream of water.

As he turned to me, I nestled my hand into the crook of his neck. My eyes cleared; the pain in my head now a faint echo. "Kade, I know I said it yesterday, but I can't stop thinking about what happened. I'm so sorry. I would never intentionally hurt you. I hope you know that."

His eyes ran over my face, my lips, my eyes before looking up to the quartz ceiling, his hair looking almost midnight blue where the sunbeams swept over it. His eyes found mine as he cupped my jaw in his hands. "Never doubt that I know that. I'm all right, truly." He slowly stroked my skin as he tucked his lips between his teeth for a moment. "Your ember is ... intense."

My heart sank as a wave of trepidation fluttered through my gut. I knew Kaden too well. He was troubled by what happened, but he wouldn't admit it to me.

I felt powerless against my developing gifts. Against the fissure creeping along the bonds of our budding relationship.

Kaden's eyes softened as he leaned forward, pressing his lips into mine. He rested his forehead against my brow, closing his eyes. "I'll leave you to—"

I grabbed his wrists as he pulled away. If he left now, the apprehension would fester, chipping away at the vulnerable cracks within me. "Don't leave."

His nostrils flared, the morning sun tracing the edges of his nose. Reaching up, I drew one fingertip down the uneven bridge, then rested my palm on his cheek, standing on my tiptoes to place another kiss on his mouth. His fingers pressed into me, a muffled growl vibrating within him.

The sound was encouraging, filling me with a sense of control—which I so desperately needed. I felt brave. Empowered.

I stepped away from him, pushing my nightgown off my shoulders. He tilted his head to the side, a few strands of shaggy hair falling over his forehead. His breathing sped up, an intense look of concentration lining his face.

The connection between us lingered as I backed away slightly, inching the material over my chest and letting it pool around my feet.

My breath quickened, now in time with the rise and fall of his chest. I dragged my top teeth over my bottom lip as the warm morning incandescence stroked over my bare skin.

He released a growl, tugging his tunic off and tossing it at his feet. His solid chest and abdomen strained, tense from holding himself in place.

One side of my lips quirked up as I turned my back to him, sliding my underwear down. Shivering, I stepped into the steamy bath water, goosebumps racing over my skin as I settled under fizzing bubbles.

With my head leaning against the back of the amber glass, I glanced at him. "Are you coming in, or do you have something better to do?"

He turned to leave, the sunlight outlining every corded muscle. "When you put it that way—"

"Kaden Larkin!" I squealed, sitting up in the tub, splashing water over the edge.

He turned in an instant, a mischievous smirk reaching his eyes. It took only two full strides for him to get to the bath, a sharp gasp rushing out of me as he plunged his broad form into the water, his trousers still on. Loud fits of laughter floated through the room as he swiftly maneuvered, stretching his long legs across the length of the tub as he sat.

Then, without warning, his hands disappeared under the froth, claiming my waist and dragging me on top of him.

His hands slipped up my soapy back. I brushed my fingers through his hair, resting them on his nape, staring at his wet lips.

We weren't laughing anymore as the water swayed around us. The sounds of our mingled breaths and bubbles softly popping floated between our bodies.

His warm exhales teased my skin, hardening my nipples as water trickled off them and into the water. He slid a hand to my breast, pinching one bud between his finger and thumb.

A sharp sensation zipped to my core, and I rocked against his wet breeches, feeling his hard length under the water. He grinned and swept the pad of his thumb over my nipple, relieving the sting and replacing it with a different type of sweet torture.

I sighed, my breath faltering as I moaned, "Kade."

His smile faded as he seized my nape with his other hand and pulled my head to his, his lips claiming mine in a bruising kiss. My lips opened immediately, our tongues clashing.

My hips pressed into his, dragging over his erection repeatedly as we devoured each other. I couldn't get close enough, the water frothing around us.

I caught his bottom lip between my teeth, dragging them over its plumpness.

Kaden groaned, using both hands to squeeze my bottom. His fingers pressed into the rounded cheeks, helping my sex rub over his. Heat built in my center, spreading outwards until its vibrations radiated over my limbs.

I leaned into his wet skin, my breasts rubbing against the

hard contours of his chest. He licked and sucked my neck, tasting my skin without abandon.

My need condensed, and when I began pressing harder into him, his grip slid to my waist, spinning me. My backside pressed against his cock as I reclined against his hard torso.

Brushing my wet strands over one shoulder, he glided his hand over my neck, my shoulder, and then my breast. Kaden played with my nipple, stroking and tugging, his teeth and mouth nibbling and kissing my neck. His other hand slid down to the apex of my thighs.

My thighs quivered and tingled, and I gasped as he plunged two fingers into my warm heat. My hips followed his fingers as he pumped them in and out, in and out.

His thumb pressed against my throbbing clit, circling and flicking while his fingers thrust.

"Kade, I … I'm going to …"

"Yes, come for me, sweeting," he mumbled against my neck, his teeth nipping just under my ear.

A wild moan fled my throat, followed by a whimper as I shattered, my sex tightening around his thick fingers.

"Fuck, Ser," he rasped, sliding his fingers from my body, slipping up my stomach. He cupped one breast tenderly, gently squeezing before he whispered, "I'll die happy dreaming of your cunt clenching around me."

A languid grin spread across my lips, my face flushing as I wiggled against him. He gulped, his erection pulsing.

I turned in the water, standing between his legs. Water dripped, my skin shining and pink with arousal.

My body hummed, any restraint or shyness long forgotten. At this moment, I was in control in a way I hadn't been before.

I cupped my breasts, teasing my tender nipples. "Your breeches. Off. Now," I demanded.

"Yes, ma'am." He fumbled out of the tub, sloshing water everywhere.

Grabbing blankets and towels, he made a haphazard pile on the floor as I stepped out of the basin.

Kaden pushed his sodden trousers off and stood in the center of the makeshift bed, his manhood thick and stiff, begging for attention.

My mouth watered while I pulled in a deep breath of the lavender-scented air.

"Lie down." I took a step forward, goosebumps rippling over my skin.

He complied, propping himself on his elbows as I kneeled between his strong thighs.

His body was a piece of art. A sculpture of carved perfection that I wanted to explore every inch of.

I ran my hands up his shins. Over his knees. His thighs. His muscles flexing at my touch, his cock twitching. My gaze focused on the rigid length.

I drew my tongue across my bottom lip as I wrapped my hand around the base of his shaft, resting my other hand atop his thigh. He grunted, his hips rising a bit to push into my palm.

"I ... I'm not sure exactly what to do," I whispered, my heart hammering against my ribs.

His mouth tipped up, his eyes glinting. "Sweeting, whatever you want to do to my cock will please him and me. Just no teeth, please." He winced, chuckling.

I sucked in my bottom lip, running my hand up his shaft, our skin still wet. Kaden sucked in a ragged breath, his abs tensing. My hand slid down with a firm grip. His hips lifted again, a bead of cum pebbling at the tip of his cock.

My body leaned forward, and I licked the salty wetness, gently squeezing the base of him.

"Torture. Plain and simple," Kaden whimpered. I smirked and then wrapped my mouth around him, tasting as I pushed down as far as possible, my lips meeting my hand. His cock jerked in my grip, and I began sucking and pumping him.

He moaned, burying his fingers in my wild hair. Pleasuring him made me feel powerful. My body was on fire, and with every guttural sound he made, my core trembled, wishing it was wrapped around him instead of my mouth.

"I'm going to come. Fuck!"

My mouth left him, my hand still moving up and down his cock. His body tensed, his eyes closed, and his brow creased.

A sensual, garbled sound rumbled from his chest as he came, his seed spilling over my hand and onto his stomach.

As I released him, his body fell limp. I cuddled into his side, his arm wrapping around me protectively.

"Well, that's one way to get rid of a headache," I teased.

He laughed, kissing my forehead in between each word. "Best. Morning. Ever."

"I think you're just pleased that you finally joined me in the tub."

"I won't deny it. Unless you want to torture me some more." He grinned as I swatted him on the chest and then placed a kiss on his jaw.

We snuggled for a bit atop the damp linens, neither of us wanting to leave the satiated bubble.

Contentment seeped into my muscles, relief working through each sinew. Any remaining feeling of being powerless was nudged aside. I sighed, kissing Kaden's collarbone.

My stomach grumbled, breaking the silence.

"Ah, time to feed the monster in your belly," he joked.

We cleaned up, and he wrapped a towel around his waist, taking his soggy trousers back to his room for a fresh pair.

I slipped my new dress over me, the fabric just as soft as my previous attire. I ran my hands down the black skirt, wishing it wouldn't call attention to me.

"Hungry?" Kaden asked from the hallway. As he met me at the door, he took my hand in his.

"Always."

18

FATED KHORDA

"Ah, new attire, I see. You've been branded a mystery, I dare say," Rhaegar stated, taking a seat next to me and placing a plate of bacon and eggs on the table.

"Wonderful," I grumbled.

"I'd look at it as an opportunity. Keeping others on their toes … or *off* them, in my case," he joked, flashing me a broad smile.

I returned it and touched his arm briefly, grateful for his encouragement and sense of humor. "I'm sorry. I recall tossing you through the air." My shoulders slumped.

"Ah, don't vex yourself. It was bloody brilliant." He chuckled, digging into his food.

"He's right, you know. People may think twice before messing with you. I call dibs on you for the Winnowing Trials." Breena pointed one finger at me, squinting. "That was a given anyway." She took a big bite out of a banana.

"All right, spill. People keep dropping hints without saying much." Letti looked around the table, her stare landing on Xeni, whose mouth quirked as she chewed slowly. Swallowing, she rested her spoon in her empty bowl.

Now that Xeni spent more time with the group—or rather,

Letti—we had learned that she was part of Gavrel's unit and had been for the last two turns. She was from the easternmost edge of Haadra.

"There's often chatter about the festivities before the Elders gather everyone. Gossip spreads like Pyria fire throughout the training field." Her voice was soothing and composed. "Basically, we celebrate the end of the Dormancy with various events, a ball, and a competition. The tournament is only for Druiks and Draumrs who wish to compete. There is often some sort of highly desirable prize for the victor."

"Thank you," Letti said, placing a kiss on Xeni's cheek. Xeni smiled, embracing my sister's hand on top of the table. Her rune tattoo, in the shape of three small interconnecting decagons, flashed silver between her thumb and forefinger.

"Whatever the prize is, we're in. Dibs on you and you and you," Breena insisted as she pointed the last bit of her banana at me, Kaden, and Rhaegar. "Xeni, I'd absolutely put dibs on you, but I heard we can only have four per team. You in to be backup?"

"Ah, I'll probably sit this one out." Xeni bowed, her mouth curving faintly.

"Feck. I'm gonna hunt down Gavrel for my reserve," Breena mumbled, brow furrowing and fingers snapping as she left us.

Kaden plunked the cup he was holding on the table. "What in the ever-loving void just happened? Were we just volunteered for the tournament against our will?"

"Yep." I laughed, kissing his cheek and jaw. Lettie's big eyes widened, and she smirked, her shoulders dancing up and down. Shrugging, I blushed as I savored a particularly juicy peach.

Lately, everyone was aware or suspected that Kaden and I were more than friends. I sighed, knowing that I might as well get used to it. I was tired of denying it anyway.

"Come here, you little humming peach monster." Kaden

wrapped his arm around my shoulders, squeezing me into his side.

I nestled there, basking in his warmth, smiling when I realized I'd been humming again. Well, peaches were my favorite.

Letti reached for my hand across the table. "Join me in the library?"

"Sure, let's go. I'm sure Mr. Burlam would love to see me on my day off." I chuckled, wiping my fingers on a cloth napkin.

As we headed to the library, the palace was quiet this morning. Most people were probably sleeping in if they could or wandering the grounds.

"So, you and Kaden. Hate to say I told you so, but—"

I interrupted, "You and Xeni, huh?"

"That's old news, but yeah. She's pretty amazing." Letti was beaming, her hazel eyes lighting up with flecks of sparkling gold.

"I'm happy for you, sis. Xeni is wonderful. I like how she watches out for you." I gave her a side hug. "And yes, Kaden and I are … having fun," I muttered, heat prickling up my neck. Thoughts of this morning prodded my mind.

Letti giggled, "I bet. Twenty-one turns is a long time to wait."

"Oh, hush. I didn't always think of him this way."

"That doesn't mean he didn't," she stated, raising her brows and pinching her lips together.

As we walked in silence, the weight of her comment pressed into me, my spine stiffening. Glimpses of moments spun through me. Lingering looks. Touches. How Kaden had always been within reach. Was I that clueless? If he had wanted more than friendship for—however long—was it selfish of me to be with him now? We were both consenting adults …

I wasn't entirely sure of what I felt. Of course, I loved him. I'd always loved him because he was my best friend. My rock. I was terrified of losing my heart to him in an entirely different way. In a way that caused me to lose my footing. That shook my entire world.

But then again, we'd forget all this when the Dormancy was over.

I chewed the inside of my cheek, confusion and anxiety washing over me. If I let myself fall down that endless, coiling hole, I feared I'd lose my mind without ever recovering it.

My cheeks puffed as I blew air out. I muttered, "Maybe. Am I that oblivious?"

"Yeah. You are." She laughed. "A couple of summers ago, I thought something was going on with you and Gav. Kaden was so moody then."

"What?" I squeaked, distracted from my spiraling worries. "Bollocks. I've never had anything more with Gavrel. He's like our big brother."

She smirked, holding up her hands. "Well, he's *not* our brother. And he's ridiculously good-looking." Her fingers tickled my side, and I squealed, swatting her as I ran ahead.

Our laughter immediately hushed as we stepped into the library. Mr. Burlam was at his desk, one bushy eyebrow raised as we passed him. "Can't stay away, I see," he grumbled.

"Never, Mr. Burlam. I'd miss you too much," I chirped, grinning brightly. His head swung from side to side in disbelief, papery cheeks turning a pallid shade of pink as he shuffled papers on his desk.

We made our way to the back of the library, collecting a few books and settling at my favorite table tucked near the curling staircases.

"Aren't you afraid?" I asked, pausing mid-sentence in the book I was reading.

Letti's eyes found mine. "Hmmm?"

"Of getting close to someone when you're going to forget your time here."

She shrugged. "A bit. But this *is* our life. Half in. Half out. I don't want to let fear stop me from living any part of it. Stop me from experiencing joy when I can. If this is all a dream, we might as well enjoy it."

My lips curled. "How'd you get so wise?"

"Not my fault I was born with all the brains," she jested, and I snorted, picking my book up.

Throughout the morning, we read, joked, and talked about life in a way only sisters could. Spending time with Letti was a balm to my frazzled edges. Her very presence often offered comfort to everyone around her.

My eyes softened as I tipped my head to the side, studying Letti. I was so proud of the person she was. Loyal and honest. Supportive and hardworking.

She looked up from her book and stuck her tongue out, her eyes squeezing shut. Shaking my head, I laughed.

She set down the novel she was reading, her brow furrowing. "Do you think Mama and Father were khorda? I don't," she murmured, concentrating on the pages splayed open on the table.

There were tales throughout history of three sister Fates helping the Ancients weaken Druiks so that mortal ember would not become overwhelmingly powerful. It was believed that Druiks were born with half their soul, the other half cleaved from them and gifted to another—Druik or human.

Their mirrored soul.

Their fated khorda.

I shrugged. "Why do you ask?" I didn't think our parents were fated, but I waited, seeing where Letti was going with this train of thought.

Letti traced over the yellowed page, her fingertip leading her. "It says here ... 'If a Druik unites with their fated through the Kollao Ceremony, their soul and ember become whole again. The aging of their bodies and lifespans tied to one another intricately.' Downside—when one dies, the other dies not long after." She leaned back, regarding me. "I mean, father isn't dead. So, either Mama is alive, or they weren't khorda. Or they never went through the ceremony."

"Or all of the above," I muttered, closing the book I'd been perusing. "I've never heard of anyone finding their other half, but I suppose in Midst Fall, most Druiks hide, go missing, or are recruited to the Akridais." I slumped in my chair, the wood rasping beneath me. "You think Mama was a Druik?"

"It would make sense. You inherited your gift from someone, and I doubt Father has any. If he did, he'd be best buddies with the Elders." She snorted.

A frown pulled my mouth downward. "You're probably right. Well, I'm surprised the Fates gave us mere mortals a choice. With the Kollao Ceremony, that is."

Letti's face fell. "Mortals? You'll live much longer than me if I'm not a Druik ... or if I don't undergo the ceremony with my fated Druik." Her voice hitched, catching in her throat. We both knew the odds of finding one's khorda were infinitesimal. Letti swallowed, tucking her golden hair behind her ears. "There's always a choice, Ser. The Fates can bugger off."

I tucked my lips between my teeth, words sticking within my chest. Awkwardly, I reached across the leather tombs, stretching my upper body over the table and scooping Letti into a clumsy hug. "I love you. And will always be with you, no matter which realm our souls wander."

She exhaled, her body deflating within my embrace, and then wrapped her arms around my shoulder blades, nuzzling her face into my hair.

"You're bloody right you will. Love you, sister," she murmured after a moment. When we pulled apart, our eyes were shining mirrors, reflecting our bond back to one another.

19

BLOOD OATHS

"Through Dormancy, we blossom!" The frenetic chant echoed throughout the Great Hall. Those who chose to sit nearest the platform were completely enraptured with the crowd's energy, their food and drink neglected as they pumped their fists in the air.

Their fanatical devotion was both confounding and understandable. When people were at their lowest, they leaned on those with perceived power—the loudest in the room, whether through words, actions, or intimidation—hoping they would be uplifted.

Melina raised one hand, a satisfied grin carving across her face as she stood from the grand throne atop the dais. The crowd silenced immediately. The other Elders sat on either side of her, jaws churning slowly as their teeth ground each bite of food. A long wooden table was set before them. They had started attending dinners over the last month—eating silently, glowering, or scrutinizing the assembled as if deciding which of us were prized stock.

"With only two months left until the spring equinox, I'll go over the Winnowing Trials!" The crowd cheered, eager to receive details instead of only knowing whispered rumors. Melina scanned the room, one eyebrow raised. After everyone settled, she announced, "In a month's time, a grand ball will be held to celebrate the upcoming spring equinox marking the Dormancy's successful end—and to honor the chosen competitors."

More whoops and applause rippled through the room. Breena grinned at me from across the table as she bit into a cheese wedge. She wiggled her eyebrows, plopping the rest of it onto her plate. Next to her, Letti smirked at Breena while leaning into Xeni, politely joining in with the crowd. Rhaegar, on my right, cupped his chin and mouth with his hand, his massive shoulders shaking with mirth.

"Only Druiks and Draumrs may compete—the trials are not for the fragile. You'll need both power and strength to secure the victory," Melina sneered, making eye contact with a group wearing white. My fingers clutched the black fabric of my skirt, looking around in confusion. *Doesn't her flock realize she's mocking them?* Sitting to my left, Kaden put his arm around me, rubbing his thumb soothingly over my shoulder.

"Failure is a one-way ticket to the Stygian Murk." Gasps and dropped silverware permeated the air. "Can you handle being caught in limbo for what equates to several weeks—or longer? For everyone else, with the fall of the full moon, your pods will awaken and beckon your astral forms home. For those who have lingered there this entire time, or those who fail during the trials … only the Fates know where they'll call home after the Dormancy. I'll let you chew on that through this week."

Breena gave Kaden, Rhaegar, and me two exuberant thumbs-up, which Kaden and I ignored, shaking our heads.

The tipped-up corners of my mouth fell as I thought of my mother and father. It was a miracle that Father had survived the Murk and returned home in previous turns. I prayed he'd do so again. If only Mama had been so lucky. My heart squeezed, and I drew in a deep breath.

I surveyed the room, wondering where Gavrel was as Melina's voice faded out of my awareness. He'd made himself scarce since the day my ember devoured Kaden's.

That was a couple of months ago.

I'd seen him briefly in passing a few times, but he had only offered me a polite nod or a dour expression before going about his business. Maybe he was disappointed in me. Or worse, repulsed.

A few of my peers, Druik and human alike, were wary of me after they had witnessed my gift's revelation. I tried disregarding their apprehensive looks, disapproving glares, and blatant avoidance. But it was wearing on me, like a thousand little pinpricks under my skin.

Meanwhile, I had been diligently practicing daily, spending hours learning how to manage my power.

Control it.

Tether it.

I stretched my neck to one side and then the other, trying to relieve the tension within my muscles.

An overabundance of thoughts fell heavy upon my shoulders, pinning me to my seat. My fingers fidgeted with each other on my lap as I took a deep breath. Shifting toward the stage, my body extricated itself from Kaden's embrace. I exhaled, feeling lighter without his hand resting on my shoulder. Melina's words came into focus again.

"... choose to compete, every team will undergo the first test —the Weeding—which could transpire any time after this week. With the fruition of each trial, survivors will advance to the next challenge." An unkind smile oozed over her face before she hid it behind steepled fingers.

She dipped her chin, dropping her hands to the tabletop. The pads of her fingers rested upon it as she composed herself, her face settling into indifference. Slowly, she lifted her eyes to the crowd.

"Now for the prize. Each competitor on the victorious team will be rewarded with a turn's supply of extra food rations." Sharp intakes of breaths scattered throughout the hall. Kaden grabbed my hand, nodding at Breena and then Rhaegar. It appeared we'd need to take Breena seriously about participating in the tournament.

"Before the Ancients disappeared, our runemaster was extensively trained in the art of celestial-blessed symbols." Melina paused, stretching her arms wide. "The victor alone will be granted a rune tattoo for their efforts—gifting them a portion of enhanced ember." The crowd responded raucously.

Melina settled on the throne, lifting her pewter goblet and taking a delicate sip. She glanced to her side. "Ryboas?"

Elder Ash rose from his seat, his chair creaking with relief. His frown seeped into his dark eyes as they studied the crowd, pale hands gripping the lapels of his crimson robes. His voice spilled over us like dry, rough grains of sand. "At the end of this week, an oath ceremony will be held at the Elysium Tree. Each competitor must submit a blood offering to the sacred banyan. This participation oath is binding. If you break it, you will be sent to the Stygian Murk."

He raised his chalice and recited, "May you withstand the currents of the Winnowing. For only the worthy will remain." He sat heavily on his chair, his face drooping in total boredom as the citizens rejoiced.

I took in the people around me. Some had eyes shining with tentative hope. Others, crazed with it. My nape tingled, energy anxiously vibrating. My skin itched as if someone was watching me.

My eyes drifted to a male Akridai skulking in a shadowed corner of the stage. We all knew him—Balor Drent—as he often lurked near Melina. As one of her favored enforcers, he wasn't someone I wanted to be caught alone with. His very presence made my skin crawl. He'd recently returned from a mission, but I wished he had stayed away. Balor played with a long strand of his slick, dark hair as he stared at me unabashedly.

An aura—slippery black grease swirling in a buttery stew—seethed around him. His tattoo burned against his neck's sickly yellow glow. Rhaegar had recently informed me that the locust rune not only enforced an Akridai's oath to the Elders but also tainted their ember, resulting in the oily, neon-like slurry of their auras.

Kaden followed my gaze, wrapping his arm around me and glaring at Balor. The male grinned, his crooked teeth gleaming, and then slinked after the Elders as they left the room at the back of the stage.

I pushed my plate away, leaning into Kaden's chest. Suddenly, I wasn't hungry anymore.

THE END of the week arrived too hastily.

Ten sets of potential competitors consisting of Druiks and Draumrs were strategically placed around the Elysium Tree. Various auras glimmered among the teams. No one was actively using their gift, so I knew I was the only one privy to this display.

Rhaegar appeared to be the only embered warrior from Gavrel's unit among the candidates. I stood with him, Breena, and Kaden at one of the ten designated points, staring at the golden, oval-shaped petals resting upon the moss. Gilded rays reflected off them, melding into their delicate cups. They created a twinkling line between each team, connecting us and forming a decagon.

Numerous guards surrounded us at the edges of the wide

canopy, separating us from the onlookers. The sun peeked through the flame-colored leaves above. A gentle breeze swept through the tree, making the leaves rustle and the mossy vines sway around us. I breathed in, enjoying the fragrant scents washing over me.

The crowd was copious, its restless energy buzzing through the mass in waves. An anxious flutter vibrated under the raised star on my nape. I widened my stance, focusing on the gorgeous, twisting bark of the tree before us. Its power called to me, waves of golden shimmers flickering over its gnarled surface. As if it knew unbreakable, blood-bound promises were about to be made.

"I can't believe we're doing this," Kaden muttered, squeezing my chilled hand with his warm one.

Breena winked at him, her smile stretching wide. She was about to burst with excitement. A warm, russet shade swept across her chest and rounded cheeks.

"There wasn't a choice. We need to do all we can to win those food rations for our village," I whispered from the side of my mouth.

He looked at me, his eyes softening. "I know, of cour—"

His words morphed into a grunt as Rhaegar thumped a heavy hand on his shoulder, interrupting him. "We will prevail, my friends. I'm quite sure of it." The warrior didn't bother to whisper, the deep bass of his voice lilting. Nearby, competitors glared at us, scoffed, or rolled their eyes.

"That's the battle fever we need!" Breena praised, clasping Rhaegar's wrist as he reciprocated the gesture. They shook each other's wrists enthusiastically before releasing each other. The corners of my lips threatened to lift before I turned my attention to the team on our left. I stopped myself, pulling my mask of indifference firmly in place.

A tall, stout woman leered at me. Her hands tightened on the leather baldric across her chest, and her Draumr uniform strained at her shoulders as if she were ready to pounce. I refused to break away from her gaze and squinted my eyes. She sneered, flicking her wavy, sand-colored hair behind her and widening her stance. Ignoring her, I looked ahead.

Rhaegar leaned closer to me and rumbled, "Don't mind Sebille. She is as spoiled as a rotted mirberry." I nudged his biceps with my shoulder, giving him a small smile in response.

My focus wandered, thinking of what could come in the weeks ahead. I was terrified of being sent to the Stygian Murk, but after we'd learned about the extra food rations, there was no doubt I'd enter the competition. This was something I could do for our realm.

Something tangible.

Something useful.

A rustling and shifting of bodies broke through my thoughts. The crowd parted as Gavrel strode through, stepping over the flower petals. He looked at Kaden, and then his eyes skimmed over me, his eyes softening. In the next instant, his mouth buttoned together tightly as he pulled his attention away from me, scanning the crowd. He positioned himself next to the enormous trunk and looked into the distance, his face a mask of disinterest. I gritted my teeth, frustration bubbling in my belly.

A wisp of smoldering smoke twirled around the twisted trunk in front of us. The tree's glittering aura stilled, its glow shrinking into shadowed crevices. The haze condensed before peeling away, and Melina appeared out of the billowy cloud. A collective gasp swept through the audience. Those farthest from the tree strained to see what was happening. Basking in the crowd's attention, Melina lifted her chin, a feral grin creeping over her mouth.

Ryboas marched into the center, a dour expression on his face as he stopped next to Melina. Not one for theatrics like his peer, he proceeded. "Welcome, competitors. I commend those brave enough to make this blood promise," he announced, reaching into an inner pocket of his robes and revealing a mesmerizing dagger.

The dagger's blade was made of smoothly chiseled obsidian, the edges carved into a wavy pattern that gently tapered into a razor-sharp point. Its hilt was brilliant platinum with intricate swirling patterns etched into the liquid-like silver. Radiance reflected and sparked off its lustrous surfaces, making it appear to be a living creature with its own aura. The pommel was made of a large, faceted diamond. Each time a speck of light touched its clear edges, dazzling rainbows scattered in all directions.

Everyone's eyes were glued to it.

Ryboas' voice rang out as he held the dagger above his head and slowly walked around the trunk. "This dagger is the only one in existence and was forged long ago by the founding Elders as a gift to Morpheus. It is rumored that the Ancient had little use for it, so he infused it with supreme ember, making its blade stronger than steel and allowing it to bond with keepers over the centuries…" He paused, stroking the blade reverently.

He closed his eyes, frowning. "But alas, we can't believe every fairytale we are told as children." He sniffed, one corner of his mouth curling in disdain. "However, its lore makes it the perfect ceremonial blade. Let's begin." He turned to face the team to our left, waving the dagger toward them and then to the tree.

Sebille lifted her chin, breaking from her team and striding forward confidently. Her teammates followed: two male Draumrs and one male Druik. Ryboas poised the knife, its glossy blade glinting. His eyes pierced into each of theirs as he recited, "Your blood is your bond. Broken promises reap consequences. The Elysium Tree is rooted in our beginning and our end."

The female guard held out her palm, and Elder Ash promptly swept the blade across her tender flesh. She squeezed her fingers into the pooling blood, dripping it onto the sacred roots below. The tree shivered as its roots drank it in. A shimmering wave of energy crept over its trunk as the crimson pool vanished. The rest of her team did the same before returning to their original position.

With each participant who made their vow, the crowd cheered. My knees were soft as my arm wrapped around Kaden's back for support. He held me close, still and composed. The team to our right was almost finished as Ryboas sliced the last male Druik's palm.

The man's form trembled as he pulled his wounded hand toward his chest. His teammate placed a hand on his shoulder, whispering in his ear. The man jerked his head frantically, clutching his limb for dear life as his ichor stained the fabric of his yellow tunic. His teammate mouthed something to him, digging his fingers into the man's shoulder. Shaking, the Druik thrust his hand forward.

His face lost all color as he gulped and snapped his hand back, stepping away from the tree and his team. He cried, "I can't!" It was too late, though. As if in slow motion, a drop of his blood had escaped, falling to the base of the tree with a splatter. It trickled down the bark like a scarlet tear before seeping into the wood.

The man's face fell, his head shaking. "No! I didn't—"

Dazzling light burst through every crevice of the trunk; the exposed surface roots blindingly bright. Everyone covered their faces, the beams too intense to behold. My heart pounded, and the air was sucked from my lungs. The man shrieked, and I knew the chilling sound would never leave my memory. Then, all at once, the radiance was absorbed into the tree, and everyone stared, wide-eyed, at the scene before us.

All that was left of the Druik was a cloud of twinkling cinder in the shape of his form. As the glow of it dwindled, the dust gently fell to the moss. A flower-scented breeze brushed against my cheek, rustling my hair and carrying away the rest of the ash. I felt sick, deep within my very soul.

"The Elysium Tree has spoken. Is your team prepared to compete with only three?" Melina's dulcet voice rang through the shocked silence as her hands clasped in front of her chest. It wasn't a question. The three remaining competitors bobbed their heads, mouths hanging open. Silently, they went back to their designated spot. "Marvelous. Let's get on with the final team. Ryboas?"

Breena turned to me, grasping my hand. She placed her other hand on Rhaegar's shoulder. Looking at each of us, she whispered, "Last chance. Yay or nay?" Her tone was sincere, lines crinkling around her eyes. I knew she would be all right if any of us backed out. I tucked my lips between my teeth, lifting my chin and staring at the vivid canopy and swaying vines above.

Counting to five, I breathed in and out, my fingers flexing in time with my breaths. We needed to do this. For all the people we cared about at home.

"I'm in."

"Same," Kaden replied.

Rhaegar nodded, and a wide grin swept across Breena's face. We moved to the center. Gavrel's brow furrowed, his eyes closed and skin tight across his cheeks and jaw. Ryboas began his speech, but I was distracted as Melina licked her lips, leaning into the commander.

I clamped my molars together and looked at Ryboas as he finished, "... rooted in our beginning and our end."

We all held our hands out simultaneously. Ryboas cut across our palms, marking us for certain misfortunes ahead. I grimaced at the sharp tinge of pain and stared at the ruby liquid pooling in my hand. Before I could change my mind, I pressed my fingertips into it, feeling it slip along my skin, staining it.

As our promises plummeted to the earth, energy zipped

from my scar. Down through my legs, it melded into the ground as our blood sank into the moss. The buried roots glowed, pulsing and shining under the earth, inching toward me. My iridescent aura flared around me, nuzzling the blessed ember flickering beneath my feet. The tree's power tingled through my limbs, dancing with mine. It felt welcoming. Eager to connect and share its secrets.

Kaden, Breena, and Rhaegar gathered closely behind me. I smiled, letting them know I was all right. My fingers, still wet with blood, uncurled. My hand stretched toward the tree, wanting to commune with it as if it were a long-lost friend. A twirling halo buzzed along my skin as the tree's energy shimmered around my body in a radiant embrace.

In response, my aura brightened. I closed my eyes, savoring the connection. The weight of something filled my palm, my fingers curling around it without thought. My arm settled at my side as I opened my eyes, gaze fixated on the tree's glittering luster. The trunk illuminated and almost sighed briefly. Around my body, its ember dissipated into the air in a burst of twinkling sparks. My aura sputtered, sinking back within me.

I turned to my team and found them gaping at me—along with everyone else. Kaden ran his hand through his hair, letting his hand rest on the back of his neck before it fell to his side. He looked at my hand. "Seryn—"

"I ... I ..." Stammering, I clenched my hands into fists, realizing I was still gripping something solid. I gulped, taking in what it was.

Morpheus' dagger.

I held the weapon in front of me, its dark blade glinting. My blood, melting into the burnished hilt, disappeared entirely. Coiling, iridescent mist languidly filled the stunning diamond. When finished, it resembled a liquefied version of my aura, swirling and glittering within the faceted globe. I blinked in disbelief.

"Woman, that blade nearly sliced off Ash's hand trying to get to you," Breena whispered enthusiastically.

My mouth dropped open, forgetting how to speak.

Gavrel positioned himself behind Kaden. Concern etched into his face, his chest rising and falling rapidly. The glow of his rune diminished as he grasped his drawn sword at his side. He lifted his tense jaw, strands of dark waves falling over his forehead. He sheathed his blade and then left the way he had arrived without a word.

Staring at me, Melina looked surprisingly bemused, her head tipping to one side; a fingernail tapping the pressed seam of her lips. She squinted her eyes at me and then followed after Gavrel, her dark dress slithering behind her.

Ryboas' brow wrinkled, a tinge of red flashing over his glassy eyes, his lips pressed flat. He seemed to catch himself and relaxed as he looked at his empty hand and back at me. He closed his fingers, making a fist. He didn't demand the dagger back. "It would seem that the Weeding has commenced," he barked, stepping closer to me.

His stale breath brushed my cheek as he rasped, "That dagger hasn't chosen anyone in centuries. Do be careful, Ms. Vawn. We wouldn't want anything … untoward … to befall you." He sniffed, one nostril tipping up, and then marched off, scattering a line of golden petals as he barged through them.

20

MEADOWS AND MIRAGES

The woods beyond the veil lingered at my back. I sprinted through a meadow of vibrant flowers painted in shades of neon pinks and yellows. They were tall, some stretching up to my collarbone. Their candescent auras glittered, sparking into the shimmering atmosphere as I brushed past.

My new dagger, sheathed at my hip, thumped against me in time with my racing heart. My lungs burned from exertion.

Well ahead, the meadow bled into the edge of a gleaming, black cliff. Kaden dashed toward the jagged precipice, his arms pumping. His sleek, dark hair swept back, flicking his ears as he ran.

"Wait!" I cried, my voice cracking against a blast of wind as it pushed against my body, slowing me. My heels dug into the earth, trying to move forward, but the gale surged into me, yanking me backward in a fit of effervescence.

My mind spun. A memory of when I was very young washed over me.

I had been learning how to swim.

But I was too far into the pond, my limbs cramping. I sank, submerged underwater, trying to claw my way up for air. My limbs churned the water into tiny, frantic bubbles as I thrashed about.

The image of a hazy form swam toward me.

Our bodies surged toward the open sky.

Blinking away the memory, I refocused on Kaden and struggled against my invisible fetters. He halted at the brink of the abyss, turning around and staring blankly in my direction.

The wind released me, its glittering zephyr rolling in currents toward my best friend. My arms spun in the air as I tried to find balance; instead, I fell unceremoniously on my backside. My fingers clawed at the hovering stalks around me as I pulled myself up and slapped my wild tresses out of my eyes.

As I chased after the embered flurry of air, a trail of blooms shifted unnaturally several paces away on my right. Sweat slid down my spine, and I sobbed without thinking.

Something was following me through the field.

My teeth bit down hard, and I withdrew my dagger, willing my legs to move faster. I had to reach Kaden before I met whatever was stalking me.

With glazed eyes, he opened his arms wide. His name tore from my lips.

Emerald green flashed over his usually clover-colored eyes. A whoosh of air left me, dragged away on a wave of confusion. A line creased the skin between my eyebrows.

The sound of swishing flora prowled closer, the crunching of stems like thunderclaps between my pounding heartbeats.

I whimpered, concentrating on Kaden. Within one blink, his face morphed into Gavrel's. A look of clarity washed over his face, and he reached one hand toward me, his muscles straining against an invisible force.

My feet were steps away when a wall of air slammed into him. I screamed and screamed as Gavrel's body crumpled and flew backward off the stony cliff.

Bursting from the flowers, I fell, my knees scraping on the

stone of the cliff, my dagger dropping. Out of my reach, he transformed into Kaden once more, a look of utter panic imploding as he faded into the void.

I shrieked in devastation, my hand still reaching out into the darkness. Tears poured down my cheeks.

Out of the corner of my eye, a slithering movement whipped past me in a blur. I spun on my knees, fumbling for my dagger, and with a trembling arm, I held the weapon up.

All at once, the wind ceased, and the sparkling energy in the air stilled. The meadow stopped dancing.

An all-consuming silence enveloped me; all sound being sucked into the emptiness beyond the cliff.

I stilled, emulating the towering flowers, but did not see any further movement. I scrubbed my hand over my face, wiping away the salty wetness.

And then, at the edge of the crag, nestled among the meadow, something quivered. A sharp intake of breath hit the back of my throat. I rubbed at the foggy blur settling over my sight.

And there it was.

A single monochrome orchid. It stood fearlessly among the neon giants looming above it.

Firm, dark-gray leaves erupted from the dirt on either side, anchoring it in place. Perched on the tip, a delicate, drooping petal cluster bent the neck of its bowed black stem. Each velutinous petal gradually blended from the darkest black at the base to the lightest gray at the brim—speckled with glittering silver dots as if they were pulled from the night sky.

It looked like the Ancients forgot to paint the plant; its colors were entirely grayscale in a sea of electric hues.

I shuffled closer to it on my knees, yearning to touch it.

To see if it was real.

Just as the pad of my pointer finger was about to brush against its downy petal, a skittering of feet sounded behind me.

I twisted, rocks cutting into my knees, as a flash of colors and glinting teeth and claws smashed into me. My head cracked into the stone beside the hauntingly beautiful flower, and suddenly, everything went black ...

My eyes snapped open as I jerked upright in bed, lungs heaving and sweat matting my curls to my face and chest. One hand covered my galloping heart. Panic and my agitated aura hissed over my skin and logic. *It was just a dream, Seryn.*

Concentrating on breathing, I inhaled deeply for four seconds, held it while feeling the beat of my heart, and blew out through pursed lips for four more seconds. *You're safe,* I repeated to myself.

Over.

You're safe. It was a dream.

And over.

As I worked through my meditation, my heart slowed, and my aura evaporated. I hung my feet over the side of my bed, facing the circular windows, and pushed my hair behind my stooping shoulders. Brushing my fingers on my quilt, I stared at the tranquil sea. The sunrise barely peeked over the horizon as the full moon faded into daybreak.

A faint knock sounded on my door.

I padded to the door, my soft black nightshift whispering against my skin as I moved.

"Good morning. I thought perhaps I heard you yelling in your sleep. You okay?" Gavrel murmured, leaning against the door frame.

"Uh, I'm fine. Just a nightmare. Actually, the same nightmare I've had since the oath ceremony." I shifted, crossing my arms over my chest. "Need anything else?"

"Ah, no." He hesitated, pressing his lips together for a moment. "You know I would break down the door if I thought you were really in trouble, yes?"

A flush of heat swept over my chest. "Maybe that was true before I almost destroyed Kaden."

"Little Star—"

I held up a hand. "I don't need any explanation. Your absence has been loud enough." I began to close the door, my eyes shifting to my feet. "Take care of yourself, Gav—"

"Wait." He put his palm on the door, stopping it from closing. "Please."

I sighed, looking at him from the small gap between the door and frame, my fingers wrapping around the edge of the metal.

Gavrel leaned his forehead against the door. "I ... There are reasons. I can't—"

He paused, snapping his attention to some sound in the hall. A low rumble sounded in his chest. Looking at me, Gavrel whispered gruffly, "I have to go, but just know that not everyone dreams when they're already dreaming." With that, he let go of the door and walked away.

Eyebrows squishing together, I muttered, "What the void?" as I clicked the door closed. My fingers pushed through my messy hair and then rested on the back of my neck. I huffed, shaking my head, and readied myself for the day.

***

"WHAT DO YOU THINK IT MEANS?" Letti asked Rhaegar and Breena as I approached the barracks. She stared at a crumpled parchment tacked to the stony arched entrance. I shuffled closer to her as a small crowd gathered.

Rhaegar answered, "Looks like the start of the Weeding."

"What?!" Breena shouted, tearing the paper from the wall. Protests rumbled through the crowd. "Bugger off!"

She stared at it, shoving it near my face as Kaden sidled up to me. As I focused on the paper, my fingers covered my mouth.

It was a rendering of the monochrome orchid from my dreams.

My hand dropped, and I pushed out of the crowd as Rhaegar took the parchment from Breena and placed it back on its nail.

Kaden touched the small of my back as he walked beside me. "What's wrong?"

"Nothing. I—"

"Wait a bloody minute, Ryn." Breena stopped in front of me and placed her hands on my shoulders. "Have you seen that pretty 'lil flower before?"

"Uh, I ..." I looked at my feet and then at Kaden. I scrunched my eyes, picturing Kaden leaping off the cliff.

Or Gavrel.

Both.

"Give her some room, Breena. For the love of Ancients," Rhaegar muttered, causing Breena to huff and drop her hands from me.

I opened my eyes, hugging one arm across my chest and gripping my biceps. Letti stood still on my other side in a wide stance.

Rhaegar continued, one hand absently tapping his burly chest with every sentence, "In recent turns, the mission has been announced in this way. An enigmatic phrase or drawing is posted. Teams must figure out the what, where, and how of it before presenting it to the Elders."

"Thank you for your brilliant assessment, Rhaeg," Breena scoffed, still irritated with her friend for scolding her. Rhaegar rolled his eyes, one side of his mouth quirking.

Breena scrunched her nose at him, looking at the ground, fidgeting with the hem of her tunic.

She lifted her chin, rubbing her forehead and looking at me with more gentleness than she was accustomed to. "Ryn-Ryn, what's going on?"

I took a deep breath, looking around to make sure no one else was within earshot. "I've been having dreams all week about that flower. Among other things."

"Excellent, that gives us a leap ahead. Tell us more as we head to the musty place with the old books."

"Indeed," I mumbled, making sure not to wince at the word "leap".

"Research time?" Kaden asked, wrapping his arm around my waist.

"Research time," I confirmed, one corner of my mouth lifting.

As we entered the library, Mr. Burlam was puttering around his desk as usual. "Never can stay away on your days of rest, eh?" he grumbled without the usual bite.

I approached his desk as Breena, Rhaegar, Kaden, and Letti went to the stacks. "Never, Mr. Burlam. I wouldn't want you to miss me too much."

One side of his bushy mustache twitched. He brushed bent fingers over his nose as if it was an itch and not the beginning of a smile that bothered him. He huffed, looking at me. "What is it then? Be off bothering your sword-swinging friends, why don't you?"

"Ah, Mr. Burlam, but I thought you might have some insight —a man as sensible and clever as you."

"Get on with it," he mumbled after a moment, placing his reading spectacles on top of the papers on his desk.

I described the flower and meadow from my dream. As I did, his thick eyebrows raised, making me realize how big his gray-blue eyes were when he wasn't scowling.

"Of course I've heard of the Mirage Orchid, girl. It's the rarest flower in all the realms. Said to have Ancient-gifted ember, but not a soul has seen one in over a century. Did you go through primary education, girl? My Ancients, future generations are doomed."

"Thank you for the information, Mr. Burlam. I knew you wouldn't lead me astray." I tapped his desk, turning to return to the others.

"Wait, girl. Is this part of that nasty game the Elders do every Dormancy? Those flowers—if they exist—are said to be guarded by vicious monsters somewhere past the veil." He puckered his lips, a puff of air from his nose rustling his mustache hairs.

"Aw, Mr. Burlam. You really do care. Never fear. I'll have my sword-swinging friends and my new dagger." I winked, patting Morpheus' blade strapped to my waist, and walked away, leaving Mr. Burlam sputtering.

I settled next to Kaden, updating the group as Xeni found us. She took a seat next to Letti. "In my dream, a creature stalked me through the meadow." I left out the part about the Larkin brothers falling off the cliff.

"Wonderful. Always love meeting new monsters that might tear us apart," Kaden grumbled. I rested my hand on his knee.

Xeni scratched her chin. "As a child, I heard tales of this flower. It's rumored to possess immense power, but the stories about its capabilities are inconsistent. Alette and I can look into it more while you prepare for your journey." She pulled the books closer to her on the table as Letti nodded. Xeni paused, pursing her lips, her brow dipping. "I've never come across the meadow you described, but I have only been on a few missions beyond the veil. Hale?"

Rhaegar shook his head. "If this Mirage Orchid is along a cliff, we should explore along the coast through the Reverie Weald."

"Brilliant. We leave tomorrow." Breena smacked her hand on the table, causing Letti to jump in her chair and grimace. Xeni put her arm around my sister, rubbing her shoulder.

Kaden leaned back in his chair; his arms crossed across his chest. "On to the next adventure."

My lips scrunched together as my hand left Kaden. I tucked some curls back and then rubbed my palms against my skirt as I thought about my recurring nightmare. My jaw set, fingers curling into fists.

I wouldn't let anything happen to Kaden. Or Gavrel.

We'd find the orchid and then compete in the remaining Winnowing Trials. There was no other option.

A sense of determination flowed through me as I stood, piling volumes in my arms out of habit. I noticed some other competitors trickling into the library. "Let's put these away and get on with it. We have a head-start ... for now." I nodded to our opponents.

Kaden followed me to the stacks as Breena and Rhaegar went to reshelve their books. Letti and Xeni delved into their tomes. I was grateful for their help.

Kaden took a book from me as I struggled to return it. He slid it onto the higher shelf and then adjusted my hair out of the way so he could place a warm kiss on my neck.

"Wanting to recreate our first kiss, huh?" His hands ran around my waist, hugging my hips.

I turned in his hands, leaning against the shelves and bracing my palms against his chest. "Of course, Mr. Larkin. But we have a quest to prepare for." I smiled, stretching up to kiss him.

His chest rumbled as he pressed his firm body into mine. "Fuck the quest." He wrapped his fingers around my backside and pressed his lips onto mine hard. As if he couldn't get close enough.

I pushed against his chest, smirking. "I'd love to continue this, but we need to prepare for tomorrow."

He sighed, resting his forehead on mine. "You're right. But that doesn't mean I like it. I wish we didn't have to go find this damned flower."

"Me neither, but we're all in now. Let's make the best of it." I snapped my fingers, my eyebrows rising. "If you play nice—I'll let you share my tent."

He let go of me, grinning as we made our way out of the library. "Now that's a quest I can get behind."

21

BEYOND THE VEIL

"Only two tents?" Breena grumbled.

"The less to carry, the better," Rhaegar responded, shifting a rucksack on his shoulder. A wicked battle axe was strapped to his back, its blade glinting in the shafts of light sprinkling through the tree canopy.

"I know, but you snore. Ah, perhaps I can share with Kaden." She wiggled her eyebrows.

"Uh, I'm spoken for." Kaden chuckled, fiddling with the baldric across his chest, his sword hilt bobbing behind his back.

"Bollocks. Sharing is caring. Right, Ryn?"

A snort escaped me as Kaden huddled closer, his hand clinging to the thigh of my black trousers. I tapped my finger against my lips. "Hmmm. Let's see if he misbehaves and revisit the sleeping situation."

"How dare you," Kaden gasped. "I'll have you know that I plan on misbehaving"—He swatted my bottom—"*and* sleeping in your tent."

Rhaegar swung his head side to side, a small smile playing over his lips, and a whoop of laughter fell from Breena. I grinned, stretching on the toes of my ankle boots to kiss him on the cheek, but he turned quickly and met my lips with his.

"Up ahead." Rhaegar tipped his chin forward.

All morning, we had traveled along the edge of the coastal cliff. Little critters frolicked or flew out of our way as we hiked through the woods. Ahead of us, the veil swayed and glittered. A quick intake of breath raced through my nose.

"Well, that's fecking impressive." Breena jogged ahead, her rucksack bouncing.

As we reached the boundary, Kaden grabbed my hand, holding it tightly. To our left, waves churning and crashing against the sea cliff mimicked the trepidation rolling through me.

I looked at each of them, nodding, and we stepped through. The familiar energy in my scar vibrated, and heat swept through my body. All our eyes were glowing brightly, little beads of swirling light stuck to our clothing.

Breena's mouth was agape, her fingers fluttering over the tiny orbs as they leaped off our bodies and back into the twinkling shroud. She spun, laughing, as the sparkling air twirled around her, the moss illuminating where she danced.

She paused, the glow in her eyes—in all our eyes—fading. "Is this what you see all the time, Seryn?" She slid her finger over a nearby tree, its glimmer following her touch.

"Not exactly. I see auras of living things when I want or when they're feeling all the feels." I shrugged. "This place is something else. The colors are insane and the sparkles—so many sparkles." I spun one finger through the glittering air, and Breena smiled bemusedly, watching as it frolicked.

Breaking our trance, Rhaegar walked forward. "Shall we? We've got a lot of ground to cover."

"We shall," Breena agreed, putting her arm through his elbow.

We didn't get far before a disembodied rasping voice flitted through my mind.

Little Staaar.

A shiver ran over me, and I gritted my teeth, shoving my hands through my curls.

"Gran?" Breena murmured, her eyes glassing over as she tried to pull away from Rhaegar.

I grabbed her forearm before she had the chance to wander. "Steady yourself, Breena. It's a mare wyrm."

Kaden drew his sword, rolling his shoulders back, his jaw set square. He marched toward the creature's call, his biceps tense and fist clutching the hilt of his weapon.

Breena struggled against her friend, trying to run forward and calling for her grandmother. When she cursed at him and went for her curved daggers, the warrior dropped his rucksack with a sigh. Around it, moss lit up as it landed. Then, Rhaegar picked her up by the waist and positioned her wriggling body over his shoulder.

"You bloody bastard! Unhand me!" Breena yelled.

He nodded toward Kaden, and I drew my dagger, trailing after him. She needed to see the beast to understand better that it wasn't her loved one, just its cruel power playing tricks.

As we approached, Rhaegar set Breena down, barring one enormous arm around her to keep her in place as she reached her arms out and cried, "No!"

Kaden strode up to the Void creature and, without hesitation, stabbed through its belly. I winced at the sight of my mother being impaled but lifted my chin as her image quickly morphed into that of a gelatinous leech writhing and screeching.

As it slumped to the ground, Breena calmed, falling limp in Rhaegar's arms. He released her, and she smoothed her hands over her red tunic and trousers. She scrubbed her hands over her face, huffing. "So, those are the fecking worst."

I rested my hand on her shoulder. She was still a bit rattled, but probably wouldn't admit it. It wasn't pleasant seeing someone you loved being hurt.

"I'll be fine. Let's move." She put her hand on top of mine and dipped her head, blowing out a breath. After a moment, she walked away with Rhaegar to gather his rucksack.

Kaden came to me and wrapped me in his arms. Calming myself, I buried my face in his chest, breathing him in. My pulse slowed as the image of my mother faded. I looked up, kissing him on the jaw and rubbing my hands up and down the sides of his waist. "You did well. You okay?"

He kissed me on my forehead and nodded, jaw clenching. I couldn't imagine what it had been like for him to stab what looked like his mother. But I knew Kaden, and I was sure his heart was crumbling at the edges even if he wouldn't admit it. I put one hand on him, gently sliding my thumb over his cheek.

Breena and Rhaegar returned, and we continued our journey.

We walked for hours with no sign of the meadow. The sun was dipping low, shades of magenta and orange coloring the forest.

As we entered a small clearing, Rhaegar said, "This will be good for tonight. Let's set up camp before sundown."

Breena and Rhaegar worked fluidly, each moving around the other in a silent dance, completing tasks without talking as if they'd done it a hundred times.

It didn't take long before we had a small fire going.

"What do you know about the trials?" Kaden asked the warrior as I settled between his thighs, leaning against his chest. He adjusted the thin blanket we shared over my legs.

Rhaegar reclined against a log next to Breena. "It's typically variations of combat tasks against your opponents or beasts. There have also been tests of endurance, strength, and ember. Different every turn, so I wouldn't try to set expectations.

However, working together and utilizing each of our strengths will have the best outcome." He bent forward, poking the fire with a long stick, sparks flying.

"Dream team right here." Breena laughed, waving one hand in a circle at each of us. Rhaegar smiled, the flames reflecting in his dark eyes.

"Have you ever competed before?" I asked.

"Not since I've been Gavrel's second. And before this," he said, holding up his tattooed hand, the silver ink blinking in the firelight against the deep, rich color of his skin, "recollections elude me, naturally."

"What's different this time around?" Kaden asked, leaning his chin on my shoulder.

The warrior held the stick in the flames, the end smoldering. "A turn's supply of rations will help many. If that were the prize in the past, I would've participated. Alas, Ancients know I've never been gifted with such spoils. Otherwise, my family's story may have been different." He tossed the stick into the fire, leaning back and watching it burn.

He hadn't mentioned his family much, but when he did over the last few months, it was clear that they were no longer in the mortal plane. He'd shared stories about his sister and how she'd become ill when they were young and didn't have the nourishment required to bounce back.

I wrapped my arms around my middle, my eyelids shuttering against a rush of sympathy mingled with dread. Kaden embraced me.

I couldn't fathom Letti being taken away from me, especially due to her basic needs not being met. But I understood losing someone you loved. I rubbed my chest, trying to soothe the ache spurred by Rhaegar's heartbreaking history.

If he felt anything similar to the unshakable, prickling grief I had experienced, he didn't need words right now. It was a constant companion whispering to our hearts. So, I stayed silent, as did the others, letting the peace we were blessed with tonight offer solace. At least, in this moment.

Tomorrow would be a new story. I glanced up, wishing upon the glittering stars peeking between the leaves that we all made it safely through this journey.

We stayed up for a bit, caught in silent memories and the bonfire's crackling flames before sleep beckoned. Breena and Rhaegar claimed the first watch, so Kaden and I bid them good night as we retired to our tent.

I settled on the bedroll, snuggling into Kaden. He curled his arm over my waist, pulling my back into his front. His warmth sunk into me, and I sighed—a welcome, dreamless sleep quickly overtaking me.

My body was swathed in a stifling heat. I groaned and shifted, trying to free myself from it. *Is there a rock digging into my backside?* A particularly stimulating moan flitted across my ear. My eyes flew open, adjusting to the early morning dimness.

Not a rock.

Kaden's fingers burrowed under my tunic, rubbing my belly as he pressed his hard length into me. A sleepy smile slipped across my lips, and I pushed back, enjoying the sensual sounds he made in his half-asleep state.

His gravelly chuckle vibrated into my back. "I see *you're* the one misbehaving, Ms. Vawn."

"Are you going to make me share a tent with Breena?"

"Only if you stop what you're doing."

I smirked, grinding my bottom into him. He growled, slipping his hand along my skin, shoving my tunic and linen breastband over my chest as he cupped one heavy breast. A small moan fled my lips.

He kissed my shoulder and then nipped it. "Hush now. Unless you want our friends to hear."

My hips moved faster, and I bit my lip in an attempt to keep quiet. He stifled his sounds of need, his biceps straining as he left my breast and slowly skimmed down my stomach. His fingers slipped under my trousers and underwear, two skilled fingers circling the needy nub at my apex.

I gasped, feeling how slick my skin was against his.

"That's it, sweeting. You're so wet for me." His teeth slid over my earlobe, and I reached my hand behind me to cling to his neck, my nails digging into his skin and hair.

He thrust two fingers into my core, and I started to cry out before he bent his upper body toward me. I turned my head, my mouth meeting his so he could ravish my lips and swallow my moans.

My whole body quaked as he pumped his fingers in and out, his thumb twirling and pressing against my throbbing clit.

I tried to be quiet.

I really did.

But it was too much when he bit my bottom lip and dragged his teeth over it.

A garbled whimper flew from me as I exploded around his fingers. He grunted, thrusting into me one last time, his cock expanding.

"Damn it, woman. When I'm with you, I'm an inexperienced fledgling." He chuckled, adjusting himself as I sat up and righted my clothes.

"Aw. How I pity you."

"As you should." He curled over by me while still lying on his side and bit one round cheek. I squealed, scurrying away.

He added, "I'm lucky I have an extra pair of breeches, you saucy wench."

"Wonderful. Time to put them on so we can take the second watch."

He grumbled as he did so, his large body bumping into the top of the tent the entire time.

Breena met me outside. "Well, well, well. Sounds like someone had a *pleasant* awakening."

A ruddy warmth swept over me, all the way to my hairline. I swatted her arm as I looked around our camp. "Any trouble last night?"

She grinned, "Unfortunately, no. All was quiet in fairyland."

"Love to hear it. Enjoy your sleep."

"Oh, I will," she said, stretching her arms and yawning.

She wiggled her eyebrows at Kaden. He smiled as we sat near the extinguished fire.

I nibbled on a piece of jerky I'd brought and offered some to Kaden. Between his teeth, he took the small bite I held, running his lips over my fingertips.

Coughing, I shifted on the log and pressed my thighs together as he smirked. It would be several hours before daybreak, and we were on high alert now that we'd gotten some sleep.

Hyperaware of our surroundings, every sound made me jump. We'd gotten lucky so far—but with various Void creatures wandering around and possibly opponents, our luck was bound to run out.

The Reverie Weald was equally mesmerizing in the dark as it was in the day—embered air and flora shimmered in a moonlit display as if the stars were dancing among us. Every step brought about an incandescent glow that whispered over the touched surfaces.

After several hours, the pink rays of the rising sun consumed the moonbeams, stealing into the shadows.

My head drooped. As my eyelids fluttered, something pinched the tender skin of my backside. "Bloody void!" I yelped, jerking forward.

Kaden leaped off the log, twirling, his sword ready. "What the—"

I spun around, my hand rubbing my bottom. "Something poked—"

Out of the corner of my eye, a flurry of kaleidoscopic colors whizzed by. A burst of air swooshed past my right cheek, my curls stirring against my skin. My attention snapped to the side, but only coiling sparkles lingered.

Kaden jumped, swatting one hand at his shaggy hair, his sword clattering to the ground.

Breena's head popped out from her tent, yawning. "What's the ruckus?" She rubbed her eyes before lurching forward as Rhaegar tumbled out behind her.

"Blasted pixies!" he shouted, his bulky frame wriggling on the glowing moss beneath him. A frenzied blur of shimmering movement bounced on his stomach. When he whipped his hands toward it, the glowing shape zoomed into his forehead, knocking him back.

I swore I heard a tinkling titter as a trail of luminescence rushed away from him and then vaulted off Breena's nose.

A strand of my hair was tugged from my scalp. "Ow!"

Kaden and the others were flailing around, cussing, and slapping at the space around them. Another flash of shifting colors whizzed by my face.

A snarl of frustration shot from me, and I stomped my foot. My hands snapped out in annoyance, iridescent energy sizzling from my scar. It rocketed over my body and flared as I bellowed, "Enough!"

Everyone froze, looking at me with wide eyes and mouths gaping.

Rhaegar sprawled on the earth; one arm extended as he gripped a wriggling, winged creature between his thumb and forefinger while another yanked on the toe of his boot.

Breena knelt, her suspended hand clutching a chunk of her dark hair as another twinkling beastie pulled the end of it.

Kaden stood, his arms limp as he stared at me. Two glimmering sprites tugged at each of his ears, their tiny squeaks of exertion streaking through the silence.

With its fisted hands on its waist, a pixie—as Rhaegar had called the little fiends—materialized in front of me, four lucent wings flapping like a hummingbird. A frenzied swirl of splintered, rainbow-like hues gleamed around its figure, which was no bigger than my hand. With each puff of air, wispy white hair fluttered around its shoulders. With a seafoam green complexion, its features—neither feminine nor masculine—were strangely humanoid except for pointed ears and a flattened nose, which comprised two narrow slits in the center of its face. One of its light eyebrows cocked, copper eyes glowering.

My mouth twisted, my glare narrowing. I mirrored its stance and thrust my knuckles upon my hips. "If you would be so gracious—please call off your friends."

The little beast huffed and crossed its arms over its chest. Then it stuck its tiny, jade-colored tongue out.

"Now," I insisted, allowing my gift to flicker and ripple over my body in warning.

It flinched, squeaking and showing its palms to me. Turning its head, but keeping one metallic eye trained on me, the pixie let loose a string of anxious chirps. The others ceased their mischief and gathered around their leader with tilted heads, ogling me warily.

Rhaegar sat up, scratched his jaw, and grunted, "Well, I'll be …"

The corners of my mouth tipped up, my aura dissipating. "Thank you." I bowed to them, an idea weaving through my mind. "Would you happen to know where a meadow of giant flowers dwells?"

Furtive glances were shared between the winged troublemakers. Nervously, one pixie stabbed a finger in the direction catercorner to the coast, its bottom lip trembling. The group began to twitter anxiously as if scolding the defector, flitting around the creature and pulsing with light.

My brows rose as I glanced at Kaden, my fingers steepling in front of a barely contained smirk. His eyebrows rose, eyes twinkling with amusement.

Breena hoisted herself up, taking a few steps in the direction the pixie had indicated. She began to look toward me, but then her gaze snapped back as she withdrew her daggers and dashed off into the woods.

"Damn it, woman," Rhaegar grumbled as he followed her, battle axe in hand. In the distance, the glow of footsteps lingered upon the moss where someone or something had spied on us from behind a gnarled tree, its bark's radiance still gleaming from where it was handled.

"You all right if I go with them? They might need help," Kaden asked, unsheathing his sword.

I nodded. "I'm fine here. Go ahead—I'll watch the camp."

Hesitating, Kaden pressed his lips together.

"Truly, I'll be okay. Go on."

He turned reluctantly, running after our friends.

The pixies suddenly stilled, hovering above my head, eyes unblinking. A grim line settled across the leader's mouth, and it darted this way and that in front of my face. I waved my hand, trying to shoo the creature away, but it clenched its fists and yanked on the collar of my tunic.

"Okay, okay. You want me to follow you?"

It chirped, beaming—exposing teeny razor-like teeth—and zoomed past my shoulder, the others following. As a unit, they zigzagged through the forest, and I followed behind at a brisk pace. Their energy trailed behind them like shooting stars leading the way.

We only moved for a few moments before they reared up,

circling above me. My neck strained to look at them before one swooped down, tugging one of my curls. "Hey!" I cried at the sharp sting. The little monster gave me a toothy grin before flying forward and landing on the outstretched hand of a young girl.

I blinked, my heart thumping. *Is this a trick? Another Void demon?*

The girl studied me with inquisitive, golden eyes, her aureate waves wisping in the twinkling breeze. She wore a simple gossamer dress that swept down to the moss, pooling around her feet in a puddle of white. She giggled, smiling fondly at the pixie sitting in her palm. "Much obliged, sweet one," she praised in a dulcet tone.

It looked at her adoringly before hugging her thumb and flitting away. The other pixies followed, scattering among the luminous flora in a flurry of multicolored streaks.

Without thought, I stepped back, resting my hand on the hilt of my dagger.

"I mean you no harm, Seryn," she said, her voice caressing me. I stiffened, head tilting to the side, eyes squinting.

"How do you know my name?"

"Let's just say I'm a friend. For countless turns, an encounter with you is something I've dreamed of. I dare say—you remind me of Maya."

22

THE DAWN DOES NOT FEAR THE NIGHT

Breath whooshed from my lungs as if I'd been punched, and I stepped forward. "What? How do you know my mother? Who are you? Aren't you, like, eight turns old?" The questions tumbled from me in quick succession, leaving me even more breathless.

If she had any information about my mother, I needed to know.

I'd take my chances.

What was one more risk in this Ancient-forsaken dreamland?

A kind smile spread across her ethereal face. "Here, come. I've got a gift for you." She reached her delicate hand toward me, a gentle smile pulling at the corners of her lips.

My boots moved of their own accord, my heart hammering. I ran my thumb over the faceted pommel of my weapon before curling my fingers around the cool metal of its hilt.

As I approached, the girl brought one hand to her other, fiddling with a black stone ring on her thumb. It seemed out of place, something midnight dark marring the pastel, otherworldly look of her.

An arm's length away, I paused, my lips pressing into a line. Her eyes softened, and she nodded, guiding her petite form upon a sizable, mottled rust-colored stone. There was another boulder next to her, and I sunk upon it slowly, keeping my senses alert for any sudden movement.

She shifted toward me, her eyes shining in the morning sun. "A gift from the Ancients," she spoke softly, her words chiming.

I gulped, stuttering, "I ... I don't understand."

Her hand rested on my shoulder, feather-light. A soft, gilded glow shimmered around her, the energy of it tingling against my skin. "It is as it always was. The Fates do as they please; it is not for us to question it."

My mouth pinched together for a moment, and I dragged in a breath, my ribs swelling with the force of it.

I was weary of the Fates. Fed up with people insisting that I shouldn't doubt them or question what my people endured each and every day.

If all they had time to do was play games, I didn't want any part of it.

The muscles in my limbs stiffened, and I lifted my chin. "The Ancients abandoned us long ago."

The girl shifted even closer to me. My feet stayed rooted to the earth. Maintaining steady eye contact, a small smile pushed into the corners of her mouth. Her features softened even further, her tone placating as she whispered, "They never left you, and to believe such is to surrender."

Bewildered, the subtle arches of my brows rose, my bottom lip and shoulders wilting. Where were the Ancients if they hadn't forsaken us? I rolled my eyes to the sky and then huffed. Cynicism kindled within as my eyebrows fell, and I lifted my frame from the boulder, straightening my spine.

She held out the ring, gently taking my hand and placing it in the palm. Its intricate design glinted—delicate, interlacing branches carved into tourmaline.

My skin hummed where it touched, the feel of it substantial. I breathed in, rubbing the sleek, wide edge of it with the tip of my index finger. A slow, deep throb stroked under my scar in wave-like laps. The sides of my mouth dipped as insistent shadows of recognition prodded at the corners of my mind.

"You must not, under any circumstances, give it to another. It is yours and yours alone. Do you understand?" Her face settled into a grave urgency, hinting at mysteries well beyond her turns.

"Yes, but—"

"The dawn does not fear the night. For it knows both light and shadow are needed—the balance protected." The white of her eyes disappeared as the liquid metal of her pupils took over, swirling. "It simply waits for its moment before rising. Always persevering, freeing the darkness. Persevere, Belladonna."

I huffed, my fingers clenching around the tourmaline. "What does that—"

"Heed your terminus." She tipped her head to the ring. "For a safe passage."

"What the—"

"Seryn!" Kaden's panicked bellow startled me, and I jolted toward his voice, my hair whipping around my cheeks.

"I'm here!" I called, slipping the ring over my left forefinger. It warmed against my skin as the pulsing in my neck settled. Contented.

I turned to where the girl had been sitting, but only a shimmering eddy of air remained. An exasperated sigh fell to the moss as I shook my hands, relieving the tension coursing through the ligaments. These days, doubt and confusion were my constant companions.

Kaden met me as I moved toward him. His face pinched, and he took a deep breath, probably to scold me, but words spilled from me in a rush before he got the chance. "I know, I know. I'm sorry. The pixies wanted me to follow them ... There was a little girl." I waved my hands in the air as I spoke, thrusting my pointer finger out. "Well, not young. Not really. She gave me this ring; said it was a gift from the Ancients ... And a lot of other things that made no sense," I muttered.

"Uh ..." The slashes of his brows met above the bridge of his nose, his mouth tucking between his teeth.

My shoulders lifted, one hand following them, palm up, my lips twisting.

"Well, I suppose we'll see what this bobble can do at some point." He smiled, grasping my hand and running a thumb over the ring. "I'm just happy you're safe. Also, you're adorable when flustered." His grip squeezed mine, and my cheeks burned as I puffed them out with an exhale.

"Rhaegar said those pixies are from the forest—not the Nether Void. I'm not sure I believe him," He chuckled, rubbing one ruddy ear lobe as we returned to camp.

"That's the end of our head-start," Breena grumbled, angrily spinning the fabric of a tent in a messy ball around her forearms. The linen kept flopping all over the place, and she groaned before throwing it to the ground.

I picked up the shelter, folding it and rolling it into a compact bundle. "What did you find?"

Breena grunted, and Rhaegar smirked, filling me in. "It was one of our opponents from Sebille's team. He's been tracking us. It was a smart move if they suspected we had any idea of where we were going. Would've gotten more information out of him, but Breena scared him off." One eyebrow arched as he glanced at her from his peripheral.

"Not my fault he's afraid of some light-hearted coercion."

"So, that's what we're calling it nowadays? Threatening to slice his jugular and waving your blade around?" Rhaegar's bark of amusement echoed through the trees as he shook his head and worked on packing things into his rucksack.

Breena's nostrils flared, and she whipped around, her stick-straight hair twirling. She began ramming things into her pack, emphasizing each thrust with a huff.

For the rest of the day, we continued our journey, so near the coast that I could hear the waves of the Insomnis Sea hurling against the cliff face. I empathized with the beaten crag—each fruitless hour was a lashing to the wall of hope I'd built around myself. My mind and confidence were battered mush.

The sun crested above the tree canopy, its smoldering peach-colored rays painting the leaves.

I swallowed, my stomach grumbling.

When we reached a long bend along the coastline, I tugged on the hem of Kaden's tunic and then shifted my bag on my shoulders. He looked over, and I nodded to a nearby tree near the stony precipice, retrieving some bread from my rucksack. He informed the others it was time for a break.

I slumped to the ground, leaning against the bark, its ember warming my skin through my dark clothing. The ocean was relentless, waves tumbling into the horizon. Peaking. Breaking.

I dropped my head into my hands, chewing on the bread. Kaden quietly sat next to me on my right, the sea breeze ruffling his shaggy hair around his ears.

"We'll find it, Ser."

"Your confidence knows no bounds," I said, a wry chuckle trapped within my chest.

Kaden sighed, rubbing his palm on the top of my thigh. I lifted my head, resting it against the tree as I looked at him. "I'm sorry. I feel like a disappointment. I want to win those rations so badly. To find this damned flower."

"I know. Don't ever apologize for feeling." His hand lightly squeezed. "You are not a disappointment. We wouldn't have come this far without you. If we push forward along this coast, we are bound to find it. Hopefully sooner rather than later." He smirked then, running his hand through his thick, black waves.

I watched as a particularly stubborn strand flopped back

over his brow. His lips had a certain curl at the sides, his dimple peeking out. Seeing this, I knew he was about to be ridiculous. "I also wouldn't have come in my breeches—in a tent of all places—without you."

"Kade!" I slapped the back of my hand on his chest, my face flushing. A hoot of laughter pushed from my throat. The tension within my body deflated as I settled, the wind stroking and cooling my cheeks.

He was right, though ... about the orchid. We had to keep going.

Out of the corner of my eye, neon pink flickered among the green. My heart skipped a beat as I jolted to my feet, using Kaden's shoulder for balance.

He thrust his hand into the moss, bracing himself against the force of my movement. "Woah—no need to get in a tizzy. It happens to a lot of men."

"What?"

"Well, when a man *really* enjoys a woman—"

I glanced at him briefly, rolling my eyes and cupping my palm against his warm lips. My feet brought me closer to the edge as I tried to get a better view across its huge, curving bend.

There, in the distance—partially hidden behind a vibrant shrub, its pearly magenta mirberries gleaming—was a tall, pink flower swaying in the breeze. A few steps beyond that was another but with bright-yellow petals. And then another. My gaze followed the line of flowers as if they were lookouts leading the way.

I waved my hand behind me, absently trying to get everyone's attention. I tapped Kaden's head, pointing when he looked up. "Uh, the meadow."

Breena ran over, gawking at the flowers. "Fecking void, woman. I think you're right."

Rhaegar stopped next to us, drawing his battle axe. "If that is

OF WITHERING DREAMS

your meadow, we'd best be prepared for whatever beast guards it."

Kaden stood, brushing off his trousers, and then sighed, readying his sword.

Leaving our supplies nestled between the trees, we hastened forward, renewed vigor nipping at our heels. We reached our destination within fifteen minutes. A breathy, relieved laugh dropped to my feet as we approached the bloom. I ran my fingertips over its rigid, silky petals, each one as big as my hand.

"Well done, you beautiful, beautiful bird." Breena laughed, smacking a loud kiss on my cheek as we moved forward.

We followed the flowers until more of them scattered among the trees. Soon, a sprawling meadow lay before us, shades of pink and yellow dancing in the shimmering wind.

"This is it," I murmured. I gulped, wiping my hands on my tunic and clutching the hilt of my sheathed dagger. My ember vibrated just below the surface in anticipation.

"Where was the Mirage Orchid in your dream?" Kaden asked, shifting closer to me.

"It was near the very edge. To the right, where these flowers meet the stone." I pointed to the general area in the distance where the slick black stone marked the edge of the meadow like a jagged ink stain.

Scanning the intimidating expanse before us, my pulse quickened, and my breaths became more shallow. I clenched my eyes, thinking of the end goal. Thinking of everyone we could help if we succeeded.

Letti.

I pushed my shoulders back, running my thumb over the cool metal in my hand. My thoughts drifted as I tried to distract myself from spiraling emotions.

Letti and Xeni had found little information about the Mirage Orchid, but what they had sounded impossible. I shook my head, curls dancing around my shoulders.

Not as impossible as everything else I've been through.
As me dreaming of this exact place.

My cheeks scrunched, crinkling my closed lids. Mr. Burlam had been right; this orchid was the rarest in existence. Letti and Xeni had learned that a single bud bloomed every half century or so, shedding in the winter months. Aside from its rarity, it was also temperamental—sometimes, it refused to blossom, and one could only harness its power by using fallen petals. Legend said it could reverse an embered curse upon your mind or body.

If it hadn't flowered in over a century, it was no wonder the Elders wanted it. Mystical attacks were not reversible ... unless you were an Ancient. But even so, our history detailed the consequences to anyone—even celestial beings—for intervening in the Fates' plans.

To nobody's shock—it was never pleasant.

"Fecking scheming trackhounds," Breena growled. My eyes snapped open, darting to where the curve of her dagger's blade pointed.

Far to the right, in the middle of the field, several of our opponents spilled from the trees, Sebille and her team among them. There looked to be about twenty of them, perhaps less. It was hard to tell with the flowery heads swaying up to their shoulders and chins.

Sebille whispered something to her team, and they stayed back as the others lumbered forward, shoving stems out of their way, crunching the flora without abandon.

"Those idiots. They're making too much noise," Kaden snarled, sweat gathering on his brow.

Rhaegar stepped forward, his sword rising. "They are, indeed. Whatever is protecting the orchid will surely find—"

All at once, several people collapsed, slicing a jagged line down the center of the throng. As they disappeared under the towering plants, screams of terror rent the air. Horrified cries and gasps tore from those nearest to the fallen, heads whipping this way and that, as if something was brushing past them, bending and cracking the shoots sharply as it went.

Sebille raised her sword, preparing to charge forward. Her three team members froze, one dropping his weapon and the other two shaking their heads and then fleeing back into the forest. She screeched, "You cowardly mouth-breathers!" at them before rushing into the fray. The third man stiffened, petrified where he stood next to his dropped blade.

"Let's go. Skirt around the edges while it's distracted," Rhaegar commanded. "Slow and steady. Quietly as you can."

We followed him, gently moving, nudging stalks out of our way, eyes glued to the group on the other side. People were still flailing.

Crumpling.

Shrieking.

Stabbing at whatever was attacking them.

A hazy, twinkling cloud of cinder billowed around the mass of our opponents as their astral bodies were destroyed. Banished to the Stygian Murk.

My pulse thrashed within my chest, and I felt it—*everywhere*.

My neck, my temples. My scar. Wrists. Under the skin of my ring. It was as if I were made of a single, giant muscle whose only purpose was to pound a hole into the earth.

The screaming ceased all at once as the cinder dimmed, its dust sprinkling over a still meadow.

"Bloody void," Kaden swore.

As I gulped and then sucked in a deep lungful of air, the toe of my boot stepped into a deep crevice. My body flew forward, and I yelped. Across the meadow, I glimpsed the flowers as they trembled, the ash being tossed off the petals.

Rapidly, I fell, and my aura skittered over me as my hands flew out to break the impact, my dagger still clutched in my palm.

It was as if time unraveled—my descent in slow motion. My

ember zipped over my arms, the branch-like patterns glowing over them. The tourmaline ring burned as if it was branding itself onto my finger.

My eyes squeezed tight. And then, as I nearly slammed into the ground, a bright snap of light burst and engulfed me.

I was an orb, condensing and twisting and churning, with a body made of fractured rainbows and mist—splitting through time and place. My mind tore apart. Through a coiling tunnel of flashing colors and radiant streaks, my being hurtled.

With another burst of brightness, my form plopped onto solid ground.

I gagged, not able to get enough air, but then wheezed, breath tearing through my throat. Coughing, I rolled onto my hip and then liberated the boiling sick within my gut. I wiped my mouth with my trembling hand, glaring at the sculpted ring as it cooled, my aura shivering and sinking within me.

The neon flowers loomed over me, mocking me with their swaying splendor. I threw my hand down and met an unyielding, smooth surface. I gasped, scooting away from whatever I had smacked.

My brows furrowed as I beheld a sizable golden egg. It gleamed in the shifting rays sneaking through the heads of the flowers. *It must belong to the beast*, I thought, frantically listening for any sounds approaching. Only the whishing of leaves met me.

Sheathing my dagger, I slowly stood, my guts still roiling from—*what? Transporting through time and space?*

Oh, my fucking Ancients.

My shoulders stooped as I peeked over, scanning my surroundings. Kaden, Breena, and Rhaegar were across the vast field. The ring had transported me to the opposite side, near the cliff's brink, where the meshed Larkin brothers had fallen in my dream. Which meant I might be near the orchid.

My eyes were drawn to the clearing between us as the stalks

separated in a swerving line, the flora trembling and swishing as the orchid's protector scraped past them.

Without much thought, I whimpered, scooping up the gilded egg. It was warm as I wrapped both arms around it, hands clasping on opposite wrists.

I dashed toward the exposed, glossy stone ledge, hollering loudly as I ran, "Over here! Look what I have! Come on, you fiend!"

My team waved their arms frantically, and I suspected they were cussing and cursing me to the Nether Void for what I was doing. I didn't let that stop me, though.

I planted my feet on the black rock as I stumbled from the meadow, the rigid leaves snagging the fabric of my clothes.

"Shut up, you fool," a rasping voice hissed. I immediately drew my dagger as I spun around, balancing the egg in one arm. Whatever was inside wiggled and shifted, the shell twitching.

The female Draumr emerged, her sword aimed directly at me, glinting in the sunlight.

"Sebille, wait." I held up my dagger with only my thumb and forefinger, the other fingers stretching wide in concession. "We need each other in this moment."

"I don't need you ... or anyone, you vapid imbecile." She had an excellent vocabulary. I'd give her that. She glared down her slightly hooked nose, gesturing with her blade's tip at the egg. "What do you have there?"

It was true that I had used it to divert its beastly mother from attacking my friends. From the corner of my vision, I didn't notice any further movement, so I suspected it had worked ... for now.

My other truth was that I didn't wish any harm to befall the innocent, unborn offspring. There was too much suffering as it was without hurting other living beings who were just trying to survive—like all of us.

I took a tentative step back.

"Ah, no, you don't." She followed as I took another stride. And another. "Halt, or I will impale you right through that damned egg. I swear it."

I believed her, but there was no other option. She would most likely impale me if I stayed where I was, or the creature would make itself known. I didn't want to linger when it did.

As I reached back once more with the heel of my boot, it caught a jagged piece of stone. The unwieldy vessel shifted in my arm, the movement upsetting my balance.

My dagger dropped with a clatter as I tripped, my bottom slamming into the ground. Wincing from the pain, I swung my arm around, clasping my wrists together again, ensuring the cocooned creature was protected.

My nose scrunched as I attempted to focus, my eyes peering through Sebille's shoulder-width stance. A quick intake of breath filled my chest because there it was—the Mirage Orchid—just as I had dreamed it.

23

BLOOD AND REBELLION

It proudly stood against the backdrop of its brethren's inflexible stalks. The heartbreaking beauty of the tintless orchid stole my breath. For the first time in over a hundred turns, it had flowered—had chosen this moment to bless us with its otherworldly presence as it perched precariously close to the precipice.

Sebille lunged forward, breaking my trance. A menacing, low growl rumbled across the stretch of rock between the meadow's threshold and us. The towering flowers trembled as something moved closer to the edge. Sebille squeaked, freezing in place as I hugged the quivering golden egg closer.

The stems shivered and parted, and two flame-colored eyes scrutinized me, Sebille's outstretched sword threatening to skewer me and its bairn, and my hands protectively cradling the egg against my heart.

A puff of glittering air sucked into a pair of bulbous nostrils that sat atop a boxy, elongated snout. With a snarl, its breath billowed out, currents of sparkles frantically spinning about the air before it.

From the dark depths, the monster inched forward. Two

broad forelegs, each with three intimidating, dark claws, dug into the moss-covered stone before advancing further.

The creature was strangely beautiful and dreadfully fierce at once as it fully emerged from the edge of the meadow. My heart hammered when a hint of recollection flashed through my thoughts. I'd seen a rendering of this Surrelian being during my studies. Its existence was the stuff of frightening childhood bedtime stories.

A wyvern.

A long, serpentine body and tail propelled the beast forward, muscled forelimbs assisting its trajectory. As it came fully into view, a set of wings sprouted from its back, each as big as me. Silky, olive-green feathers covered them, blending into cerulean tips.

Suddenly, it stopped and rose, balancing on its midsection. It was as long as six adult humans stacked head to toe. With wings spread wide, it stirred the sparkling air around it. Lustrous indigo feathers encased the top of its massive form from the top of the reptilian head to a spade-shaped tail. The rest of its face and underbelly were covered in gilded scales the size of my hand.

Sebille shifted closer to me, her eyes fixed on the creature, her sword precariously close to the egg. The beast growled, baring pointed teeth.

I whimpered; my aura flickered over my body, no longer able to be contained. From my peripheral, the metallic hilt of my dagger glinted.

I scurried back, pushing against the stone with my boots. The movement caught the Draumr's attention, and she looked at me from the side of her eye, snarling, "Don't even think about it, Vawn."

A tiny crack split down the front of the egg, the incessant tapping from within becoming frantic. "I think we have bigger things to worry about right now. Pretty positive *that's* the mother."

I held my hand up, cradling the egg in one arm. Sebille squinted but nodded once as I shifted and gingerly set it to my right side.

The monster shuddered, feathers ruffling, as a snarl rumbled through its gullet, scaly lips quivering against razor-sharp teeth. The fissure widened, pieces of the gold shell flaking off.

A reptilian head poked out of the crevice, squeaking in victory, aqua-colored eyes blinking in the sun. Fluffy scarlet feathers fluttered atop its head as it clawed at its confines with stubby, golden-colored forelimbs.

"It's stuck," I murmured, reaching to help it break free.

"Don't you dare. It's one of them." Sebille nodded to the monster, slithering closer every second, her eyes fixated on it. "We have to kill it."

My hand crept past the newborn creature, reaching for my dagger—just out of reach—as I used the other hand to help the egg fracture further.

"No, Sebille—"

Within my next breath, everything happened at once.

Without warning, she turned, jabbing toward the egg as the little beast emerged, its teal wings unfolding.

The mother roared as its wings tucked against its body and raced toward us.

My fingers lunged, iridescent light flashing over them, beckoning to the matching liquefied mist within my dagger's crystal pommel. It heeded the call instantly, the diamond's swirling haze stilling and splendent as the weapon snapped through the air and into my palm. I swung it in an arch, blocking the sword's attack as I surged forward onto my knees.

Sebille's sword flew from her hand, the edge of her blade nicking my left forearm as I held it up to protect my body.

She fell back, screaming as fizzing liquid shot from the creature's maw, coating her shoulder and side.

The monster's massive tail whipped around, flinging Sebille aside as if she were rubbish. The warrior's body crumbled and rolled to the edge of the cliff, her leather armor and uniform bubbling and disintegrating where the poison spattered—her skin angry and curdling.

The creature's snout was inches from me. I set my dagger down slowly, holding my hands out in front of me. My ember shimmered, stroking over the wyvern's snout. "I mean no harm to you and your baby."

The mother's eyes squinted, a huff of air puffing from its nostrils and tossing my curls back.

Kaden, Breena, and Rhaegar stumbled out of the meadow, weapons drawn.

"Stay back," I demanded, my aura flaring. Thankfully, they listened, halting where they stood. They were too far away to reach me if the monster attacked anyway.

I leaned to my side slowly, gently picking at the shell, helping the newborn break free from the egg. I scooped up its wiggling form, needing both arms to hold it as it squirmed and licked my hands with a flat, black tongue. It was like trying to handle a squirming, floppy cat as I held it out. The baby mewled, sniffing and licking its mother's snout.

A purring rumble came from the monster's throat. It regarded me, shelf-like brows relaxing over its watchful gaze. It bowed its head to the ground, and I took that as my cue to step to the side tentatively, setting its baby on the mother's neck. Its downy feathers tickled my arms.

Shuffling back, I showed the beast my palms, my aura evaporating. Its wings ruffled, and a pointed tail flicked back and forth a couple of times before it veered toward where it came from, slipping away into the meadow with its newborn.

I let out the breath I'd been holding, wiping my hands on my trousers and then bending to pick up my dagger. Kaden and Breena ran to my side as Rhaegar went to check on Sebille.

Kaden pulled me into an embrace and then held me at arm's length away, inspecting my body. "Are you okay?"

"I'm fine."

"Holy monster shite, woman. I almost soiled myself." Breena sheathed her sword, swatting my arm as we went to Rhaegar and Sebille.

"She's alive. I'm not sure how deep the poison went," Rhaegar informed us.

"Here, let me try." Kaden knelt next to Sebille's motionless form. Aura shimmering, he held glowing hands over her back and shoulder. His brow furrowed as he closed his eyes in concentration.

Her exposed, raw skin bubbled as he worked, a milky substance seeping from the wounds. Once the poison was expelled, her skin slowly knit together. Kaden slumped, his energy waning. Through her ruined clothing and leather armor, all that was left of her injuries was shiny, thick scar tissue mottled with puckered ridges as if coated in melted candle wax.

"I suppose that's what she gets for threatening you," Breena muttered, propping her hand on her hips while studying the guard's injuries.

"Yikes, Breena," I scolded. Sebille was nasty, but I still wouldn't wish such harm on anyone.

"What? No one messes with my Ryn-Ryn and gets away with it." She shrugged, one side of her mouth quirking. I dipped my head, slightly swinging it from side to side, a muffled snort sneaking out as I touched her shoulder. She glanced at my arm. "You're bleeding, by the way."

"Ah, just a flesh wound." I shrugged.

I helped Kaden stand, securing my arm around his waist. He leaned into me, accepting the assistance. "So, you can transport, huh? Like Melina," he mumbled, putting a glowing hand on my cut. It sealed over in an instant.

I cringed, curling my fingers into my palms. "Now we know what the ring can do." I sighed, swallowing my unease, realizing that was why the ring was familiar ... because Melina had something similar.

"Once again, never a dull moment with you, my friend. That will come in real handy during the trials." Breena chuckled.

I clenched my jaw together, nodding once. "There's the damned orchid, by the way."

"That's just ... just phenomenal," Rhaegar murmured, crouching beside it. "It hasn't released any of its petals yet." He pressed his lips together, scrunching his brow before looking at Kaden. "Think your gift would help?"

"Let's find out." Kaden kneeled in front of the mystical flower, calling upon his ember, guiding it over its form. The orchid's aura flashed silver as Kaden's energy tried to commune with it. After a couple of moments, he pulled his power back, frowning. "That's a no. That thing is blocking me."

"Makes sense, considering its capabilities. Perhaps the orchid is immune to ember manipulation," Rhaegar said. Kaden and Rhaegar stood, similar looks of puzzlement lining their faces.

My scar vibrated as I regarded the bloom. I kneeled and couldn't help but run my fingertip gently over the dark stem. It was as if the flower was calling me, yearning for my touch. A glistening crimson drop ran down its shoot, pooling in the moss where the earth met rigid, gray leaves. I looked at my arm—the blood from my cut had dribbled down my ring and finger, depositing itself on the divine plant. I swiped my hand over my breeches.

A shiver ran down my spine and spread over my skin, goosebumps sweeping over the surface. The orchid quivered in response, its metallic aura sparkling around. Its bent stem bobbled momentarily, and then three petals released, floating to the moss. I scooped the precious gifts into my palm.

With a grin spreading wide across my mouth, I stood and presented our victory to my friends. I chortled, seeing their mouths hanging open, gently tucking the petals in my pocket. "Looks like you were right, Breena. We are the dream team."

WE CARRIED an unconscious Sebille out of the meadow, and fortunately, the three men from her team lurked among the trees. With sheepish looks galore, they vowed to get her back to safety.

Once we retrieved our supplies, I securely wrapped the petals in a small black leather pouch, positioning its long cord around my neck. It was daunting to think of the immense power I carried. It thrummed against my breastbone with every step.

Was it wise to hand over such a gift to the Elders? Over the last few months, my distrust of them had flourished. If I was honest with myself, I had been wary of them and the Dormancy for far longer. My thumb swept back and forth over the pommel of my dagger as my thoughts spun.

With their abilities nearly reaching celestial levels, I worried how the orchid would be used. I didn't believe for a moment that Melina, Lucan, or any of them would use it for the good of the mortal plane. I lifted my chin, stacking my spine, and took a deep breath.

"So, how do you all feel about handing these over to the Elders?" I lifted my necklace, letting it sway back and forth.

Breena puffed her cheeks, blowing a dramatic exhale from her lips. "I thought you'd never ask. I say—feck 'em."

Rhaegar chuckled, shaking his head as we walked.

Kaden rubbed his palm over the stubble lining his jaw, raising one brow. "You know what? I agree with Breena. Why should they have something so powerful when they already have such divine ember?"

Rhaegar's face fell as the last of his amusement dropped to the earth. "Do you not fear accusations of treason?"

"Rhaeg, you haven't told them?" Breena responded. My brows lifted, fingers dropping the necklace back in place. The warrior glared at her, his eyes flashing. The message was clear. And it was that he wanted her to shut up.

She did not. "Oh, bugger off. I'm appalled you haven't broached the topic already." He heaved a sigh, staring up at the forest canopy.

"So … do tell," Kaden encouraged, his voice raising an octave. His fingers pushed through his hair, his eyes going back and forth between Breena and Rhaegar.

"Oh, nothing much. Just a 'lil rebellion is all." Breena laughed, waving her hands through the air.

Kaden's mouth dropped and then snapped closed as he stood taller. "I'm in."

I smacked him on the chest. "What the void, Kade? You don't even know what she's talking about."

"I don't care. If it's to help Midst Fall and to stand against the Elders, I'm in."

Rhaegar sighed, "All right. Yes, there is a small network of like-minded people throughout the realm—those who agree that the Elder Laws and the Dormancy are unmerited. That the Elders abuse their power. If word gets out, you know what will happen."

"Like I said—I want in." Kade clapped a hand on Rhaegar's shoulder.

"Well, it won't matter anyway … you'll forget about this when the Dormancy ends," I added, looking at him as if he'd eaten a bug.

"That's where Rhaegar comes in. He won't forget and will communicate with you through our contacts," Breena countered, smiling smugly.

"Bloody void." I rubbed my sweaty palms down my tunic, the soft fabric itchy and stifling.

This expedition was unfolding in ways I never imagined. My mouth clamped shut for the rest of the journey. My thoughts distracted me, and I barely paid attention to Kaden or the others.

I gripped the leather pouch around my neck, stroking the soft leather. We agreed to hide the petals. I'd hide them somewhere deep in the library or perhaps in some shadowed cranny of the palace.

If none of the teams were successful during this Weeding, it was highly probable that they'd have to allow those who remained to compete. I'm sure they wouldn't want to upset the masses. Keeping the majority distracted and content seemed important to the Elders—at least while we were in Surrelia.

Melina and the others already held too much power. It wouldn't be an issue if I believed they had truly tried everything to help our world. But I suspected that they had not, and this nagging suspicion burned within every cell of my being. Something had felt off from the very start—I knew it in my gut. My ember constantly tried to communicate with me, but the answers were always just out of reach.

Was I ready to be a part of a rebellion? I ran my thumb over the ridges of my stone ring, thoughts whirling, trying to find the answers in shadowed corners.

It didn't surprise me that Kaden was all in. He was always more vocal about his aversion to the Elders.

Was this the right path to help Midst Fall?

There was too much information knocking around my skull. Too many fears. Too many truths bared. Too many doubts.

Just too much.

24

TOXIN AND TONIC

"Citizens! You see before you undeserving, disgraceful failures," Melina scorned, her singsong voice bouncing through the Great Hall. Half the crowd stood wordlessly, shifting their feet, suppressing looks of sympathy. The others, packed in the front, jeering, their faces twisting into wretched masks of contempt.

The control Melina and the Elders exerted over their flock left a foul taste on my tongue. My fingers dug into my pockets, my thumb pressing so firmly into my rune stone that the etching would surely leave an imprint. It was disheartening that my peers were so fickle—so easily maneuvered like puppets on oligarchic strings.

The other Elders were situated at the base of the stage. Gavrel, other Draumrs, and Akridais stood beside them lining the surrounding walls. My gaze fixated on the back of Gavrel's thick, ebony waves, his form still and unyielding. The dense muscles of his shoulders were tense, the dark fabric of his uniform straining across his back and biceps.

Blade-like, dark nails sliced through the air as she passed the surviving competitors, holding her palms up. She moved before the line of us on the platform, her snug dress shifting over her body like molten oil with each step. When she slinked past me, her smoky, powdered floral scent invaded my senses—like nightbloom roses and bitter almonds.

Or poison.

I had once read about a toxin that smelled similar to almonds. Sweet, woodsy, and acrid.

Deadly.

The muscles of my jaw flexed, and my tongue clamped precariously between my front teeth. I would never be able to tolerate the smell of roses or almonds again.

"Nevertheless, six teams have returned, and the tournament must go on." The horde cheered, and Melina raised her hand to silence them. I stared at the tourmaline ring on her thumb, my left hand curling around its counterpart in my pocket.

Her dainty nose sniffed with disdain as she glanced back at me. *She really doesn't suspect.* A wry smile pressed into the seam of my lips, holding in the secret. Our minor victory. Praise the Ancients for her lowly opinion of everyone. In her eyes, we were all worthless from the very start.

The Elders believed that we failed, barely escaping the Mirage Orchid's keeper by the skin of our teeth. I pictured the delicate orchid petals sandwiched between the pages of my beloved tome. The one that tumbled from the shelves in front of me on that first day in the library. *Ancient History: An Unabridged Bridge into Divine Yesterdays.*

My eyes met Letti's in the crowd—golden, hazel pools like Mama's. Concern etched on her angelic face. She was like the orchid. Resilient even when burdens pressed from all sides, trying to squash her. I yearned to have her confidence.

My eyes clamped shut, fists tightening around my ring and my talisman as Melina droned on. I was certain she loved the sound of her own voice.

What if there had been another way to defeat the decaying of our world—to delay the Withering? What if there still was?

Too much had been lost. Too much had been taken from those I cared about. Because of the Elders and their deals. The laws they implemented.

I thought of Rhaegar's sister.

Breena's grandmother.

Father.

Hestia Larkin.

Mama.

I could do this. I could figure out how to change Midst Fall for the better. Why should it be someone else and not me? Why should other people take risks while I drowned in my own worries, doing breathing exercises to avoid crippling panic? The good thing about breathing ... I could do it anywhere, even while snooping, scheming, stabbing—or whatever one did to topple unjust tyrants.

My eyelids snapped open, eyes like impenetrable ice, focusing on Melina. Her hand fell to her side, a false smile hanging off the tips of her incisors. "In a fortnight, the celebration ball will take place. After this, the final two trials—the Wilting and the Winnowing—are sure to entertain us all." She lifted a sharp chin, tossing her sleek hair behind her. "You'll be notified of the opportunity to choose formal regalia in the Great Hall—the only requirement is that you choose something in the same color as your current attire. Elder Law decrees such identification. Dismissed!"

She departed, accompanied by enthusiastic applause—without mentioning or offering condolences to the fallen competitors. My mouth pressed into a grim line, unsurprised.

With any luck, the Elders and their unjust rule would be ancient history one day soon. Maybe the Fates had already written it in the stars. If not, then *feck 'em,* as Breena would say.

My ember purred under my skin and through my sinew.

Yesterday's hesitations were whisked away—the soggy heft of them expelled. I bounced softly on the balls of my feet. Perhaps I could stomach a little rebellion after all.

"It's a shame, it is." Derya nonchalantly hung some fresh clothes in my pewter armoire, peeking at me from the side of her vision. Waiting for me to take the bait.

My eyes glinted, one eyebrow lifting. "Whatever do you mean?"

Her lips quivered as she struggled to hold back a smile. She spun around and made her way to the window where I stood, trailing her fingertips along the end of my bed. "Well ... if someone *had* secured themselves even a morsel of the Mirage Orchid, they'd be fortunate indeed." Her words were measured, lacking their usual brisk melody, as she fiddled with the buttons of her cobalt dress. "So, what a shame that no one did, is all."

Glancing at her, my mouth scrunched to the side, suppressing a chuckle. I didn't know how, but the woman often knew more than she let on. As I turned to the window, one hand reached across my chest, resting on my upper arm, while the other cupped my chin in mock contemplation. The sea was particularly calm this morning.

"Hmmm, that *is* a travesty."

Derya made an impatient chuffing sound, dropping the button she'd been so focused on. "Yes, well. If someone were to have such a prize, I'm sure they'd be tickled to know how to use it."

My eyes widened, giving away my interest. Derya clucked her tongue, wiggling her eyebrows, wrinkles creasing around her bright eyes. "Ah, yes. That would be a useful tidbit. Wouldn't you say?"

I sighed, "It certainly would. Let's say, hypothetically, of course, that it was found. How would one use it?"

She clapped her hands together loudly, making me flinch. "Oh! Aren't we the curious cat? Well, I'll have you know, I am quite a skilled alchemist, I am. Been working at the craft for as long as I remember, especially once I learned I could influence liquids and what's in them."

I blinked several times, my mouth gaping open. "Derya, how did I not know this about you?"

She sniffed, "I suppose you never asked. It brings me joy to have some secrets, my dear." She waved her hand dismissively. "Anyway, now hush and listen. Hypothetically, of course, spells that reverse ember are rightfully quite rare. They often require a blood offering to activate them. So, I would think the best course of action would be to muddle the petal into a powder, add a few drops of blood, dead nettle, and mugwort." She eyed me, one eyebrow raised. "Quite convenient that the ingredients can be found here *and* in the mortal plane."

"Quite."

"I'd guess that one petal could provide a tonic for two. Then, wait until the full moon and bottoms up!"

I cringed, my heart beating a tattoo against my chest. "My, my, Derya. That was very ... informative. Thank you."

"Always happy to help," she murmured, brushing her palm along my arm and squeezing my hand. Her brows shot up along with the volume of her voice. "By the by! Are you looking forward to the ball? The trials? To returning home?"

I laughed, "Not really. Not at all. And yes. What about you?"

"I enjoy the Winnowing festivities as much as anybody. They really shake things up around here, but they also sadden me. I have to say farewell to those I've come to care about. It can be quite boring during the summer months until you all return."

My brows furrowed, my mouth twisting in confusion. "What do you mean? You don't return home to Haadra?"

She tittered, cuffing me on the arm she had just rubbed, "Haadra? Oh, my Ancients! I haven't been there in nearly a century."

"I don't mean to be daft, but I ... I don't understand. Where do you go home to then?"

"My dear child. I am *home*. My astral body has been here since I passed on. I've worked in the palace for decades. I even knew your mother!"

"What the void!" I cried.

"No need to shout, dear. I'm standing right next to you."

I ground my molars together, clamping my eyes and my fists shut for a moment while my mind spun.

"What is it? Are you feeling unwell? Do you need me to make you a potion for nausea?" She placed the back of her hand along my scrunched brow.

A frustrated groan fell from me as I swatted her away and sat on my bed, glowering at the flighty chambermaid. "All this time, I thought you went through the Dormancy like all of us. I didn't know you had ... passed on. That you studied alchemy." My voice raised to a level I couldn't control, exasperation vibrating my chest. "That you knew my mother!"

"You seem rather vexed."

"I am vexed!"

"I know a tonic for—"

My glare was biting, and she stopped mid-sentence. Derya tucked her lips between her teeth, sitting next to me on the velvet coverlet. "I ... I'm sorry, Miss. I didn't realize that you'd be so distraught or even didn't know. I've been here so long that I often forget how to behave. It's difficult caring for so many and them not remembering you every turn." She stroked a hand down my curls, tucking them behind my ear like Mama used to. "I did know your mother. She stayed in this very room many times. She was kind. And thoughtful. *Strong*. I've watched you from afar over the turns. Always such a hopeful, sweet child, you were. It was easier for me to stay away—not bring up Maya because I didn't want to cause you more pain. I ... I didn't want to carry more pain. I suppose that was selfish of me, it was." She bowed, clasping her hands in her lap.

I sighed, putting my hand on her shoulder. "It's all right. I understand. I can't imagine having to bear your memories turn in and turn out while everyone else forgets. Everyone grows older—mortal reminders of the passing of time. I'm sorry, Derya."

She swiped her fingers over damp cheeks. "Thank you. I'm always here for you. Quite literally." A small, watery smile lined her lips.

"Who else, um, resides in Surrelia?" I shifted, crossing my legs, leaning forward in interest.

She tapped a neatly trimmed, bare nail on her lips, looking up in thought. "Well. Most of the seasoned palace workers. Mr. Burlam, of course. He's a dear friend. Such a sweet man."

An amused breath fell from my lips as I rested my chin upon my fist, elbow digging into my thigh. "Naturally."

She continued, completely oblivious to my droll tone. "Ah, and the Elders."

I jerked up, coughing on my next breath. Derya patted firmly on my back. I wheezed, dragging in air, and croaked, "The Elders live here? In Surrelia? As in their physical bodies are here?"

"Isn't that common knowledge?"

"Um, no. Everyone believes they live on Pyria Island and are soul-wandering with the rest of us." A seething heat shuddered under my scar. I breathed in and out slowly, soothing myself.

I had learned more than I bargained for this morning. Although I was frustrated with Derya's flightiness, I knew she would never cause me harm intentionally. I sighed, flexing my fingers. I'd have to process what she told me later.

"Oh. Oh my. Seems like everything has gone wibbly wobbly today, it has."

She crushed me in her warm embrace. Sniffling, she held me at arm's length by the shoulders. "Now, don't forget what I told you about that wee flower. Hypothetically." She gave me her version of a jaunty wink—with both eyes because she couldn't wink with just one. I huffed a laugh as she popped to her feet. "And don't forget to pick out your dress for the ball today."

I grumbled, flopping back on the bed as she spun out of my room like the overwhelming whirlwind she was.

"Mind repeating that. I think I just suffered an apoplexy and misheard you." Kaden crossed his arms over his thick chest, grinding his teeth together.

"The Elders never leave here. They live—*physically*—in Surrelia."

"I fecking knew it," Breena hissed, snapping gowns out of her way as we skimmed the available ball attire.

"What does it matter if they live here or on the mortal plane? I didn't even think your physical body could be here," Letti whispered, holding up a pretty white dress.

Kaden huffed, his ears turning a ruddy shade. I put my hand on his arm, leaning into Letti, watching those around us. "It matters because they force their laws upon us. We have to sleep half our lives away. Scrounge for food. Survive. All the while, they live here in a thriving paradise with food aplenty."

"Oh. When you put it that way ... What the void?" she whisper-yelled, her delicate features crumpling. A few curious glances were tossed our way as I covered her mouth, sweeping my head back and forth. She blinked in understanding, and I released her.

"Exactly. Also, it would seem that their ember is so divine that they can be here physically. Who knows?" I shrugged, absentmindedly tugging the only black gown I could find off the wooden racks strewn about the Great Hall. "Did you know most of the seasoned palace staff are deceased and live here in their astral forms?"

"What?!" Letti cried, collecting more than a few curious stares now. I frowned at her, and she grimaced sheepishly, cheeks turning pink.

Breena laughed. "I mean, it makes sense. We are in Surrelia." My chin lifted, puckering my lips as my brows furrowed. She had a point. "Most of the deceased live in the capital far beyond the Reverie Weald. There is a whole realm outside Morpheus' little bubble."

My mouth dropped open. "Bree, how the void do you know all this?"

She beamed. "You read. I persuade people to tell me stuff. It helps that they know it's the most effective way for me to stop hounding them and/or waving my blade close to their tender bits."

Letti and I snorted at the same time. This woman was absurd. Absolutely, delightfully absurd.

"I've got to get out of here. See you later, Ser," Kaden grumbled, pecking me on the cheek before stomping away with his green formal attire.

I sighed, knowing that he was most likely going to chew Gavrel a new orifice. I couldn't fathom how his brother hadn't known about this—as an elite commander in the Order. Just another secret he'd kept locked away.

"That is gorgeous, Ryn. That's the one," Breena said, holding up a ruby-colored dress. "Now, do me."

I chuckled. "You're going to look astonishing, Bree."

"Yes. Yes, I will."

"Also, this is the only black gown there is. So, yes—it is the one."

"And what a stunner it is." She called after me as I left with my dress bundled in my arms, chuckling.

As I entered my room, a glimmer caught my eye. A satchel and four glass vials, each the size of my pinky finger, sat on the end of my bed. I picked up the folded parchment next to the gifts, reading the looping, feminine script.

> Seryn,
> Keep the vials safe at all times. A little birdy found what we were talking about. I thought whisking these up would be an excellent Winnowing gift for my favorite girl. Albeit a sneaky one, you are. There is one still left where you hid it, by the by. The little birdy won't sing for anyone else, so don't you worry.
> Now, if you recall, all you need is to add a few drops and then drink it under a full moon. It may take some time for the tonic to work.
> I hope this isn't too forward, dear. But I also made a special tea blend for you ... in case you were in need of a ... preventative. Just use it the day after you take a roll in the garden. I know how these grand balls can be.
> Hugs,
> Your favorite alchemist

It was indeed too forward. My. Cheeks. Were. On. Fire. How did Derya know I hadn't ... rolled in the garden ... with Kaden yet? I brushed my fingers over the tea satchel and then covered my face, groaning into my hands. The woman didn't waste any time when she set her mind to something. Did she have a store of ingredients lying around somewhere? She never ceased to amaze and exasperate me all at once.

A dry chuckle escaped, and then I shrugged, storing the blend in the drawer of my nightstand. Forward but thoughtful, considering I wasn't ready to have children yet ... especially if I wouldn't remember how they were made. But did it matter that we were in our astral forms? I suppose it wouldn't hurt either way.

Sighing, I picked up one vial, shaking the fine gray powder within. In the light, it sparkled with flecks of silver. Derya had made the Mirage Orchid concoction sans blood. I rolled the smooth glass between my thumb and first two fingers, struggling to swallow the lump in my throat.

The possibilities were endless. We could save these for any mishaps during the trials. Or was it possible that they could heal memory damage caused by the Dormancy pods? Would it work on an astral form?

Heart twitching in nervous anticipation, I found my black leather pouch and secured the vials. I dug my talisman from my pocket, and as I ran my thumb over it, its usual prickle of energy met my skin. I dropped it in the pouch for good measure, wrapping the long cord around it and tying it tightly.

We'd need all the help we could get.

25

PRUNED

Over the next few weeks, our team prepared as best we could. Sparring. Working with our ember. Researching various creatures and how to defeat them.

Preparations for the ball and Winnowing Trials had the palace staff, including Letti, in a tizzy. The Great Hall, the library, and everywhere in between were far more busy than I'd ever seen.

My eyes stared absently at the wide expanse of grass ahead of me. The training field was abuzz with excitement and activity, people moving in and out of the forest.

My ember hummed along my skin as I practiced with it. I looked down at my forearms, the glowing branches slowly spreading from my fingers to my biceps, my nape thrumming eagerly. Kaden and Breena were on either side of me, their auras whirring over their bodies. They'd been helping me work with my ember methodically since I lost control all those months ago.

My gift had something to do with absorbing other Druik's auras. What that meant, I wasn't entirely sure yet, but little by little, I'd loosened the reins on it to see what my limitations were. To sharpen my control.

To avoid hurting anyone again.

"... and I heard rumors there's an underground cavern." Letti's giddy voice broke through my wandering thoughts, the toes of one slippered foot tapping upon the grass.

Xeni nodded. "Accurate." Letti squeaked with glee, and the warrior's lips quirked. "It's so large that it spans the entire training field." She stretched her hand as far as she could toward the far tree line. "It's only used during the final trial and is otherwise secured with various spells. The main entrance is hidden behind the barracks."

"Ah, that's why people keep wandering in and out. I thought I was missing some party in the woods," Breena said, concentrating on her aura as mine lapped at hers.

On the other side, my energy drank in Kaden's, too. My brows furrowed as I focused on tethering my ember's hunger. It shuddered in spasms throughout my muscles. I expanded my lungs, held my breath, and expelled it slowly, counting my measured heartbeats.

You've got this, Seryn.

"Are you both okay?"

"Never better, firefly." Breena smiled. Kaden bobbed his head, sweat beading on his brow. Xeni took a step away from me, grabbing my sister's hand. I wasn't offended. I'd rather have Letti protected in case this got out of hand.

But it wouldn't.

I'd made progress.

Or at least I had struck a truce with my ember—I let it play so long as it didn't take control. Until now, that tepid deal had held.

Clover-and-cherry-colored radiance mixed with my iridescent glow. I channeled the consumed energy through my arms, their mingled hues rippling through the boughs. My ember sifted through theirs as it churned within me, creating something entirely different.

I widened my stance, toes curling in my boots as I sensed the transmutation. My focus went to the invisible cord joining me and my friends, and I imagined snipping it.

My aura flared—disgruntled—but I severed the connection nonetheless and pushed my attention to my throbbing, burning palms. The creature within me relented, seemingly more interested in the kaleidoscopic light contracting in my hands.

With stiff joints, I moved my fingers, weaving the energy into a spinning, pulsating ball. Tiny sparks ruptured from the orb, popping and fizzling.

Kaden sucked in a gulp of air, the skin that dipped above his jaw flexing. Breena moved to him, resting a hand on his shoulder and squaring her stance. Letti and Xeni moved a few more steps away.

This was the first time I'd coaxed the temperamental power into a distinct form. Bound it in a way that could be useful.

I grinned, digging my top teeth into my plump bottom lip. A shiver ran through my arms, scurrying through my bones and down my spine. My shoulders pushed back, and I lifted my chin. Warm, silent excitement jumped in my throat, and a giggle slipped out in a whoosh of air. "I've got it. Don't worry."

"Of course you do." Gavrel walked over, distracting me. We hadn't interacted since after my meadow nightmare when he had checked on me. The orb wobbled, its shape now more of a wiggling blob. "But it needs to be expended now that you've pruned it."

"Was getting to that, you fun assassin," Breena mumbled.

Eyes wide, my gaze snapped to Breena, voice raising an octave. "What do I do with it?"

"Well, you could try to call it back and disperse the ember."

She stuck her bottom lip out, propping a hand on her cocked hip as she scanned the area.

My heart thumped in time with my scar. I was losing focus, and the shimmering, molten-like blob sloshed around my fingers. Panic was intruding. My thoughts raced. "I ... I can't."

Breena yelped, noticing my chest heaving erratically, and rushed to my side. "It's okay, Ryn. Throw it into the water," she ordered, putting her hands on the back of my waist and pushing me toward the edge of the training field.

As we reached the railing, my upper body bent over it, and I released my ember creation into the abyss. My aura fizzled and then seeped within me, my body slumping from the exertion of handling my gift.

The energy globule zoomed downward, slicing through the crashing waves. A spinning vortex sucked in behind it as it sunk, and then suddenly, a towering column of water exploded upward, the obsidian walls on either side of the river vibrating. Shining slivers of stone fell from the cliff faces.

Breena and I turned, looking at each other with wide eyes, mouths forming shocked circles. I gulped and murmured, "I hope I didn't kill any fish."

Breena blinked rapidly a few times and then burst out laughing, holding her stomach.

Letti ran up and threw her arms around me. "That was amazing, sis."

Xeni approached, nodding in agreement. A reserved smile curved her mouth.

"Well done," Kade said, patting me on the shoulder. His smile not quite reaching his eyes.

I tilted my head, my eyebrows drawing together. Before I could ask him what was wrong, Gavrel bowed, rubbed his lips together, and then walked away to a group of guards sparring, readying his sword. I sighed, focusing on the group.

"Winnowing, here we come!" Breena pumped her fists in the air excitedly.

I began to roll my eyes but thought better of it, smiling instead and rubbing my tingling hands down my dress. Progress was a good thing, and it was time I recognized it within myself.

26

FATED PROMISES

My ballgown swished rhythmically against the floor as I walked to the balcony overlooking the foyer. I rested my hands upon the smooth banister. Its surface—along with the staircases on either side—glittered like the night sky as the obsidian reflected hundreds of lantern orbs floating about. Luminous moonbeams nudged at the quartz ceiling, peeking through the prisms. Bursting with radiance, the star-shaped crystals of the chandelier sprinkled splintered rainbows over every surface.

My lips parted, a sigh slipping past them as haunting, melodic chords drifted over me, flowing out of the Great Hall. Closing my eyes, I swayed with the glowing spheres for a moment, letting the harmonies consume me. When the music paused, my shoulders slumped, and I looked down.

Kaden was waiting for me in the center of the foyer, studying me from below. I grinned, sliding my fingers along the banister as I walked down the stairs to my right. His eyes tracked my unhurried descent, the tip of his tongue sweeping across his bottom lip as a look of admiration settled across his features.

The midnight velvet of my dress matched the stone below my feet, and for a moment, I wondered what it would be like to melt and become one with it. The dress was magnificent, but I wasn't accustomed to dressing in such finery—and the intensity of my best friend's attention was overwhelming.

Made of crushed, black velvet, the full A-line skirt swelled from my hips and plunged regally to the ground, a modest train caressing the stairs behind me. From my left hip, the fabric overlapped and parted seductively, a slit running from just below my hip to the floor. With each step of my satin slippers, the air brushed against the front of my entire exposed leg.

Velvet flowed up my waist in a corset, the plush-covered boning creating vertical banding up my middle. The fabric then gathered in a softly pleated line that swept across my chest. Above this ruching, silk, rhombus-shaped appliqués—covered in glittering, black beadwork—cupped my breasts, creating a V-shaped cutout between them. The velvet shirred to the side of my left breast and split into two sections, with one section swooping over my left shoulder and the other draping over my left biceps.

As I met him, my ribcage was full of trapped, fluttering butterflies. I nervously touched the sides of my hair, ensuring it was still secured. Derya had helped me wrangle the fiery tendrils, sweeping the sides back and securing them in place with a pair of dark, bejeweled hairpins. They were the only accessory I wore aside from my embered ring.

Kaden's penetrating gaze swept over every inch of me and then met mine as we stood under starry luster. "Seryn, you are breathtaking," he rasped, adjusting the pewter cravat tied neatly around his neck.

"Thank you," I murmured, dipping my chin as warmth colored my cheeks. "You clean up well yourself."

He chuckled, wiggling his eyebrows, "Ah, nothing like a steamy bubble bath to set things right." He held his arm out, the muscles stretching the fabric of his forest-green, double-breasted tailcoat. Silver buttons along its lapels and that of the mossy-hued waistcoat glinted in the chandelier's light.

A rosy blaze crept down my chest at the memory of our intimacy. I bit my bottom lip and threaded my arm through his.

Jovial, bouncing music spilled through the doorway of the Great Hall, which had morphed into a grand ballroom. People danced and twirled in the center of the room, the colors of their attire streaking in a jumble of vibrant hues across my vision.

Thousands of lantern orbs continued into and around the room, hovering at various levels throughout the space. The vaulted crystal ceiling sparkled, stuck between the flaming globes and the moonlight.

I allowed the reins upon my ember to slip—just a bit—so I could see a multitude of auras flickering and shimmering around the Druiks. I smiled, enjoying the mystical ambiance of it all as I scanned the ballroom.

To the right was a small stage, a quartet of fellow citizens positioned upon it with their various string instruments and pianoforte. My hips gently swung to the carefree tune bouncing through the room.

Kaden smiled at me and stepped forward, leading me into the revelry. We meandered through the crowd, a mixture of polite smiles, head nods, and wary glances meeting us as we made our way to the left, where various refreshments were laid out.

The Elders perched atop the platform, Melina's tight black sheath dress wrapping around her like thick, silky strips of bandages. Her gaze raked over me as if she wished it were her claws doing so, her full lips twisting snidely.

I averted my eyes, willing myself to ignore her attention. To take no notice of Balor's slimy gawk as he stood with the other Akridais in front of the stage.

Tonight was for celebrating.

Melina could watch me until her eyeballs fell out of her face.

A slow smile stretched across my mouth at the thought.

"What has you grinning like that? Or who do I need to punch?" Kaden whispered near my cheek, his hand warm as he pushed my loose curls over my shoulder.

A breathy giggle left me. "No one. Just enjoying myself. Dance with me?"

"I thought you'd never ask." He took my hand and led me onto the dance floor.

He held me, one hand at the small of my back and the other wrapped around mine as we bounced and skipped around the floor to several lively tunes.

Letti and Xeni breezed by us, Letti's delighted titters streaming in her wake as Xeni held my sister's hand and twirled her in place. They were a sight to behold, with Letti's silky snow-colored dress fluttering around her and Xeni's formal Draumr uniform pressed to perfection.

A flash of ruby caught my eye at the edge of the dance floor. Breena, in her magnificent, mermaid-cut dress, and Rhaegar, also in his dress uniform, were deep in conversation. She winked at me as we waltzed past them.

When the song finished, Kaden and I stepped apart, my hand resting atop my racing heart. "Mind if we take a moment? Unless you want to chop off my feet."

"Best not. They might be useful later," Kaden teased, leading me from the dance floor with his palm on the small of my back.

"Bree, like I predicted. Astonishing," I said, waving my hand from the floor to her bare shoulders.

"You're bloody right." She rocked her hips from side to side, her hands propped on her waist. "And you look positively delicious."

I smiled, grabbing her hand and squeezing it. "Rhaegar, won't you dance?"

"Two left feet, I'm afraid."

"More like two massive slabs of meat," Breena muttered, bending and rubbing the toe of her ... boots. I pinched my mouth together to hold in any laughter that was trying to flee.

Kaden patted Rhaegar on the shoulder in solidarity, offering to get some refreshments for us all. "Four honey wines coming right up."

The first bittersweet chords of the next song echoed through the room. My head tilted to look at the beautifully forlorn notes drawn across the musician's strings.

I knew this melody.

Where was it from?

Without thought, my feet shuffled toward it. My heart pumped wildly, its pulse drumming under the star on my nape. My ember chafed under my flesh, and I trapped the air within my lungs—not wanting to miss a single note.

My concentration was so fixated that I didn't realize I stood in the center of the dance floor, my hand covering the spot where my heart should have been. The spot where tiny shards were breaking off with every haunting harmony. Tears gathered as faint words surfaced above the shadows of my recollection— the corpse of a buried memory exhumed. My eyes fluttered closed. The haunting lyrics echoed in my head to the rhythm of the ballad.

> *There it shall linger,*
> *In the void where shadows creep.*
> *Beyond Nether,*
> *The nightmares decay sleep.*
>
> *Here you'll find me,*
> *In the withering mist between trees.*
> *Among shattered*
> *Hopes and phantom breeze.*

There, I'll find you,
In the blooming embers of your dreams.
Fated promises,
Sealed in moonbeams.

"It's the song you hum when you eat—Maya's song." The words whispered across my cheek, bringing me back to the present, my eyes snapping open. I drew in a deep lungful of air, remembering to breathe again as the sound of my mother singing faded into the shadowy corners of my mind.

Gavrel's warm, solid frame stood close, and he shifted from just behind my right side to face me. His dark, formal uniform rustled against the velvet of my skirt. He looked at me, his brow drawn together.

People danced around us, swaying and swirling as if we weren't even there. Steel-colored, braided tassels swung from his squared shoulders, the only things moving on his person. The only thing ensuring me we weren't frozen in time.

He was so tall. So sturdy. My icy blues studied his emerald greens, and he gently cupped one cheek, brushing a calloused thumb under my eyelashes to swipe the lingering tears away.

Warmth swam over me, and I swiped my other cheek clumsily. "You're right," I murmured, the words catching in my throat. "I haven't heard it since I was a child."

"I'd know it anywhere. I hear it when you're enjoying a meal," he smirked.

A smile teased the corners of my lips. "You do not. We barely see each—"

"It's a bewitching melody for a bewitching woman. Dance with me, Asteria."

My breath hitched, catching in my throat. His hand enveloped mine, and I leaned into his warmth. His other hand rose to wrap around my waist.

"Thank you for saving my place, brother," Kaden snapped,

stepping between us, his hands replacing Gavrel's. My feet stumbled, and Kaden's grip tightened, keeping me upright.

Gavrel's lips settled into a thin line, his jaw firm. His shoulders tensed as if he was going to step forward, but before he had the chance, a wispy vapor orbited us to the sound of startled intakes of breath and faltering steps. Melina materialized next to the commander, her claws digging into the biceps of his stiff overcoat.

She glowered down her nose at Kaden and me—but mostly at me—the moonlight flashing across her metal irises.

Kaden's scowl softened as he studied his brother and the Elder. A look that resembled something close to pity glinted across his features before it settled into one of indifference.

Melina's voice, so melodious, was jarring, considering its edges were wrapped in barbs. "This song—*Fated*—always stirs something in me. Reminds me of home. Of course, it's rare for the mortal realm to yield such a masterpiece, but when it does, you can be certain it's from the Perilous Bogs. Wouldn't you agree, Gavie?" She licked her bottom lip, sidling up to him and stroking his arm.

A curling smog of disdain coiled in my belly, the acidic burn rippling over my throat and tongue. Kaden's fingers pressed into my waist. I hadn't realized I'd edged forward but was grateful he hindered me.

Melina's movements were unhurried as her palms inched over Gavrel's thick muscles. Her lips curled, and her aura smoldered as she noticed my reaction. Deliberately, she scanned those around us, one brow raised. Everyone immediately averted their eyes and began dancing once more.

The skin beside Gavrel's nose twitched slightly. He pressed the line of his lips together so tightly that they paled. He bowed to us and then left without a word, Melina's touch extracted. The dancing couples swept him from my view.

A satisfied grin split Elder Harrow's exquisite face before she sauntered away, following the path the commander had taken. The crowd shifted and split around her like a stone slicing through a current.

I blinked a few times, almost forgetting where I was.

Kaden made a low, resonant sound in his throat, pulling me closer and bringing my attention back to him. He positioned our joined hands next to us and steered us around the floor, his brows furrowed. The silent, circling box steps were making me dizzy as I tried to make sense of what had just happened.

"Kaden."

He didn't look at me.

I waited, my hand clinging to his.

He glanced down, his jaw ticking.

"Kaden."

"What?"

"What's wrong?"

"I'm feeling punchy."

I choked on a laugh, feeling a bit *punchy* myself. His response soothed my frayed nerves. My palm slid from his shoulder to the side of his neck, rubbing my thumb in circles. "There's no need to punch anything. Or anyone."

"If you say so." His head tilted, the furrow disappearing under the hair flopping over his forehead. After a moment, he said, "I've heard that Bogs song before."

"It's the song my mother used to sing."

"Ah, the song you hum." He smiled sweetly, his eyes softening. "Want your mead? I left it with Letti. Might be gone. You know how she can be with libations."

I rolled my eyes, snorting. Letti didn't drink. "I think you're confusing my sister with you, you sot." He gasped, clutching a hand to his chest in mock offense.

"Here's your drink, Ser. Well, half of it. Kaden practically threw it at me when he went to you," Letti scolded.

Kaden laughed nervously, rubbing the back of his neck. "See, told you she was in her cups."

I snickered, sipping the rest of my drink. Letti stuck her tongue out at Kaden before she and Xeni went to dance.

"Wasn't that slow tune just the saddest, most lovely melody you've ever heard? I'm gutted," Breena murmured. She snapped her fingers after a moment. "Your humming song, right? I knew it sounded familiar. Was hard to tell since you're usually gobbling down your food."

I cuffed her on the arm without any real heat behind it, and she grinned. My fingers brushed away some errant curls, and I sighed, not wanting to think anymore tonight.

Not of Melina.

Not of the song or its summoned lyrics.

Not of Gavrel or his brother's reaction to his presence.

So, instead, I drank another goblet of honey wine with Kaden.

27

SHATTERING

In my quarters, Kaden unbuttoned his waistcoat, shrugging it off and letting it fall to the floor. He fumbled with the knotted cravat as he mumbled, "Bollocks."

"Here, let me help," I smiled, brushing his hands aside and untying it for him. "Did you have fun tonight? Feel celebrated like the big, strong competitor you are?"

He chuckled, wrapping his hands around my waist and pulling my body flush with his, candlelight and shadows dancing over the plains of his face. "Indeed, I did. Call me big and strong again. Emphasis on *big*."

Letting the silky fabric slip from my fingers and flutter to the ground, I reached on my toes to press my lips against his. He tasted of honey and the faint bite of liquor. "You're so strong," I purred, squeezing his biceps and drawing out the words. "And *big*."

He grinned, grabbing hold of my bottom through my gown and lifting me. I squealed, laughing as he twirled me around and then carried me to the bed, tossing me on it.

I propped myself on my elbows, bending one knee and placing my foot on the edge of the bed. He sucked in a gulp of air, raking his eyes over my figure, and then fixated on the deep slit in the velvet exposing my bent leg.

He wrapped his hand around my foot, pulling it toward him and kneading the instep. "You were the most beautiful creature at the ball tonight."

A disbelieving snort left my exhale, followed by a small moan as he worked a tender area. "Maybe it was the mead."

He paused until I focused my eyes on his face. I had a pleasant warmth from the drink, but his expression, lined with sincerity, anchored me to the bed. "I mean it, Ser. Or, at least, I think so because I couldn't see anyone but you."

I smiled, heat rising over my chest as my eyelids fluttered. "Thank you. And thank you for whatever witchery you're doing to my feet."

He chuckled, picking up the other foot and giving it the same treatment. When he finished, I stretched, my toes curling and fingers stretching wide. I sat up, my heart forgetting how to beat as he looked into my eyes intently, head tilting, one hand rubbing his chest.

"Will you help me?" I asked, reaching for the ties at the back of my dress.

"If you're asking for me to unwrap the present I've been waiting for all damn night, I wouldn't dream of doing anything else."

Slipping off the bed to stand before him, the corner of my mouth curled. "Well, less talk. More action."

His hands bracketed my waist, squeezing as he held in a laugh, the green of his eyes glinting as he bent toward me. My breath hitched. I swallowed as his lips hovered above mine, his breath tickling my skin.

"I've no objection to taking action with you," he whispered, echoing his words from the tête-à-tête we'd had before we'd crossed this muddied line between friendship and intimacy.

My eyes closed.

Waiting.

My heart galloped. It was a restless beast trapped within the confines of my corseted bodice, heat pooling in my belly, anticipating.

He straightened abruptly, my body swaying in a daze before he spun me around by the waist. I braced my hands on the edge of the bed, and he swept my hair over the front of my shoulder, gliding his hand from my nape down to the interweaving bindings. With nimble fingers, he unraveled the ties, the velvet fist around me releasing.

He took a quick intake of breath, its release skittering down my exposed spine. "You're bare under this?" he rasped, stepping into my space.

I turned my head, smirking and shimmying my shoulders so the fabric slipped further down. "This dress was an all-in-one kind of situation. I can just keep it on if it bothers—"

He grabbed me by the hips, pulling them against his rigid body. The air fled from my lungs, and I reached my right hand up to hook around his nape to steady myself. His fingers dug into the plush material. "Don't you fucking dare," he growled before leaning down and nipping my neck. A startled mewl fell from my lips, and I pressed my rear into him, wishing there wasn't a barrier between us.

His left hand slid up the loosened bodice as he feasted on the curve of my neck. My fingers dug into the soft waves at his nape.

The callouses of his fingertips scraped up my arm, a shiver chasing them, fleeing over my chest until my aching buds pressed against the corset. He pushed the two draped-cloth bands from my shoulder and biceps, and I shifted my arm, freeing it completely.

His mouth moved to my ear. "You taste like salted honey. And I'm starving."

I gasped as he shoved my bodice down to my hips and then

grazed his fingers over my belly. My ribs. Cupping my breasts, heavy with need, in his palms. His right hand gently squeezed before slipping down, burrowing under the waist of my gown. His left hand plucked at my puckered nipple, and I bit my bottom lip to keep in another whimper.

He groaned, resting his temple against mine when his fingers tunneled between my thighs, realizing that my womanhood was bared. I grinned, my front teeth refusing to release my bottom lip. "Fuck, woman. You're going to end me."

In fitful circles, he twirled his thumb around my clit, his first two fingers gliding through my wetness, driving into me.

My body buzzed and vibrated, an inferno building at the apex of my thighs as he worked me, pumping and pinching.

Coiling, molten waves rippled from the base of my spine as I cried out, thrusting my chest forward, my toes curling into the stony floor. His left hand cradled my breast; his other slowly continued slipping around my pulsing nub and in and out of my sex until I drooped forward, my limbs languid and spent.

"That's my girl." He slipped his fingers from me, moving his hands over my skin and carefully pushing the wide skirt from my hips and down my legs. As it puddled around my feet, he shifted. The whisper of his shirt brushed against my back as he removed it, dropping it to the ground. My frame wobbled, my bones almost liquefied, as he scooped me into his arms and placed me on the bed.

He untied his trousers, shoving them off. His length stood rigid. My mouth watered, my thighs pressing together and shifting. I needed more. More friction. More of his hot skin gliding against mine. More of him.

Kaden crawled onto the bed, positioning himself between my thighs as I opened for him. He placed a soft, lingering kiss on the ribs in the middle of my breasts.

A brief memory of our first intimacy together flitted across my mind. The decision I made, then, under the Elysium Tree—

buckling to whatever the Fates had planned. And accepting that I'd be broken into a million pieces.

But I was ready. It was time to shatter. But in a way similar to the sunset upon rippling water, its rays splintering and dancing into the horizon.

Always the same.

But also new.

Something ever-evolving.

"Kaden," I whispered, "I ... I think it's time for the main course."

His eyes snapped to mine, his voice deep and husky. "Are you sure?"

"I want this. I want it to be with you."

He stared at my lips. "It'll be taken from us, Ser."

"But not in this moment."

Reverently, he rested his forehead against my ribs, his hot breath floating over my stomach. I wiggled my hips and sucked in a breath at the mild friction it ignited on my sensitive clitoris.

Kaden looked up at me, grinning and quite pleased with himself. He pushed himself up and crawled over my body, pausing to draw one nipple between his lips. My mouth opened partially, my breaths quickening and echoing through the air.

His tongue circled the peaked bundle, and he sucked it before letting it pop from his lips. Molten electricity zipped through my channel, and my hips bucked once more, greedy for attention. My nails dug into the bedsheets.

"So impatient," he murmured, gliding his right hand down my side, then to my hip. He braced himself on his other elbow, fingers twining with the loose curls next to my ear. Sweetly and tortuously, his mouth lowered slowly to mine. I held my breath, heart hammering in anticipation laced with nerves and desire.

He looked into my eyes, an ocean of emotions sweeping through his before tenderly kissing me. My tongue met his as his right hand cupped between my legs, two thick fingers sliding back and forth over my opening.

My hands gripped his hips as his ragged words breathed over my mouth. "You're so wet, sweeting. So fucking beautiful. Let me hear you ask for what you want. I need words."

My legs trembled as his thumb caressed my clit, and I shook my head, pushing into his touch. He flicked the throbbing bud, and a gasping groan fell from my throat. He kissed me hard, taking my pleasured sounds within him.

"Words, Seryn," he growled, sliding two fingers into me. Slowly pulling them back out.

"I ... I want you. Inside me."

"But I am." He thrust his fingers back in, and my nails clamped into his flesh, tugging at his hips.

I moaned, "Please, Kaden. I need *you*."

He smiled as his fingers left me, and he positioned the head of his cock at my entrance.

For a moment, my breath was stuck within my chest as nerves reared and tension flooded my belly as he braced himself on both forearms.

"Breathe, Ser. Look at me." He brushed his thumb over my temple, and his tender gaze penetrated deep into mine, soothing me.

Achy longing swept over my limbs, my muscles relaxing. My desire pushed aside any worry, my sex pulsing. He smiled before his mouth crashed into mine, his hips pushing forward with a powerful thrust.

There was a sharp pinch of pain. I gasped, but the garbled sound was trapped between us. He stilled, fully seated within me, strained concern washing over his face. "I'm sorry, Ser."

I bit my lip, adjusting to the odd sensation of fullness. The pain eased, and I shifted, feeling the weight of him. Of what we were doing.

I closed my eyes, sliding one hand over his tense back

muscles and then his shoulder. I lifted my head, and he met me, joining his mouth with mine. I kissed him deeply, slowly, tasting him as our tongues danced with each other's. My fingers pressed into him, encouraging him to move.

He pulled out, the friction of his hard length dragging along my core. A moan hummed within my throat, and he grunted, pushing back in.

"Oh ... oh, Kaden. More. I need ..."

"Fuck, Ser." His hips moved faster. The sounds of our joining echoed through the space. I opened my eyes, flames casting waves of light over our slick skin as I looked down to where we were joined.

The sight of his thick cock sliding in and out of me was too much. I was going to combust. Heat raced down my back, and I clenched around him, relishing in the exquisite friction of him inside me. He groaned, sweat dripping off his brow and onto my cheek.

A new, agonized throbbing vibrated at the base of my spine as my hips met his, desperate for more. My fingers dug into his skin as every muscle within me strained.

Kaden thrust into me. Hard. And my limbs trembled. I cried out as a fiery explosion ignited deep within me, stars exploding behind my eyes.

My sex convulsed around his hard length, and he reared up on one elbow, biceps straining as he slipped from me. He took himself in his other hand, pumping twice as a throaty groan rumbled through and from him, his seed painting my stomach.

He fell limp on top of me, his cheek resting between my breasts. I grinned, feeling wonderfully boneless and enjoying his weight atop me. My fingers played with the ends of his hair as his arms wrapped around me.

He rolled to his side, positioning me in the crook of his arm.

"Kaden ..."

"Hmm?"

"I think I'd like dessert later."

A choked laugh rumbled in his chest, and I tucked my head against his chest, grinning as we drifted into a deep, sated slumber.

LATER, his soft breaths brushed against my cheek, loose tendrils of my hair tickling my chin. I squirmed in his arms, and his grip tightened around my waist. The heat of his bare skin pressed against my back, and I sighed, allowing my deliciously sore body to sink further into the twisted sheets. Into him.

"Ser, there's something I need you to know." His raspy voice drifted over me, goosebumps sweeping over me. "You know I ... I love you, right?"

Something fluttered apprehensively through my belly. I turned my head toward him, gripping his hand over my stomach. My eyes searched his, softening. "Of course I do. We're best friends."

A huff of air left his nose, and he rested his forehead against my temple. "Not what I meant."

"What are you saying, Kade?"

"I love you as my best friend. *And more.*"

My heart dropped into my gut, panic tunneling into its vacancy.

"No."

"No?" His arm slipped from me, and he sat up, resting his arms on bent knees. I rolled on my back, gnawing on the inside of my cheek.

"After the Dor—"

"I don't care about the bleeding Dormancy," he growled, shoving his fingers through his messy hair. "I care about you. I love you. I think I have for a long time. Just to be clear—more than just my friend."

"Kade ... I don't know what to say." My pulse thumped clumsily as if drowning in a sticky vat of honey. It's not that I didn't feel deeply for Kaden, but I wasn't certain I felt how he needed me to.

He hung his head. "You don't need to say anything. I can read between the bed sheets." His words felt like a slap to the face. My brows whipped to my hairline; my mouth dropped open.

"That's not fair, and you know it," I snapped, sitting up while clutching said sheets to my breasts, throwing my feet over the side of the mattress.

He hoisted himself off the bed, huffing, and burning indignation bubbled at the back of my skull as I watched him. We'd shared something significant. I gave myself to him. Trusted him with my body. My vulnerability.

Plucking his breeches from the floor, he jabbed his legs into them. He didn't bother tying them, and despite my growing ire, my mouth watered at the sight of them dipping low on his hips.

Stop. I wrapped my arms around myself in frustrated confusion, tucking my lips between my teeth. Chastising my tactless desires. I was self-centered. I'd hurt my best friend.

He bent to pick up his tunic, handing it to me as he stared past me and out to the unyielding sea. I slipped the tunic over my body as I stood before him, my center still sore from what we'd shared. The embarrassing burn of tears threatened me, and I inhaled deeply through my nose. Refusing to give in to the emotion.

The wrinkled hem rustled against my knees as I reached for him, my palm brushing over the strained muscles of his biceps.

His jaw tensed, and he cursed under his breath. "I know. But I don't want to feel this way—I don't want any of it. I knew what I was doing when we started this. I've always known that

I'd rip my heart out just to be with you ... if even for a moment. That is on me, not you."

He turned to leave, but I slid my hand to his wrist, holding firm. "Kaden, please. I care about you; I need you. You're my best friend—one of the most important people in my life. But I don't know if I can promise anything more than what we have now. Even if ... even if we remember after we wake up."

"It's him, isn't it?" he murmured, still facing the door.

"I don't know who you're talking about."

He scoffed.

"Kaden, I don't ..." I choked on the words. "My mind and feelings are my own—no matter how muddled. I thought we were on the same page with being intimate."

He whipped his focus back to me, his gaze burning into mine. "We were—until we weren't. Like I said, that's my fault." He shifted his eyes to the rumpled bedsheets and then back to me. "I made our bed. Laid in it. And now we can end with that. Thank the Ancients—wherever the fuck they are—I won't remember any of this."

I flinched, crushing the fingers of my free hand into my palm to steady myself. His words were a bitter arrow, and it had found its mark right between my ribs. He scrubbed his free hand over his chest as if he, too, had been stabbed, the skin turning pink.

"This—all this—meant a great deal to me. *You* mean more to me than you'll ever know. Please hear me. I'm just trying to be as honest as possible, and I'm sorry. I ... I never meant to hurt you."

"You never do." He tugged his wrist away from my grip and strode toward the door. My aching heart lurched, hurtling to the black stone beneath my feet. The door slammed behind him, rattling in its frame—the metallic clang echoing through my hollow bones.

I had wanted to break—into something new.

Transformed.

My body wilted, a strangled cry ripping from my throat as I gasped for air.

It was no use blaming the Fates. This was *my* doing. I deserved to weep under the crushing consequences of my choices.

I'd gotten what I wanted.

Kaden didn't.

Yet we had both shattered anyway.

28

GOLDEN BRIDLES

"You love who you love, my dear." Derya rubbed gentle circles on my back as I lay on my side, lost in the churning sea beyond my window. "There wouldn't be so much heartache if everyone could force it to beat for just anyone."

"He isn't *just anyone*, though. I …" I choked on my words, forcing down the swelling sob that wanted to break free. "There's something wrong with me. Why can't I love him like he needs me to?"

A faint click echoed through the room, and my body lurched. Letti and Breena walked to the bed, settling on either side of me. Letti scooped me into a hug. A dry sob clawed from my chest, knocking into her shoulder.

Derya must have called for reinforcements.

Letti released me, taking my hand in hers and resting it on her crossed knees. "There's nothing wrong with you. Just give him space to work through what he needs to. You can't take away his pain, but Derya's right—if you don't feel the same, being honest was the kindest thing to do." She rubbed her delicate thumb over the inside of my palm. "And it's okay for you to feel however you feel. You're your own person, with your own mind and heart."

"Don't beat yourself up, Ryn. You're allowed to have a tumble without getting all the feels involved." Breena rubbed my shoulder.

I sniffled, my lips hiding between my teeth. My throat was raw, my chest hollow and achy.

Wordlessly, Derya handed me a warm cup of tea. The preventative tonic. A watery lump formed at the base of my throat. I nodded, sipping the bitter brew, allowing it to wash my grief away.

All day, my doubt and guilt had hurtled through my racing mind. Overwhelming shame consumed me—for not seeing the depth of my best friend's feelings before it was too late. Before he was in such pain.

For allowing my desires to take the lead and ignoring my own feelings.

Or had I not wanted to acknowledge the truth? I wasn't sure anymore. Either way, this is where we were, and I'd have to deal with it.

Just not now.

Exhaustion slithered through my body, hooking into my very soul and calling for surrender. I set the empty cup on my nightstand and laid back, settling my head on Letti's thigh. She stroked my hair as I soaked in her quiet comfort.

"How will we get through the rest of the trials?" I whimpered.

Breena leaned forward as if sharing a secret. "In time, the little holes in both your hearts will heal. In the meantime, it might help to focus on all the holes you'll stab into others during the trials. Nothing like a good ol' dagger fight to get over heartache."

Letti narrowed her eyes, and Breena shrugged, her eyebrows squashing together as she silently mouthed, "What?"

A wry, soggy giggle bubbled from my lips, making them vibrate.

My sister blew out a breath and tucked my hair behind my ear. She wrapped both hands around mine. "You just will, sis. It's what you do. You're stronger than you realize—and so is Kaden."

I sighed, knowing she spoke the truth. But it didn't mean any of this hurt less.

Time and patience. Why was it that the things we needed the most were always in short supply?

"Thank you. I'm sorry I'm such a mess."

Derya clicked her tongue, running her hand over my cheek. "Don't you ever apologize for that. You're alive—living is a messy business."

THE FINAL TEAMS and Elder Craven stood in the center of the training field. Around the edges, hundreds of our peers gawked—not at us or the Evergryn Elder, but at the majestic, winged horses brushing at the grass with their hooves, nostrils flaring, teeth chomping on gilded bridles.

Thick, golden rings shackled their necks. A black mare lunged forward, her wings flaring as she soared to a chorus of mesmerized gasps. The other equines shuffled, signs of frustration stiffening their massive forms. The mare's body unceremoniously jerked, her muscles straining as her hooves dug into the space around her. Realizing that there was an invisible chain tethering her to the earth, she brayed, huffing and reluctantly floating back to the ground.

"I didn't think they existed," Rhaegar whispered, his eyes wide.

None of us did. Pegasi were the stuff of legends—mortal-bred horses gifted wings by the Ancients once they reached Surrelia. My gaze lingered on a chestnut-colored stallion, my heart dipping and breath catching. It looked just like a younger version of my old horse, Alweo.

"Such elegant creatures shouldn't be chained," a wiry Druik muttered next to us, tugging at the sleeves of his wine-red tunic. "It isn't right. They have earned their freedom."

He wasn't wrong. It was clear that these majestic creatures weren't meant to be chained.

"Fortune has smiled on us today," Lucan bellowed, his gang of Akridais flanking him. "As you can see, we've acquired six Pegasi. They are quite rare, of course, but the Ancients kindly guided them to our part of the Reverie Weald for such an occasion."

"More like they were hunted down and imprisoned." Kaden stood well away from me, his eyes refusing to stray my way. He'd kept his distance for the last week, and I couldn't blame him. I'd give him as much time and space as he wanted.

My brows dipped heavily as my fingers played with the pouch in my pocket. I'd kept Derya's gifted vials on my person since receiving them, aside from when I attended the ball.

My head drooped thinking of the ball. Of that night. I tucked a loose curl behind my ear, resting my palm against my neck. A defeated breath fell from my mouth, and I dropped my hand, focusing on the majestic steeds before us.

I'd only told the team, Letti, and Xeni about the vials, and we all agreed it was best to wait. To hold on to them in case we needed them during the tournament. I wasn't afraid to admit that perhaps we were afraid to use something so powerful without knowing exactly what it would do.

Lucan's rough voice continued, "Teams, choose your champion for the Wilting. This will be a joust, of sorts. No ember will be allowed during this trial—just your wits, your weapon, and command of your Pegasus. They are bound to this area but can still fly a good distance. The joust continues until only one competitor remains."

"I can do this. I spent quite a few summers riding," Breena volunteered.

"Riding, not flying. Not jousting," Kaden remarked, crossing his arms across his broad chest.

"It's all in the hips." Breena's eyebrows wiggled. "And the pointy end of the big stick."

Kaden rolled his eyes. A small laugh stuck in my throat, escaping through my nose instead. Kaden glanced at me with a smirk, but then he quickly looked away, the corners of his mouth dropping.

"If you're certain, then I'm confident you'll succeed, Bree." I touched her forearm, pushing aside the ache in my chest.

She grinned and stepped forward with the chosen competitors from each team—two male Draumrs, two female Druiks, and the male Druik who'd been upset about the chained animals earlier.

"Here." Lucan's twisted cane thumped against the grass, demanding the six to join him. "Allow the Pegasi to choose their champion."

As they moved closer, the chestnut stallion sidled closer to Breena, sniffing her outstretched hand. She uttered soothing words, and he whinnied when she gently placed her palm on his long snout. Still murmuring, he allowed her to glide her hand along the expanse of his neck. He watched her progress with one eye; his wings, the color of baked wheat, ruffled at his sides. He huffed and then looked forward, chin lifted, as she mounted him.

The others succeeded as well despite the agitation and shuffling of the winged equine. Each player was given a long, wooden lance with twisting patterns carved down the length of it, leading to vicious points.

None of the competitors wore armor. Swallowing my

unease, my fingernails dug into my skirt as an image of Breena being impaled skittered through my mind. The players arranged themselves in a wide circle, and the rest of us joined the crowd at the edge of the field.

"Let the joust commence!" Lucan shouted, raising his gnarled staff in the air. The Pegasi and their riders shot in different directions, some in the air and some on the ground.

Breena kicked her heels into the side of her steed. It snorted in response, charging forward. One of the male Draumrs galloped toward her on his white-winged stallion.

I bit my lip, not wanting to scream, holding my breath as she leaned forward, aiming her weapon at him determinedly. The male's horse was distressed, and it shifted, causing his lance to fumble. Breena's aim was steady, though, angling herself as if she and the spear were one.

Just as she'd taught me with blades.

The wooden tip met its target, skewering the guard's chest. Breena grimaced, wrenching her lance from his body as he toppled off his animal. Screaming in agony, he clutched at the gaping hole in his torso as the frightened Pegasus bolted. Before the man slammed into the ground, his body burst into a cloud of cinder. Breena's face crumpled, but she gripped the reins tighter and directed her steed toward the sound of a woman.

The black mare that tried to escape earlier furiously reared up on its hind legs, its forelegs churning the air. The female Druik lost her hold and flew backward, her neck catching the ground with a reverberating crack.

Dismay rumbled through the crowd as the woman whimpered, apparently unable to move. Breena rode toward her, jumping off and tossing her lance down.

The dark horse bucked, its hooves thrashing in all directions. Breena swooped toward the woman, grabbing her under the armpits and dragging her shrieking form away. But the mare was too distressed, and as it thrashed down, its hooves crushed into the woman's ribcage, her body crumbling into dust.

Breena fell backward at the sudden shift in balance, coughing and swatting away the ash coating her face. She jumped to her feet, holding her hands up, her lips moving as the Pegasus writhed. The wild-eyed creature brayed and snorted, then ran off into the woods when Breena slapped its flank firmly.

Bile burned in my chest, and I sucked in air, realizing that I was forgetting to breathe, not wanting to miss a moment despite the shock and gore before us.

My eyes flew up as a powdery haze sprinkled from above. The other male warrior stabbed the second female Druik, her Pegasus tearing through the air as her disintegrated body scattered.

The Pyrian Druik guided his animal to the back edge of the field, terror lining his features. The Draumr looked at him, then at Breena collecting her lance from the ground below. He turned his airborne beast, diving directly for her.

"Breena, watch out!" I screamed, and she dove toward her Pegasus just as the tip of the guard's lance jabbed the soil. She jumped to her feet with her spear, climbing atop her stallion. They galloped in a half-moon shape before she shifted her weight forward, squeezing her knees. The mount's massive, downy-feathered wings swept open, and they shot into the air just as the guard reached them.

With a whoop of laughter, Breena soared with the creature, its mane and hers fluttering in the wind. The male followed, determined to destroy my friend. Breena drove her Pegasus up and up, its wings and powerful legs pumping through the air.

As the Draumr followed, Breena's beast nosedived unexpectedly, nearly colliding with her opponent. The male recoiled, pulling on his reins exorbitantly. His airborne steed thrust its wings forward, abruptly jerking and causing the guard to spill from his seat.

As he plunged to the earth, Breena was ready. He fell beside her, and she thrust her wooden spike into his soft underbelly. His roar of pain was cut short as he exploded into fragments, fine grit raining onto the field.

The chestnut stallion landed gracefully, Breena looking like a regal warrior queen atop its back. Her eyes met the last challenger shuffling toward her from the trees, dropping empty golden bridles and collars at his feet.

He'd freed the other Pegasi. The corners of my mouth curled in admiration.

He showed Breena his palms as he approached, shoulders stooping. "I'm done. Don't bother." He turned to the crowd, glaring at Lucan. His voice reverberated over the field. "Do you hear me? I am done with this madness—with these useless games! Stand up, you fools! The Elders lie! The Elders—"

His body ruptured, the breeze carrying the remains away—his blood oath broken.

But not soon enough to prevent the wave of uncertain whispers rippling through the masses.

"Enough!" Lucan demanded as a jade light flared around him. It was the first time I'd witnessed his aura. Splotchy, needle-shaped burned-ocher shades snapped within, like a tornado of dead grym needles. His cane sprayed grass as it cracked into the dirt, and the ground trembled under our feet.

My hands flung out to keep my footing, but Kaden grabbed me from the side, steadying me. He grumbled an apology as he straightened, rolling his shoulders back in irritation, and stepped away from me once more.

The fleeting sensation of my heart filling with prickly grym needles surfaced, but I filled my lungs with fresh air, stacking my spine.

My palms slid over my tunic as the Akridais and Draumrs

on duty edged closer to the Elder. "We have the Wilting champion. The final test will come soon enough. Now, be gone!" His face was an unhealthy shade of purple as he stormed toward the palace, his bristly nimbus pricking the air.

We went to Breena as she removed the restraints from her Pegasus. The creature pushed into her palm as she stroked its ear.

I rubbed her shoulder, offering a sympathetic smile. "You okay?"

"Yeah. We need to win these trials. One way or the other." She shrugged, tucking her messy hair behind her ears.

"And that woman who broke her neck? Your chivalry was showing, my friend." One of Rhaegar's eyebrows lifted as he drifted to the Pegasus, looking at Breena from the corner of his eye.

Breena's lips puckered. "Don't go to mush. Didn't think that was the way to go out. On her back." She looked at her feet, shoulders slumping. "Didn't matter anyway."

"Your flying skills were impressive," Kaden admitted after the silence stretched out too long. Rhaegar nodded, petting the stallion, his eyes soft and lined in awe.

Breena grinned, the corners wobbly as she smoothed her breeches. Her shoulders pushed back, and she brushed her fingers over her cheeks, her face streaked with her opponent's dust. "Told ya. It's all in the hips."

29

ENTOMBED IN AMBER

My brain refused to rest. I huffed, tossing my blankets off my body. It was the night before the final trial, and numerous outrageous scenarios ran amok. The unknown of what the Winnowing could bring stalked me through every corner of my mind.

Over the last six months, I'd learned that anything was possible—especially in a dream realm. It didn't matter, though, because everything I went through, every relationship I'd lost or gained ... it would all be erased.

Kaden's mischievous smirk flashed behind my scrunched eyelids.

Maybe it was for the best. If I was a coward for wanting to take his pain and anger away—for not wanting to feel the crushing guilt—so be it. I was exhausted down to the marrow.

He was still avoiding me, and icy sections of my heart chipped away with every passing day.

I missed my best friend.

The scrape of metal against metal echoed in the hallway while the soft radiance of the full moon filled my room. I slid from bed, quickly pulling on my training breeches and sliding my dagger into its scabbard. I tucked my silken nightshirt in the waistband and pulled on my socks and ankle boots as a rustling noise shuffled further down the hall.

Tiptoeing toward my door, I cracked it open, wincing as the hinges creaked. I froze, met with silence. Air rushed in through my nose as I slipped through the small gap, nerves rattling through my limbs.

A stretching shadow raced around the corner that led down to the foyer below as I pulled the pewter barrier closed with a soft click.

As I rushed over the stone in pursuit, my boots were soundless. I peeked over the balcony, glimpsing the shadow gliding toward the Great Hall.

After descending, I snuck into the room, avoiding the center where the moon cast its beams through the line of windows depicting its phases. I felt along the left wall as my eyes adjusted to the dark.

A soft tick sounded ahead of me like a pebble bouncing off a stone. I gulped, taking a step back. And bumped into something solid.

My startled squeak rent the air before a large, warm palm covered my mouth and another wrapped around my biceps.

"Keep quiet, Little Star." Gavrel's warm breath rushed across my cheek.

"Bollocks," I snarled, turning to face him and swatting his shoulder, which was like slapping a boulder. I flexed and shook out my hand, frowning at him. "Why the bleeding void are you lurking about?"

He scratched his stubbled cheek, his shoulders dropping. "No reason. Just a late-night stroll?" His words lifted as if he was asking a question.

"You're a terrible liar."

His mouth set in a firm line. "I need to check on something—and I need to do it alone. Go to bed, Seryn."

Irritation skittered up my back, forcing my spine straight and lifting my chin. I squinted my eyes at him. All my anger and confusion and frustration and embarrassment from the past months ... all of it boiling together in a frothy vat of acid.

I stepped into his space, my voice spitting venom. "Do *not* tell me what to do. Where do you get the nerve after ignoring me for months, you ... you arrogant wanker?!" I poked his rigid chest, my silky nightshirt rustling against his black tunic. A rush of heat fled up my chest, my breathing ragged. "Now, tell me what is going on, or I'll have to figure it out myself."

His brows rose, eyes blinking rapidly, and he licked his bottom lip, contemplating his next move. His nostrils flared, jaw ticking. He opened his mouth but then snapped it closed, pulling us deeper into the shadows.

I squirmed in righteous indignation but then froze as Melina slinked onto the stage from the right with a silky, dark robe wrapped around her. Lucan and Ryboas followed, their faces set in mirrored apathy.

We watched as her aura smoked around her. She splayed one hand across the back of the throne. Her front was painted in a quivering glow before she and the others walked right into the obsidian, disappearing from view.

"What the void?" I hissed.

A heavy sigh fell across my shoulder. "I overheard Melina telling Lucan to meet her here during the full moon. Something about a dungeon." My eyes widened so much I thought they might pop out of my face. He stood tall, scanning the room and cautiously stepping toward the stage. "I need to figure out what exactly is happening—it's my last chance until the next Dormancy. Would you listen if I asked you to go to bed politely?"

"Not a chance."

"That's what I was afraid of." He scrubbed a hand over his face, pushing his fingers through his thick waves. "Stay close."

Behind the throne, he placed his hand on its intricate carvings, his star rune lighting up brighter than any in the night sky. The back glowed, shimmering and flickering before a fissure split down the center as if the stone was vapor.

I gasped, staring down a chiseled obsidian passageway. Gavrel nodded once before entering, my feet trailing after him. The opening sealed behind us, and I gripped the back of his tunic, not wanting to be left behind.

His tattoo was the only light guiding us through a twisting, descending maze of tunnels and stairs. He disentangled my nails from his tunic, wrapping his warm fingers around mine. The chilled air pressed into my skin as we pushed forward, urging us to turn back. I squeezed Gavrel's hand, my heart beating erratically.

As we approached an archway, flickering radiance swayed within its opening. Gavrel crouched, his mouth close to my cheek. Tingling heat washed over my skin. His words were solemn as he whispered, "Please be as quiet as possible and keep your aura from surfacing. I'm not trying to be an … arrogant wanker." The corner of his mouth quirked, his dimple peeking out. "I just need you to be safe, yes?"

I bobbed my head, cheeks flushing. The thumping under my star-shaped mark was relentless. I brushed over it as I concentrated on my respirations.

At least Gavrel was with me. His steady composure offered some relief. Just knowing he was near smoothed the ruffled edges of my anxiety—the prickling dread that we'd be trapped within the dark stone surrounding us.

A cavernous well burrowed down the center of the open space beyond the arch. My knees wobbled as I stared into the bottomless void, my feet retreating until my heels pressed into the stone wall.

Gavrel looked at me, taking my hand again and leading us down the spiraling ramp carved into the walls. Hovering lantern orbs lit our way, exposing various tunnels, stairwells, and barred cells. I wondered where they all led. How many had been kept prisoner over the centuries?

I inhaled the cool, damp air, concentrating on each step. My ember tapped at my nape incessantly, trying to get my attention. I exhaled, my left thumb grazing the smooth boughs of my tourmaline ring upon my forefinger.

Deeper and deeper we went, the temperature increasingly frigid, the atmosphere buzzing with frenetic energy.

Seryn.

I leaned forward. "What?"

"I didn't say anything," Gavrel whispered, peering over the edge of the narrow slope.

Was I going insane? Why did this place seem familiar?

Below.

"Obviously," I countered.

Gavrel paused, looking at me with pursed lips, his eyebrows squashing together. "Obviously?"

"You said 'below' like it wasn't obvious that it's where we're heading," I scoffed.

"I didn't say anything."

"Well, then I'm going insane." My whisper went up an octave. "It was nice knowing you before I lost my marbles."

"You heard someone?"

"Yeah, he … he said my name and 'below.' Why does it feel like I've been here before?" My power was thrumming, tossing within me, wrestling my pulse. Trepidation slinked over my skin in itchy swells.

He cupped his palm on my cheek. "Take a deep breath, Little Star. You aren't insane. Let's keep going and—" He stopped abruptly, grabbing me around the waist and tucking our bodies against the cold, black wall.

"Open ...." The Elders' muffled voices wafted up the pit.

We crept ahead, keeping to the shadowed curves along the path. Once we came to a tunnel perpendicular to the Elders several feet below, we nestled within the safety of its darkened arc as we watched them.

"After all this time, this is quite tedious," Ryboas grumbled, the key scraping as he unlocked the barred door in front of him. The gate groaned as it rolled away—its edges concealed within deep grooves carved into the stone.

Lucan snorted. "It's a small price to pay." His lips puckered as a woman in soiled blue robes stumbled from the cell, collapsing to the ground. Her eyes were unfocused, pained confusion sweeping over her features.

A gasp crept up my throat, my hand covering my lips to keep it in. It was Haadra's Elder, Marah Strom.

My eyes snapped to Gavrel, and he shook his head, his mouth a steely slash across his face.

As I returned my attention below, Ryboas opened a second cell, and Endurst Guust, the Pneumalian Elder, staggered out. Bracing his hand against the cavern wall, he brushed his disheveled robes the color of rotten lemons.

"Get up!" Melina snapped.

Marah glared at her, her eyes clearing in lucidity, her chin jutting forward as she pulled herself up on unsteady legs. "The Ancients will cast you all to the Nether Void." Her voice, although feeble, was laced with animosity. "And I look forward to that day, knowing you'll writhe in nightmarish pain for all eternity."

Melina tittered, clapping her palms on her upper thighs, and bent forward. "Ah, I see you are well-rested. It's a shame our divine ember and blood oaths somewhat mend your memories—but after all these turns, your minds are scarred. It'd be much simpler if my shadows stuck like they do with everyone else. At this point, your minds are just piles of scabs I need to keep picking, aren't they?" Her lips curled as she wiggled her eyebrows at Marah and Endurst.

"Always such a ch-child, Melina. Hasn't this gone on long ... long enough?" Endurst stuttered, his deep voice imploring.

"If you mean your sentences, then yes."

His jaw stiffened as he focused on the male Elders, his body twitching. "You know very ... well ... we-we ... We were never m-meant to continue this long. What about Midst Fall? Have you no ... no pity left in you?"

Lucan's upper lip curled as he looked away, sniffing. Ryboas tucked the iron keys into his pocket, the metal clanging as his feet shifted restlessly.

"Enough. I tire of you both. You *forget*"—she snickered—"that you did this to yourselves. If you had played nice, you'd be free. Free from these cells. Free to keep your memories. But alas, I can't trust you to roam without spurring bothersome rumors and unrest among the mortals." The last word fell from her lips as if it tasted of refuse. "Selfish of you both, considering we took a vow that impacts us all—decides if we lose our gifts." She snapped her fingers in front of Endurst. He blinked slowly, unamused.

Marah wailed, "We aren't meant to rule or live forev—"

My shoulders flinched as Melina's aura flashed over her in a billowing haze, shadowed tendrils curling around the unwilling Elders' necks and heads, their eyes clouding over, mouths snapping shut.

"That's better. Let's get on with it." Her captives looked around in confusion.

My heart stomped against my ribs, energy stinging through my muscles. Gavrel rested his warm palm on my shoulder blades under the curtain of my hair.

"What are we doing here?" the Haadra Elder whimpered, rubbing her temples.

"Ah, my dear friend. Just the usual—Elder things. Follow me, and we'll be done before you know it."

"I do hope so. I'm ... I'm quite fatigued," Endurst mumbled, staring blankly at the stone wall.

"You can rest after we're done."

A subtle whirring resonated against the gleaming walls of the cavern. Propelled by an inky energy coiled around its edges, a sizable saffron-colored disk levitated up the pit. The edge swerved over to the ledge where the Elders stood. Once they boarded, it sank into the boundless shadows.

Gavrel put a finger to his lips, tipping his head to the side. I followed close behind as we rushed stealthily down the abyss, the unending corkscrew making me dizzy. Time escaped me as we descended, my breaths puffing out in chilled wisps as the temperature plummeted. My nape throbbed, almost unbearably, but luckily, my aura acquiesced to my requests for restraint.

We stopped at a safe distance when we finally saw them, our bodies concealed in the shadows. The circular glass conveyor hovered at the perimeter, above what resembled curling black lava—hazy white smog and liquid silver snaking within the molten undulations. In the center, a hulking mass of raw amber protruded, its roughly chiseled edges blurring the bulky form suspended within.

"What ... what is that?" I whispered, squinting as I tried to figure out what I was looking at.

Gavrel squatted, leaning forward. "It looks like something—or *someone*—is entombed in that stone."

I angled my head, brow furrowing. He was right. I could just make out the outline of a well-built figure, back arching as if they had jerked forward before freezing within the boulder.

Melina's sooty fumes flared to life, slithering around the others, igniting their smoldering auras. She closed her eyes, guiding their power until the hues tangled together. A churning gray clot floated between them and the solitary boulder.

Melina's eyes snapped open, her irises burning silver as she immersed their combined energy into the twisting pool. The igneous substance sparked and thrashed, rolling frantically as tendrils latched onto their ember. All at once, liquid shadows rose, spilling outward over the platform and their feet, seeping over the entirety of the massive, uncut gemstone.

A blinding flash washed upward, illuminating the cavern as if the sun had exploded. The Elders stiffened, their necks craning and eyes clenching as the irradiation enveloped them. It coursed through their veins, glowing and pulsing. Within the amber, a throbbing, golden brilliance vibrated, fractured light boring through the natural fissures of its surface and spraying over every dark, gleaming surface.

As the power gradually faded from the imprisoned being, the Elders' bodies wilted, shuddering while their auras sunk within their forms. A healthy afterglow painted their cheeks.

Melina shivered, licking her crimson lips. "Always a pleasure," she purred toward the boulder. It glimmered once, trembling angrily and sending ripples throughout the well.

Gavrel grabbed my hand, tucking me into the stairwell, his firm body sheltering mine in the shadows as the Elders began ascending on the embered disk.

I held my breath as they whooshed past, my cheek pressed against his chest. His pulse thumped rapidly in my ear, and my breath rushed out as I looked up at him. Even in the dark, his eyes glimmered, the rich green of them studying mine. He stepped back, the chilled air seeping into me. His warm palms grazed down my arms. "Let's move," he murmured.

I brushed past him without a word, my nerves frazzled and buzzing. Whatever we had just witnessed, it wasn't good. It took much longer on the way up; each crevice, tunnel, and level blended, making it difficult to tell where we'd originally arrived.

We passed the cells where the two Elders were held, my heart fluttering, but they were unconscious—two piles of brightly colored robes shoved into their separate chambers.

Gavrel shook his head, pushing his shoulders back as we continued. There wasn't any way for us to help them in this moment.

"What do you think they were doing? And why are Marah and Endurst imprisoned?"

"I don't know yet, but I fear it isn't for the benefit of Midst Fall or its people."

I grimaced, fists clenching. On that, we agreed.

As we neared the top of the corkscrew path, my scar thrummed, the nagging suspicions resurfacing. "I think I've been here before." I paused, turning to Gavrel and putting a hand on his wrist. His head dropped, the muscles of his throat bobbing as he swallowed. "And there's things you're keeping from me still."

"Seryn..."

"I'm tired of this. One moment, you're *my* Gavrel; broody and sweet and trying not to smile. The next you're—well, you're always broody—but you're disgusted by me or ignoring me or talking in riddles."

He stepped closer, brows furrowing. "I'll never be disgusted by you. Also, your Gavrel?" One corner of his mouth lifted, the flickering flames of the lantern orbs swishing over his face. I huffed, and he chuckled, tucking a loose auburn curl behind my ear. I leaned into his touch, and his lips pressed between his teeth. "I told you at the start, there are things I can't share with you. There are things I must do—have done—to keep those I care about safe."

"But what does it matter anymore? After tomorrow, I won't remember any of this. Let me help carry your burden for at least one day. Tell me why I can't remember being here before." My forehead scrunched, jaw jutting forward. "Melina did something to me, didn't she?"

He brushed his thumb over my cheek and then dropped his hand. "If there were a way to keep you safe, I would tell you everything."

"There's always a way." My hand thrust into my pocket in frustration, my knuckle bumping into leather.

Drink.

I flinched at the distant, weak voice flitting through my skull.

With a quick intake of breath, I eagerly pulled out the pouch, plucked out a vial, and shoved it in his hand. "Take this."

"What is this?" He held it up, eyeing the silvery powder, wrinkling his regal nose.

He watched me in bewilderment as I stuffed the pouch back into my pocket and withdrew my dagger, pricking my finger with the tip.

His eyes widened. "What are you—"

"It's the way." I grabbed the container from him, tugging its stopper out with my teeth and letting it drop to the stone floor. Blood beaded on my fingertip, and I held it over the glass, letting a few drops fall. It melted into the powder instantly, its ruby hue turning silver as the tonic frothed and sizzled.

I bit my bottom lip, and Gavrel's mouth fell open as the concoction's color morphed—it was as black as this bottomless pit but with shimmering, star-like specks swirling within.

"We didn't fail during the Weeding." His mouth snapped closed, and he shifted closer. I took a step back. "If you can't or won't help me figure out what's going on. Maybe the Mirage Orchid will."

He called out my name as I gulped the potion, its effervescence prickling my throat.

A rush of stinging heat swept from my belly and radiated

through my limbs. My skin tingled as if I was freezing and burning up simultaneously.

Then nothing. My fingers flexed, and I looked at Gavrel. The look of concern and irritation he gave me was palpable. "That was ridiculous. I hope you're pleased with that little show."

I chuckled. "To be honest, I thought it would be worth it." My shoulders dropped. "But I don't think it's work—"

A searing burn ravaged every corner of my skull, and I screamed, clutching my head.

Then the world blinked as if I had never existed at all.

30

BITS OF ASH

BACK THEN

... THE NIGHT AFTER MY EMBER ALMOST DEVOURED KADEN.

The day had been terrifying. My ember almost seriously hurt Kaden, devouring his ember like a famished beast.

Correction. I *did* hurt him.

My shoulders sagged as Gavrel and I approached Melina's quarters. I thought I had learned how to regulate my abilities, but clearly, I was wrong. My ember still controlled me when it spun out of control. Thank the Ancients Gavrel had been there.

He knocked once, and Melina bid us to enter. He led us to the center of her impressive sitting room. It was drenched in gold-and-black silk. She perched on a silky black settee, her legs crossed and head tilting.

"Stay, Gavie," Melina instructed, her eyes squinting and scanning me as if mentally peeling the skin from my bones.

The commander hesitated before stepping closer to my side. Her mouth pinched. My nose chilled, the air temperature dropping another notch, lungs prickling with the frostiness of it.

"Here," she snarled, one pointed nail tapping on the cushion's glossy material. She uncrossed her legs, her long gown falling open at the slit in its side, exposing one shapely leg.

Gavrel sat, keeping as much distance as the sofa would allow. Leaning her hip and side into the tufted seat, Melina crossed her legs toward him, draping her elbow over the top of the settee.

She stared into my eyes, testing me like Mr. Burlam had done when I first met him, but it was clear this wasn't the same game. The air was heavy and menacing, pushing into my pores from all angles.

I shifted so my weight was balanced across the bottom of each foot. My gaze didn't waver as I fortified the mask of indifference across my face, fingernails pressing into my palms.

"Ah, yes. There she is," Melina purred. She placed one hand on her knee, her fingers toying with the shiny fabric, drawing circles, her tourmaline ring glittering on her thumb. Her other arm inched closer to Gavrel, the backs of her fingers grazing his shoulder.

Gavrel's jaw locked, his gaze never straying from mine. His pulse hammered in his temple.

"Little pet, what are we to do with you? Your ember certainly doesn't hail from Evergryn."

"I ... I don't know, Mistress." The less I said, the better. Easy enough when I didn't have a clue.

"Ah, but of course. Your mother wouldn't have divulged anything. So untoward to have lost her at such a tender age. How long ago now?"

My teeth were going to break if I clenched them any harder. "Fourteen turns. I was seven."

She scrunched her nose, an insincere pout pulling at her

bottom lip. "I can't imagine ... being that young again." Her fingers stopped circling her knee as she glanced to the side in contemplation.

My nails dug into my skin, willing my ember to stay locked within me, its energy incessantly poking at my nape.

Her penetrating gaze bored into the depths of mine. I pulled in air deeply through my nose, counting in my mind and then exhaling.

Seconds ticked by.

Melina was studying me in an unnervingly familiar manner.

It was how I scrutinized others when sparring, waiting for weaknesses or signs of attack to reveal themselves.

"Well, perhaps it's for the best. You're the person you are now because of it. You must be someone of worth for our dear commander to be so protective of you." She moved like a spider, her hand gliding over his shoulder and down his arm. Her claws clamped onto his thigh.

His thick muscles tensed, straining against his trousers. She leaned forward, one arched brow rising as she stretched her other hand out to me. "Come."

Gavrel started, "Mistress—"

"Melina!" she snapped, her eyes flashing silver. "If I must remind you again, our little pet will be disciplined."

My molars ached. I stood in front of them, the pads of my palms bruising.

Gavrel's lips pressed together so hard that they disappeared entirely. "Melina. I've known the girl since she was an infant. It's only natural we'd be on friendly terms. She's my brother's friend and our neighbor. Otherwise, she's of no consequence to me."

His tone was steady. Convincing. It cut through delicate threads within my chest, my heart no longer attached, the organ sputtering and plopping into my belly.

She scoffed, smacking his thigh, "Enough. It's too late for all that. I know what she is to you."

Gavrel froze, his already stiff body went motionless, and his breath caught in his throat.

A sneer cut across her beautiful face as she continued, the metal in her eyes swirling and scrutinizing my body. "I won't have it, Gavie. Won't have you pining for each other like you were the summer before the last Dormancy."

I shifted my position, confusion pushing my brow downward as I glanced at Gavrel. A quiet breath left him as his shoulders relaxed. His jaw ticking again.

"You've been misinformed."

"Enough," she hissed. "Not only do I have eyes everywhere, but I already sifted through her mind after her little mare wyrm encounter …" She counted on her fingers, continuing, "And her dungeon adventure … and last winter. She makes it so easy—constantly creeping around the grounds and palace alone. Just like her mother. Some things never change," she tittered; waving her fingers toward me.

My mouth fell numbly, sagging into a defeated line. Her words weren't making sense. Memories weren't clicking into place.

Dungeon? Does this place have a dungeon?

What happened last winter?

Just like my mother?

I reached into the shadows of my mind, scratching at the darkness. Nothing but a blurred murk greeted me.

"Well, aside from her having ember this round." One delicate shoulder lifted as she twirled her hand in the air. "It matters not. Those memories are long gone, Commander. Along with some other tidbits. I must say, it was quite convenient your brother is so appealing."

Gavrel's teeth were bared, a rumbling snarl carving into his mouth. His hand moved for the dagger strapped to his belt, but his fist clenched before reaching it. His burning emerald glare tore into her profile.

She rose—either oblivious or disinterested in Gavrel's reaction—her nose mere inches from my body as she did so. My focus was entirely on her again, my muddled thoughts bouncing around their bony cage.

Her hot breath skittered over my skin, along with her rosy, smoky scent. She looked down at me, her refined chin a few inches above the crown of my skull.

Goosebumps swept over my arm, my right hand reaching for my hip—for a weapon that wasn't there.

I rubbed my palm against my dress instead, the soft white material offering me comfort. The hard bump of my talisman nudged me through my pocket.

"Sit." Melina circled me as I complied. A slinking cat toying with a mouse. "It's a shame you haven't a clue. The torment of yearning for someone can be so pleasurable in itself." She sighed, behind me now, her fingers tracing my wild strands.

I swallowed, pushing down the dread rising within my throat, my mouth dry as the broken land in the Stygian Murk.

"My ember is quite effective, of course. Well, not with Gavie. It's been quite frustrating not being able to see inside that naughty head of his." She tugged a stray curl. "Nevertheless, at least you haven't any recollection of how foolish you both were."

Her hand left me, trailing along the back of the settee above my shoulder. "Our predicament is this: First, the commander is mine. He does as I command," she purred, eyeing Gavrel as she moved to my side. "Has she even a clue of the things you've done? You've been quite the wicked boy—I doubt she'd want you if she knew, Gavie."

His nostrils flared, scowling.

She poked a pointed tip into my upper arm and dragged it

down my flesh. "Second, it's a shame that you're more useful alive. For now."

My heart crashed inside me, matching the pace of my spiraling thoughts. I clamped my sweating hands onto my thighs, holding myself together—trying to alleviate the incessant scratching at the back of my mind.

She paused beside me, her claws digging into the cushioned sofa arm. "Maya Vawn. She also interested me. You see, it isn't every day ember originating from the Perilous Bogs makes itself known. We are a rare breed, after all."

I blinked rapidly at the swift change in topic, my head drawing back from the shock of her words as if she'd slapped me. My mouth was agape, my head shaking.

Melina was lashing me with information—none of it fitting into place. Her words were misshapen and disordered. My brain was unable to stack them neatly to make sense of anything.

Flashes of a distant memory prodded my awareness as my hands fell to my sides.

My mother had been whispering in the woods with Hestia. I was six turns old, hiding behind a grymwood, waiting to jump out. Giggles caught behind my hands as the words "bogs," "scion," and "fates" trembled through the night air.

The memory scampered into the shadows of my mind as Melina stepped in front of me, lifting her chin. "It's the only explanation, pet. There are occasional exceptions, I'll admit. Druiks can have mixed ember that's distorted—its origin a mystery." She tipped my face up with one sharp nail. "But alas, I can practically taste your ember. It calls to me, just like Maya's. In the end, your mother denied it, and look where that got her. Too bad my ember couldn't break through her mind. Would've been so much easier."

Heat flared over my face. My aura surged over me, my fingernails digging into the slippery cushion. "What do you—"

She whipped her hand up, closing her eyes, her smoky aura seething over her body. My mouth snapped closed. She opened her eyes, sparking metal piercing into the ice of my glare, now ignited with my bitter ember.

Her voice was barely above a whisper. "We are going to have a little fun, you and I."

I didn't like the sound of that. A barely perceptible growl vibrated through Gavrel. He shifted toward me, his shoulders widening as if bracing for an impact.

Melina snickered. "Ah, Commander. Settle yourself. We've discussed what will happen if you interfere. Her memory will be corrected in whatever way I see fit. Otherwise, she'll meet a fate worse than a little *historical revision*."

"What?!" I yelped, no longer able to contain the muddled agitation within me. My aura vibrated along my skin, yearning to spill free.

He squared his jaw, the pulse in his neck thumping against the tanned skin. "I've kept my word to you and will keep my distance from her. She means nothing to me." Bile coated my throat as he whispered, "Please, Melina."

A healthy flush spread over the milky skin of Melina's chest and neck. She ran one hand over her hip, biting her bottom lip and letting it slip from her teeth. "Since you asked so nicely, darling, I'll only erase the important bits. She can handle it once more." Her smile was the most feral thing I'd ever witnessed as she looked at me, holding her palms in front of her. "Her memories are a risk I can't abide."

Gavrel jerked forward, but oily black and yellow ropes of ember slithered over him, pulling him onto the settee and tightly fastening him.

My head whipped back, seeing a slinking Akridai male who had slipped into the room unnoticed. Bright glee lit up Balor Drent's blunt features, his tongue running over the thin slash of his lips. His long, dark hair as limp and greasy as his aura.

"Thank you, Balor," Melina purred and then looked at me. "Well, pet. This might hurt a little. But the fun part is seeing if you can stop me."

Wild rage shot through me as I spun back to Melina, my ember ravenous and frantic.

But it was too late. She was a billowing eddy of soot-colored mist. In the next second, a sphere of twirling smoke condensed between her palms and then sprung toward my face. It clung to me, seeping into my eyes, nose, mouth, and ears.

I slapped wildly at my head, my aura throbbing, failing to dispense the fog invading my skull.

It was of no use.

The image of Melina thrusting her chest forward as her head and arms flung back burned into my senses. And then a turbulent rush of unbidden memories flashed behind my shuttered eyelids.

It was like when I'd watch the Evergryn woods at night during a lightning storm—intense bursts momentarily painting the dark, neglected trees in a ghastly white.

"Hestia, I fled far from my home. He told me never to tell a soul. To be someone else. I never wanted any of this for her. Thank you for everything you've done—"

Her words drifted away in the recesses of swirling smoke.

"Damn the Fates. She doesn't have to be the one—"

The flash evaporated.

"I won't be the Scion—"

Darkness.

A disembodied voice trapped underground.

"There will be no ascension—"

Fleeing through glossy black tunnels.

Melina outside my door.

The memory crumbled away into the haze.

Gavrel's eyes.

Several different days, times, and moments spinning together. A chaotic fusion of verdant shades—

A hesitant smile teasing his full lips.

His eyes.

His sturdy arms around me.

Moments vanished into the mist, smoke clogging every shadowed crevice as my ember worked to mend the damage.

"Seryn!" Gavrel roared, his tattoo blazing as he struggled against his embered restraints.

"I'll only erase the important bits. She can handle it once more."

Melina's teeth glinted through the smog.

"Her memories are a risk I can't abide."

The embered smoke smoldered through my thoughts as if they were nothing but rotting grym needles being incinerated.

And then. Nothing.

Nothing but the lingering black ash of memories drifting away into the night.

31

UNBIDDEN MEMORIES

NOWADAYS

*J*erked upright as my aura buzzed and thrashed over my body like splintered prisms. I dragged in air, greedy for a ragged breath as if I'd been drowning. My pulse hammered in my ears, matching the throbbing over my scalp.

A frantic vortex of dread slammed around my mind as I tried to collect my scattered senses.

Where am I?

My nails dug into plush velvet, and I blinked several times—colors and shapes coming into focus, outlined by the early morning sun spilling through the oceanside windows.

I was in my room.

What had happened?

A whimper scurried from my lips, and I cupped my hands on either side of my jaw, feeling my frenzied heartbeat.

"You're safe, Little Star. Take a deep breath." Gavrel's gravelly tone washed over me, and I flinched in the direction of his voice.

I stared at him, not believing he was sitting on the edge of my bed as if he were a cosmic apparition my mind conjured. A shadowed look of apprehension drifted over his eyes, making his emerald irises look nearly black.

"It's okay. You're okay. Breathe."

My body heeded his words, pulling in breaths until my lungs were about to burst. Then releasing. Over and over until my heart slowed to a consistent thump. My hands rested on my midsection as my ember evaporated, leaving behind the remnants. Fragments of memories shuffled through my mind like loose pages scattered from a torn book.

When the fog cleared, everything crashed into place—murky shadows chased away by a stunning clarity.

The Mirage Orchid.

I'd taken the potion. And then...

"I remember."

"Say more." His nostrils flared, the skin of his temples and jaw ticking rapidly.

Derya chuffed from the end of the bed, and I startled, realizing she was there. "Don't be daft. She took the tonic. You know that whatever curse was forced upon her has been lifted. Isn't that right, Miss?"

My heart sank as vivid memories flooded my mind, each one as clear as the day I lived it. A stream of unbidden tears streamed down my cheeks. I let them fall, not caring if I drowned in them.

Pain.

Fear.

Confusion.

Burrowing into my bones from every angle. Trying to dig out the very essence of who I was.

Breathe in.

Breathe out.

My gaze fell on Gavrel, icy irises boring into his soul. "I

mean—everything." Acid roiled in my throat, and I paused, swallowing.

I shifted to the side of the bed, legs hanging over the edge next to his massive frame. "I remember every erased thought. Every moment. My time during every Dormancy since I was a small child. The memories that Melina stole from me."

Derya gasped, one hand gripping the bodice of her dress; the other hugged a pile of clothes to her chest.

"Seryn..." Gavrel breathed, shuddering.

"The memories of you."

He closed his eyes, forehead crumpling as if he were in an immense amount of pain, his fingers digging into the tops of his muscled thighs.

Derya swooped around, oblivious—or perhaps not—to the cloud of tension between Gavrel and me. Distressed, she barely breathed between her sentences. "I'm pleased the tonic worked—but you gave us quite the scare, you did. Gavrel carried you up here and summoned me through the gem by the door. I've never run so fast in all my life—living or dead! Do you mean to tell me that it reversed the effects of the pods? This is quite miraculous, indeed!" She flapped her hand in front of her flushed face. "We've been waiting since this morning for you to wake. Sweet Surrelia, I was worried I'd put too much mugwort in! Of all the ridiculous things to—"

The door slammed open, and Breena darted in, Derya clucking her tongue in annoyance and setting the clothes on the bed. Kaden lingered outside. He scowled as his eyes landed on his brother. Jaw clenching, he stomped away down the hall.

At that moment, I knew I should care, but I didn't know how to. I couldn't. Too many emotions and thoughts spinning through me. A soothing numbness seeped over the raw edges of my mind, and I welcomed it.

Breena's confident gait slowed as she neared me, her head

tilting. "Uh, I hate to interrupt. But we have to get down there. It's starting soon."

"All right." My voice sounded like an echo from another room. I slipped from the bed and gathered my clothes. "Please leave," I murmured to no one in particular, watching the sea beyond my window. Wanting to be at one with its relentless rolling; feeling that I already was.

"Sure. We'll meet you in the foyer," Breena said in the softest voice I'd ever heard her use, brows knitting together as she left.

Derya sighed, pulling my wilted body in for a hug and brushing a hand over my hair. She whispered in my ear, "Good luck, my dear. I'm always here if you need me."

I hugged her back, wet saltiness lining my eyes. "Thank you for everything. I remember you, Derya. How kind you've been over the turns." She gave me a watery smile, touching my chin before departing.

Gavrel stood, his hand reaching out and then falling. "Seryn, I—"

"I can't do this now. Please go." The words burned my windpipe.

His shoulders slumped. Resisting the urge to comfort him, I turned my back to him as he hesitated; the rustling of his clothes following him out of the room.

I didn't want to deal with everything I remembered. All the turns and moments. The emotions tied to them. It was too much.

Concentrating on washing up and dressing, I willed myself to exist in the moment, not allowing myself to be dragged into the endless sea of unveiled recollections.

My undergarments were soft, and I relished the feel of them against my skin, thinking they might be the last small comfort I'd have for a while. I slipped the short-sleeved charcoal tunic over my head, the sleeves looser near the shoulders and more fitted on my biceps. My breeches were made of soft black leather and moved against my curves like a second skin as I shifted and bent at the knees a few times, warming up my joints.

A snug black leather vest wrapped around my upper body, the V-shaped neckline dipping low in the center of my chest. Breathing came easy now, my disquiet lulled by the mindless repetition of lacing the front ties of the garment.

Last, I slipped on sturdy midnight-hued leather boots that went up my calves and fastened with various straps and pewter buckles. My dagger was sheathed in its scabbard on my right, the belt hanging around my hips. A smallish satchel nestled on the other side, also secured to the belt.

Despite knowing they'd disappear once I was pulled back to my pod, I tucked my leather pouch—filled with my rune pebble and the remaining orchid vials—inside. After plaiting my hair, I tossed the thick braid behind me.

Gleaming light bounced off my ring's branch carvings on my left forefinger. I ran my thumb over it, relishing the vibrations under my skin.

One last time, my eyes scanned the exquisite beauty of my room. It had been exceedingly more comfortable than the barracks I'd stayed in during my previous Dormancy spells. Much more extravagant than any home I'd seen in Midst Fall.

My shoulders pushed back, and I lifted my chin. I hoped Melina, Lucan, and Ryboas enjoyed their time here while it lasted.

I went to the door, my mouth pressing into a tight smile, thinking of how I'd like to destroy them. My ember strummed over my spine, its strings vibrating along my nerves. It was enjoying my burgeoning spite. I shook out my hands, breathing deeply through my nose as my teeth clenched.

I'd cope with the memories and what clung to them later. All the fury and regret and shame and grief.

Later?

A wry laugh fell from me. There'd be no later—the pod

would once again wipe my memories of Surrelia regardless. But it couldn't take the ones from home. Of Gavrel.

I had told Letti he was like a brother—that we'd never been anything more. But that wasn't true. Not even a bit.

A sour taste lined my tongue, and I swallowed it and hurried through the halls. My boots creaked against the stone like a clock marking the seconds. With eyes boring into the path ahead, my jaw set tightly.

If I kept taking steps, one in front of the other, the seconds would carry me until I reached the end of the day. I'd get through whatever lay before me.

Through the Winnowing and beyond.

***

Was it my imagination, or did Mr. Burlam have a slight sparkle to his grayish-blue eyes?

I nodded to him as I walked past, already set on my destination.

"Wait, girl," he grumbled, hobbling around his desk to meet me. He squinted, his bushy mustache wobbling over pursed lips. His rich brown aura shimmered around him as he reached my hand, placing the last Mirage Orchid petal within it.

Exactly what I had stopped by the library to get. My mouth dropped as I eyed the petal's dried, ombre surface, pressed flat from hiding between the pages of our history. My brows rose as I looked at him, a small smile curving my lips.

"Derya said your memories have returned. Won't be saying anything to anyone." He sniffed; one corner of his mustache lifting. "And, well ... I ... Good luck." He huffed, his knobbly knees shifting uncomfortably in his trousers.

Memories flit through my recollection. I'd worked in the

library for several turns, and Mr. Burlam had always been the same. Rigid. Cantankerous.

Loyal.

Oddly endearing.

I took his hand and squeezed it gently. It felt oddly sturdy for something that looked so breakable. His brows lifted, his eyes softening. "That means a lot, Mr. Burlam. I do remember, and I appreciate you and our time together over the turns."

A warm glow flushed his pale cheeks before a grumpy breath puffed them out. He exhaled, grumbling, shuffling away, and flapping a hand at me dismissively. "Oh, don't make a show of it, girl. Go on and play with your swords and imbeciles."

My head swayed from side to side as I chuckled, departing and making my way to the foyer to meet Breena, Rhaegar, and Kaden. The dried petal nestled safely in my necklace pouch, separate from the vials and rune stone within my belt satchel.

"Excellent, everyone ready to give them a show?" Rhaegar asked cheerfully.

Breena grinned. "When am I not?"

Kaden let a subtle smirk tip his mouth before remembering himself. "Let's get this over with." His mouth pursed as he rolled his shoulders, moving toward the palace entrance.

32

FRAYED

*E*lder Melina Harrow was going to reap the consequences of her wickedness.

That much was certain. I'd never felt such deep conviction before. But I knew it to be true because *I* was going to make it so.

I bit the inside of my cheek, maintaining my mask of indifference—*of ignorance*—as she prattled on before us on the training field. She wore a dark, gossamer cape that fluttered behind her, snagging on the weathered wooden fence as if trying to claw its way off her shoulders. Her long black dress skimmed her body, draped sleeves dripping off her wrists.

I huffed a breath of disgust out of my nostrils. There were still plenty of unknowns bouncing around my head, but I certainly was no longer oblivious to the unjust cruelty and selfishness of the Elders. Well, maybe not Marah and Endurst. They stood behind Melina in a stupor, teetering between Lucan and Ryboas.

We'd have to figure out a way to free them.

Repulsion swelled through me, cresting along my spine at the thought of Melina's ember repeatedly slicing through our minds time and again for so many turns. Picking at scarred wounds until it crippled our very essence.

My fists tightened, one wrapped firmly around the hilt of my dagger. I widened my stance, digging my heels into the grass.

She had no clue I evicted her cursed shadows. They had covered my mind like layers of cobwebs over the turns—the bits in between erased by the Dormancy.

Lost memories continued to weave through the cleared spaces like spider silk, their delicate webs greedy as they seized onto passing recollections. With one impulsive decision, I'd unearthed the missing half of my life.

I recounted her cruelties—not just against me but countless others. All the times Lucan and Ryboas participated or followed but did nothing to stop her wanton savagery.

I shifted my gaze to the sea beyond the cliff and then dragged along the inky line of its edge, the roar of the cascading waterfall to our left goading me.

Nineteen coils of rope were piled along the precipice beyond the fence. My stomach churned. An image of me spiraling into the angry river below stole my breath.

I focused on Melina's voice. The sickly, sweet tone grating along my nerves. "Congratulations on making it to the grand finale." She waved her hand toward the fence. "The rules are simple: Find your way into the arena without using the main entrance or your ember, and then do whatever it takes beyond that to be the last one standing. Using your power is permissible once you've entered the cliff. Everyone will be watching your every move from the amphitheater below—so do try to make it fun." Her lips curled as she turned to the Haadran and Pneumalian Elders, nodding. Lucan leaned, snarling something at them.

Marah jerked forward as her powder-blue energy enveloped her. Liquid-like orbs reflected within her halo like mirrored balls. A film of swirling blue water materialized between her hands, moisture pulling from the damp air. It expanded, and a citrus haze burst around Endurst as he directed its wisping yellow currents toward it. His ember supported the watery membrane, guiding and suspending it. Its blurred screen sharpened, clear fluid rippling over it like liquefied glass.

A faint hum vibrated under our feet as an image of a cheering crowd flickered on the screen's surface. Endurst flinched, the film splintering into various hovering globes, the spectators fading in and out of their undulating curves.

The Elders moved toward the barracks, Melina flicking her fingers in the air, dismissing us. "May you withstand the currents of the Winnowing. For only the worthy will remain."

My teeth ground together as everyone moved toward the fence. The floating water projectors, or whatever they were, soared around us in the background and over the abyss, broadcasting our every move.

It was clear that the ropes were for us. Breena and Rhaegar hopped over, handing Kaden and me our bundles. I stared blankly at the rough coils, the bristly threads scratching my skin. A deafening buzz vibrated in my ears. Was it my heart or the roiling water?

Quickly, Kaden knotted one end of his rope to the nearest fence post along with the others. He glanced at me, his eyes crinkling just a fraction. I felt the weight disappear from my trembling hands, and without a word, he fastened mine to the post as well.

"Thank you."

"No problem," he grumbled and threw his leg over the fence, easily shifting to the other side. My knees numbed, tingles running up and down my calves. He rubbed his lips together, his shoulders dropping as he held out a hand. "It'll be okay. Come here."

My feet fumbled, and I put my hand in his, his warmth

sinking into my chilled fingers. He helped me over the fence and handed me my line.

"Listen." He rested his hands on my shoulders, his brows furrowing at the contact. I looked at him, my mouth tense. "You are going to be all right. Remember that one summer with the rope swing over the pond?" I nodded, releasing a shaky breath. "Just hang on like we did then. Use your feet to brace the rope between them. You can do this, Ser. Just follow me."

I gulped, bobbing my head as if dazed and not in full control. It had been so long since he had spoken to me. Said my name. We were so far from the days of playing on the rope swing.

Melancholy and fear lumped together, sticking in my throat. I swallowed, weak legs shuffling closer to the precipice as I craned my neck to peek over.

Kaden gripped his rope, positioning his body on the edge. Most of our opponents were shimmying over the brink, some already rappelling down the cliff face.

Breena winked at me before the top of her head disappeared, Rhaegar's massive form unseen.

Stone bit into my knees as they met the ground, my fingers digging into the rope's taut fibers.

As I inched over the stony threshold, my heart slammed into my throat, the skin under my scar pounding. The twisted hemp dug painfully into my hands as I squirmed, the full weight of my body and dread pulling me down into the rumbling abyss below.

As a breeze pushed into me, my rope creaked and swayed. I yelped, desperately clamping my boots around the cord and crushing my eyes closed.

Each terrified, ragged breath was a prayer to the Ancients—their response lost in the crashing waves.

"Ah, might as well piss yourself now, you gutless twit. Even better while your team is below." My eyelids snapped open as my temper flared. Sebille was several feet to my left, her long legs bunching as she descended with ease, a cocky sneer carved into her face.

My nose crinkled, lips puckering as I turned away from her, scowling at the black rock glinting before me. With a determined growl, I forced the air from my lungs, chin jutting. My molars clamped tight as I sucked in a full lungful through my nose.

You can do this, I repeated in my head. Over and over.

I slackened my feet, letting the rope slide through them, my hands clutching and releasing as I moved.

"You got this, Ryn!" Breena shouted from several feet under me.

One hand over the other, I inched my way down, letting the movement repetition and muscle memory take over, tucking my fear deep within my belly.

Droplets of water sprinkled upon my leather-clad chest, and I paused, licking a drop from my bottom lip. Narrow waterfalls were scattered across the wall, spouting or trickling from various hollows. My fingers squeezed tighter, beads of dampness sinking into the rope threads.

As I met my team, I looked up at the top half of the cliff, sunbeams blinking off the dark brim. Then my gaze dropped to the river's currents, closer now, flicking like grasping fingers.

"Well done." Rhaegar's deep timber drew my focus as he leaned back, his feet anchored on the cable, one beefy hand holding it.

Breena grinned, "I think there's a cave over there." She nodded to the right, and I gulped. A gaping opening sat several lengths away, a thick ledge protruding and a stream gushing over its lip.

"We'll need to swing over and grab onto the others' lines," Rhaegar rumbled.

A flash of movement to my left caught my eye, my attention drawn to two bodies screaming and plummeting toward the raging water, flicking coils of rope and a few dripping projector orbs trailing behind them. I looked at Sebille, following her glare as her mouth twisted.

Farther up and to her left, an average-sized Druik with short, curly brown hair and wearing navy leather armor sheathed his knife, his tongue tucked into his cheek as the frayed remains of hemp jerked beside him.

The severed rope taunted me, trying to unravel my tightly bound nerves like its tattered threads swishing in the breeze.

A look of determination washed over Sebille's face as she pushed her feet against the stone, her rope swinging precariously close to mine. Our opponents mimicked her, either realizing the danger they were in or where the entrance was. I was mesmerized, staring vacantly at the oscillating ropes as if they were the sweeping pendulums of several chiseled clocks.

"Move!" Kaden barked, snapping me out of my stupor. A sharp stab of panic shot into me, and I slipped down my rope before gripping tightly, my body jerking on the line. My mind clicked off, limbs and muscles shifting, pulling, and pushing in time with my best friend's movements.

Kaden's fingers stretched and then grasped the wiggling rope to his right, holding both cords tightly. As I swung toward him, his hand shot out, grabbing my rope. From my peripheral, another person crashed into the river, and I vaguely saw two forms to the right grappling, spinning, and lurching down as they wrestled and jabbed into the spaces around their opponent with blades. They both fell, one hurtling to their demise, the other snatching a line just in time, his back slamming into the cliff with a thud.

My lips pressed inward, nostrils flaring as I grabbed onto the braided cord Kaden held. His hands and feet were positioned below mine as he released the other two ropes.

Rhaegar and Breena were close to the hollow now. Sebille latched onto my discarded rope.

Kaden moved, our rope swinging and creaking with the extra weight of two bodies. He grabbed the next line. "Go now. I'll be right behind you."

My pulse and ember thrummed under my skin as if I were one giant heartbeat, but I kept swinging, advancing, and clutching the rough braids—one after another—despite the burn on my already raw palms. As I reached the last rope before the entrance, my grip slid down the damp hemp before I twisted my boots in the slack below. My body wrenched, muscles screaming and limbs shaking.

After hurtling toward the cave's lip, Breena heaved her body on top of the ledge. Rhaegar grabbed her hands and helped her the rest of the way. His massive boot upset the flow of the rivulet, its water flinging over the edge in broken torrents.

She brushed her snug red leather trousers off, droplets flinging from them, and then stretched her arms out to me, her leather breastplate pushing against her armpits. "One more. You can do this, Ryn-Ryn!"

As I ran along the cliff, building momentum, the Draumr, who'd been brawling earlier, landed near Rhaegar. The guard swiftly drew his sword and jabbed it at Rhaegar as he jumped out of the way, crouching and circling an outstretched leg into the man's ankles. Rhaegar righted himself as the guard toppled over, falling into the gorge, his holler chasing him the whole way down.

Cringing, I leaned the full weight of my body into my swing. With one last impetus, I released the rope, fingers and boots clawing at the empty space around me as I vaulted toward the jutting cave entrance.

My breath sunk within my ribcage, acid rising to meet it. Everything seemed to slow as I pitched forward, a raven cawing and soaring past me as I flew.

Rhaegar gripped the back of Breena's ruby leather armor as she lunged forward, our hands locking around each other's forearms. They pulled me in, our bodies tumbling into the cavernous opening in a mound of flesh and rawhide.

"Well, that's one way to do it. If you wanted to jump my bones, all you had to do was ask." Breena chortled as I rolled off them, shuddering and whacking her in the stomach with a limp arm.

Rhaegar grunted, jumping up to help Kaden as he landed on the ledge behind us and patting him on the back. The warrior promptly stalked into the cave, drawing his battle axe. "Let's move."

I jerked to my feet, muscles groaning. As we journeyed deeper into the cave, shadows engulfed the sunlight, the chilled atmosphere thick and dank. Our footfalls echoed around us, mixing with the sounds of the rippling creek.

One of Marah's orbs zipped ahead, bursting apart. Its pieces melded with the current and dripped down the cave walls, winking at us. My lips crushed together, thinking of everyone watching us through the embered water. I sighed, stretching my neck from side to side.

The glow from Rhaegar's rune tattoo bounced off the glassy chips and crevices, the space lengthening as we progressed. All four of us fit comfortably; the ceiling and walls were tall and wide enough to accommodate double our number.

At the back of the cave, a gentle aqua pool gurgled, a stony shelf bordering it. Behind this, three darkened passages branched off, sputtering water flowing from them into the sparkling pond.

I studied each ingress, my gift thrumming under my scar when I looked to the left. "This is the one," I said, confidently moving my feet along the ledge. Hurried steps echoed through the darkness behind us, prompting my team to follow me hastily.

We scurried through the carved stone, Rhaegar and I on one side of the stream, Breena and Kaden on the other. The warrior's rune glowed, and the rest of our auras shimmered around us. My ember bubbled gleefully at its freedom.

Crossroads lay ahead of us, the channel splitting into two. To our left, the tunnel narrowed around the stream, its flow slapping the curving sides.

We turned to the right, the water sparse and trickling. Before long, the faint sound of wet, smacking footfalls reverberated ahead of us.

"Snuff the lights," Rhaegar whispered, his clipped words echoing. His rune's radiance extinguished. I nudged my energy aside, willing it to recede as well. It sunk into my skin, but the hum of it lingered along my nape.

We lurked in the blackness, the trickle of water mingling with our bated breaths. A wobbling glow painted the archway of another crossroad. It was well ahead of us; far enough that our halos had not yet revealed its existence.

The light grew brighter, its edges jerking frantically. A shrill scream tore through the air, bouncing against the crags. Soon, a female Druik sprinted past the arch, her rosy ember flashing around her as she flung balls of it behind her.

We pressed our bodies against the walls, my breath sticking inside my ribs. In the fading aureole, something substantial skittered in front of the opening. Breena's darkened outline flinched, her breath sucking in. She hissed, stepping back in the direction from whence we came. "What the fecking feck was that?"

"Let's not find out," Kaden muttered, following.

Another terrified shriek sliced through the air—promptly cut short by the sound of squelching. The rose hue blinked out, leaving us in total darkness once more.

Rhaegar's palm met mine as he silently urged me to move. We rushed, my fingers grazing the wall for guidance, our feet splashing.

A strange, resonant clicking sounded behind us. I held my

breath as my heart plummeted into my belly, acid consuming it. The scuttling grew closer.

"It's following!" I cried, my aura bursting forth. There was no use hiding any longer when the beast was already pursuing us.

"Almost there," Breena grunted, arms pumping. Her power burned around her, mixing with Kaden's luminosity beside her.

We fled into the other burrow; its width only big enough for us to move in single file. Its rushing water licked at our calves.

A screech, frustrated this time, chased us down the tunnel, but not the monster to which it belonged. The clicking waned as we pushed forward.

We paused, my chest heaving as I braced my hands on the tapering walls. My ember pulsed around me, its energy growing more insistent as we progressed. I looked ahead, and the tunnel continued to contract, our torsos stooping, water splashing against our thighs. My lips scrunched into my cheeks as I exhaled sharply. "We have to keep on this path."

"What now? This tunnel is already feeling a bit cramped," Breena groused.

"Believe me, I know. But something is calling to my ember, and I trust it." I shrugged, wading forward.

"All right, firefly. I'll pick drowning in this bloody tunnel with you over being eaten by whatever that thing was."

"I'm happy to hear that our friendship is so meaningful." Rhaegar's head swept back and forth, his shoulders shaking.

The aqua liquid rushed against my hips, undercurrents ramming into my legs, trying to knock me off my feet. My teeth clenched—I needed a distraction. "You know, there are only so many cave-dwelling creatures in Surrelia that grow to such a large size."

"Don't say it. I'd like to stay in denial a bit longer," Kaden grumbled, his chest touching the water as he bent double. He huffed, his forehead wrinkling. "Bollocks. Say it."

A nervous laugh puffed from my mouth, warmth spreading

up my spine at his droll tone. He sounded like himself. "Well, there are trolls, various hollow sprites, some species of wyrms, burrowing wyverns ..."

"The children of Arachne," Rhaegar stated, his massive frame bent and submerged to his thick neck.

"That's right." My smile faltered as I looked at the bleak set of his mouth. An image of the half-woman, half-spider beast crawled through my mind. It was said that a mortal weaver challenged an Ancient to a weaving contest and was punished for it when she bested them—cursed to live as a monster for eternity. "You don't think ..."

"Don't say it," Kaden moaned.

The Draumr nodded. "I do. I think it's a chasm spider."

"He said it." Kaden's eyelids crunched, his bulky frame stalling as water lapped at his chin.

"Uh, hate to break this up. But we have bigger problems." Breena and I were treading water now, our limbs swishing through the nippy liquid, tiptoes skimming the floor.

For a moment, panic scratched my chest, the memory of almost drowning when I was young trying to break my concentration. I drew in a deep, slow breath as my chin tipped up. My eyes squinted, peering down into the scurrying fluid. My heart skipped a beat. "Everyone, switch off your ember."

A dim, otherworldly glow pierced the shadowed depths ahead, fractured reflections dancing in the turquoise currents.

"Ready?" My brows rose as I looked at my friends.

"Nope." Kaden balked. Breena splashed him in the face, and he growled.

"Let's do this." She snickered as acquiescence lined Rhaegar's face.

A lungful of air inflated my chest, and I dove toward the light, my friends following in a single line. As I approached the submerged exit, my body strained against the vigorous flow. Air bubbles fled from my nostrils, burning my lungs. The sound of my heart thumped in my ears. I kicked with all my strength, my arms stretching.

With one final drive, my fingertips clamped onto the edge of the opening, the obsidian slick and jagged. I yanked myself forward, ignoring the bite of the stone along my palms. My boots pushed off the rock, and I propelled headfirst, breaking through the seemingly endless current.

Lungs screaming for air, I clawed through the liquid. Just as my body was about to surrender, spasms tugging at my ribcage, my face broke through the surface, the cool air slapping my cheeks and tumbling down my throat.

I sputtered, coughing up salty water and gulping down much-needed breaths. I rubbed my stinging eyes and then pushed some sopping, errant curls off my face.

Breena and Kaden broke the surface, doing much the same. Rhaegar popped up behind them, swiping his hands across his face and bouncing his head to the side to rid his ear of water.

The din of muffled ovations echoed through the cavernous space looming around us.

We'd entered the arena.

33

WINNOWING

I flopped backward onto the glittering black sand—broken, glossy shards crunching beneath my leathers. To my right, the tributary sloshed past my boots, escaping through various hollows and crannies in the stone wall. Breaths flowed in and out of my damp, parted lips, soothing my aching lungs as I stared above.

An undulating bubble of glassy fluid curved over the arena, thousands of lantern orbs circling its edges and casting a fiery glow over its cyan tint. A giant, turbid image of my exhausted face and the others projected across its surface, our movements broadcasting for the horde's entertainment.

I sat up, following its boundary as it bowed over the opposite side of the river, separating those in the arena from the audience perched on long steps cut into the obsidian.

The Elders were positioned in a circular partition at the front, frigid silver flashing over Melina's eyes when they met mine. Her upper lip curled, baring her incisors. I smirked, dragging my eyes over her horridly beautiful face before looking away, snubbing her.

Gavrel, various guards, and Akridais stood along the dome's

edge. The thick slashes of his brows pressed together, his penetrating gaze twisting my guts. Pleading.

My throat bobbed as I swallowed, a stagnant chill pressing into me as I forced my eyes away from his.

I couldn't find my sister. Part of me wished that meant she wasn't here, but I knew better. My lips pressed inward, sucked between my teeth as I looked away—reeling in my focus.

Water dripped under the neckline of my tunic, my sodden plait sticking to my nape as I hoisted myself up. Absently, I licked my lips, tasting the salt as I studied the arena, beholding its ovate magnitude. Its oblong borders spanned the entirety of the training field above. My forehead crinkled in wonder, a warm breath slowly dragging over my bottom lip.

Directly across from the spectators, a barrier was carved along the Reverie Weald. It was shrouded in dense, gnarled roots that coiled through dark stone and compacted soil. Its sides wrapped around, the roots dwindling and receding into the solid rock of the cliff.

At the opposite end, a darkened archway cut into the wall, a gilded metal door blockading it. Flickering light danced along the ridges of its centered etching—a pair of spears in an X, crossing in front of a torch flame, its cinder fluttering off to the side.

I blinked; the golden sheen seemed out of place in this glassy pit of dark, chipped stones. Movement caught my eye. Sebille and the male Druik from her team stumbled from the stream. A few others scattered over the coliseum floor, their boots rasping against the splintered gravel.

As my opponents oriented themselves—recalling that only one of us could remain—the slide of metal rang through the space, hands gripping various weapons. Other than Rhaegar and Sebille, three other Draumrs remained.

The male beside Sebille flared in a burst of cobalt haze. Three other Druiks released their auras, one the color of wheatgrass, another buttery yellow, and the last violet. My brow rose at the purple hue swirling around the petite female. I'd never noticed her before. Although uncommon, Melina had mentioned that power could be blended, an inherited anomaly.

The corners of my mouth fell, remembering what Melina had done to me. I wasn't an abnormality as I once thought. My gifts were rare, stemming from my Perilous Bogs heritage.

My mother had lied.

Kept our past secreted away.

Uprooted my identity before it ever got the chance to sprout.

My hand clenched around Morpheus' dagger as a kaleidoscope of energy shimmered over me, humming in anticipation. Breena and Kaden positioned themselves on either side of me, their bodies glowing and weapons drawn. Rhaegar's battle axe balanced in his palm, his rune's light coating the blade as he stood beside Kaden.

The twelve of us inched toward the center, forming a circle as if we were the warped numbers of a clock. Wary eyes darted around, seeking signs of attack. A metallic creak sliced through the air, and everyone stilled.

Our images fizzled from the dome, its rippling surface no longer transmitting our performance. *So everyone can see our annihilation in real time,* I thought, teeth grinding.

The gold doors lurched open, scraping against the pebbled grit, hinges groaning. My heart plummeted at the gummy clicks flitting through the darkened passage.

Without warning, a colossal, bulbous mass lunged from the hollowed void, eight segmented legs crouching and then leaping onto the guard closest to the door in a dark blur. The man's weapon was knocked from his hand as the beast pinned him to the ground, one wickedly pointed leg stabbing him through his thigh.

The crowd beyond the wavering dome audibly sucked in a

collective breath. And then cheers and cries of distress became one.

A symphony of clacking spilled from the tunnel before three more cottage-sized creatures skittered out—slightly smaller than the first, which I suspected was their alpha. Metallic streaks shifted over their armored membranes as they passed through the doors. Their copious, rounded bodies had camouflaging abilities, gilded streaks wrapping around the dark hues. As they circled us, muted shades of gray, azure, and umber shifted over burnished black.

Chasm spiders.

"Fuck. I fucking hate spiders," Kaden grumbled.

I chuffed nervously, my insides churning.

The monster reared, its bulging underbelly reflecting hues from the wood and watery dome as a juicy hiss spewed from its gaping maw. Two long, curving fangs the size of my arms flanked on either side, stretching wide to reveal several needle-like teeth within a cavernous jaw. Putrid strings of slime dripped onto the man's face, and his skin curdled and steamed at the contact. His blood-curdling scream was cut short as the spider plunged, its fangs clamping around his head, teeth sinking into his face with a crack and a squish.

I covered my mouth with my hand as bile coated my tongue.

As the spider suckled, the man's body crumbled into dust, sinking into the stony gravel. The creature screeched, its oozing face whipping up.

A flurry of movement exploded as competitors ran away, the smaller chasm spiders chasing and leaping. Sebille's teammate fell, rolling out of the way when one beta tried to impale him. Sebille swung her sword, slashing through the bottom joint of one tubular leg and then stabbing into the spider's underbelly as it stumbled. It hissed, snapping its fangs at her as she pulled her blade free before darting away, tugging her peer toward the river by his shoulder armor.

It followed and then stilled as they got into the water, its jaws grasping at the air angrily. Limping, the aggravated beast scampered along the shore, avoiding the liquid along the edge.

The alpha cornered the Druik in yellow and a Draumr near the door at the opposite end. The warrior yelled, jabbing his broadsword as taupe-tinged ember flowed from the male at his side. Forcefully, a mystic gust of air pushed against the creature, its legs vibrating as it skidded back, gravel grinding.

My heart galloped as I backed away, eyes darting toward any movement.

The spider closest to us feasted on a twitching body beneath it—the Druik in green. Before he disintegrated, Rhaegar and Breena took advantage of the beast's distraction and rushed behind it.

Kaden grabbed my arm, pulling me toward the root-covered wall as I watched a fiery orb spin between my friend's palms. Breena thrust her hands forward, the ball slicing through four of the spider's legs along the juncture of its abdomen. The excess energy crashed into the side of the dome above my head, its power smothering the flaming ball with a sparking sizzle. Kaden and I ducked as the sparks rained down.

The spider shrieked, falling to its side, legs thrashing in the air. Rhaegar leaped in an arch, his blazing axe swinging into the monster's belly. It squealed, legs convulsing as it plopped on its back and stilled.

Rhaegar freed his blade, turning toward the largest spider as it leaped sideways onto the wall to escape the embered wind. Scampering along the wall, it stabbed a leg through the Pneumalian Druik's belly. The howling male, still skewered on the leg, whipped through the air and hammered into the Draumr, knocking him down. The spider slammed another leg into the guard, impaling him while his sword clattered onto the stones.

"Watch out!" Kaden bellowed, pushing me to the side as a

chasm beast landed between our fallen bodies. He jumped to his feet, his sword swinging as Breena rushed toward us.

My aura throbbed, my chest heaving. Dusty puffs of earth fluttered around me as my back pressed into the contorted wood. My vision shrank, shadows creeping around the edges. It was as if I was watching the scenes from far away.

As if I was no longer in my body.

Time slowed. The ticking of the chasm spiders and the chiming of metal stretched and echoed between my ears.

Click.

Bodies exploded into cinder.

Kaden and Breena feinted in opposite directions, slashing and jabbing at the repulsive creature.

Others were being skewered by pointed legs, fangs, and their opponent's blades. The clang of metal and streaks of ember whooshed throughout the space, the dome glinting with every impact.

Click.

The dome that kept the crowd and Elders safe but trapped us within, ensuring our slaughter.

Click.

My breathing slowed as ember zipped over my spine, branch patterns creeping from my elbows to my wrists. For a moment, I wondered if the roots at my back had burrowed under my skin.

My head tilted, staring blankly at the carnage surrounding me. My hands stopped trembling, and I slid my dagger into its sheath, my vertebrae locking in a column.

Click.

A burning rage enveloped me, blazing through every fiber and tendon of my body.

I'd had enough.

Enough of lies.

Of being afraid.

Of not fighting back.

Enough.

Dazzling light exploded from my palms, radiating iridescence overtaking my icy eyes. In this moment, my ember and I were one. I felt at peace—confident as I flung its tethers away. My power stretched before knotting its cloying puppet strings around my soul.

A sense of unease bubbled along my nape, but it was too late. My will, sinking deeper within the corners of my mind, was no longer my own. I'd willingly given the leash to the thing inside me.

Fractured rainbows twirled between my outstretched palms and then latched onto Breena's aura. Cherry hues swirled into the emerging orb, its power thrumming against my palms.

My power drank and drank.

More.

Breena stumbled, her aura dimming as she tried to jerk away from me, daggers still slashing at the spider with determination.

Kaden thrust his blade into the monster's maw as it lunged toward him. It squealed, collapsing. Kaden pulled his slime-coated weapon free as Breena dropped to her knees.

"Seryn, stop!" he roared, catching Breena as she tipped over, convulsing.

I couldn't, and the Ancients weren't responding to my desperate pleas.

My unleashed ember consumed hers, her golden, olive-toned skin turning sickly and ashen as she convulsed in his arms.

More.

It was too late. My arteries ripped from my bleeding heart, tying around it. Strangling it. My mind raged against its chains.

But I couldn't stop it.

Breena's eyes fluttered closed, her back arching like a bow.

And then she ruptured into fiery ashes, coating Kaden in gleaming dust.

My heart dissolved along with her. Unshed tears choked me as my body moved against my will.

From somewhere trapped inside my skull, I watched helplessly as Rhaeger fought the alpha spider. It lurched forward as his axe swung behind him, its leg piercing through his heart.

Silent cries ripped through my mind as he jerked, blood spilling from his lips. With a thunk, his lifted axe cut off the monster's leg. The fiend screeched, jumping back as my friend fell to his knees. Rhaegar tipped forward, his form bursting into cinder as it smashed into the ground in a glittering cloud.

The limping beta spider Sebille had injured earlier scurried toward us, its gait lopsided. My hands pushed forward, flinging energy at it. Slamming into its side, smearing across its body. It spread, seeping into every crevice and wrapping around every limb. Light blazed, contracted, and then exploded—the being crumbling like the gritty sand beneath our feet.

The crowd was hysterical. People jumping and yelling. Whooping and laughing.

Piles of dust and steaming gore scattered over the black sand.

The ashes of my soul sank into the earth with Rhaegar's.

With Breena's.

I slipped deeper into the dark void I was imprisoned in. Adding my own shackles and nestling within my ember's chains.

Even if they survived the Stygian Murk and escaped to Midst Fall, the vileness of my true nature was already exposed. I was a vicious monster. Brutal, aching pain seared through me as the images of my friends' destruction replayed in my eyes.

I did that—I destroyed them.

My aura shimmered, petting my skin. I recoiled deeper within myself.

Something was broken inside me, and now my gift would also devour me.

And I deserved it.

Movement caught my eye. Gavrel's fists pounded against the watery dome, his yells muffled. A smoky haze slithered around Melina, her brows pinching.

Numbly, I looked around the arena.

Everyone was consumed or slain.

Everyone but Kaden and me. And the female Druik, who was sloshing through the river, water up to her knees, as she avoided the last chasm spider.

Violet mist swept over her as the limping alpha stalked her along the shore, her dark-blond hair whipping around her indigo leather tunic.

"Bloody void." Kaden pushed his shoulders back and raced toward the towering predator.

My body sauntered after him, aura blazing.

Kaden whipped toward me, hearing the crunch of gravel. His face crumpled, a look of disdain coating his features. "Get back."

My head tilted, but my body stilled in the center of the ring, light pulsing through the patterns on my arms and hands.

As he turned around, a zap of shining purplish light zoomed toward him. My mind screamed, wrenching against my tethers. My aura flared.

The lines of time slackened, and everything around me moved sluggishly.

Something cracked within me, and a glint cut through the looming shadows inside my skull. I reached out, digging my nails into the fissure, tearing at it until my will breached the vibrating prison walls.

In the next moment, my thumb—under my control once more—swept over the tingling stone of my ring. It hummed against my skin, and the melodic words of the little girl from the Weald twirled around my head.

Heed your terminus.

My eyes locked onto Kaden as my fingers closed into a fist, the tourmaline branding my forefinger.

In a flash, my body splintered and reappeared next to him—time tugging the line taut once more. He yelped as I shoved him out of the way, and the female's attack splattered against the dome. I sprung up, the energy once again coiling between my outstretched palms.

Melina was standing now, her eyes blazing silver, fists clenching at her sides.

Gavrel was gone.

From the corner of my eye, Kaden's clover aura flared as the alpha spider skittered in our direction.

My eyes shifted back to the Druik. She squinted, rosy lips pressing together. Hastily, she shifted, leaving the river and lobbing power at the spider. Radiance splashed on its back like lavender-colored water but clung to it and ignited. The creature squealed, a series of angry clicks echoing through the stadium.

Kaden's ember tugged the roots in the wall, and while they were heeding his call, they were moving too slowly. Too tangled within the soil and stone.

Another flare of purple raced toward me, and I spun, the orbiting sphere in my hands snapping and slurping as it gobbled up her ember before it got the chance to ram into me. She was closer now. My halo latched onto hers, shock painted on her pretty face.

Energy shoved at me from all sides, trying to bury me once more. But I was more concerned about Kaden's well-being. My power stopped sparring with me once it realized I wasn't preventing it from draining her. Within moments, she fell—completely depleted—and burst into ash as I turned, her energy weaving through mine.

The urge to touch Kaden was overwhelming. My ring vibrated, heating at my touch and transporting me to his side.

He jolted away, but not far enough as my palm clamped onto his forearm. My ember poured into him. His head flung back, both eyelids fluttering.

As my power waned to a faint shimmer, his expanded, the green of it vibrant and pulsating around him.

His eyes snapped open, irises igniting as he thrust one hand forward, verdant hues spilling into the roots he'd been calling upon. With a reverberating crack, a massive wood spike ripped free of the wall, contorting and bending.

As the last spider leaped at us, Kaden flicked his wrist, and the jagged root skewered the beast.

He turned to me, shoulders slumping. Confusion swept across his face as he gaped at me. He looked down, stretching his fingers wide as they shimmered.

A searing blaze of pain burned through my side, jerking me forward.

"No!" Kaden roared, catching me as I stumbled. The hilt of a dagger stuck in my flank beneath my leather vest, blood seeping.

I'd been wrong. Not everyone had been destroyed. Sebille propped against the wall. Bracing herself on the stone with one hand, her other outstretched arm dropped to her side. Streaks of blood and grit coated her face as she sneered.

Kaden's hand snapped out, calling upon another root and slashing it over our heads.

Sebille screamed as the jagged wood found its mark in the dead center of her chest.

Her attention whipped to me, her mouth hanging open in disbelief.

Within one blink, she shattered into cinder.

Kaden gently set me down. "This is going to hurt," he murmured before withdrawing the blade swiftly. It clattered to the stones, and I cried out, biting my bottom lip and trapping the agony behind my teeth. He hovered his glowing palms above me, a wash of green draping over my injury.

The dome above flickered and popped, its liquid vestiges sprinkling over us as if the Ancients wept above.

"Kaden. I'm ... I'm so sorry. For everything." The words were faint—fading away into the darkness lurking at the side of my vision.

"Stop. You're going to be okay." The gruff words rumbled from his chest, a boiling well of emotions were finally frothing over. His shining eyes widened, disbelief and desperation sweeping over them, a severe line of concentration creasing between his brows. "The Murk hasn't taken you yet—it can't have you."

I whimpered, aches pricking through my cold limbs.

"We have a victor!" Melina's voice fluttered over me like a distant echo. The crowd cheered. Kaden growled as he urged the last of his power into my wound, his torso slumping over me as his body drained.

"Come on, don't you give up on me. Fight, Ser!"

Warmth spread through me, the bite of ice stinging my fingertips as fire scorched through them. Midnight cloaked my eyes, and my eyelids fluttered shut. My mind slipped into the void, the distant sounds of crunching pebbles lulling me into oblivion.

"Well done, brother. Stay here ..." My limp body lifted into solid, unflinching arms. Indistinct words were snarled as if I were underwater, my senses ebbing before blinking back on as Gavrel barked, "Enough." His chest rumbled against my cheek. "Play your part so I can get her out. I've got her."

It was the last thing I heard before my mind drifted away, following all the others—like dust swept into the Winnowing currents.

OF WITHERING DREAMS

Not remaining.
Not worthy.

34

MIDST FALLING

*E*verything was black.
    Every bit of me ached. Muscles. Bones. Guts.
My side twinged with each breath.
Breath?
Wasn't I dead?
Bloody void. I'm in the Stygian Murk, aren't I?
I scrunched my brow, hoping my lashes would knot together so I'd never have to open my eyes again.
Drip.
Drip.
Drip.
A groan tumbled through my throat, my hand swatting at my face. At the droplets splashing onto my cheek. A wafting breeze fluttered against my chin, and a soft whirring hovered somewhere above my chest.
It's probably a shade. Just fucking do it. Suck me dry.
"While this is extremely amusing," Gavrel muttered wryly as the sound of metal sliding into leather rasped, "we need to get going. No, you're not in limbo. And that most definitely is *not* a shade."

My shoulders jerked at hearing his voice, eyes blinking open. I yelped at the pixie floating above my chest, its semi-transparent wings flapping in a blur. It was the leader I'd met during the Weeding. It wiggled the fingers of one hand as the corners of its dark lips curled. The pixie's seafoam cheeks flushed a pretty shade of jade as it tossed a dewy flower on my chest, the remaining moisture beading on my leather vest.

A low chuckle left me as I swiped away the drops on my cheek, pushing myself up. My laugh turned into a grimace as I did so. By the Ancients, my side burned with every motion. The little fiend squeaked, eyes furrowing as it grabbed the end of my messy braid with tiny, spindly fingers and tugged as if trying to help me.

A grateful smile broke across my face. "Thank you." It chirped, grinning.

My mouth fell as I stood with effort, gripping my aching flank. Neon radiance gleamed under my feet, the glow of the moss rippling away from me. It was nightfall, the full moon steeping through vibrant orange leaves.

A deep, shaky breath left me as gloom clung to my spine, pulling on my frame. Breena was gone. Rhaegar was gone. "Where's my sister? Kaden?"

Gavrel rose from the boulder he'd been sitting upon, moonlight bathing one side of his chiseled face, the other hidden in shadow. "They should all be home."

The pixie perched on the boulder, its head bobbing between us as we talked, copper eyes wide, mouth gaping.

"How long have I been out?"

"A few hours."

"How did we get here?"

"I carried you."

I snorted. "All the way from the arena?"

"Correct." He shrugged, running his hand through his thick hair. I stared at the dark waves streaked in midnight blue where the light kissed it. "Marah and Endurst's dome collapsed after Melina thought you were destroyed. The barracks exit was wide open."

My cheeks flushed. An image of Gavrel holding me close, his breath fluttering over my neck, intruded my thoughts. A vision from two summers ago. I shook my head, my damp braid plopping off my shoulder and down my back.

"Well, thank you," I mumbled. "Mind filling in any other blanks so we don't give this little beastie a neckache?" The pixie squeaked in agreement, folding two delicate hands in its lap.

Gavrel wrapped his large hands around his baldric, skin stretching across his knuckles. He sighed. "Kaden healed you. Lucky, considering your injury was surely fatal."

My chin dropped, my heart tender and aching.

His fingers met my jaw, lightly pushing up so my eyes had no choice but to meet his. "You lost control of your ember, yes. But that doesn't make you a monster. You'd never intentionally hurt those you care about. In time, you'll learn to be in harmony with your gift." I turned my head to the side, disbelief puckering my lips as his hand fell away from me.

I'd already hurt those I cared about. Physically *and* emotionally.

His nostrils flared. "At this moment, I know you are incapable of seeing how extraordinary you are. But I'll believe it enough for the both of us until you come around." My eyes narrowed at him, my heartbeat accelerating.

He turned his attention to the pixie as it stared adoringly at him. "Mind showing us the way, little one?" The creature zipped up, its wings flapping furiously. It twirled and pointed ahead.

"Thank you." He took my hand. "Let's move, and I'll explain more."

We followed the trail of zigzagging iridescence through the Reverie Weald, my stomach sore from my healed injury and cramping from hunger.

I rested my hand in Gavrel's warm one, soaking in the comfort. His encouraging words stroked my ravaged soul, trying to seal its cracks.

Promising me that I wasn't a monster.

"As I was saying. Your injury—you should've broken into dust, but you didn't." His eyebrows pinched. "Kaden realized it. I realized it. I'm hoping Melina was too upset after seeing your powers to realize it. But we most likely won't be so lucky." His hand squeezed mine, and he sighed, watching the creature before us.

The pixie paused, flitting in front of a giant banyan tree, scratching delicate fingertips along the trunk's gnarled bark. A wide grin spread across its face as a translucent amber archway presented itself—embedded in the trunk. Mossy vines swayed before the swirling and twinkling center, inviting us in. It looked just like the portal gate near the palace. My head turned, eyes fixing on Gavrel's profile.

"What are you saying?"

"You aren't in your astral form, Little Star."

"What?!" I cried, yanking my hand from his.

"For one, you didn't disintegrate after a fatal injury. For another, your body wasn't pulled back to your pod at midnight." My belly gurgled. He smirked. "And that's a regular occurrence."

I huffed, "You're still here."

His shoulders lifted. "My team is always the last to leave. As the first day of the Spring Equinox draws to an end, we do our final rounds, and then the pixies help us find the exit portal after everyone is gone. It often moves, but they can find it. Between you and me, I think the beasties just want us to leave—Rhaegar has had a void of a time with them." He smiled at the pixie, which clapped its hands together.

My shoulders slumped, picturing his second-in-command impaled. Gavrel's forehead dropped, wrinkling. "This little one was waiting for us outside the barracks. I think it likes you. Have you met before?"

A reluctant curl tweaked the corner of my mouth. "We've met." It smirked, tugging on a stray curl next to my cheek. "Thank you," I called after the creature as it waved and zipped away. One brow lifted as I studied the commander. "You sure seem to be in good spirits, considering everything that's happened." I stepped away from him. "And strangely forthcoming."

A distant smile lined his lips, his tongue pressing against the inside of his cheek. "The currents are turning. Perhaps the Fates are in our favor for once." His eyes bored into mine. "Perhaps we'll never have to suffer the Dormancy again."

My eyebrows shot up, but before I could question him further, he wrapped his arm around my waist and flung our bodies through the hazy mist, its firefly-like orbs spinning frenziedly as we plummeted.

My mind somersaulted along with my body through the aether—the Ancient's ethereal firmament. It swathed me in a swirling, opaque mist. Glittering orbs of light clung to my skin and hair. I had no clue where Gavrel was.

Did the original mortals name our realm Midst Fall because the Ancients chucked them out of Surrelia and they just fell to the earth?

And fell.

And fell some more.

After everything I'd been through, my emotions were dulled. Their usually sharp edges scuffed away, leaving only a blunted detachment.

I should have felt horrified that I'd been fully in Surrelia and could have died numerous times in the last six months. But I didn't. All that was left was a smoldering vat of ire and the need to lash out. Was this how Kaden always felt?

My belly grumbled again, not appreciating being left out. No wonder I was hungry and tired all the damn time. You had to actually eat and rest when you were alive and walking around in your Ancient-forsaken body. I huffed, my breath immediately becoming one with the mystical haze.

The abyss tore at my battle clothes, and I gulped in a lungful of cool, honeyed air before a new sensation suctioned at my body. The nothingness suckled at my skin, consuming me.

Without warning, I jolted forward, my spine bouncing and locking mid-air. Inky tendrils crept around me like shadowed fingers, claiming me and shooing away the lively beads of light. The dark mist slithered over my body, under my clothes, and I squirmed. Unable to move. It spread up my neck. Over my chin, as I clamped my lips closed, my nostrils flaring.

My ember thrummed under my skin wildly, my scar knocking against my nape. Just as the sticky darkness was about to seep into my mouth and overpower me, my power blazed like iridescent barbs. The haze reared back, slinking from whence it came.

My aura expanded, illuminating the amber egg encasing me. It pressed against the barrier, and a rainbow-like shimmer rippled over the glass before it rotated and vanished.

"Welcome back," Gavrel murmured, the edges of his emerald eyes glinting as he studied me. He held out a hand, and I took it, lifting myself from the Dormancy pod, opaque mist spilling at my boots.

My gaze swept around the conservatory. With a hissing whoosh, the glass of my tomb revolved back in place, transforming into a solid, glossy black cell like all the others.

Their starburst shape still resembled a gleaming, sinister flower. A flower that had poisoned our dreams and torn apart our very souls. The line of my mouth scrunched, the bridge of my nose wrinkling.

I looked at Gavrel, his plump lips ever in a firm line, mimicking his straight spine. My chin lifted, and I mirrored him, my vertebrae stacking perfectly atop one another. "It didn't take my memories."

"I thought as much." We looked into each other's eyes. But I'm not sure what he saw in mine or if they reflected what was in his. He turned, waving his arm toward the exit, and I gave him a curt nod.

Running to my cottage, my pulse drummed in my ears. The sturdy, grymwood frame called to me. A flickering light danced in my and Letti's circular bedroom window, cutting through the early morning dawn. A broken sob tore from my lips as Letti dashed around the side, her body colliding with mine. I shuddered within her warm embrace.

She held me at arm's length, head tilting and hazel eyes searching my face. "What's wrong? I was so worried when you weren't there when I awakened. I've been waiting all morning for you. Thank the Ancients, you made it back." She wrapped her arm around me, leading me to our home. Gavrel followed silently behind us like a wraith bathed in twilight.

As we entered, the reassuring scent of timber, candle wax, and astra poppies hit me. My shoulders fell, and I leaned my weight into Letti as unshed tears lined my lower lashes. I was finally home—the same as I'd left it.

But I wasn't the same. I was broken. Made of ragged fragments that I feared would no longer fit together.

My sister guided me to a kitchen chair, the seat creaking as it took my weight. She lit a candle, its delicate flame frolicking along the red-orange petals of the astra poppy adorning a vase on the table. I looked at Letti as she sat beside me, Gavrel standing near my shoulder, palms resting on the back of my chair.

"Are you all right, sis? You look rattled." My eyes fixated on the dainty bloom. "Don't worry, I didn't pick it. I found it lying on the grass in the backyard." She shrugged.

I murmured, "Do you ... do you remember anything?"

One golden brow rose, and she snorted. Heavy footfalls marched down the hall, and my back stiffened. Gavrel's fingers tightened, making the chair's dowels squeak.

"What is going on? Why are you all sneaking around in the dark?"

"Hello to you as well, Father." My lips pressed together as I lifted my jaw. I sat taller, leather rasping against my seat.

He squinted as he looked down his nose. "I see you've made it back. What a relief." His brittle tone begged to differ. I leaned back with a sigh, his words not burrowing into me as they once would have. I wasn't sure if that was because I now knew there were greater things to fear or if I was still numb.

"Thank you, you as well."

He sniffed, tightening his thread-bare robe around him. "Yes, well. What were you on about?"

Letti stood, rubbing her hand on his shoulder. "Ser asked if I remembered anything from the Dormancy."

"How absurd." He arched a light eyebrow, his trimmed blond hair swept back. Even when he slept, there wasn't one single hair out of place.

I rose from my chair, the pads of my fingers pressing into the table. "Yes, you're right." Something stopped me from telling them about my memories, my nape tingling.

He gave us a curt nod, squeezing Letti's shoulder, and turned back to his room. "Get some rest. We've got a lot of work to do." He left without waiting for a response, his feet thunking against the floorboards.

"Letti, have you seen Kaden?" Gavrel inquired, stepping closer to the flickering light.

Her hand fluttered up, resting against her collarbone. "Oh

no. No, I haven't. I woke up alone." Her eyes widened, nails digging into the collar of her nightshirt.

His jaw clenched. "All right. I'll watch for him. Good night." He bowed and departed hastily.

I didn't want to alarm Letti, so I put my arm around her. "Let's get some sleep. In the light of day, things will be clearer." I wasn't sure whether I was convincing herself or myself. If my cryptic words confused my sister, she didn't show it as we went to our room and tucked in for a few hours of rest.

Gavrel and I both knew Kaden should have been reeled back in at the same time as everyone else. But we couldn't do anything about it right now, especially without rest or sustenance.

As soon as my head hit my feather pillow, my eyes drooped closed, and I fell once more—this time into a blessedly deep and dreamless sleep.

35

SHEDDING SKIN

Daylight spilled into our room, its midday beams cutting a straight column down the center of our room. Fresh spring air sifted through the open window. Something dug into my hip, and I flopped onto my back, the dark leather a tight fist around my torso.

My hands glided over the clothes I hadn't bothered removing, mystical tourmaline branches glinting on my forefinger.

My dagger.

The satchel at my belt.

I sucked in a breath, sitting up and unfastening it. My trembling fingers dug within.

"What is that?" Letti yawned, stretching her arms above her head. "And what are you wearing? Didn't get a better look at you in the wee hours of the morning." She shrugged, shuffling and sitting on the end of my bed. It squeaked under her weight.

My front teeth bit into my bottom lip as I tipped the necklace pouch, three vials, and the talisman into my palm. A long breath expelled from deep within my chest, my heart bouncing. "Good thing you're already sitting." I chuckled, the sensation scratching up my throat.

"Spill."

My hand cupped the back of hers, turning it and placing one vial in her palm. She held it up, studying the gray and silver-speckled powder.

"I lied before. I remember everything ... from every Dormancy we've ever been through. And that"—I pointed to the tiny glass container—"is how I know."

Her mouth dropped open. "What the void are you on about? Are you unwell?" She put her other hand on my forehead, but I swatted it away.

"Listen, don't tell anyone. I mean it. I don't know who to trust except Gavrel, Kaden, and you." I huffed, untying the laces of my vest, feeling less confined as I did so. "I'm wearing these clothes because it's what my physical body was wearing when I came back ... from where we go during the Dormancy." My eyes rolled to the ceiling in frustration. I didn't know where to start. I sighed, looking back at her. "There is too much to go over, but I will if you want me to in the coming days ... or you can take that tonic."

Letti watched me with an intense focus as I tried to summarize where we went during the Dormancy—in our astral bodies—and how I was there physically somehow.

I ran my thumb over the black sliver in my palm, its energy zinging against my skin. My ember revealed itself after it was bitten out. I suspected this rune had tethered my body to Midst Fall during our long mandated slumbers, but I wasn't sure why or how. Yet.

I went over when and how to use the orchid potion. Considering what I told her, Letti's bottom teeth dragged over her top lip. "I'll take it. You know I'll believe whatever you tell me regardless, and if this will bring back my memories—it's what I want."

"Okay, sis, but know that it may unearth painful things. Things you've done or said. People you've loved or hurt during the forgotten moments. It isn't easy." The corners of my mouth wobbled.

She grabbed my hand. "Then we'll take the hard path together. It's the last day of the full moon. Do you think it'll work now?"

I smiled, the feeling foreign but not entirely unpleasant. "There's only one way to find out. Be warned—it gave me an awful headache. It was like I'd been run over by a horse. I was knocked out for several hours as well, but I'll be here. Promise."

"I know you will. I'm ready." Her voice was full of conviction, heading to her bed. She pricked her thumb on my dagger, letting a few drops spill into the vial. Once the potion resembled a starry midnight sky, she tipped it down her throat, reclining on her mattress.

Her eyes widened at some sensation brewing within her. I whispered and took her hand, "It'll be okay. I'm here."

She nodded but then bowed off the bed, her face contorting in pain. Her fingers dug into the back of my hand, and I smoothed her golden curls off her face. Then she settled, her features and limbs sagging into a mystical sleep.

While she slept, I informed Father that she was feeling unwell and resting. He didn't question it, directed me to care for her—as if I wouldn't—and then left the house to go about his business.

It felt good to wash off the grit and sorrow from my skin. There was still so much, so many emotions, colliding within me. But I felt like I could breathe again. The familiar warmth and scent of the grymwood trees. The creak of one particularly whiny floorboard in the hall.

As I slid my worn chemise over my head, I grimaced. The scratch of its fibers along my shoulders felt foreign, as if it were old skin my body wanted to shed. I slipped my knee-length, mud-colored kirtle over it, lacing it up and ensuring my membrane settled over my muscles and bones.

Once more, I checked on Letti, her face serene in slumber. I went to my bed, picking up the necklace pouch. The dried petal needed to be put somewhere safe. My mouth twisted to the side as I scanned the room before my eyes landed on the bark and catbane-reed box my sister made for my thirteenth birthday.

I plucked it from my nightstand, nestled the pouch inside, and lifted a loose floor plank under my bed, tucking it in the exposed hole before clicking the wood back in place.

Throughout the rest of the afternoon, my fingers disturbed our garden soil at the side of our cottage, dug into the earth, and sprinkled seeds.

My body moved without thought, the monotonous work soothing my jagged musings. I arched, pushing my hands into my lower back, wiping a bead of sweat from my brow, and wiping my hands together to rid them of the clinging dirt.

A soft breeze caressed my cheek, my auburn curls fluttering against my neck. It carried with it a sweet, musky scent. The aroma of wood and grass—living things—trying to draw breath through all the decay.

My eyes closed, arms wrapping around my waist. I breathed in to the count of four. Could I move forward after everything I'd done? Everyone I hurt?

I exhaled.

Four.

Three.

Two.

One.

Did I have the strength to endure my memories?

Hold. Breathe in.

My eyes opened at the sound of flapping wings. The scratchy, gurgling caw of a raven swooped through the garden, nestling on a thick bough on a tree near the conservatory. It stared at me intently, tilting its head. I chewed the corner of my top lip, a tinder of hope kindling, yearning to chase away the shadowed doubts.

One step—one second—at a time. The Ancients bestowed the gift of existence upon mortals, so the least I could do was endure. Survive my ember. For living was to survive whatever dream or nightmare drifted across your path.

I could use my jagged edges to carve a new space for this version of myself... in this realm and all the others.

BEFORE DUSK, Letti awoke with a groan, her body rolling to one side and curling in on itself. I lit the candles on her nightstand and then rubbed her back. "It'll be all right. Give yourself a moment. You're safe."

She whimpered and sat up, mouth grimacing as she rubbed at her temple. "I ... It's all jumbling around. You weren't kidding." She grabbed my hand, crunching her eyes closed for a moment.

"It'll take some time."

She shook her head as if trying to dislodge something lingering. "I'll be all right. Yay for potions!" Her dry chuckle fell to the floor.

On my way to the kitchen, a hurried knock rapped on our front door.

"Gavrel?" I welcomed him in, his sword and a rucksack swaying against the back of his black tunic. It was startling to see him in civilian attire for once.

I blinked a few times before noticing his jaw ticking, his cold eyes surveying. "Where is Gideon?"

"Hello to you," I griped, lifting my chin. "I have no clue. Why?"

"Good, we've got to go. Now."

My nostrils flared, and I stepped back. "What? No, thanks. Did you find Kaden?"

"He's missing." He squeezed his eyes closed for a moment, sucking in a breath and then releasing it before looking at me. "Please, go grab a pack of clothes and your boots. We've got to move. I'll explain as we go."

I growled but stomped to my room, his heavy steps following. If he was saying we had to leave, there was a good reason for it, but I wouldn't make it easy on him.

Letti shifted on her bed as we entered. "Hey, Gav. Any luck with Kaden?"

His eyes and voice softened as he looked at her. "Unfortunately, no. But I'll find him."

"Letti remembers everything. No need to tiptoe around her." I held up the remaining two vials, shaking them.

"Bloody void."

"It was her choice," I retorted.

He clenched his teeth.

"What's going on?" Letti asked, sliding onto the floor and standing at the end of my bed.

He scrubbed a hand down the stubble of his jaw, head tilting as he looked at my sister and ignored her question. "You know what? The Vawn sisters' impulsivity just might work in our favor this time."

My sister laughed. I huffed, stuffing my leather clothes and dark tunic into my rucksack. I put on my boots, grumbling the entire time. The woolen fabric of my kirtle swished as I tightened the belt. Gavrel's lips pinched together as I glowered at him, securing my dagger. My talisman and the two vials were safely tucked within the belt satchel.

Letti stifled a laugh, her brows lifted, the corners of her eyes wrinkling. "How can I help?"

Our heads swiveled to the rounded window, its pane still ajar. The rumble of a heated conversation slipped into the room. All three of us crept to the window, Letti and I crouching under the sill and Gavrel hiding to the side. His fingers gently lifted the curtain's hem as he peered through the gap.

"I'll ask you only once more. Where is Seryn Vawn?" Irritation and authority lined the female's voice. They were somewhere near the conservatory, their voices audible but distant.

"As I've said, she could be inside or anywhere for all I know. I've just returned home myself." I pictured Father's lips puckering, his inability to control the situation riling him.

"You've done well over the turns, Gideon. It isn't a lack of gratitude on the Elders' behalf. We're just doing what we're told. That is, we need to bring her in. The less struggle, the better for you and your daughter." The male's tone dripped with artful insincerity.

Letti and I held matching expressions of concern and confusion. Gavrel let the curtain fall in place, crouching beside us. His whispered orders were urgent. "Seryn, once the backyard is clear, we run." He nodded at the window. "Letti, you'll need to stay here. I'm sorry ... It's too dangerous without ember; you should be safe here. It'll also be more useful if you stay. Keep an eye on your father, and do not disclose that you remember anything. If Breena or Rhaegar come to the house, pretend you don't know them in front of Gideon, but get a message to them that we've gone to the Perilous Bogs. Rhaegar will find us."

"What?" I hissed, hearing the shuffling of feet against grass. Letti nodded in agreement, completely trusting what he said.

"Gideon is one of the Somneia. He reported my mother. He also hasn't had to undergo the Dormancy since Maya disappeared."

Letti and I gasped, my hand flying over my mouth, an exclamation trapped behind my fingers. Rage burned through me, consuming the shock. Of course, Father was part of the Elders' spy network.

My teeth threatened to break as I clenched them. He was

safe in Midst Fall every winter—not trapped in the Murk. Spying. Getting other people culled. "That fucking piece of—"

"It's time. Let's go." Gavrel stood, glancing behind the curtain, the voices passing the back of the house.

Letti and I jumped up, wrapping our arms around each other fiercely. "I love you. Take care of yourself. I'll be back for you before the next Dormancy." It was a whispered promise I hoped I wouldn't have to break.

Letti nodded, her thumb running along my cheek and brushing away a stray tear I hadn't realized had fallen. "We've got this. Now go." She spun, walking down the hall hastily, her golden curls bouncing behind her.

Gavrel opened the window and climbed out stealthily. I scooped up my rucksack, my ring vibrating against my pointer finger as I slipped through the window just as the rasp of our front door sounded.

Letti chimed, "Welcome home, Father. Who do we have here?"

Gavrel's strong hands wrapped around my waist, helping me safely to the ground. My body slid down his front, tingles grating along my chest at the contact. He jerked his chin toward the trees as he released me and pulled the window closed swiftly.

Then we ran, the forest enfolding us in its embrace.

36

ASTRA POPPY

The stars twinkled over the meadow. Chalky smudges from the moon dusted the tall, dancing grass and reeds. Shades of deep purple and inky blue painted the spaces in between. A symphony of chirping insects rippled through the field, pausing as we passed, only to hum behind us when the turf settled.

"So, my father is a disgusting excuse for a human, huh? I suppose that isn't a surprise. I'm so sorry about Hestia." The crickets silenced abruptly at the sound of my voice.

"Thank you, but it was long ago." He moved efficiently, his steps never faltering as they whooshed past the long blades of dry grass. "I'm sorry that Gideon is part of the Somneia. Though it'll offer Letti some protection before you can get back to her."

I sighed, worry buzzing in the back of my mind. "Where is Kaden, and why are we going to ... to the Bogs?"

He stopped, turning to face me and shifting his pack on his shoulder. "You aren't the only one who dreams, Little Star."

A rush of air flit atop my chuckle. "Everyone dreams."

"No, they don't, or if they do, it's rare. Do you recall anyone talking about a dream they've had lately?"

"That's a ridic—" My words fizzled as I bit my bottom lip, head tilting in thought. This gave a whole new meaning to Kaden's favorite idiom. He always said he wouldn't dream of this or that. And, well, I suppose he wasn't.

The moonbeams skimmed Gavrel's forehead, one raised eyebrow peeking out of the shadows. "Exactly. People might mention a dream, but they're often describing some bizarre fever dream or a nightmare—mild or otherwise."

I sucked in a breath, my heart speeding. "But ... I've dreamed over the turns. Especially while in Surrelia."

"Indeed. But they're different, aren't they? Like the voice in the dungeon ... a call from the aether. And always during a full moon. It makes sense. Ember is at its most potent during the full moon. Portals between realms at their weakest."

My eyebrows rose, eyes crinkling before I nodded slowly. My scar tapped eagerly, but I ignored it. Any trust I had in my power had deteriorated, my nerves still raw after the Winnowing.

Gavrel ran his hand through his dark strands, his words spilling freely. "After searching the village unsuccessfully for Kaden, I rested before coming for you. Visions of your father with Akridais plagued me. A reflection trapped within his eyes of my mother's body exploding into ash. And your image in her place. Your body tearing apart."

My shoulders contracted into a cringe, and a replay of my dream invaded my mind—the Larkin brothers tumbling into the void beyond the Reverie Weald.

His forehead crumpled as he continued, "I saw Kaden screaming and drowning in the swamp." Dipping his head, he moved forward again, and I walked briskly beside him. "I've often suspected Gideon, doubting his whereabouts and absence from Surrelia during the Dormancy. Over the last several turns, I've learned to trust premonitions."

"You think the Oneiroi are sending us messages?"

"Yes. Them, or perhaps the Fates."

My mouth dropped, a snort of disbelief falling at my feet. "Well, aren't we special—dream Ancients taking notice of us. Fates even."

He shrugged, his scabbard groaning against his spine. "The warning helped us tonight, didn't it? And after everything you've been through and now can recollect, is it so bizarre?"

My cheeks flushed, and I was grateful for the night cloaking my face. He cleared his throat. "I'm sure they've helped you before. You know they have. That's why we're going to the Bogs. Kaden is either there, or the information we need is. And I wasn't about to leave another person I care about to be culled." He rumbled deep within his chest, fists clenching. "Never again."

My pulse hammered, and I swallowed, my mouth parched and wordless. I couldn't argue with his logic. Because we were operating in a surreal reality, weren't we? And everything he said was true. The whims of Ancients and Fates ruled our paths, coated in ember and blood.

"You know, maybe I preferred it when you didn't tell me things."

He smirked. "I know better than to say I told you so. But as long as you remember saying it, I'll be content."

A snapping twig echoed behind us. Gavrel grabbed me by the waist and tossed us to the parched moss, his back breaking our impact. A wall of tall catbane stalks shielded us. My face pressed against his muscled chest, the scent of timber and an earthy, rich spice swept into my next inhale, heat racing over my chest and belly.

My eyelids fluttered, memories of his warm embrace seeping into the crevices of my brain. I gritted my molars, trying to expel them.

We'd been something once. Something that had started to

bloom two summers ago. But it didn't matter now. He'd torn it out by the roots and discarded it. Discarded *me*.

Too many jumbled moments and emotions spun together, but it was glaringly clear that I had once felt something more than friendship for Gavrel. For longer than I'd like to admit. Well before he stomped on my heart a couple of turns ago.

My palm pushed against his sternum, his heart bumping against it rapidly. His arm tightened around me, his words tickling my cheek as he whispered, "Don't. Be still and let them pass."

For a moment, I thought he meant my memories until heavy footfalls trudged along the border of the field, the female from earlier grumbling, "We'll never find the damned dirtling at this rate. These bloody trees go on forever." A glimpse of a flapping pewter cape gleamed through the reeds as they marched past. Akridais. Melina had sent them for me. I sunk into Gavrel, his thumb rubbing gently against the fabric above my belt.

"Well, we can't go back empty-handed. You know what she'll do. We'll search for a few more hours and then make camp. Pick it back up tomorrow."

Their voices faded as they continued in the direction we had been heading.

"We should be good," Gavrel murmured, his arm not lifting. My face tilted to his, my front teeth running over my bottom lip. His hips shifted, a soft breath whooshing from his parted lips.

An image of Kaden snapped through my mind, and a small sound of distress fell from me. My hands pushed against Gavrel as I rose, his thick arm slipping from me. "Uh, sorry. Which way should we go now?" He'd traveled all over Midst Fall, so I assumed he'd know several paths into the Perilous Bogs.

He stood, looking in the direction the elite enforcers went and then to the east. "I don't want to risk crossing their path. We could head toward Haadra. I doubt they'd expect us to travel that direction. They'll probably stay in this area and along the borderlands. I'm sure Melina told them to check the Bogs, considering that's where your mother was from."

A resigned inhalation swept into my chest. "I think you're right. East it is."

We moved like silent wraiths in the shadows of the night. We were nocturnal creatures. Both hunting and being hunted. I wasn't ready to sift through my history with Gavrel. Or what Kaden and I had shared. Or my feelings connected to them both. For now, I'd concentrate on finding my best friend. On finding out who I was—so far from the woman I had been before.

The old Seryn was harvested and consumed like all crops were during the Autumn Equinox ... but spring was here, and it was a time for planting seedlings.

For clinging to hope and believing that they would sprout. For taking the time to nurture them while they grew and flourished.

My shoulders pushed back, and my hands ran down the itchy fabric of my skirt, one rummaging through my pouch and taking out my stone.

The pebble's etching stared back at me, humming with lingering energy. There was a reason my mother put this in my neck. I looked ahead, my eyes bright with determination as I tucked it away.

There were buried reasons for *everything*. And I was going to unearth them.

As we came to the edge of the meadow, a single crimson bloom beckoned to me. Its delicate stalk stretched out of a patch of crushed, desiccated reeds.

I knelt, stroking the pad of my finger down its silky, vibrant petals. It shivered as a cerise-colored aura glittered over it. My mouth curled at the astra poppy's verve. The bloom's absolute will to endure.

I rose, my spine mimicking the flower's resilience.

I caught up to Gavrel, and we were once again surrounded by towering grymwoods, their bent branches sheltering us from the aether.

Without question, I now understood that a mortal could be shattered beyond recognition and still persist. Still fight.

My ember quivered at the back of my neck, humming down my vertebrae.

One step at a time.

We'd find Kaden.

We would dismantle Melina and her minions.

And I would exhume every dormant truth. One by one, until I understood this new version of myself and how to heal Midst Fall. If I had to shatter realms—and my soul—apart again and again, I'd do it.

I'd just have to make sure the pieces were sharp enough to carve through the nightmares.

NOT YET THE END ...

GLOSSARY/PRONUNCIATION GUIDE

CHARACTERS/CREATURES

- **Akridai (Ack-reh-die)** – very powerful, elite Druik enforcers who wield their power at the discretion of the Elders and the Elder Laws.
- **Alette Vawn (A-let Vawn)** – a.k.a. Letti. Younger sister of Seryn Vawn. From Evergryn.
- **Alweo (Al-weh-oh)** – Seryn's chestnut stallion.
- **Ancients** – powerful gods who created the mortal realm and gifted magic to certain mortal bloodlines.
- **Breena Cadell (Bree-nah Kah-dell)** – friend of Seryn Vawn. Lives in Pneumali City, but originally from Pyria Island. Possesses red, fire-related magic.
- **Chasm spider** – giant, cave-dwelling spider beasts with camouflage abilities.
- **Derya Atwater (Dair-yah At-water)** – friend of Seryn Vawn and her chambermaid. Lives in Surrelia, but originally from Haadra. Possesses blue, water-related magic.

GLOSSARY/PRONUNCIATION GUIDE

- **Draumr (Draw-mer)** – warriors in the Elders' warrior legion, the Order of Draumr. Uphold laws and order within realms.
- **Druik (Drew-ick)** – one who wields magic. Lives longer than non-magic mortals/humans.
- **Elders** – extremely powerful, chosen/ascended Druiks granted extra celestial powers through the Ancients' Ascension ceremony and rule the mortal realm as an Oligarchy. They hail from divine lineage from one of the **five founding bloodlines**:
    - **Aerides (Air-id-eez)** of Pneumali
    - **Celosia (Suh-low-sha)** of Pyria
    - **Lotus** of Haadra
    - **Nightshade** of Perilous Bogs
    - **Oleander (Oh-lee-an-dur)** of Evergryn

    Current Elders:

    - **Endurst Guust (En-derst Goo-st)** of Pneumali – possesses yellow, air-like magic.
    - **Lucan Craven (Loo-can Cray-ven)** of Evergryn – possesses green, earth-like magic.
    - **Marah Strom (Mar-ah Strawm)** of Haadra – possesses blue, water-like magic.
    - **Melina Harrow (Meh-leena Hair-oh)** of the Perilous Bogs – possesses smoky, memory-erasing magic.
    - **Ryboas Ash (Rye-bow-es Ash)** of Pyria Island – possesses red, fire-like magic.
- **Elysium (Eh-lis-ee-um) Tree** – the oldest and most sacred, banyan-like tree in all of existence. A source of life-giving ember. A place to pray or offer oaths to the Ancients.

GLOSSARY/PRONUNCIATION GUIDE

- **Emmet Larkin** – Gavrel and Kaden Larkin's father. Husband of Hestia Larkin. Died shortly after his wife was culled.
- **Fates** – three powerful sister entities who write, alter, and determine the destiny of mortals, realms, creatures, and Ancients alike.
- **Gavrel (Gav (like have)-rel (like fell)) Larkin** – Seryn Vawn's neighbor and friend. Brother of Kaden Larkin. Elite Commander in the Order of Draumr. Has a rune tattoo on his right hand that grants him some ember and enhanced strength/stamina.
- **Gideon Vawn (Gid-ee-on Vawn)** – Seryn and Alette Vawn's father. Husband of Maya Vawn.
- **Harbinger starling** – starling-like birds that deliver missives across the realm.
- **Hestia Larkin (Hess-tee-ah Larkin)** – Gavrel and Kaden Larkin's mother. Wife of Emmet Larkin. Was culled when Gavrel was eighteen turns old and Kaden was thirteen turns old. Possessed green, earth-like and healing magic.
- **Iben Burlam (Eye-ben Burr-lamb)** – librarian and begrudging friend of Seryn Vawn. Lives in Surrelia, but originally from Evergryn. Possesses brownish, earth-related magic.
- **Kaden Larkin (Kay-den Larkin)** – Seryn Vawn's best friend. Brother to Gavrel Larkin. Possesses green, earth-related and healing magic.
- **Mare wyrm (worm)** – Nether Void, leech-like creature that tricks you into thinking it is your loved one. Once they have you in their slimy hold, they suck the life and magic out of you.
- **Maya Vawn** – Seryn and Alette Vawn's mother. Wife of Gideon Vawn. Disappeared when Seryn was seven

GLOSSARY/PRONUNCIATION GUIDE

turns old. Has some sort of magic related to the Perilous Bogs, where she was originally from.
- **Morpheus (More-fee-us)** – the supreme Ancient of Dreams. Presides over Surrelia.
- **Oneiroi (Oh-knee-roy)** – the dream Ancients. Siblings.
- **Order of Draumr (Draw-mer)** – the Elders' warrior legion.
- **Pegasus (Peg-ah-sus)** – Surrelian winged, horse creature. Mortal-bred horses that were gifted wings by the Ancients once they reached Surrelia. Very rare.
- **Phantasos (Fan-taz-ohs)** – Ancient of Illusions (and surreal dreams). Wanders across the realms and likes wild landscapes.
- **Phobetor (Foe-beh-tore)** – Ancient of Nightmares. Presides over the Nether Void.
- **Pixie** – mischievous, winged creatures that are as big as a mortal hand. Reside in Surrelia in the Reverie Weald. Skilled at finding portals in Reverie Weald.
- **Rhaegar Hale (Rag-ar Hail)** – friend of Seryn Vawn. Gavrel Larkin's second-in-command in the Order of Draumr.
- **Scion (Sigh-on)** – descendants of one of the five founding bloodlines. The only type of Druik that can undergo the Ascension to become an Elder. Only one exists at a time.
- **Seryn (Sair-in or like the name Erin) Vawn** – Our main female leading character. Alette is her younger sister. Gideon and Maya are her parents. Has some sort of mysterious magic that hails from the Perilous Bogs. Has lived in Evergryn her whole life.
- **Somneia** (Som-nee-ah) – the Elders' covert network of spies.

- **Wyvern (Why-vern)** – Surrelian creature that lives along the cliffs in the Reverie Weald. Massive, reptilian-like creature with wings, feathers, scales, and two forelegs. It can spray poisonous spit. Protects the Mirage Orchid.
- **Xeni Reed (Zen-ee Reed)** – friend of Seryn Vawn. Girlfriend of Alette Vawn. Warrior in Gavrel's elite Draumr unit.

PLACES

- **Evergryn (Ever-grin)** – Northern, wooded region of the mortal realm. Magic that hails from here is earth-related and often shades of green and brown.
- **Haadra (High-druh)** – Eastern, water-ridden region of the mortal realm. Magic that hails from here is water-related and often shades of blue and aqua.
- **Insomnis Sea (In-sawm-niss Sea)** – fabled dream realm sea that surrounds Surrelia.
- **Midst Fall** – the mortal realm
- **Nether Void** – Ancient nightmare realm. Phobetor presides over this realm. It is a terrifying, dark realm where those who pass on may live out their eternity in eternal suffering.
- **Perilous Bogs** – Western and center, swamp/bog region of the mortal realm. People avoid this area and not much is known. Magic that hails from this area is mysterious and can manifest in many different ways and is often shades of black or iridescent.
- **Pneumali (New-mall-ee)** – Southern, desert region of the mortal realm. Magic that hails from here is air-related and often shades of yellow and orange.

GLOSSARY/PRONUNCIATION GUIDE

- **Pyria (Pie-ree-ah) Island** – Southernmost, volcanic island of the mortal realm. Magic that hails from here is fire-related and often shades of red.
- **Reverie Weald (Rev-er-ee Wheeled)** – a beautiful and neon-colored forest that separates Morpheus' land and palace from the rest of Surrelia.
- **Stygian (Sti-jee-uhn) Murk** – a colorless portal realm or limbo between realms where time slows and travelers easily get lost while their will to survive and exist is drained.
- **Surrelia (Sir-el-ee-ah)** – Ancient dream realm. Morpheus presides over this realm. It is a beautiful, vibrant realm where those who pass on live out eternity.

TERMS

- **Ascension** - the ritual in which the Scion metamorphoses into the new Elder.
- **Dormancy** – the process the mortal realm is mandated to undergo from every Autumn Equinox to Spring Equinox in order to preserve resources.
- **Ember** – magic that was gifted by the Ancients to Druiks and is inherited through bloodlines.
- **Fated khorda (Core-duh)**– a Druik's mirrored or twin soul. The three sister Fates helped the Ancients weaken Druiks so that mortal ember would not become overwhelmingly powerful. It was believed that Druiks were born with half their soul, the other half cleaved from them and gifted to another—Druik or human.
- **Kollao (Kah-lay-oh) Ceremony** – the ritual through which a Druik is bound to their fated khorda and

becomes whole in soul and magic. Their life is also bound together.
- **Turn** – one year
- **Winnowing Trials** – a Surrelian festivity at the end of the Dormancy where Druiks and Draumrs can compete to win a grand prize.
    - **Weeding** – first trial of the Winnowing Trials
    - **Wilting** – second trial of the Winnowing Trials
    - **Winnowing** – grande finale trial of the Winnowing Trials
- **Withering** – the progressive decay of the land in Midst Fall.

ACKNOWLEDGMENTS

This story is one that I've been dreaming of for many years. But without the love, support, and persistent encouragement of my husband and closest friends, I doubt I would have found the courage to write it. So, here's a massive thank you to my husband who is always there, even in the wee hours of the morning, to listen to me rant and ramble my way through brainstorming and fixing plot holes.

Thank you a billion times over to my friend Lana who read this entire thing even though it was her first fantasy AND first romance novel. Her insights and honesty were beyond valuable and helpful on this writing journey. I truly couldn't have done it without her support and relentless encouragement.

Thank you to my friend Bethany, who introduced me to one of my favorite fantasy romance authors, Sarah J. Maas, years and years ago. Her thoughts and guidance on this as one of my beta readers were indispensable especially because she loves fantasy romances with open-door spicy scenes just as much as I love to read and write them.

Katie (Spice Me Up Editing)– my fan-freaking-tastic editor who whipped this book into shape. Her humor, perpetual optimism, cheerleading, and support kept me going when I wanted to chuck my computer against the wall. My computer, mental well-being, and I thank you into eternity and beyond.

Thank you to all of my readers, my beta readers, my Wicked Dreamers Street Team, ARC readers, and reviewers who took a chance on a debut indie romance author with a dream and a magical, steamy story to tell. I appreciate each and every one of you for reading, reviewing, sharing, making reels/posts, and generally just being amazing humans.

I can't even with my character art. Thank you to the amazing Sarah of Spooky Yeti Art (IG handle: @spookyyetiart) and Hope Garrity (IG handle: @hopegarrity). You should check them out because, I mean, their art is freaking gorgeous and brought my crazy characters to life. Thank youuuu.

WANT MORE?

Of Blooming Embers (Fate of the Embered Book 2)
Ember Sparks. Passion Ignites. Fate Burns.

Don't miss the next thrilling chapter in the Fate of the Embered series by Rowyn Adelaide—a spellbinding tale of passion, peril, and profound sacrifice—where love and power come at a devastating cost.

ORDER OR READ YOUR COPY HERE:

FOLLOW ROWYN HERE:

IG/TikTok/FB/Goodreads/Amazon: @AuthorRowynAdelaide

JOIN THE WICKED DREAMERS NEWSLETTER HERE:

ABOUT THE AUTHOR

Rowyn Adelaide is an insatiable romance reader, advanced practice MSW social worker, and the author of the *Fate of the Embered* series. Her debut novel, *Of Withering Dreams*, launched the dark fantasy romance series with a haunting blend of passion and peril. Her work fuses atmospheric world-building with emotionally driven romance, often exploring themes of transformation, angst, and resilience. When she's not writing or devouring stacks of romance novels, she's usually globe-trotting, rocking out at concerts, counting down to spooky season, or singing karaoke (very poorly). She lives in the Midwest with her favorite creatures: her husband, their dog Audrey Shepburn (aka the goodest girl that ever lived), and their chaotic cat Stormy, who is equal parts villain and sidekick. For more information, visit www.AuthorRowynAdelaide.com.

Get your books, follow Rowyn, get updates, & join her newsletter!

Made in the USA
Middletown, DE
28 November 2025